EVERYDAY
Lies

TANYA ANNE CROSBY

Published by Oliver-Heber Books

0 9 8 7 6 5 4 3 2 1

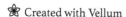 Created with Vellum

PRAISE FOR TANYA CROSBY

Praise for Tanya Anne Crosby's The Girl Who Stayed:

"A beautifully written, page-turning novel packed with emotion." – #1 *New York Times* bestselling author Barbara Freethy

"*The Girl Who Stayed* is a deeply moving story. I am fascinated by the concept and by Tanya Crosby's stunning storytelling."
– Stella Cameron, *New York Times* bestselling author

"Crosby tugs heartstrings in a spellbinding story of a woman trying to move beyond her past."
– *New York Times* bestselling author Susan Andersen

And Redemption Song:

"Crosby's second foray into women's fiction (after *The Girl Who Stayed*, 2016) is a quick read with charm and quirk."
– *Booklist*

"A woman searches for closure, meaning, and maybe revenge in Tanya Anne Crosby's latest, *Redemption Song*. Delving deep into the core of a damaged soul, Crosby cleverly contrasts the warmth and harmony of a family not so different from the protagonist's own. Masterful."
– Pamela Morsi, *USA Today* bestselling author of *Simple Jess*

"Packed with raw, emotional power, *Redemption Song* is an insightful and moving exploration of one woman's triumph over grief. When you come to the last chapter, you'll feel breathless as you reach for the tis- sues. This is Tanya Anne Crosby at her very best and marks her as a strong new voice in women's fiction."
– Julianne MacLean, *USA Today* bestselling author

This one is for my sisters around the globe. Together, we've navigated rough waters and, though some have been lost amidst the storms, and some of our sails are battered and worn, finally there's Terra Firma ahead. Now, altogether, let's fill our sails and glide into port, a fleet of intrepid sailors.

And also to the men who stood ashore to cheer us on... my husband being one. Thank you, Scott.

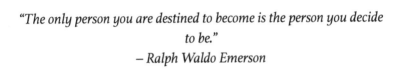

"The only person you are destined to become is the person you decide to be."
– Ralph Waldo Emerson

1

THE VIRTUES OF CATS

Gillian's husband left. That's who she was. She was the girl who'd married too young, whose husband couldn't, or wouldn't, stick around. As far as pity parties went, there must be worse, but it didn't stop Gilly from celebrating her desertion with impunity.

And oh, how she celebrated.

For one, she'd witnessed enough sunrises by now for that miraculous event to seem mundane, although it wasn't always that way.

A memory teased her—Kelly, high atop the roof of her grandmother's house, and all that natural beauty sending her fifteen-year-old pulse into overdrive. Arm in arm, they'd lain, watching a Texas sunrise and listening to the *thump, thump* of their hearts under a pink and yellow sky. It was the first time a boy had ever put a hand in her pants.

She'd crawled out through her bedroom window in her pajamas, sans underwear, and the surprise of Kelly's exploring fingers, along with the look of shock on his face when he discovered her moist, trembling bud, was enough to make them pull apart, like polarized magnets. Afterward, they'd lain staring at the sky, enjoying God's mastery, as the electricity produced by their bodies relayed pleasure across their synapses. Funny how she could still feel those spectacular currents coursing through her body with but a memory, and still the notion of pursuing similar results under similar circumstances was about as thrilling as a Neti pot.

Gillian also visited local animal shelters the way some people toured cemeteries, but not out of some misplaced sense of social responsibility. It wasn't anything so noble as that, because Gillian realized long before walking in the door, she wouldn't be taking home a new pet.

Nor would she be volunteering at a sidewalk adoption, because, let's face it, she was usually too hung over in the mornings. It was all she could do not to puke.

The most good she ever did along that vein was to push prospective adopters toward taking home a fur baby of their own. "Aww, he's adorable," she said to woman at the shelter this morning.

A bit overweight, with frazzled red-gray hair, she stood petting a three-year-old male Maine Coon. The feline was far too lovely to end up in a shelter. Either he'd gotten lost, or he'd peed on somebody's socks one too many times. If it were the latter, it served his master right for leaving clothes all over the floor.

Her husband used to do that. Kelly would leave his clothes everywhere, shedding them like snakeskin the minute he walked through the door. Gillian hated that habit of his so much, and yet she'd spent a great majority of the past three years drinking too much, and alternately hating him and daydreaming he would come back to do it some more.

Clearly, ambivalence had become her MO—her marital operandi—because she certainly didn't display that sort of contradictory emotion where anything else was concerned. She loved her grandmother. Loathed her father. Felt sorry for her mother. All strong, straight-up emotions without the least bit of a willy-nilly mixed in.

Rubbing the inside of one brow to will away a lingering headache, she eyed the wilting man standing behind the cat-loving woman, his expression bored as he waited for his wife to decide which kitty to buy. Her shirt was generously smudged with garden dirt and much too tight, revealing extra lumps on top of her natural breasts, like a second pair of boobs. Evidently, she didn't pay much attention to her appearance, and yet she still managed to keep her man.

Unlike you, Gillian.

"Isn't she lovely?" the woman asked. She smiled as Gillian reached out to caress the cat's lush fur. *How hot the poor thing must be?* It was 107 degrees in the shade. After two weeks of one-hundred-plus-degree temps, the city was considering brownouts. The back of Gillian's neck was damp and her hair stuck to her skin as she continued to pet the cat. The woman's smile faded. "I'm sorry," she said. "Were you considering this one?"

Considering him? As in taking him home? "No." Gillian shook her head. "I already have three." *Not true. She didn't have one.* Gillian sighed. "But I would . . . if I could." *No, again. She would not.* Three years of visiting pet shelters and she still had an empty house, because Kelly was right: she had an unhealthy fear of commitment.

The woman knit her brows, looking confused. "Do you work here?"

Gillian shook her head. "No," she said, and smiled, though there must be something innately wrong with her that she didn't run like wildfire from moments like these. To the contrary, she was like a self-flagellating priest, punishing herself for even considering the joys of communing with another warm-blooded being. This was how she knew she wasn't a sociopath, because sociopaths weren't compelled to self-recrimination.

The woman frowned. "Well, if you don't mind . . . I think I'm taking him home." Smiling nervously, she pulled the cat out of Gillian's reach, as though she suspected Gillian of being some peculiar breed of cat burglar, lying in wait to steal other people's prospective pets. "Sweet baby," she cooed, dismissing Gillian.

And that's usually the way it went, with Gillian looking on as another potential fur baby shuffled off to a new home, feeling inexplicably resentful and thrilled for the animal's good fortune.

But this was the inalterable truth: in her current condition, Gillian wasn't fit to adopt. In fact, some part of her longed to be adopted herself. So this was why she visited shelters, not because she longed to save animals, but to commiserate with them and comfort them, because she understood full well what it felt like to be rejected. Someday, she hoped to provide a stable home for a pet, but until she fixed herself, she didn't trust herself with an innocent creature's life.

"Good luck," she called after the woman, waving as the trio wandered over to speak to the handler, who in turn smiled companionably over at Gillian—it wasn't the first time her presence had incurred a sale for Operation Kindness.

"Honey? Do you like him?" the woman asked her sweaty husband.

"Uh? Yeah. I do," he said, more animated now that the wife had chosen her cat. Probably because now he would get to go home and put his feet up in his La-Z-Boy, somewhere near a window unit that would blast cold air directly into his face.

"Here," said the lady, dumping the hairy cat into her husband's hairy arms. "What now?" she inquired of the handler.

"Do you have any other cats at home?"

"Only one. She's a baby," the woman said. "They'll get along fine."

Without missing a beat, the handler said, "If not, he's welcome back. You may return him for a full refund within seventy-two hours. After that, you can bring him back, but we'll be unable to refund the adoption fee."

"How much is the fee?"

The woman cast a glance at Gillian as she stuck a finger into another cage containing a highly adoptable young tabby—the question annoyed her, because under no circumstances should you be allowed to take home a living being on a trial basis. Sometimes life threw curve balls, but you had to know up front that you were willing to play for keeps.

The kitty in the cage immediately came forward to sniff Gillian's finger and she nuzzled the cat's wet nose, pretending to ignore the woman adopting the Maine Coon.

"One hundred twenty, but that includes neutering, a microchip, and all vaccinations, including FeLV and FIV. Plus, all our cats have been treated for fleas and dewormed."

"Wonderful!" the woman said, pulling out her wallet.

The handler asked, "What will you name him?"

"Maurice," the woman said, smiling at the husband, who now had his overlarge fingers threaded into the animal's thick fur. "What do you think, honey?"

The husband nodded dutifully, repeating, "Maurice."

Gillian probably would have named him Charlie. He looked like a Charlie. Oh, well. She hoped he'd found a stable home. She had been visiting him for a week, even though she'd realized the cat wouldn't last. Heartsick over the fresh loss, she pretended to duck into the store for pet supplies.

It was a particular form of torture, putting herself through these visits; simply because she never brought one home didn't mean she didn't grow attached.

Once inside the store, Gillian paid a visit to the fish, peering at them through smudged glass. Fish would be easier . . . safer. But she didn't believe in putting living beings into a bowl for one's viewing pleasure. Fish were meant to swim free. She'd rather see them out in their own habitat, diving through the reefs. Kelly always said he would take her snorkeling, but in all their years together, not once had they ever come close. It was always work, work, work.

Gillian also hated zoos. Animals belonged in the wild. It was different with cats and dogs, because cats and dogs had domesticated themselves. They craved human contact.

Point in fact: You couldn't pet a fish, could you? No. Nor did fish aspire to living in bowls, where they were at the mercy of humans. On any given day, what if its human was lazy? Leaving excrement to swirl about in the bowl. Poor fish would suffocate in a PH nightmare—a fate only slightly worse than living with a man who couldn't look you in the eye.

In the end, that's how it was with Kelly.

He could barely acknowledge her, and whenever he did, he'd had that intensely unhappy look in his deep, dark eyes—part fury, part disgust, part pity. But it was easy for him to judge. He was a paragon of virtue, always taking the high road, while Gilly opted for the low road—but then, of course, shouldn't that be expected? She was a Frazer, not a Noble.

Damn you, Kelly Ruby.

Bored with the fish, Gillian moved on, opting not to wander aimlessly through the remainder of the aisles. Only this time, before heading out the door, she did something she didn't normally do: She made her way over to the tag dispenser and chose a tag—you know, those silly name tags pet owners stuck on the collars of their newly acquired best friends. She chose a black bow tie. Going through the process a bit aimlessly, she engraved the tag with the name "Charlie" and then gathered up her items and took them through the line at the register.

After that, she left the store, quietly amused by her purchase, because, what the hell? She could buy a name tag, but not a cat.

Gilly, Gilly, Gilly . . . what is wrong with you?

Something, for sure.

She felt the proof of it like a black hole, straight through her soul. It wasn't so much a thing that could be defined, or a tear with boundaries. It was like a great sucking vacuum, threatening to pull her inside. If she let go, she might never be seen again—and worse, the entire event would probably go unnoticed, like a stray cat who'd come around now and again, only to vanish, his absence as insignificant as the squashing of a mosquito on the back of your arm. It would be gone for months before someone idly noticed, and then, in passing, wondered what befell him.

Someday she would stop just being a visitor and bring a pet home, she promised. *Someday. But a cat. Not a dog.* Dogs were too needy, and though Gillian loved the idea of needing and being needed, she couldn't bring herself to cross the line, not even in her head.

Out in the parking lot, she unlocked the door to her Z-3 and slid inside, tossing her purse onto the passenger seat, along with her brand-new purchase in its royal purple velvet bag. No sooner had she climbed inside and settled behind the wheel when her phone rang. Wondering who could be calling so early on a Saturday morning, she fished the cell phone out of her purse— the instant she saw the name on the caller ID, she wished she hadn't bothered.

It was her dad. Joe Jr. was not someone she ever aspired to talk to. *Ever.*

Letting the call go to voicemail, Gillian checked her other missed calls—two more this morning, one from an unknown number. Sensing the calls must be related, she waited for the phone to beep with her father's message, and then proceeded to check them all at once. "Gillian." His voice was stern. "Call me."

Not in this lifetime.

Not unless she must.

The next message was from a woman whose voice Gillian didn't recognize. "Hello, I'm trying to reach Ms. Gillian Frazer, concerning Ms. Rebecca Frazer. Please call as soon as possible."

Gillian's heart thumped. She blinked, staring at the number, then hung up and punched call return without bothering to listen to the second message.

"Texas Health Presbyterian Hospital, Plano."

A sudden tremor appeared in Gilly's voice. "Hi, uh, this is Gillian Frazer. I understand you're trying to reach me about my grandmother, Rebecca Frazer?"

The woman was silent a long moment, presumably checking her records. "Please hold," she said. All the while Gillian waited for the woman to return, she chewed the inside of her lower lip, feeling tension build in her shoulders. *Thursday.* That was the last time she saw Gigi—a quick stop before going to happy hour. *But she was fine then, wasn't she? Why was she in the hospital? Why hadn't Gigi called?* Had the hospital called Joe because they couldn't reach Gillian? Despite Geeg having two sons, Gillian knew good and well that Gigi would have referred them to her, which only meant her grandmother wasn't alert enough to speak. A sick feeling settled in Gillian's gut.

Thursday, Friday, Saturday.

She counted days on her fingers. It had been two and a half days since she'd last talked to her grandmother. Two whole days. No missed phone calls. Guilt mixed with fear and gurgled in her belly—she was an awful granddaughter. Self-medicating had taken precedence over caring for the people she loved. Quick on the heels of guilt came a massive dose of self-reproach.

Stop drinking, Gillian. What the hell are you doing to yourself? Stop drinking.

It was an interminable moment before another voice appeared on the line, and the woman's tone bled with sympathy. "Hello. Ms. Frazer? This is Karen Hobbs, a nurse with Texas Health Presbyterian Hospital, Plano. Your grandmother . . ." She paused. "Well . . . I'm afraid she's had an . . . event. Can you please come in?"

"Is she okay?"

"I'm sorry, I'm not at liberty to discuss that on the phone."

Gillian fought a tidal surge of nausea. "I'm on my way," she said, and hung up. The instant she ended the call, she unlatched the car door, shoved it open, and leaned her head outside, puking on the white striping of the asphalt parking lot. After she was finished, she shut the car door and stabbed her key into the ignition.

2

JEFF & JOE

Gigi's "event" was a massive stroke.

Evidently, this was how they referred to potentially life-altering cataclysms that befell old folks—an event, not like a concert but more like a total eclipse, after which, when the light returned, things might or might not remain the same.

Upon Gigi's arrival in the ER, they'd given her a tissue plasminogen activator through an IV, followed by a mechanical thrombectomy, during which they'd removed a large clot. Fortunately, the procedure stopped the brain bleed. However, because of her condition, as well as her advanced age, they'd opted against more invasive surgical procedures. By the time Gillian arrived, she was resting in a drug-induced coma. They had her stabilized and Gillian was allowed to see her for a total of thirty seconds—eyes closed, mouth twisted horrifically, stretched across a wheeled bed—before they whisked her away for more tests. Her grandmother wasn't gone five minutes when Gillian's father and uncle arrived, arguing emphatically. Her Uncle Jeff marched into Presby waving her grandmother's DNR like an eviction notice. "Says here she don't want to be susitated," he announced to Gillian, his lip curling with contempt as he pointed to the document he held in his hand.

Meanwhile, her dad attempted to wrest the legal document from his brain-dead brother, lowering his voice, but hardly approaching a whisper. "I ain't saying no. All I'm saying is we ought to read the damned thing afore we hand it over. Give it to me, eegit!"

Jeff shook his head, but with one quick tug, Gillian plucked the document from her uncle's oil-stained fingers. "Resuscitated," she corrected. Then, ignoring the complaints that erupted at her back, she marched Gigi's will over to the nurse's station, handing the document over to the nurse on duty. Afterward, she returned to banish her father and uncle to the waiting room, where, presumably, they would continue to argue the merits of keeping their mother's end-of-life wishes to themselves.

"She's your daughter," her uncle said in response to something her father said.

Gillian didn't catch Joe's muttered complaint, but she wished she had; anger toward the men in her family was a welcome distraction. As for herself, she opted for the hall, pacing while she awaited the doctor's return.

At this point, Gigi's vitals were stable; a DNR wasn't applicable or necessary. But that wouldn't stop Jeff or Joe from continuing their debate, to little avail. Her grandmother's living will provided that Gillian, and Gillian alone, was authorized to make decisions on Gigi's behalf. Leave it to her father and uncle to go searching for a will for all the wrong reasons. Both of Gigi's sons were testosterone-impaired sperm donors. Neither had the good sense God gave a rattlesnake. At least rattlers intuitively understood the consequences of sparring with another of their species. No good ever came of two poison-fanged creatures locking jaws, and yet those two did at regular intervals, no matter who stood by as witness.

Fight. Impregnate women. Sleep. Fight some more. This was the life cycle of a Frazer male. During their fifty-some years, both men together had ruined more women's lives than a Catholic all-girl's prep school and a high school prom, combined. With Gigi gone, Gillian felt utterly and hopelessly alone. The thought alone made her long for a good cry, but luckily, she was particularly adept at keeping tears in check. If, at any given moment, she dared give in to her grief, she would end up in a quivering mass on the floor, worthless to everyone.

In this way, she was not unlike her grandmother. Gigi never bowed to her circumstances—unlike Gillian's mother. Both women had married good-for-nothing men, but Gigi had brushed herself off, held her head high, and kept on living as best she could. "Don't be a woman who needs a man," she'd said. "Be a woman a man needs."

On the other hand, her mother would say, "Gilly, honey, it's a woman's lot to suffer. That's the way of the world." And even more insidious was this: she'd often said such things while trying to convince Gillian to compromise herself, something Gillian was not predisposed to do. So, she took her examples from the woman who'd raised her, not from the one who'd given birth to her.

Nevertheless, she forgave Maria everything, because Maria was a victim, who wore her badge willingly, though not wittingly. There was a difference. One accepted her lot in life, because she couldn't conceive of shedding it. The other wore it vengefully, pinning the same badge on her only daughter, because she believed: "I am screwed, and therefore we are both screwed."

To Maria's credit, having realized who she was, she had driven six-year-old Gillian to Gigi's house one day, tearfully acknowledging her inability to be the parent Gillian deserved, and then she'd left, returning only now and again for misty-eyed reunions Gillian mostly endured, though not so much because she was angry. Deep down, even as a child, Gillian had suspected her mother's days were numbered, and so she'd braced herself for the inevitable outcome every time she walked out the door. In the end, the abandonment had been a good thing, because Gillian only ever understood "normal" after living with Gigi.

It was close to 1:00 a.m. There was something about walking the empty halls that exacerbated Gillian's sense of loss. As she paced, she had the most incredible yearning to call Kelly—a longing she realized she shouldn't cave to. He was probably sleeping in anticipation of an early meeting, and the last thing he needed was a phone call from his ex-wife about a woman who was no longer part of his life. But it didn't escape her that, even now, he was the only person she longed to call.

Finally, they wheeled Gigi back into her room and Gillian caught another terrifying glimpse of her grandmother's face, and then it was a good forty minutes longer before the doctor reemerged into the hall. Crossing her arms, Gillian's throat constricted as she listened to the doctor's explanation. Because of Gigi's stroke, much of her brain was compromised. Her motor skills were affected. So were the language areas of her brain. She had what they suspected was global aphasia, a condition in which individuals were unable to understand language in written or spoken form. She was also affected by paralysis—hence the alarming facial expression.

"Is she going to be okay?"

The doctor's smile was barely discernible. There was a note of sympathy in her tone. "I don't know. We're running tests . . . she has yet to speak or show signs of cognizance. I'm sorry, Gillian. We hope to know more soon. Her vitals are strong," she offered as reassurance.

Gillian nodded, swallowing past the knot in her throat. Her eyes burned like twin coals on fire. "So . . . how long will you keep her?"

It was a dumb question, because Gigi clearly wasn't in any condition to go anywhere, much less home. But it seemed pertinent, somehow—not for the least of reasons: the simple act of asking implied the situation must be temporary, and therefore her grandmother might eventually wake up and go home. More to the point, Gillian realized hospitals no longer kept patients for extended stays—especially not old people with no hope of recovery. There would be next steps to consider, and soon.

"Ms. Fraser . . . it's simply too early to say." The woman reached over and placed a comforting hand on Gillian's shoulder.

Gillian nodded again, peering in through the open door at Gigi's contorted face.

The woman who'd raised her—who'd bandaged her skinned knees, who'd made sure she never went without a meal—looked perpetually on the edge of a heart attack, even during sleep. The unsettling countenance made Gillian want to go home and shove her head beneath a pillow.

Later, she would kick herself for not asking more questions, but at the moment, all she could think was that Gigi needed her. "Can I go sit with her?"

"Yes, of course. We'll move her into a private room in the morning, then you can feel free to stay as long as you like while she remains here."

Gillian crossed her arms. "Thank you. Okay. Thanks, that's what I'll do," she said, and peered down at her sandaled feet, because the carefully guarded sympathy in the doctor's gaze threatened to unravel her composure.

"I'll let your father and uncle know they can join you."

Gillian hugged herself tighter, wishing she wouldn't do that, even though it was as much their right to see their mother as it was hers. "Thank you," she repeated, and she stood rooted in place for a moment as the doctor moved away. Steeling herself, Gillian waited until the doctor was out of sight and then pushed open the heavy door and walked into the antiseptic-smelling room.

"Gigi," she called softly.

The woman in the steel-framed bed, dressed in faded green

cotton, lay so still, her resting body and terrorized expression so at odds that it made Gillian's stomach burn—or maybe that was the headache powder she'd slipped into her coffee an hour ago? It hadn't touched her headache, but, thankfully, she had an extra one in her purse.

Gigi looked smaller than she had only a few days ago, diminished in a way a loose cotton gown and a tightly fitted twin bed shouldn't accomplish on their own. Her metal-framed bed was surrounded by blinking, beeping apparatuses, one connected to her finger, some to her arm and some to her torso. "I'm here," Gillian said, heartbroken, approaching the bed and taking Gigi by the hand.

"Have dinner ready. Plan ahead, even the night before . . . Most men are hungry when they come home . . . The prospect of a good meal (especially his favorite dish) is part of the warm welcome needed."
—*The Good Wife's Guide, Housekeeping Monthly*

6:00 p.m. Tuesday, July 5, 1960

The air was dry and stale. The kind of dry that left nostrils feeling baked and the back of the throat raw. No matter how many times you swallowed, you couldn't get past the feeling that one more speck of dust would throttle your windpipe.

Something has to give.

A small army of black ants marched across the pale-green Formica, disappearing into a crack at the edge of the counter, where the chrome trim buckled away from the wood. They weren't there an hour ago, but now they were, carrying' on as ants must, putting one spindly leg in front of the other, searching for something better—like Rebecca's parents, running away from Black Sunday. Lured by the promise of black oil and cheap, dust-ravaged land, they'd stopped short of clear skies and settled in McKinney, Texas. Believe it or not, they were the lucky ones.

Sometimes people got stuck.

Rebecca observed the ants a moment longer. Good little soldiers, all doing their part. But it wasn't their day. Fishing under the sink for the chlorine bleach, she groped about for the new plastic bottle, and then, finding it, she hoisted it up, unscrewed the cap, and doused her washcloth over the sink. Now, with a more streamlined shape and a four-fingered grip, it was so much easier to handle than those amber-glass bottles.

Her already parched nostrils flared against the sharp scent, and she glanced up at the clock on the wall as she swept the washcloth over the kitchen counter, sweeping curled, dead ants into the sink. *Poor little things.* They looked like granules of black sand. She brushed a few off the counter and onto the floor, then turned on the faucet to wash the remaining ants down the drain.

Perfect.

Pristine.

That's what Joe expected. No amount of bemoaning the lives of God's little creatures was going to soften his heart. Her pa had warned her; she didn't listen. She'd been hoodwinked by that Frazer charm—sweet talk that dried up like a stingy oil well the minute her parents kicked up their toes. Now, the mill was failing, so too was the ranch.

What were they supposed to do?

Some folks were taking money to burn fields, drive up prices, but that didn't set well with Rebecca. And Joe—that n'er do well —he'd gone and bought himself that car!

However, Rebecca didn't believe in crying over spilt milk. Even so, a bit of her bristled over marrying him still. Her husband was a grifter. No amount of do-gooding on her part would ever change that fact. Loving him, not loving him, made no difference at all. She was a married lady now, with two small boys, and she had a responsibility to her ranch. She was excited about the new job prospect, even if Joe wouldn't like it none at all. As far as Rebecca was concerned, they'd been struggling for too long. He might just be greedy enough to allow it, if only she could present it just right. Southwestern Bell paid very well, the pensions were wonderful.

For Pete's sake, Dottie Shepherd said she knew a woman who retired at the age of forty-five with all her benefits and a salary to boot.

More ants emerged from the counter crevice, recoiling from the bleach, stumbling away like drunken little men. As much as they didn't cotton to it, there were far too many to turn back. Rebecca took a bit of the washed-out gum in her mouth and shoved it into the hole in the counter, stopping the invasion once and for all. "Evenin', Joe," she said, practicing her lines. She rinsed the washcloth, rinsed out the sink, and tried again. "Evenin', honey."

No. That was no good.

What would Joe think if she suddenly up and spoke to him that way? No, he liked her best when she was . . . motherly, he said. Not formal, 'cause then he claimed she was stiff—whatever that meant. Boards were stiff, dead folks were stiff, Becky Lee Frazer was not stiff.

"Evening, honey."

Making ready for her husband's eminent arrival, she rushed about the kitchen, swiping at everything within reach. "You need Clorox to get out the dirt suds leave in," the ads all said. "When it's Clorox clean, it's safer for family health!" Well, Rebecca's family was her priority. *Why else would she take a job outside the home?* Even Joe must appreciate her willingness to work.

She went to retrieve his newspaper from the porch, folding it just the way he liked, with the front-page headlines front and center. Today's top headline read: *Johnson Finally Makes It Official —He'll Run.* On the same side of the page, close to the bottom: *Bandits Rob Euless Bank.*

Rebecca sighed. These were desperate times. If only she had the gumption to do such a thing; all they needed was a bit of help to get ahead.

She placed the paper on the table in front of Joe's chair, sharpening the crease. Sometimes he enjoyed reading while he ate, although she wished he would talk more to the boys. Never mind, the dinner hour was over. The boys were outside playing.

Stopping now to peer out the kitchen window to see if she could spy them in the field, she marveled over how big they were growing.

At eight and six, Joe and Jeff were so much like their pa, right ready to scuffle at a moment's notice. She supposed that must be part of a man's personality, but she didn't like it all that much. God knew, she wouldn't need any job at all if those boys were more inclined to help.

Outside, the sky appeared as though it were on fire—beautiful in a frightening way. They were due for a good rain. Droughts always put the fear of God in a body, 'cause everyone knew how that story went. There wasn't a natural born Texan over the age of twenty who didn't have a dust-storm story to tell. Although Rebecca had been young, she could still recall the day her family fled Farwell after the worst day of the year. *Black Sunday.* Her pa used to tell stories about that day, when a wall of dust five hundred feet high came rolling through town. On the first clear day afterward, her pop loaded up the truck. They left so quick they raised up a dust storm of their own. All the kids, Rebecca included—well, she must have been two or maybe three—all named the place they'd left Farewell, Texas. "Farewell, Farwell," they'd said, waving from the back of the truck.

"Good riddance," her pa always grumbled at the end, no matter how many Sundays that story was told.

Outside, there was no sign of the boys and Rebecca worried they were up to no good. Last week, Joe Jr. took a hammer to the chicken coop and Jeff stuffed piles of hay into her father's old cotton gin. The only thing those boys ever paid any mind to was their daddy's belt, but that was something Rebecca was never inclined to subject them to, so they ran about, wild as coyotes.

Shaking her head, she continued cleaning, sweeping her bleach-soaked rag over the countertops. The smell was awful, but Joe loved a clean house. And this was something she knew she would have to keep up with, with or without a new job. It wouldn't matter much if she was tired by the end of the day, Joe wasn't going to be any help. Anyway, she wouldn't dare ask. She could tell straight away where that would lead—nowhere good, and fast.

The bleach bottle in her hand jiggled a bit. Some of the bleach splashed out, onto her blouse. She frowned, guessing that "no-drip" promise was too good to be true.

Glancing again at the clock, she returned the bottle beneath the kitchen sink. It was her last one, so she must be sure to get more the next time she made it to the store. But now, it was nearly six. Usually, Joe came home straight after work to get a bite to eat before heading back out the door. He was late.

One last time, she ran her bleach-soaked cloth over the enameled sink, then rinsed it out and hung it over the edge to dry. Better yet, she should put it outside, because as much as Joe appreciated a clean house, he hated the smell of bleach—especially when she reeked of it herself. Lord, she was smelling like a freshly scrubbed toilet right now. The aroma of dinner would mask the scent in the kitchen, but it wouldn't help Rebecca.

After a quick check on the roast, she hurried into the bedroom to freshen up and change her blouse. She'd barely made it into the room when the front door opened and slammed shut so loudly it shimmied the floorboards. "Becky!" her husband roared.

Rebecca tugged a pink gingham blouse off the hanger in the closet, shrugging into it as quickly as she was able.

"Goddamn it, Becky Lee! Where you at? Dinner ain't gonna serve itself!"

3

DARKNESS VISIBLE

On the bedside table, the spines of *Darkness Visible* and *Blackout: Remembering the Things I Drank to Forget* stared back at Gillian. Both books sat beside an empty glass that once held two ice cubes and a few fingers of tequila. Annoyed, she turned around, reaching into the space her husband used to occupy. Palm flat, she absorbed the coolness of the sheets.

Damn you, Kelly.

It didn't matter.

She had more important things to consider right now—like, they were moving Gigi into a senior care and rehabilitation facility. Her vitals were still strong, but Rebecca Frazer was never coming home. Her stroke had left her unable to speak, and in its aftermath, the expression frozen on her face reminded Gillian of a Bill Burr skit, except there was nothing funny about her grandmother's condition. Her eyes remained wide, like a perpetually frightened child, and the vacant blue-green irises, once so like Gillian's, might have been glass marbles for all the emotion registered there. Her grandmother had made it eighty-four years, fending for herself; now she couldn't feed herself without help. Changes must be made.

For one, the house in McKinney was vulnerable, all its history and valuables laid bare with no one around to protect them. This, Gillian realized, was now her job—to protect the house, the cornerstone of her family, and even her life.

Her father and uncle no doubt had already ventured in to grab whatever their hearts desired, and what their hearts desired mostly had shiny gold and silver surfaces.

According to Gigi's will, the house and nearly all its contents would someday belong to Gillian, but for now, while Gigi was still alive, the thought of her father and uncle raping her grandmother's house turned her stomach worse than any hangover.

And no, it wasn't because she coveted anything of her grandmother's. She loved that house, but even more than that, she needed it to remain whole and unviolated. Like Samson who got his strength from his hair, Gillian's strength was born in that house. So as much as it disgusted her to think of material things with her grandmother in the condition she was in, if she meant to save anything for later, she would have to safeguard it today. Given the opportunity, her father and uncle would prowl the house and pawn everything that would bring a half-dollar.

Plus, there was her grandma's horse to consider. For the time being, a friend was looking in, but that was bound to get old fast.

Why bother hanging on to the apartment?

Because.

Giving up her Turtle Creek apartment was like giving up a rent-control flat in New York City. They didn't come available often. *So what?* It was just an eight-hundred-foot flat, hardly worth considering. So what if the floors were engineered satin wood? So what if the six-inch trim was above and beyond the norm? So what if the cabinets weren't pressboard and the counter tops were granite. The house in McKinney was her real home.

Rise and shine, Gilly.

It was Gigi's voice in her ear, and so, with a sting in her eyes, Gillian dragged herself to a sitting position and slid her legs off the side of the queen-sized mattress—a mattress and box spring, no headboard or frame. Because Kelly was right: she was going through the motions.

After the divorce, she'd gathered only what was necessary—enough to give her life some semblance of order, but really, just enough so she wouldn't be tempted to compare herself to her mother, a tragic figure whose downhill slide was only partly due to her father. Still, it gave her a measure of satisfaction to blame him. Joe Jr. was like his dad—a shadowy figure Gillian barely knew by name. Her grandmother had never spoken much of her delinquent husband. From the stories Gillian had heard—mostly told by a son who was too much like his dad to recognize the similarities—Joe Sr. was a grifter. After sucking the Noble ranch dry, he'd walked out the door one day and never returned.

Was it any wonder Gilly was afraid of commitment? Not one significant male in her life ever gave her a reason to see things differently. Her grandfather left her grandmother. Her dad left her mom—or rather, he kicked her while she was down, literally, and then couldn't leave fast enough to avoid arrest. And then her own husband divorced her—never mind that she couldn't blame Kelly for leaving. The fact was that he hadn't been willing to stick around to prove her wrong.

What doesn't kill you makes you stronger, right?

That's what Gigi used to say.

Only, right about now, Gillian doubted that particular nugget of wisdom. Squeezing her eyes shut over the ache in her head, she touched her toes to the Berber carpet, groaning aloud.

Stretching her neck, her gaze was drawn to the black bow tie tag she'd purchased at PetSafe, neatly placed beside the empty glass of tequila and her cell phone. The sight of it made her snort and she reached for the phone to check the time.

11:15 a.m.

Holy crap. There was so much on her plate today. Work was the last thing on her mind.

Why haven't you told him yet?

There was no rational reason.

She and Kelly co-owned a web design firm. While her ex-husband handled day-to-day operations, Gillian schmoozed customers and led the design team. Kelly managed the office, mostly because she no longer kept an office. She worked from home, giving direction via conference calls. If anyone asked, this was why they hadn't dissolved the business with their marriage. Neither had to ever see the other if they didn't wish to, though Gillian's work hours easily doubled Kelly's. Her job remained a priority, because she understood full well that a lack of regard for deadlines and responsibilities were signs of alcoholism. This, too, was why she worked ungodly hours, stopping only for "happy hour" intermissions, many of them work related.

Up until now, Gillian had been perfectly content to be a worker bee. The one thing her husband had never found fault with was her work. Conversely, he thought she was the worst wife on the planet. And maybe she was.

Shuffling into the kitchen, Gillian plucked a water glass from the cabinet, then pulled open the utensil drawer. She ferreted out a headache powder from beneath the spoons, unfolded the package, and dumped the contents into a glass. Then she opened the fridge and grabbed a water bottle, and after pouring fresh water over the powder, she stared at the white sediment that remained at the bottom of her glass. Narrowing her eyes, she swirled the contents, hearing Kelly's grumble at her ear. *"That shit's going to burn your liver."*

Gillian had given him an eat-shit glare. "Why don't you say what you really mean, Kelly?" Because what he'd really wanted to do was complain about the late night she'd kept.

Nevertheless, unlike her father—who'd dished out ultimatums over everything from skirt lengths and cleavage to the color of her mother's lipstick—Kelly had never once put his foot down. Consequently, it had been difficult for Gillian to read him, up until the end, and she'd always assumed he didn't care. "You're a grown woman, Gillian," he would say. Always *Gillian* when he was angry with her. "I want you to do what you want to do." *Passive aggressive bullshit.*

Who knew the man was keeping score, and that each failed test was a yardstick of her worth to him. That never failed to infuriate her. In fact, it downright pissed her off, even now, as she lifted her glass, swirling the water to mix her powder.

Defiantly, she chugged down the morning's hangover meds as images flashed through her head of Kelly's disapproving glare. The bitter taste of the powder made her grimace.

God knew, if she had to count how many powders she had hidden throughout the house, she couldn't do it. Whereas alcoholics hid cheap vodka bottles, Gillian hid headache powders— not that anyone was paying attention. There was no one around to count drinks or powders. Nobody gave a crap how many she opened during the course of a day—one, two, three, four. *Whatever.*

Naturally, you had to keep one handy for when you woke up with a hangover, and then it didn't hurt to take another before bedtime, on the off chance you could avert a hangover. Therefore, she always needed one in her purse, in case she didn't make it home. The prospect disgusted her, but she did it anyway.

Why?

Gillian frowned. That she didn't need a drink was perhaps the worst of the lies she'd told herself, but it wasn't the only one. Okay, so physically, she didn't crave alcohol. Her body didn't shiver and shake without it, nor did it give her sweats. If she could figure out a way to feel good sober, she would walk away and never be tempted again.

The fact was, she didn't feel compelled to hide her drinking, nor did she think about drinking twenty-four-seven, devising ways to do it.

It wasn't like that. To the contrary, Gillian simply didn't want to think—or feel—and the easiest way to accomplish that was to drink. After a few shots of tequila, everything was Zen.

Maria, on the other hand . . . Maria was a true-blue, dyed-in-the-wool alcoholic. Maria, not mom or mother—because that's how Gilly thought of her—*lived* to drink. Everything she did, every job she ever took, every place she ever lived in, she chose specifically to facilitate her addiction.

If you ever visited whatever long-stay motel Maria had chosen to "manage" because it gave her room and board and easy access to her private stash of zinfandel, you'd be hard-pressed to sit anywhere in the room and not find alcohol paraphernalia—a tall plastic cup infused with the scent of vino, a corkscrew in the cushions (for times when she might feel like splurging on bottles with a cork), and a vase in the middle of the fold-down table, filled with wine-stained corks.

It was difficult to say if Maria valued them, keeping them as tokens of bygone celebrations, or if she was simply too lazy—or too drunk—to walk over to the trashcan, and instead tossed her corks into the collection until, one day, it rivaled the collection of shoes at the Holocaust Museum.

As for Gillian, she rarely kept alcohol in the home. Last night had been an exception. Her drinking was most often pursued as a sport, or celebration, wherein tears weren't allowed, laughter was encouraged, and reverie was expressly prohibited. She drank responsibly. No drinking and driving, ever. She was good about never getting behind the wheel of a vehicle while under the influence . . . though she might ask herself why she chose to live in a tiny, cramped apartment within walking distance of West Village and its pubs.

But that was beside the point. While Gillian drank to "happy up," she suspected Maria drank to maintain a level of sadness. She had often contemplated, "Which came first, the bottle or the tears?" And, although she couldn't say for sure, she suspected which had come last. Maria died with a bottle in her hand, and a blood-alcohol level of 0.45, which no doubt had left her in a state so benumbed that it probably didn't allow for tears.

"Forget about it," she said, as she made her way back into the bedroom to grab her phone. Taking it from the nightstand, she dialed Kelly's number—at the office. Gillian never allowed herself to cross boundaries. *No drunk dialing. Ever.* Still, there were bound to be a few butt dials here and there, because you couldn't work with someone and not have their number in your outgoing calls. However, no personal conversations. No poignant memories dragged into the light of day. The past was gone, finished. Done. Gillian was very, very good about staying in the here and now.

She walked the phone back into the living room and sank down onto the sofa, staring at her closed computer on the coffee table. For some reason, she hadn't told Kelly about Gigi yet. Instead, she'd come home tired after spending time at the hospital and gone to straight to work, emailing with questions instead of calling. She was up late last night working on the Burke account. Kelly would see the time stamps on the files, and note the late work hours, but the only real red flag was the simple fact that Gillian was usually online and available for questions by 9:00 a.m.

On the other end of the line, the phone rang, rang, and rang . . .

At this hour, there probably wasn't a meeting . . . In fact, at 11:45, Kelly was probably getting ready to go to lunch. Gillian scratched the back of her head, thinking about recent events. It seemed to her . . . even before Gigi's stroke . . . he'd been avoiding her a bit. Whenever he had something to say, he wrote it in an email or gave the message to Gillian's assistant.

Could it be that he was finally seeing someone? Would he bring her to the office? Maybe she was there now, waiting for Kelly to gather his things? *Cell phone. Wallet. Computer.* Would he leave for the day?

But, of course, he'd rarely taken time off to spend with Gillian. He'd merely assumed she would be content to sit home and watch *Band of Brothers*.

When did he stop flirting? And why don't you know?

The call went to voicemail. Frowning, Gillian hung up without leaving a message. She dialed his number again, because even the thought of him dating made the little demon on her shoulder ache to reach for a drink, although it was way too early and she wasn't about to do it.

Especially not today.

"Answer," she demanded.

"Hey," he said, sounding breathless. *But why?*

It was on the tip of Gillian's tongue to ask why it took him so long to answer the phone. Only reminding herself that her grandmother's situation took precedence over any curiosity she had about her ex's lunch plans, so she said, "Hey, it's Gillian."

The bitterness in his voice was like vermouth in a martini, hard to miss. "I know," he said.

"What are you doing?"

"Working." There was a long, ambiguous pause. "What are *you* doing, Gillian?"

Gillian blew out a sigh. "Clearly, not working, as I'm sure you have discerned."

Silence.

No one else could say so much without saying anything at all. And still, Gillian couldn't tell if he was angry or worried. "Hey . . . it's Geeg," she said, forcing the words out. "She's . . . had a stroke."

Silence again.

"They're moving her into rehab today."

His tone softened. "Rehab?"

Gillian dabbed a finger to the corner of her left eye. "Yes, and no . . ."

Find your strength, Gillian.

"Is she okay?"

Asked with more warmth than he had displayed toward her in three years, his simple question came closer to discomposing her than anything else had all week. "I'm fine, but . . ." She swallowed. "Well . . . she won't be coming home."

"What happened?"

This. This was why she hadn't called him yet.

More tears sprang to Gillian's eyes, but she curbed the tide, swallowing convulsively, working the muscles of her throat until finally she could speak. "She . . . suffered . . . a stroke—massive. It left her with what doctors are calling global aphasia."

"Global . . . aphasia?"

Gillian had the impression he was having trouble getting words out himself. "Yeah." She swallowed again. "Widespread damage to the language centers of the brain. She can't speak or presumably understand speech. And . . . there's . . . paralysis."

That awful expression on her grandmother's face unnerved Gillian because it spoke of something terrible. It spoke of fear. It was as though something had frightened her and now she was trapped in the memory forever, like a horrific mental prison.

Silence again.

Gillian wished Kelly were standing in front of her so she could gauge whether he needed a hug. At one time, he had been close to her grandma, but he'd given Gigi up in the divorce as thoroughly and willingly as though she'd been an ugly set of china.

His voice was thick. "I'm sorry," he said.

Gillian tasted the salt on her own lips. "Thank you," she said. "I figured you ought to know. And . . . Well . . . I'll be needing some time off."

Even now, she couldn't admit she needed him.

"Of course. Yeah. Don't worry about a thing, Gillian. We'll handle whatever comes in. Take all the time you need." He never called her Gilly anymore.

No one could speak her name the same way he did, with that

same intonation—a heady combination of tenderness, a little playfulness, and just a hint of seduction.

Actually, she'd once broken up with a guy because he'd said her name with such brute force, as though it were a reprimand. "Gillian!" Like that.

"Thanks," Gillian said.

For a moment, Kelly lingered on the phone . . . waiting . . . probably for the right moment to hang up. No matter how you might feel about your ex-wife, it probably wasn't appropriate to hear this kind of news and simply say, "Okay, thank you for telling me, bye." And yet, gone were the days when he might have offered more than a "Yeah, don't worry about a thing."

Kelly wasn't cold exactly, but despite the fact that he'd so often accused Gillian of being frigid, he seemed perfectly capable of shutting down his emotions and moving forward with blinders on. That he'd not yet dated anyone seriously was merely a testament to the fact that he was picky about whom he chose to spend time with.

Or, maybe he wasn't all that picky and he was merely good at hiding his private life—unlike Gillian. She was an open book. "Okay. Well . . . thanks."

"No problem," he said, and the barriers went back up again, solid as bricks, only this time his tone held a lingering note of empathy. "Keep me posted, okay?"

"I will," she promised, and hung up. "Forget about it," she said crossly.

Forget about it, forget about it, forget about it.

4

BONE CHINA

"You sure you can handle it?"

The last thing Gillian meant to do was nurture doubt, but it would be irresponsible not to ask, since she was essentially sweeping everything off her plate and into Dana's lap.

"Yes," Dana said. "Stop worrying. I thought you were taking time off?"

Exits sped by—Coit, Spring Valley, Beltline—all a blur. "I am, but he's so high-maintenance. Remember, three comps, no more. Then charge him for additional iterations, unless the changes are minimal. It's spelled out in the contract, but you're going to have to enforce it—Burke has a history of asking for umpteen revisions."

"Got it."

"Oh, yeah, and remember that he wants his labradoodle in the logo, like an Alpine St. Bernard with a barrel around his neck. It's a sentimental value prop. Give it to him, please; only try not to make it look derivative."

"It's a dog with a cask around his neck. There are only so many ways to draw that. The image itself is derivative."

"Try," Gillian pleaded. "Please."

"Okay."

"What does Kelly say?"

"He says not to bug you. As far as he's concerned, so long as Burke's checks don't bounce, he doesn't care if I put a barrel around the dog's neck and a space shuttle up his ass."

Gillian laughed. Her husband's humor, even secondhand, was a bright spot this morning. "This is why he's in charge of books, not the accounts."

Dana laughed as well.

"Hey, don't tell him I called, okay?"

"I won't."

"Thanks," Gillian said. "Okay. I'll let you get back to work. I promise not to check in anymore today. I think I just needed to hear a friendly voice."

Before Gillian could hang up, Dana asked, "How are you holding up?"

Her soft Texas drawl was soothing in the way a parent's should be, in spite of her youth. At twenty-two, Dana Salvo was the youngest designer on Gillian's team, but she had the instincts of someone who'd been designing for years. If Gillian were to leave the firm, Dana could easily replace her. The thought reared unexpectedly.

"As well as to be expected."

"I'm sorry, Gillian."

"I know. I know. Alright, let me go."

Even now, Gillian couldn't talk about Gigi's condition, not without battling tears. A good cry might make her feel better, but she wasn't ready yet. She hung up, promising not to call again, and then settled her attention on the road.

Parker, Spring Creek, Legacy. More exits flew past.

No matter how many times she made the trek north, it felt as though she were traveling back through time, but times were changing. The bubble surrounding her hometown was getting the air sucked out of it. Soon McKinney would be just like the rest of North Texas—zero-lot-line houses metastasizing like skin cancer across the face of Texas.

Used to be—after JFK, but before the boom years, before the tollway, and before the endless highways and outlet centers—the thirty-minute drive north was a lonesome sojourn. Flat lands, few trees, the sunset so large it gave the impression of being on a lonely boat adrift at sea, sailing beneath a long, tall moon. Except that on this endlessly flat, dusty ocean, the boat cruised north on hot rubber tires, and the moon was a mean, fiery orb that shriveled anything standing long beneath its steady gaze. For Gillian, this was a good time to contemplate life's little mysteries, or mentally pore over the day's schedule, or even just zone out and watch mile markers fly by.

Nowadays, it was only the last few miles on Old Mill Road that offered any sense of remoteness, but once on that stretch of road, the manufactured lawns fell away and there was an overall impression of brown and white. Although these colors might not be the greatest sensory experience for most people, brown and white provided Gillian with a strong sense of home.

As a kid, it had been the rows and rows of fluffy white balls on twiggy crops that had given Gillian that impression. But the cotton fields had long since vanished by the time she was ten— like her grandfather, *poof*. And once those cotton fields were all played out, brown was the only impression for miles and miles beyond the dirty white house—brown in copious shades: redbed clay, sand-bedded tumble grass, gold-tipped sagebrush. Half mesquite woodlands, half prairie, North Texas was seriously thirsty land, so it was easy to imagine how a bit of mismanagement could whip up a dust bowl—but, hey, one guy's drought was another man's gusher, right?

At least that's how it seemed.

On the heels of Black Sunday, Henry Hayden Noble—
Gillian's great-granddad—picked up the land around Noble
Ranch, plus a small house, for something like two hundred
dollars per acre from a couple who couldn't afford to hold on to
their land. The worst of the droughts were further north, up in
the Panhandle, but with a sickly kid and another baby on the
way, the couple escaped east. Their failed investment became
Henry Noble's gusher. Not Texas tea, per se, but the next best
thing: cotton. Cotton was McKinney's version of black gold. Luckily, Henry had saved a bit of money from the sale of illegal
whisky, and with his savings, he'd made a new beginning for his
family in McKinney, Texas. But, unlike her father and grandfather, Henry Hayden Noble hadn't been a bad guy, just a man
who'd believed in searching for silver linings in dark clouds.
Some people were like that. She knew a guy who'd invested in
airline stocks the day after 9/11. Only Gillian couldn't help but
wonder if there could be bad karma in that kind of thinking . . .
karma that wove its way into the fabric of a family and inalterably
changed it.

Chewing on the inside of her lower lip, thinking about that—
about her dad and uncle, and even her mother—she drove past a
mess of new roads all paved in the sweeping, methodical fashion
city planners had. Surrounded by fresh cement dust, the embry-
onic subdivision was as yet devoid of landscaping or any defining
lots, but there was a sign that read "Welcome to Miller's Crossing." It had an historic looking rendition of the old cotton mill in
its logo. Only this new subdivision would be nothing like the old
mill community that had existed south of the factory, with parks
for the kids, bands playing, and town-wide picnics down by the
creek. Unlike the Noble house, which sat atop a knoll, these new
houses would be like hive pods, with front doors that were rarely
used. Like folks in a witness protection program, their inhabi-
tants would come and go through alleys that led to a road that led
to a job and back home again. On rare occasions, you might hear

voices in some random backyard or spot the rise of smoke from a rusted-out grill, but you wouldn't actually see anyone unless you scaled a privacy fence. And even then, it was a long shot, like spotting a bobcat in the city. However, Gillian wasn't one to throw stones. Essentially, she was a part of that rat race, creating "home" designs for binary addresses. It paid well, but she never felt the same sense of accomplishment her grandmother had seemed to feel at the end of every day. Good days, bad days, Gigi had never had time for "cocktails." She'd slept like a baby after a hard day's work. Her steadfast presence was as fierce as the Texas sun, no project ever too big for her to tackle, right up until the end. Eighty-four years old and she'd still been out there cleaning horse stalls. "Gigi!" Gillian had admonished a few weeks ago. "What in God's name are you doing out here?"

Shovel in hand, Gigi had slid her a censuring glance. "Don't use the lord's name in vain," she'd said. "I taught you better than that." And she'd continued shoveling out Baby's stall.

Baby, short for Baby Girl Blue, wasn't a baby any longer. She was a racehorse rescue some folks might have sold off for glue. Of course, Gillian would never advocate such a thing—she loved animals more than she did people—but there were places to set a good horse out to pasture that were better kept than an eighty-four-year-old could manage, feisty though she might be.

"Sorry," Gillian had said, knowing better than to rush in and take the shovel from her. Well intentioned or not, Gigi would have taken the backside of her shovel to Gillian's hind side.

"Can't get good help anymore," she'd said.

"Are you going to try another ad?"

"Maybe."

"What happened to the last guy?"

"'He was more interested in poking around his cell phone, so I told him to get on out of here and go home."

Gillian nodded. Smart phones were an employment hazard. She would have liked to say it was a teenager's folly, but age didn't seem to be any sort of criteria for addiction to technology. She argued for a bit of common sense. "Maybe it's time to give her up?"

Her grandmother's head snapped toward Gillian. "Baby?"

Gillian winced. "Yeah."

"Not on your life!" she'd said. "We girls will be kicking up our toes right here." *Right here.* She pointed to her feet. *On Noble land.* "The only difference is that Baby gets to be buried over yonder, 'neath that pecan tree, and I get to be carted off and tossed 'neath some heap of dirt I ain't never turned before. Stupid laws," she'd said. "Stupid, dumb laws. Ain't no God-given reason I shouldn't get to be buried on my own land. It's my land," she'd railed. "I don't want you to go selling it off to no snake oil salesmen. I worked too hard to keep it from going down the tubes, you hear me?"

Gillian sighed over the memory.

Plain spoken and grumpy as she was, nothing would be the same without her.

Turning onto the old dirt road that led to the main house, the two-seater hit a sandy patch in the narrow lane and spun its back tires, kicking up dust. The acreage was still mostly fenced off. The road leading to the main house had never been paved. Much like the house itself, any vehicle entering the lot would immediately accrue at least a quarter-inch of dust.

Up by the main house, nose up in the sloping driveway, Gigi's dirty, ancient Aztec-gold El Dorado sat, untouched for who knows how long. The keys were likely still in the ignition.

Her grandmother hadn't been driving much before the event, because one day she'd found herself in the parking lot at Walmart, disoriented and wondering how she'd gotten there—and, more importantly, how to get home. After that incident, Gillian offered to buy her groceries and run her errands and Gigi had relented, if only grudgingly, probably so Gillian would be forced to come by at least once every other day to touch base and pick up a list.

Sometimes she wondered whether that had been her grandmother's way of forcing Gillian to stay on the straight and narrow. Taking care of someone else did that for you; it forced you to think outside yourself. In fact, now that she thought about it, Gigi's parking lot incident had happened soon after Gillian's divorce . . . so, for three years she'd been coming by nearly every day, and this was the longest she'd gone without a visit to the house.

Home sweet home.

Same as it ever was.

Her grandmother's house was part classical revival, part bungalow, part American foursquare—something like the Burton house over on West Hunt Street, but with one significant difference. The Burton house was on the official register of historic homes.

By definition, American Foursquare architecture was "mostly plain, and incorporated 'honest' handcrafted woodwork, *not* purchased from a mail-order catalog." And therein lay the rub. Despite being nearly eighty years old, the house on Noble Ranch was a Sears "Modern" kit home, the likes of which all sported names like The Avalon, The Olivia, and The Corona.

After the first house on the property burned down, sometime around 1938, her great-grandfather had purchased a brand-new house, every board cut and fitted, from a Sears, Roebuck & Co. catalogue. It was the white-collar thing to do back in the day, but it had a blue-collar stigma—like tract homes versus custom homes, except there was nothing resembling a tract home in her grandmother's house. Among its best features was a wraparound porch with Doric columns and exposed rafter ends that begged visitors to, "grab a glass of tea and set a spell"—*set*, not *sit*, for reasons Gillian never properly understood.

Gillian also loved the stained glass transoms, but, unlike the house on West Hunt Street, which was painted in soft greens and pale yellows that properly accentuated its rich historic details, the house on Noble Ranch was painted a gritty lead white—simply white—because Gigi always said, "We don't need to impress no one, Gilly Bean. Don't go puttin' on airs."

Those people in that house on West Hunt. *The Fergusons.* "They're puttin' on airs," Gigi had said. And later, after Gillian met Tyson and Tamara Ferguson, she'd understood what her grandmother meant. The twins' mother had marched through the halls, led by the tip of her nose, into the principal's office to assure everyone who would listen that her perfect little boy and adorable little girl would never, ever, ever stick gum into anyone's hair. Certainly, her son wouldn't do it, because he was a Ferguson, and because her father was one of McKinney's original founders —didn't everyone know that? Yeah, Gillian got it. Indeed, they were putting on airs, and so, naturally they would never, ever paint a house leaden white. No matter what, they always hired professional painters who took their time to get it right, ensuring every detail was authentic—unlike Geeg, who hired out painting to teenagers because she'd believed in instilling a certain work ethic in "young folk." It had never mattered to Geeg whether the shingled hip dormers and accents were painted deep woodsy green or Terra Cotta, or whether the sashes and railings were painstakingly trimmed with golden wash. She only cared that good kids were keeping busy and staying honest.

This was how Gillian met Kelly. He'd come over one fine summer day with his older brother to paint the house, and Gillian fell for him the instant she saw him. Her passions had soared from boredom to delight in less than the time it took to inhale a breath.

At sixteen, Kelly had had a swimmer's body, tall and lean, without a pinch of fat around his waist. His dirty blond hair and dark eyes were like honey and chocolate, warm and rich. He was the sort of guy who could get away with having two distinctively feminine names.

"Hey, Ruby," one of the older boys had teased, when he glanced over his shoulder to find Kelly raking his sun-kissed bangs out of his face and smiling at Gillian. "Get your ass to work."

Hey, Ruby, the guy had said without any trace of mockery, but Gillian wondered then what kind of mom and dad named a boy Ruby. Only later, she'd discovered that his name was actually Kelly—which wasn't altogether better, but somehow he managed to be all spiders and snakes, and not one bit sugar and spice.

Even now, as much as Gillian hated to confess it, he had an easy smile that sent her pulse racing. People naturally gravitated to him, like a field of bluebonnets leaning toward the sun.

Only back then, he was the sort of guy who'd lived for the moment, embracing life fully. He'd watched sunsets from rooftops and made secret dates to go skinny dipping down at Bush Springs. He'd reminded Gillian of a classic James Dean type, living his life by a Brownsville Station song. Except that he'd never "smoked in the boy's room." And despite his easy demeanor, he'd developed a fierce "do right" attitude that ironically fell more in line with deep woodsy green shingles and golden-washed sashes. But Kelly also believed in living and letting live, and so it was perfectly understandable that her ex-husband had been content to slather on thick coats of white paint, so long as the house didn't belong to him. This would exactly mirror his attitude about marriage. Until the day they'd said "I do," Kelly Ruby had been willing to live and let live.

And then everything changed.

Parking behind the El Dorado, Gillian turned off the car. She sat staring at the house a long while. As much as she'd loved the house, she'd cried the day her grandmother told her it would someday belong to her, because as a child the mere thought of losing Gigi had been a terrifying prospect. At thirty-eight, it was still frightening.

Without Rebecca Lee Frazer, Gillian was alone in the world, and the house looked about as forlorn as Gillian felt.

Opening the car door, Gillian slid out, then marched over to the El Dorado to peer inside. As she'd supposed, the keys were still in the ignition. With Gigi out of the picture, there wouldn't be much in the way to prevent Jeff or Joe from taking the car, although Gillian didn't care about cars, vintage or otherwise. They could have it if they wanted it, so she left the keys where they were.

Aside from the house itself, she didn't hold sentimental attachments to things. Like people, things came and went. It was better not to get attached.

The front door had been left unlocked—also not unusual, but considering that Gigi wouldn't be coming home, it was careless. Anyone could have come in.

Inside the house, the living room lamp was on—Gigi usually kept it on at night and sometimes forgot to turn it off come morning, which meant that the lamp must have been burning continuously for six days or more—though maybe her father or uncle had left it on when they'd come searching for Gigi's will? Either way, she was surprised the bulb hadn't fried, especially with the house's ancient wiring. Maybe it would be appropriate if the house burned down—again. After all, a Noble built it; technically, her grandmother was the last of the Nobles. As much as Gillian loathed to admit it, she was a Frazer, which was doubtless the reason she was so screwed up.

Resigned to being the house's caretaker, she swung her purse off her shoulder as she walked through the front door. Tossing the handbag onto the brown-and-white floral sofa, she went straight for the lamp by the bookshelf. The bulb was scorching hot, singeing her palm when she tried to locate the switch to turn it off. Once found, she turned the knob to no avail—because, like the wiring, the lamp itself was ancient. The knob missed its catch, and Gillian turned it a few more times before it clicked off, giving the room respite from the heat.

The house seemed to sigh in relief and Gillian fell into her grandmother's easy chair to consider what came next.

It had been a long time since she'd spent any real time at the office; she didn't really need to keep an apartment nearby.

On the other hand, she wasn't all that sure she could live here, alone in the boonies. Never mind that it was no longer technically the boonies—it was still the boonies to most folks. Truth was, Gillian liked being near the restaurants.

And, okay, yes, the bars.

What was she going do with her downtime? Sit in her grandmother's chair and learn to knit? *Good God.* She didn't like keeping her own company; how could she blame Kelly for not wanting to be around her?

Shannon liked her. In fact, Shannon liked her so much she hardly ever went a night without calling and asking to meet Gillian at some place or another.

Dana liked her as well. But Dana worked for her, so technically Gillian couldn't consider Dana a friend—more like an employee with benefits.

Poor Dana. She sat contemplating RocketDog Brewery, Nick Burke, and the logo of the dog with the beer cask hanging from his neck.

And then she thought about Kelly's barbed response and smiled, envisioning a space shuttle crammed up the poor dog's ass. It was just like Kelly to say a thing like that, but that raw, dry humor was no longer accessible to Gillian. He was all business now, polite as he had ever been.

Whatever. What kind of name was RocketDog for a brewery, anyway? Gillian didn't know what the name lent itself to, but it didn't sound like a brewery.

Her head was hurting again. Warmed by the heat of the lamp,

the chair smelled too much like Gigi, and probably would for some time to come.

In fact, the entire house smelled like her—a blend of Vicks VapoRub, lavender, baby powder, and pecan jumbles. Her grandma was all about that Rub. She'd used it the way some folks used Robitussin and Pepto-Bismol.

Got sniffles? *Get the Rub.* Got muscle aches? *Get the Rub.* Got mosquitos? *Get the Rub.* In fact, all three items were staples in Gigi's cabinet, right alongside bleach, and of course there was the ever-present cod liver oil in the fridge. Oh, and Vidalia onions. "An onion a day keeps the doc away," she'd proclaimed.

"I thought that was supposed to be apples?"

"You eat apples, missy; I'll eat onions."

Her grandmother's sass was an endless source of amusement.

"An onion a day will keep everyone away," Gillian had quipped.

Her grandmother snorted. "Won't bother me any," she'd said. "I don't want anyone near me anyway."

Now, Gillian wondered if Vicks would get rid of hangovers. She didn't have a massive headache today, just a small one. Not enough to open another powder.

Ever since her grandmother's event, she'd been drinking at home—alone. But wasn't that a red flag? Drinking alone at inappropriate times?

She studied the bookcase, where a few of the volumes were slightly askew and out of order. But at least they'd put them back on the shelves after retrieving the will ...

Her grandmother's decoy safe was tucked behind twenty-four leather-bound volumes of the Fourteenth Edition Encyclopedia Britannica—as though it were the last place on Earth someone would disturb. And it could be true because Gillian couldn't remember ever pulling those dusty books off the shelf. So that's where the safe was stashed, the lock unchanged since her great-grandfather's day. Both her uncle and dad knew the combination, but . . . that was not where her grandmother stowed her real valuables. Only Gillian knew where those were, and if she were to die without revealing it, nobody would find them in a hundred years.

Gillian stared at the encyclopedias. On one of the few occasions her pop had spent any time with her, he'd pulled out the dried-up leather volume with the cutouts of the human anatomy, and went straight to the overlay with the human reproductive organs.

"See here, Gilly Marie," he'd said. "This is where a man gets himself a boy. Right here."

He pointed to the vagina entry and tapped the page hard, eyeing Gillian resentfully—presumably for not being male. Gillian had blushed, horrified to be learning about sex and childbirth at her father's whim—and not because he'd cared one whit about preparing her for the future. No. He'd wanted only two things: To let Gillian know, not for the first time, that she was a bitter disappointment to him. But also to peek at the safe hidden behind the books, as though to reassure himself it was still there.

Greedy bastard. So long as Gigi lived, the thought of disturbing her valuables felt cheap and tawdry. There was a tidy little sum for both her sons hidden in her real safe, but Gillian wasn't going to give it to them until Gigi was dead. The doctors hadn't wasted any time giving up on her and moving her into a nursing home, but Gillian wasn't ready to do that.

"There's nothing more we can do for her here," the doctor said. "She needs therapy . . . and she needs to know you're there for her. She's a strong woman."

They didn't know the half of it.

After her husband left, Rebecca Lee Frazer had raised two bratty boys all by herself. Word on the street was that her grandfather might or might not have left of his own accord, and that maybe he'd found his fate at the business end of a shotgun. As far as Gillian was concerned, she couldn't be bothered to find out for sure one way or the other. No matter how you looked at it, Big Joe

Frazer was a grade A jackass, and Gillian had too much respect for her grandmother to cut him any slack. He was a quitter; nothing more need be said.

Automatically, her thoughts returned to her last conversation with Kelly as she scratched at a piece of crust clinging to the arm of her grandmother's chair.

Yesterday, when he'd asked about Gigi's progress, it was the first time he'd spoken to her without that nasty bite in his tone—not that he would ever raise his voice to her. He would rather let his disappointment hang in the air, like unflappable wet laundry.

Where did everything go so wrong?

Annoyed with the question, Gillian bounced up from the easy chair. She made her way through the dining room, toward the kitchen, inspecting the house with critical eyes.

She ran a finger along the dining room trim, testing for dust. The tip of her finger turned black. Clearly, Gigi's eyes were not what they used to be.

Still, she loved all the little details, especially the picture-trim molding in the dining room, although she wasn't into all the gewgaws and clutter. If she meant to stay for any length of time, she'd have to move Gigi's stuff into the basement—or maybe into storage.

Somehow, although she couldn't put a finger on how or why, she had a sense the house itself would be her salvation. All her tethers were bound here.

Built on a pier-and-beam foundation, the original plans for the house had included seven rooms, one bathroom, a basement, an alcove, and a sleeping porch on the second floor. There was no attic space, and the basement was a rarity in these parts because the ground was so expansive. When it got wet, it swelled and when it dried, it shrank, which made for lots of cracks and shifts in the foundation. Because of this, Gillian was not allowed to go down in the basement. And, furthermore, to prevent anyone from venturing downstairs, her grandmother had taken the bulb out of the ceiling's light socket. So, any trips downstairs necessitated a flashlight. And even then, it wasn't advisable because there were no rails and the stairs were steep.

"Holy crap," Gillian said, as she walked into the kitchen, discovering it in shambles—chairs knocked over. Correction: one chair. It lay on its side near the dinette. Gillian swept it up and set it back on all fours, pushing it back beneath the table before turning to examine the room.

There were ants all over the counters—hordes marching up and down, all about. One cup sat on the table, half-filled with a dark, oily substance—likely coffee by the looks of it. Another cup lay smashed on the floor, an oasis for thirsting ants. They were congregated about a dark spot on the floor, like tiny nomads at a watering hole. Coffee too, by the looks of the stain.

Over near the counter, Gillian found more ants, all scurrying up and into a crack in the wall. But the sink was spotless, not a dish to be found—aside from a single glass that may or may not have been present during her grandmother's event. Could be her father or uncle put it there, but Gillian doubted it. For one of them to take a few extra steps to set a glass into the sink was unthinkable. Come to think of it, if there wasn't someone on hand to pour them a glass of anything, Jeff and Joe would probably die of thirst before stirring themselves. Gillian was convinced that's why her dad kept Sharon around—not because he loved her. Like his own father before him, Joe Jr. didn't know what it meant to love. Sharon was his indentured servant and his punching bag, and nevertheless, she seemed perfectly content with the role. So, whatever. You couldn't help someone who didn't know they needed help.

Groaning in disgust, Gillian turned on the hot water. The faucet sputtered before releasing its contents. With old pipes, it took a while longer for the water to heat up, so she grabbed a washcloth that was neatly folded beside the sink and soaked the rag with cold water, wetting it thoroughly, then wringing it out.

And then, leaving the water to run, she took the washcloth over to the spot on the floor, gingerly lifting up the broken coffee cup.

It was one of her grandmother's favorites—bone china she generally only brought out for guests. Creamy white cups with pink country roses. Gigi had napkin rings to match. Setting the broken pieces aside on the table, Gillian swept the wet rag over the stain. Ants scattered at her intervention and a bit of the black dissolved into red, startling her.

Did Gigi cut herself during the fall?

Gillian screwed up her face. So far as she could remember, her grandmother didn't have any cuts. The left side of her face was badly bruised, and there had been a knot at the side of her head, near the temple, but the nurse had assured Gillian those injuries were minor—a result of the fall she'd taken when she had the stroke.

Still . . . it could be that a little blood was mixed into the spill, and that would explain the ants. As far as she knew, ants didn't love coffee and Gigi didn't put cream or sugar in hers. In fact, Gigi used to put out grounds during dry weather in order to repel them. On the other hand, there was sugar in blood . . .

Inspecting the rag closer, Gillian moved toward the sink, holding it under her nose to sniff. Smelling only the faint remnants of bleach, she frowned, then rinsed the rag out under the faucet, watching the current as the brown stain washed down the drain.

It was difficult to say; maybe the red was all in her imagination?

It took another few trips to the sink, wringing the rag each time, to get up the entire spot. Then, just out of curiosity, Gillian checked the cup that was still sitting on the table and found the contents thick and oily as well.

Two cups of coffee?

Maybe her guest liked sugar in their coffee. Beyond repair, Gillian tossed the broken cup into the trash, then picked up the remaining cup on the table, bringing it to the sink to wash. Watching the coffee dissolve and run off onto the white enamel, she looked for red . . . and saw nothing.

But who was here . . . with Gigi?

Her father? *No, couldn't be.* Jeff and Joe Jr. hated coffee—especially Gigi's black brew, which at one point her father had likened to truck oil.

After washing the cup, Gillian was forced to agree, although she was loathed to agree with either of the Frazer men about anything at all.

Her uncle Jeff was only slightly less annoying than her father. Probably because A, he had no offspring and wasn't in the habit of pretending he was other than who he was, and B, he was the youngest son and had spent far less time with their delinquent father before the idiot ran off. Whatever damage had been done to Jeff's personality was all a direct result of her father's influence. He'd learned how to be a grade A jackass from his older brother.

However, it was her dad who'd called to let her know about Gigi, and Gillian made a mental note to ask him if he knew who'd made the call to 911. *Someone must have.* Or they would have discovered Gigi much later.

More to the point, Gillian would have discovered her when she came to pick up a list. It wasn't likely that her dad would have happened upon her by chance. He didn't come around unless he meant to ask for money, which Gigi had stopped providing the day he was arrested for domestic abuse. Finally, after years of putting up with his bullshit, Gillian's mother had called the cops.

"No son of mine is ever gonna hit a woman and think I'm gonna support him," Gigi raged that day, and true to her word, she'd left Joe Jr. to raise his own bail.

The sound of water gurgling into the pipes brought Gillian back to the question of her grandmother's "fall." All things said and done, Joe would never harm Geeg. She was the one woman he thoroughly respected—as much as he respected anyone. He didn't have a choice in the matter. Gigi demanded respect. Gillian stared at the floor, thinking . . .

She had only assumed, for whatever reason, that her dad had found Gigi and then rushed her to the hospital. But maybe someone else did that? *Maybe someone else was here? Two coffee cups, two people?*

She tried to recall what time she'd received her father's call, and opened her phone to check the time stamp on the call from the hospital. The hospital had called first, somewhere around 1:00 p.m., just as Gillian was leaving the pet store. It had been close to 1:30 once she'd reached the hospital. By then, Gigi was no longer in the ER. She had been moved into intensive care. So, clearly, she had been there awhile already. But how long? These were all questions that, until now, she hadn't had the presence of mind to ask.

Considering who else might have been in the house, she cleaned up the kitchen, only marginally sorry for having to dispatch so many ants. Only one of them could occupy this house, and Gillian wasn't giving it up to swarms of insects. It was only after she'd washed and put away the coffee cup that she realized she'd already mentally replaced her grandmother's dishes with her own.

Yeah, this was where she needed to be . . . but . . .

She reopened the cupboard, reexamining the cups—neat rows of saucers and teacups on the top shelf, the mix-matched coffee cups on the second shelf, and the sundry water glasses on the lowest shelf . . .

At five foot four, Gigi wasn't tall enough to reach the top shelf without help and her stool wasn't close by. It was stowed neatly in the corner by the pantry, though she could have easily replaced it there after retrieving the cups. Her grandmother was a neat freak. But this was the thing that was still bothering Gillian: there were two good china cups that had been in use.

Two.

"Hmm," she said, grabbing a water glass. And then, fishing another powder out of her back pocket, she dumped the contents into the clean glass and turned the faucet on, filling her glass.

"CLEAR AWAY THE CLUTTER. MAKE ONE LAST TRIP THROUGH THE MAIN PART OF THE HOUSE JUST BEFORE YOUR HUSBAND ARRIVES."
—*THE GOOD WIFE'S GUIDE, HOUSEKEEPING MONTHLY*

8:37 P.M., Tuesday, July 5, 1960

REBECCA'S EYES swam with tears.

The instant the first dish crashed against the wall, both boys bolted up the stairs, as if on cue. Two broken dishes and one shattered cup later, Joe exploded out the front door—cursing so loudly Rebecca was certain they must have heard him clear to the mill.

The evidence of his fury was now permanently etched into the hardwood of her dining room floor. If only he had managed to hit the carpet instead. You couldn't replace floors like these. They were special, like her grandmother's bone china.

Rebecca dearly loved that china. It was one of the few things she had remaining of her grandmother's, because everything else had perished during the fire that took the original house.

She wiped away a tear that threatened to spill from the corner of one eye.

Lord knew, she wasn't a saint. If she had been, she would never have fallen for the likes of Joe. And this was the thanks she got for giving him two children and a ranch? *What a silly fool you are.* Sometimes she wished he would leave and never come back.

What must her neighbors think? Thankfully, there was no one close by, but she knew good and well that if she got on that party line, she would catch them all gossiping behind her back. Already, she'd managed to overhear more than she wished.

Why, oh why, wouldn't he go?

Some people got divorced. It happened all the time now. Only Rebecca had two little boys to consider, so maybe an occasional flare up was worth not seeing her children grow up without a pa? *It's only a teacup,* she reasoned.

A fine china teacup from Royal Albert, in England, she argued silently. A wedding gift from her grandma's aunt, who'd lived in Yorkshire at the time. She'd bought the set in a shop outside of London—so, yes, it was irreplaceable. It was one of the few things her family brought with them from Farwell, because it was precious.

Damn, Joe.

Could he not appreciate heirlooms? How could he not see how upset this would make her? Did he value nothing? Did he have to throw things every time? What on God's earth was wrong with that man? He was getting worse; the stress was killing her.

So, okay, she wasn't going to get that job. What did that matter? She had plenty to do here on the ranch. The land wasn't gone—not yet—and she could go ahead and take the buyout, burn the crop. But, once again, could she even do that without Joe's permission?

Well, of course she could, and why should he say no? He hadn't had much interest in farming anyhow. That was the main reason the ranch was going under. She couldn't hire the help she needed to keep it going because he claimed the men would only hang around, trying to get under her skirts. But she couldn't hire a bunch of women, could she?

Though why not?

The mill hired mostly men. Why couldn't Rebecca employ

their wives? *Because she didn't have a cent to her name, that's why.* If only...

If only she could take the boys and go, but no...

This was her land, not Joe's. Maybe that man didn't care what became of it, but Rebecca sure did. Her mother and father would roll over in their graves if they caught wind of what was going on under their roof. Her papa would have put Joe out on his boots long before now, regardless of vows, and her mother would have been right behind him, shotgun in hand. Texas didn't rear weak-kneed women.

Gingerly picking up the broken shards of her teacup, she wondered again about the legalities of land ownership now that she was Joe's lawful wife and now that her parents were both dead. Did he own the ranch outright? Did she have any recourse?

Rising carefully to her feet, Rebecca took the largest fragments to the garbage bin, poring over each fragment before tossing it out. *So delicately painted. So lovely.* It broke her heart to let each one go. Tears slid down her cheeks, though not a sound escaped her lips.

The boys were upstairs playing, their voices bolder now that the front door had opened and shut one final time. The night air was cooler, the heat not quite so oppressive. The windows were open to let in a thin summer breeze. Outside, the chirping of crickets was louder than Joe's yelling had been, even despite the ponderous silence.

She closed the trash bin and went back into the dining room to sweep up the remaining shards from the floor, and while she did this, she reconsidered the idea of hiring women at the ranch. She thought about who might be interested in doing something like this... maybe for a share of the profits... Julia Hart needed money. Her daughter Mindy was plenty old enough to come along with her to work. Rebecca and Julia had been good friends since their school days, but now they only ever saw each other at

Sunday church—and not much at all since Rebecca stopped attending.

Dottie Shepherd might also be interested. She and Billy had no kids, and it seemed to Rebecca that so long as he was out carousing with Joe, that was never going to happen. There was talk about him gettin' into trouble over at the Roadhouse, and in fact, Rebecca suspected Joe was into much the same.

And, well, maybe Camilla Heard? That lady could lift near as much as any man. She was a lifelong spinster, and some people liked to say she was fond of ladies, not men. Rebecca had no inkling 'bout any of that, but it wouldn't matter to her how Camilla passed her time outside of work.

So, if she took the buyout, just this once, she could use that money to plant a full crop come March. Her pa had never bothered himself to process cottonseed, but her mother always encouraged it. Like sunflower oil, it was wonderful for cooking, and her father always kept a pile to use as feed and fertilizer.

Too bad Procter & Gamble was no longer using cottonseed in their Crisco. No matter; all she really needed was a good huller, and she could sell the cotton to Waco—so long as they didn't close their doors as well.

For extra money, they could harvest the oil to sell. Plus, she could sell the stalks for wood chips. Tough times meant you couldn't leave anything to waste. All she needed to do was find a way to get rid of the boll rinds and residual lint. And, if she could hire enough women, they could do it the old-fashioned way, by beating the stalks on a wooden mallet. Then, they could grind up the hulls for feed. Best of all, Joe would only expect money from the cotton crop, not from the rest.

There was merit to this plan, and as she repaired the dining room and then the kitchen, Rebecca continued to work out the problem in her head. Once the dishes were all washed and the leftovers were stacked in the fridge, she made a trip down into the basement to retrieve a box. She found a good, sturdy one that was half empty and hauled it back upstairs. One by one, she placed the remaining pieces of her grandma's china into the crate, wrapping each piece carefully with the good white napkins her mother had embroidered.

No need for these up here anymore.

They were far too precious to leave in harm's way.

Mean old man.

Once her china was neatly packed, Rebecca carted the box back down into the basement and found a neat spot where no one was bound to trip over it. And then she headed back up the stairs, turning around to assess what all was amassed in the basement.

Little by little she had brought down the things that mattered most. Her grandmother's quilt and the rocking chair her pa built. She'd brought the chair down the day Joe tossed it across the nursery, cracking a runner against the wall, and the quilt after he'd laughingly put out a cigarette on one of the squares. Now, she stood staring at the rocker.

Her husband was innately lazy. Just so long as she didn't give him ultimatums, she needed but place obstacles in his path. If it didn't have anything to do with money or alcohol or gambling, it didn't take much to put him off.

The original plans for windows in the basement had been scrapped. Her pa had done this to keep sand from blowing in. You simply didn't escape Black Sunday without keeping in mind that, at its whim, the earth could easily bury you alive. After the tornado in '48, her father shored up some of the walls, turned the wooden stairs into concrete steps, and placed a bib of concrete around the stairs. The rest of the basement had dirt floors, except around the bases of the piles her father erected for support.

Lifting a brow, Rebecca turned and made her way back down the stairs. She dragged the rocking chair over, beneath the single bulb in the room, and took off her apron. Then, carefully, very carefully so she wouldn't fall, she climbed atop the chair. Holding one arm out to keep her balance, she used the apron to protect her hand as she unscrewed the bulb. It remained loosely threaded into the socket when the room fell into darkness.

That should be enough.

Under cover of darkness, she smiled and got down, donning the apron about her neck again. And finally, letting her memory guide her, she dragged the chair away from the bulb. Confident now that nothing stood in her way, she went back up the stairs, closing the basement door behind her. It latched with a soft click.

5

HOMEMAKER

Inside the house, the air conditioner rattled in protest. Outside, there was a burning stillness in the air, interrupted only by the occasional whinny coming from Baby's stall. Without a trace of breeze, the air felt stale and old. No one came by. No one called. Even Dana kept her word.

Fine. It gave Gillian a chance to reflect on what she wanted out of life—not so simple a task as one might suppose. Far easier than focusing on what she did want, she thought a lot about what she didn't want. All week long, she'd remained painfully sober, and without that fog in her head, she had a clearer idea of what she proposed to leave behind.

Everything.

Before her grandmother's event, outside of a few annoying particularities, she had considered herself mostly content. The lack of a partner wasn't necessarily a problem, she'd convinced herself. Her inability to commit—even to a cat—might seem odd, though it saved her money on pet food and vets. Though at least she was aware of her shortcomings.

As for the drinking . . . it was habitual, not compulsory. She could stop any time. She'd already proven that, hadn't she? She wasn't an addict. She didn't need to drink. Alcohol only made it easier to cope with the emptiness deep down.

However, that emptiness could no longer be appeased by simply picking up the phone, or hopping into her car. She was already here, at Noble Ranch, where she would have been drawn.

Like a visitor to purgatory, Gillian longed for things past, but she had a strong desire to transcend these things and move on to a better place. Only beneath it all, there was a darker feeling dragging her down, a lurking shadow she couldn't shake. By all rights, she had no good reason to be depressed. She had a lot to be grateful for—a good job, great house full of memories of a life with a woman who'd selflessly given her all. Any problems she had in life were mostly self-induced.

So what if her father was a heartless bum? So what if her mom was a drunk? So what if her husband left her? These were all problems normal people faced, and eventually, most people weathered them with dignity. Still, ever since that day her grandmother went into the hospital, the shadows surrounding her had begun to lengthen...

Now that Geeg was gone, nothing would ever be the same. Consequently, the idea of carrying on as she had was loathsome. All those things she had been content to do before were now part of a lie she no longer wished to tell.

Shrugging off a cloak of sadness, Gillian made her way through her grandmother's files, just to be sure all her bills were paid. Staying occupied was crucial, she realized, but going back to work held zero appeal. The firm wasn't her baby; it was Kelly's. He'd pressed her into exploiting a skill set she'd only accidentally discovered she had. Graphic design was never Gillian's focus in college. She enjoyed art, but as far as application went, she'd rather do her own thing without having to worry about meeting someone else's expectations. As an afterthought, she'd pursued marketing and graphic design—but she'd done it for Kelly. Therefore, it stood to reason that she would begin to distance herself from the business as time went on. She also realized this much: she had begun to resent Kelly for pushing her in an unwanted direction.

Let him go. Let it all go, Gillian. What're you holding on to?

The question rolled around in her noggin while she took inventory of her grandmother's belongings, marking items with blue tape to be moved into storage.

She didn't have much to move over from her apartment—let's face it, not even a real bed—but she and Gigi had different tastes. Gillian's were less traditional. She appreciated clean lines and empty spaces, and she preferred her walls to be bare, with only an occasional abstract painting here and there, not a mishmash of family photos, mostly consisting of faces she didn't recognize.

Thankfully, her grandmother wasn't overly sentimental. There were but a few good portraits of Gillian, and fewer yet of her father and uncle, not a single one of her mom.

More so than Jeff, most of the photos of her father were tiny cameos, occupying random frames throughout the house. A few, tattered and torn, were jimmied into the frames of larger photos, as though her grandmother had taken them in and out, putting them away and back again.

Or at least Gillian imagined it this way, because the ambivalence was hers as well. These days, however, she mostly tolerated her father, and why should she feel differently? He was useless, like his dad.

Unsurprisingly, of all the photos Gillian pored through, none were of Joe Sr. Once you set aside the ones of Gillian, the great majority of those remaining were of Gillian's great-grandparents, with plenty of photos of their three cherubic children—Margaret, Henry, and Rebecca, better known to Gillian as Geeg.

Gillian came across one picture of Gigi in her mama's arms. She could see more of her grandma's expression in the tattered old picture than she could in the woman lying in the nursing home. It was a lovely photo of a blonde woman wearing a cream-colored dress and a mink shawl—or at least some type of fur that was no longer PC. Behind the woman sat a Studebaker pickup and a kid's back-clad leg, caught exiting the frame in a blur. The back of the photo was marked with the numbers 1937, presumably the year the family moved into to the newly constructed house. Out of all three kids, only Gigi had survived to adulthood. Henry, the middle child—it was most likely his leg exiting the photo—drowned when he was eight. They buried him in McKinney's cemetery. Margaret, the eldest, succumbed to a fever at ten. Two children gone in the space of just a few years—it was no wonder her grandmother was such a trooper, taking her lumps as they came. She'd watched her own mother bury two kids before she turned five herself.

One by one, Gillian placed the pictures into a box, intending to find them a new home once the house was returned to order. The remainder of the photos, mostly of her father and Jeff, she put into another box to be carted down into Purgatory—or the basement, as it was otherwise known.

Some of her grandmother's things could remain, but it was time to be realistic about Gigi's prognosis. Oddly enough, however, as she went through her grandmother's effects—most of them visually familiar—she had the strangest sensation that she had never actually seen some of them before. That was to say, she had seen them, to be sure. They were here, in Gigi's house, and they had been here in the house for most of Gillian's life, but Gillian had never truly seen them.

For example, take the table next to her grandmother's chair. It had a story, but Gillian didn't know what it was. There was no one left to tell it. Certainly not her dad or her uncle. As self-centered as those two were, they'd probably never asked a question about anything in all their lives that hadn't pertained to them. However, it wasn't as though Gillian had room to talk. She had grown up with this relic of ages past, setting her sweaty tea glasses on its surface, never really knowing where it came from. But the piece was fascinating. It was a table, but not a table, with glass sides revealing rows upon rows of spools with all the thread still intact. *Green. Red. White. Gray. Blue. Black. Brown. Yellow.* It was clearly a storage cabinet, but it was far too lovely to be shuffled away to Purgatory, so her grandmother had used it as a side table for her reading chair. Gillian had never once seen Gigi actually use the spools; her grandmother didn't sew, but for the occasional hem repair. So maybe the table had belonged to someone else in the family, like Gigi's mother—that elegant woman in the photograph. Gillian tried to imagine that woman seated at a sewing table, making dresses for her little girl, and the image filled her with a strange melancholy.

The cabinet was only a piece of furniture now, complete with water stains on top, most probably inflicted by Gillian herself, because Gigi had never revered it like the treasure it was.

Or maybe Gigi had valued the cabinet—who knew—but it was never important enough for Gigi to feel the need to reprimand Gillian for not using coasters.

Trying to remember the times Gigi had ever yelled at her, and remembering only a handful of spankings, Gillian's throat closed, but she didn't cry.

In fact, she couldn't remember the last time she'd allowed herself to indulge in a good, long sob—not even after her divorce. *Maybe Kelly was right?* Maybe Gillian was cold.

But if that were true, why did she hurt so much?

This much must be true: the day she finally let go, she was bound to set loose a flood to rival Noah's. And wouldn't that be a sight for thirsty old North Texas?

Come to think of it, flash floods were a thing here. Tears from Gillian might be equally as devastating. The thought turned her lips into a hint of a smile. At least Kelly would say such a thing. With that wit of his, he always knew exactly how to make her smile. But he was gone, and she was finished torturing herself. Her grandmother wouldn't have done it; neither should she.

It was crazy, wasn't it, that she and Gigi had both lost their husbands? There was little wonder that Gillian and Gigi were so much alike. Why wouldn't she be like her grandmother? Tough as nails on the outside, soft as marshmallow inside. The only difference between them, as far as Gillian could see, was the simple fact that Gigi had two kids, and the way it was looking, Gillian was bound to have none. Ironically, however, during one of Gillian's trips down into the basement, Gillian found a box of vintage magazines—a discovery that dumbfounded her, not so much because her grandmother had saved the issues, but because of what they were and what was inside. *Good Housekeeping, Life, Housekeeping Monthly, Texas Homemaker,* and *Better Homes and Gardens.* She lifted out a *Texas Homemaker* and flipped it open, surprised to find the pages marked with pen.

There was a prominent circle around a Clorox ad, with each word underlined in pen. Gillian had to look close to see that it was actually part of the print. Even so, there were notes in the margins of recipes, and checkmarks and X's above each of the articles, as though Gigi had been studying them.

Curious over the magazine contents, Gillian dragged the box upstairs to the kitchen. Only then, as she sat poring over the *Texas Homemaker* under better light, she grew more and more . . . perplexed. Nothing about the magazines matched the woman she thought she knew. *Nothing at all.* They were all about . . . subservience. That was the word that came to mind to describe what she was reading.

"Arrange his pillow and offer to take off his shoes. Speak in a low, soothing, and pleasant voice." What nonsense was that? Gillian couldn't imagine her grandmother had ever done such a thing, and if Gillian ever had, Kelly would have slid a thermometer under her tongue.

Thinking the stash must have belonged to her great-grandmother, Gillian closed the issue of *Texas Homemaker* to look for a date—October 1959. On the cover was a platinum blonde in a white sweater who looked something like Doris Day. She was peering over her shoulder with a hand at her back, as though patting herself. In the background stood a ghosted, smiling patriarchal figure—ever present and looming over her, judging her merits as a housewife.

Bizarre.

Gillian couldn't remember what year her grandparents died —both on the same day, she believed, in 1957 or maybe '58—a car accident, but Gigi rarely spoke of it. However, unlike the subject of her grandfather, the topic wasn't taboo.

She turned to a page with a recipe for pecan pie. Here, again, in the margins were notations—mostly corrections to the existing recipe—but this made her smile. "Too much sugar," it said, underlined three times. "Not good for kids." Another note read, "No good til October." Which would be right about when pecans ripened.

Seated alone at her grandmother's kitchen table, poring over magazines, with dim memories of eating pie, Gillian was reminded of *The Walking Dead*, where the world outside was lost, and worse, everyone remaining was turning into rotting, ambling corpses, and all that stood between Gillian and certain death was a weak chain on the back door and a few jars of pickled cucumbers. Her father and uncle would be the zombies, of course— both beyond saving.

Gillian tossed aside the magazine, feeling curiously ungrounded.

That might be the best way to describe it—as though she were a Chinese lantern set adrift, and now, with Gigi here but gone, she had no place to land and no one to pull her back.

Then again, Chinese lanterns didn't land, did they? They combusted in the atmosphere. *Self-destructed.* Like the Challenger on reentry. *Pieces on fire, raining down to Earth.*

The apocalyptic images only exacerbated her end-of-the-world-as-we-know-it mindset. Disgusted with herself, and her mood, she abandoned the vintage magazines.

Lately, she lived with a perpetual headache that couldn't be eradicated. Except that she couldn't blame it on alcohol, because she wasn't drinking. Although, maybe that was her problem? She wasn't drinking. It was only stress, she reassured herself. Only, how was it possible to be so stressed while surrounded by so much silence?

It must be a caffeine headache, she realized, as she reached into her back pocket for a powder. But her pocket was empty. *Ugh* . . . if she needed more incentive to get out and do the shopping, here it was.

Rising from the table, Gillian made herself a stiff cup of coffee from the last remaining grounds in her grandmother's cupboard —Folgers, not her favorite, but clearly not awful enough for Gillian to have made a trip to the grocery store. She had been holed up here, feeling sorry for herself for weeks.

"Caffeine," she added to her growing list on the fridge, when what she really meant was "headache powder." *Same difference.* The powders had a sturdy dose of caffeine, which was probably why she craved them. As for Kelly—the bone head—he hadn't called in to check on her even once. Then again, why would he? For years, Gillian had made it clear she didn't need him.

Once her coffee was prepared, she took the steaming mug out to the barn to visit with her grandmother's horse. She found Baby waiting for her, nosing eagerly at the stall door. Smiling at the welcome, Gillian set the mug down on a post and reached over to unlatch the door.

"There you go," she said.

Baby filed out, stamping her feet, as though to say, "It's about time, Gillian. Where ya been, honey?" But she didn't go far, moving off to one side, accustomed to hanging out while her stall was cleaned. After less than ten minutes in the barn, Gillian felt her nerves steady and her mood improve. She walked over and patted the horse and leaned in for a hug.

"It's just you and me, Baby Girl," she said. That was, unless Gillian should happen to decide to take in a few more strays. The possibility lingered as rudely as the scent of Baby's poo.

Except that it wasn't such a bad prospect. Not really. She had plenty of space on the ranch, and there were any number of ways she could supplement her income, if she ever got off her duff and faced the truth. She hated her job worse than she did shoveling crap.

And Baby was more appreciative of her efforts. The horse nudged the small of her back and Gillian reached back to pat the old girl's muzzle.

Baby Girl Blue was the last of a long line of rescue horses her grandmother had adopted—all female. She was like a big dog who, like Gigi, was a rarity in a field overrun by men.

Gillian had read somewhere that something like sixty-seven percent of race horses were male. Like her grandmother, Baby Girl Blue had set herself apart, coming close to winning the Kentucky Derby, a contest only three fillies had ever won since the thirties.

Unfortunately, Baby took a spill during the final race, unseating her rider. She ended up with a knee fracture that, while not a death sentence, put an end to her life in the races. Though once again, like Gigi, you couldn't tell by the horse's demeanor. She was as prideful as her owner.

After Gillian's grandfather left, Gigi hadn't wasted any time feeling sorry for herself. She'd formed a local women's union and built a thriving business, managing to keep it afloat even while others closed their doors. Due to Rebecca Frazer's thriftiness, she'd managed to survive the Waco Mill closing, as well as the mill at Love Field. And then, even after the McKinney Mill shut its doors—sometime around '69 or '70—Gigi continued to sell her cotton. At a time when men ruled the workforce, Rebecca Lee Frazer forged a path for herself and her sisters.

This is why Gillian couldn't reconcile the way her father and uncle turned out. Their characters were complete dichotomies to their mother's.

Fortunately, neither had bothered to come around since Gillian moved in, and Gillian was pretty sure they'd already pilfered whatever they'd wanted from the house—which was not to say they wouldn't expect a share of proceeds should Gilly happen to hold an estate sale. They might not give a damn about gewgaws or stoneware, but they sure would care about any money generated by a sale—all while giving equal priority to making certain neither expended one bit of energy to see anything done. She loathed to think of her father as a self-serving ass, but that's exactly what he was.

Only now, thinking about those magazines in the kitchen, Gillian grabbed a shovel and proceeded to scoop out the stall. Wondering at what changed her grandmother's attitude since jotting down those notes, she took a rake and combed the stall floor, getting rid of the soiled hay. Clearly the woman who'd written in the margins of those articles was not the same woman who'd rallied a group of ladies to form a local union.

By 1960—the year her grandfather walked out—the McKinney mill's main claim to fame was that it was one of only two mills west of the Mississippi manufacturing colored-print cloth. Later, it became a major manufacturer of denim. Using mostly locally sourced cotton—cotton her grandmother must have planted—it produced something like three hundred thousand yards of denim per week. Nine years after Gillian's grandfather left, the mill finally shut its doors, but Gigi kept her ranch going another thirteen years—all without Big Joe's help.

So, who needs a man? Not her grandmother. Not Gillian.

But you're a liar, Gillian argued silently.

She nipped at her lower lip, feeling an incredible yearning to hear Kelly's voice. Only pride kept her from dropping everything and going inside to get her phone—because why couldn't he bother to pick up his phone and call her? He said he loved her, but he let her go.

Anyway, it had been too long since she'd called him for anything other than business. She wouldn't have a clue how to begin a conversation with him—or even whether he was open to having one. Of course, he was too polite to hang up on her, so he might endure a brief chat, but it would be awkward at best, and it was bound to make Gillian feel worse than she already did.

No personal phone calls. Remember? Your rules.

The feeling would pass. It always did.

After Gillian finished with the raking, she grabbed the water hose and dragged it into the barn. She took her time, cleaned the stall right—just as her grandmother taught her to do—and then she refilled the stall with clean straw while Baby ambled around, staying close by.

Once the stall was clean, she led Baby back inside, and closing the stall door, she then stood a moment as her grandmother used to do, in no real hurry to leave.

Brushing a hand across the mare's muzzle, she let Baby sniff her, smearing her shiny black lips over the back of Gillian's hand. After a while, the mare lifted her coal black eyes, and Gillian felt a pang so deep it pricked at her soul. They were sad, knowing eyes.

After a time, Kelly had had eyes like hers.

Her grandmother's gaze had been just as canny, but without any pity. Whatever was happening in Gillian's life, Gigi always trusted her granddaughter was made of sterner stuff.

Inhaling a tight breath, she gave Baby a pat and a scratch beneath the muzzle, then she returned to the house, thinking Gigi had it all wrong: Gillian was nothing like her.

For one thing, why hadn't she realized how much work the ranch needed before now? It wasn't just the fence in need of repairs; the doors on the barn needed to be replaced and painted. Was she so like her father—selfish and self-centered—that she hadn't even realized Gigi needed more than milk on Tuesdays and a phone call to be sure she was still breathing?

Gillian was coming to realize that maybe she was guilty of, at the very least, going through the motions. As the years passed, she lost herself amidst her own marital problems, work, and the hassles of everyday life—all so far removed from the McKinney ranch. Now she realized she'd disengaged as much from Gigi as she had from Kelly.

Sure, she came by often, but when was the last time she'd asked Gigi to bake a pie together? When was the last time she'd gone out to help clean the stall? When was the last real conversation she'd had with her grandmother? And now, Gillian would give anything for one more chance to deliver her grandmother's groceries, and then "set a spell" and talk.

LATER THAT SAME WEEK, desperate for answers, Gillian found herself seated in her grandmother's chair with a stack of encyclopedia at her feet.

Freshly returned from visiting Geeg, she felt newly bereft. There was no recognition in her grandmother's eyes. Her blue-green gaze had been robbed of its brilliance. The skin on her hands seemed to have grown paper-thin overnight. The impression of her delicate fingers in Gillian's hands made Gillian feel as though one tight grip would crush it to bits. Her skin was cold to the touch, her flesh without elastic—as though all trace of blood had been drained from her veins and all that remained was a fragile glove made of papery flesh, like the filmy, inelastic layer beneath the shell of an egg.

Now, probably for the first time in Gillian's life, she pored over the volumes of the Encyclopedia Britannica to learn everything she could about her grandmother's condition.

All the while she read, her fingers traced the swollen water stains on the thread cabinet. But there wasn't much in the books, despite them having so many words. She found more details in an old Merck manual. Apparently, there were two types of strokes, the most common type being an ischemic stroke. This was caused by a blood clot obstructing blood flow to a portion of the brain. The other type—the one her grandmother had suffered—was a hemorrhagic stroke. Far less common than the other one, this one was caused by a tear in the wall of a weakened blood vessel, and once formed, the tear allowed blood to seep into the brain, killing off surrounding tissue.

The doctors had explained that Gigi was probably born with an abnormality, but it could have been triggered by chronic, long-term stress, hostility, or depressive symptoms. Except Gigi wasn't depressed, and if she had been stressed, she was quite good at keeping it to herself, which then left hostility . . .

The image of the smashed coffee cup on the kitchen floor flashed through Gillian's head. Then the one still on the table . . .

She couldn't get past the notion that there must have been someone present that day, though no one seemed to know anything about how Gigi ended up in ER. As of yet, no one had come forward—no neighbors checking on her, literally no one. Gillian had a yen to go door to door, except Gigi's nearest neighbor was an empty subdivision. There was nobody there.

Hungry for more information, she scoured the web.

The problem with therapy, or a long-term prognosis, was that ordinarily, after such a stroke, patients exhibited at least some desire and therefore, frustration, over the need to communicate. Gigi exhibited nada—no desire to speak or respond. She sat, mouth agape, eyes unnaturally wide. There could be some brain function, but her gaze remained vacant. Thus, any normal therapy—impairment-based or communication-based—was inappropriate at this stage.

She might or might not improve over time. However, with

Gigi's age as a consideration, and the severity of her impairment, her doctors could safely prognosticate that she would always need extensive personal care. It was all too painful to think about.

Gillian took a break from the books and, finally, made a trip to the store. But then, along with the coffee and sundry items, she stopped by the liquor store.

Her weeklong sobriety ended with a bottle of tequila, and just so she could pretend it was a happy-hour cocktail, she bought a jar of habanero salsa and a bag of tortilla chips. Then she proceeded to drink while poring over another book at the kitchen table, one titled *Aphasia and Related Neurogenic Communication Disorders*. It was a textbook-grade, five-hundred-page volume about the history and treatment of aphasias that had been sitting on the front porch waiting for her when she arrived home, thanks to Amazon.

She felt like crying as she studied the pages, only all that materialized was an annoying wet dot at the corner of each eye. It could have been allergies after being so long in the barn, but it was accompanied by a cloying burn in her chest that made it difficult to breathe.

Or maybe it was the alcohol?

"You're one cold bitch," Kelly had said the night he'd asked for a divorce.

All because Gillian couldn't cry.

That night, seated at their kitchen table at the M-Street house he'd seen fit to keep after the divorce, she'd sat numbly, unable to stir even a bit of fear over the potential loss of her marriage.

Though maybe she hadn't wanted to fix things? Maybe that's why she'd sabotaged their relationship at every turn? Maybe she didn't love Kelly the way she thought she should?

"I can't live like this," he'd said, and Gillian had grit her teeth.

Hardening her heart, she'd stood and, without a word, fetched the car keys from the hook by the fridge and walked out the door.

Even now, all these years later, the pain she'd felt was undeniable. It was like a vice grip squeezing her heart harder and harder and harder with every step she took toward the door. And then, once that door slammed shut behind her—a firm thud she wouldn't soon forget—it hurt so bad it felt as though she were having a heart attack. And still she'd kept on walking toward her car.

That night, she'd gotten drunk with Shannon, powering through. And later, she came home to catch Kelly sleeping like a baby, sprawled over the king-sized bed—a bed he'd claimed he didn't want, but soon discovered it gave him more space. Well, he'd claimed that space, she'd noticed. Embraced it, even. He didn't curl up into a fetal position on his side of the bed, like a wounded man-child. No, even with the sun peeking in through the lacy curtains, he'd lain on his stomach, one leg and one arm cast out into the middle, as though he were defending his territory, disallowing Gillian to come near. He didn't stir as she entered the room, and with no missed phone calls on her cell phone, she'd taken it as proof positive that he didn't care. It was the last straw. She'd moved out that same day.

Gillian rubbed her tired eyes. Really, the simple fact that they had been able to make the business work was more a testament to the fact that their relationship lived outside an emotional minefield. While most people fought about normal things—the trash, toilet seat, clothes left on the floor—she and Kelly rarely exchanged cross words.

More to the point, Kelly baited her, but Gillian didn't escalate. She stepped carefully over potential mine blasts because it was easier that way. But on the inside, she felt *everything*—every stabbing barb, every unshed tear. And this minute, she felt the loss of her grandmother so keenly that even the thought of a hangover was a welcome distraction. However, on the edge of those thoughts was an image of Kelly's face, his jaw taut and his dark unfathomable eyes hard as steel.

No amount of wanting could change the past.

She put the massive book aside and bent to pluck up another copy of Gigi's *Texas Homemaker* magazine, turning to an ad with a headline that read: "Husband-pleasing coffee." There was a woman with eyes closed, holding up a full glass pot in one hand, and a flowery cup and saucer perched in the other. From the cup of coffee emerged a Pepé Le Pew styled ribbon of aroma that drifted past the woman's nose. In bold handwriting, in what was now becoming a familiar blue pen, was written in capital letters "NO." *Just the word no.* The sight of Gigi's scribble made Gillian smirk. Apparently, there was no truth in this advertising, and her grandmother disagreed.

However, what was becoming apparent to Gillian, after paging through so many issues, was that Gigi had tried so hard to please that man—all to no avail.

"Ungrateful bastard," she said, as the cell phone on the table rang, startling her. She peered up at the window over the kitchen sink in time to see something flicker outside, though it was gone in a flash, and she couldn't be sure she'd seen anything at all.

It could be her uncle or father, lurking outside—undead zombies—but by now, she'd had had enough to drink to doubt her faculties. Only one glance at the caller ID furrowed her brow. Disappointed by the name that appeared on the screen, she flicked a glance at the window as she clicked to answer, wondering why she felt compelled to do so. There wasn't enough tequila in the universe to help her deal with her father. "Gilly Bean," he said right off, sweet as pie.

Gillian rolled her eyes. She hated when he used that endearment. It was Gigi's nickname for her, not his, and nine times out of ten, he used it when he wanted something from her.

Lifting the glass of tequila sitting in front of her, Gillian swirled the contents and chugged the last lemon-washed sip. "What . . . is . . . it . . . Dad?"

Drowned by the tequila, her words slid around her mouth, coherent, but loosely formed.

"Why's it gotta be like that, Gilly Marie?"

Jesus. How dare he invoke her mother's name, even though it was hers as well? He didn't have any right to speak Maria's name in Gillian's presence. "What do you want, Dad?"

Her father let out a hefty sigh. The sound of it punched Gillian's ear. "Well, you know, I was wondering . . . ain't you gonna get the house ready to sell?"

And there it was. Gillian reached over, gripping the bottle to hoist it up and pour herself another glass full of tequila. "No. I am not."

"Why not?"

"Because Gigi's not dead. That could be why."

As most reasons went, you'd think it would be enough to shut her father's face and maybe call up a bit of shame, but no, not him. "Gilly Bean," he said again, like a loving parent would, except it held a note of meanness. "Your grandma ain't coming home, little girl. Best you face facts."

It took Gillian a full moment to get her alcohol-dazed thoughts together, but when she spoke again there wasn't a hint of a slur. Anger sobered her quickly. It sat like a flame in her gut.

"Look, *Pop.* Even if I were to sell the house, it isn't yours, best you face facts," she returned sarcastically. "Gigi is leaving it to me —leaving, mind you—not left, because remember, she's not dead. By the way, thanks so much for ferreting out her will precisely five minutes after her stroke. Guess we all know where your priorities lie."

Completely overlooking Gillian's sarcasm, her father said, "Me and Jeff are mama's rightful sons." He meant heirs. Still, she didn't correct him. "We're entitled to our father's ranch."

"Really?" Only that pushed Gillian over the edge. She bounced up from the chair, clutching the cell phone to her ear. She couldn't believe either of them needed a history lesson, but apparently her father did. "It is *not* your dad's ranch, hence the name—Noble Ranch. It belongs to Geeg."

"Yeah . . . well, you know what I mean." Yeah, she did know what he meant. She knew exactly what he meant, and he went quiet now, trying to jump start two brain cells to formulate a coherent argument that Gillian might not easily shut down. The simple fact that he remained quiet for so long didn't surprise Gillian as much as his next words did. "I'll sue," he said.

"Really?"

"You betcha."

"Really, Dad? Your mother is still alive—the woman who raised you! All you care about is getting your hands on this property, really?"

"It's mine."

"No, it's not."

"Yeah, well, here's something I bet she didn't tell you, you goddamned know-it-all: they made her an offer she couldn't refuse."

Gillian screwed her face. "Who is *they*?"

"Developers, Gillian Marie, that's who. Don't you patrify me now."

Patrify? What did that mean?

The urge to correct him went unheeded as surprise filtered through Gillian. Only it was short lived, realizing Gigi probably got offers for the Noble property every other week. This area was a final frontier, with Dallas swiftly encroaching. "Yeah, well, clearly she *did* refuse, didn't she? Or we we'd be having a different conversation. Right, Dad?"

She liked to remind him what he was supposed to be to her, as though it could possibly make a difference. It didn't, and that only made Gillian feel marginally better for mocking him. Only for a second.

"Only because of her stroke," her father said with conviction. "She was gonna sign the papers, Gillian. Why would I lie?"

Without even trying, Gillian could think of at least twenty-five reasons why her father would lie. "No way. She would *never* sell this ranch. But, hey, don't take my word for it, you have a copy of the will. It's all in there, straight up."

"Yeah, that's what you think. We believe there might be sufficient grounds to contest the will," he said, more than likely quoting his attorney.

It wouldn't surprise Gillian one bit to learn he'd already taken his copy to someone who could advise him. He'd retrieved his documents from the nurses' station the instant he could. Gillian had been too concerned about her grandmother's health to pay any mind to what her father and uncle were doing until it was too late. But it didn't matter. She had her own copy. Gigi had made sure of that. In fact, four years ago, Gigi put Gillian's name on the deed.

"Go ahead, Dad. Do it."

"Hey," he said, changing his tune, "Wills can be misplaced. What happens then? It'll be intestate and you won't get to be her executive any longer."

"Executor," Gillian corrected, surprised only that he had managed to remember the word intestate. He must have practiced it over and over in the mirror before calling her.

"Whatever. I mean it, little lady." His tone held an edge Gillian recognized only too well—that same mean edge that nearly always concluded her conversations with her father.

"Gigi's not dead, good luck with that."

"You damned ungrateful bi—"

Gillian hung up the phone and didn't bother to answer when it rang again.

At least she knew it wasn't him lurking outside.

Good lord. For Gillian to be ungrateful, her father would have had to have done something, anything—just one little thing—to benefit his daughter, after which he might not have been fully appreciated by her. There was nothing selfless on Joe Frazer's parental docket—not even one solitary after-school pick up that didn't come with an ulterior motive—like, for instance, he wanted to leverage the good deed with a loan he hoped to get from Gigi.

"This is why I don't do more," he'd railed to Gigi. "Because I don't get no satisfaction. You take that cunt and shove her up your wrinkled ass. You deserve each other!"

Gillian had stood there, wide-eyed, wondering what she had done so wrong to make her father scream so loud. At six, she hadn't understood the word cunt, or that it wasn't about her.

Nothing he ever did was about her. "Who's your daddy and what does he do?" folks used to run around asking when Gillian was a kid, mimicking Schwarzenegger's Austrian accent. "I don't have a daddy," she'd wanted to say.

She didn't have one then.

She didn't have one now.

Tossing the cellphone onto the kitchen counter, Gillian walked out the back door.

6

CASSIOPEIA

B *low it off,* she told herself. *Blow it off.*

Standing on the back porch, looking over the barnyard, Gillian inhaled a good lung full of scorching Texas air. It was uncomfortably warm at 11:00 p.m.—not unlike the inside of an oven someone forgot to turn off. Sweat trickled down the inside of one breast.

There was a certain clarity that came with a tequila high.

Edges were crisper, colors richer. Tonight, she welcomed the warmth that seeped into her gut. It crept through her limbs, relaxing her, so that not even the conversation with her father indelibly upset her. It was par for the course, so they said.

Off in the distance, a coyote howled, a mournful sound all too familiar to folks living up north. The flash of movement she'd spied earlier was a trick of the moonlight. *No one around for miles.* Even the coyotes were three miles out, burrowed deep inside the tangle of mesquite brush that grew on the outer edges of the cotton fields.

Tonight, the moon hung low, neon in its brilliance against a black-velvet sky. The stars were clear and bright.

Across the yard, the columns holding up the awnings on

either side of the pole barn were no longer white. They were dingy gray. The barn doors remained on the original hardware, hanging slightly askew, the rich oak soaking in the moonlight.

Her grandmother preferred to leave them open, pulled to one side, so that both doublewide panels dragged at the ironwork bars. Time to get them repaired.

This far away from ambient light, you could see the constellations clearly. Gillian had forgotten how peaceful it could be.

"There's Cassiopeia," she heard Kelly whisper at her ear, the memory materializing, like dust from a distant star. It brought a new sting to Gillian's eyes. "And there's Cepheus. See?" A ghostly arm pointed to a cluster of stars to the right of Cassiopeia. "Husband and wife, banished together for eternity."

That night, Kelly had promised to put a ring on her finger and she'd smiled, laying her head atop his chest. She turned and peered up at the rooftop.

Right up there, on the gently sloping roof of her grandmother's house, they'd spent many a night. Here, below on the porch, her grandmother had often swung open the kitchen door and come out with broom in hand. She and Kelly would place their hands over their mouths, trying not to laugh.

Everything was funnier back then.

All these years later, Gillian had little doubt that her grandmother had known exactly where they were, but she'd never said a word. She'd milled about the porch, sweeping loudly, reminding them of her presence, shuffling the broom about the deck before going back inside. And then the screen door would close again with a soft thunk.

She and Kelly would then go back to staring at the stars, feeling contented in a way Gillian couldn't remember feeling ever again. "Doesn't seem much of a punishment," she'd said one night after Gigi went away, and Kelly had taken a long lock of her hair and twirled it about his finger.

"Hmm?" he'd said.

"Cassiopeia."

"Actually," he'd said with a lazy smile. "Seems more like a windfall, doesn't it? Stuck up there, all by your lonesome . . . with the one you love . . . forever and ever . . . and ever . . ." He'd whispered the last words into her mouth as he'd pulled her beneath him, pressing his body tight against hers until she could feel every granule of the black tar roof beneath her bare shoulders.

Gillian's body had come to life, nipples aching for his touch, her pelvic muscles tightening with longing. Her voice was husky with desire. "You might sing a different tune if—"

"No," he'd said. "We'd come up with plenty to do." And he dipped his pelvis against her in a suggestive way that made her cheeks burn.

"Shhh," she'd said. "You'll bring Gigi back outside."

He had silenced her with a long, passionate kiss that made her swallow now at the bittersweet memory.

Tonight, the sky was equally brilliant as it had been that night, moonlight glinting off the static weathervane on the barn. She craned her neck to examine the old roof and then turned to go back inside, inhaling deeply and exhaling a sigh.

Closing and locking the door behind her, she felt weary to her bones—she missed Kelly. She kicked out the stool next to the pantry and seized the bottle of tequila, still more than half full, then climbed up and placed it high in the cupboard, next to a deep fryer she would never be tempted to use. Then she pushed the stool back into its corner and flipped off the kitchen's overhead light before making her way across the room by the silvery light of the moon.

All at once, she felt the puncture of vulnerable flesh in the arch of her right foot. Crying out in pain, Gillian stumbled to her knees. Stunned, she sat on the kitchen floor with the moonlight shining in through the kitchen window, and after a moment felt a warm puddle slide beneath her leg, and smelled the coppery scent of her own blood.

With a furrowed brow and slightly detached sensation, she watched as a shiny patch of black spread across the pale floor.

3:00 P.M., Friday, July 8, 1960

"YOU THINK SHE KNOWS?"

"Well, if she don't, she ain't so smart as she likes to think."

It was Mary Claire speaking—the snotty witch.

Instinctively, Rebecca sensed the conversation was all about her, despite the fact that they had yet to speak her name. Neither woman had acknowledged the click when Rebecca picked up the line. Clearly, they were so entranced by their gossip they didn't care who overheard.

Placing her palm firmly over the receiver, steadying her breath as she listened, Rebecca didn't feel the least bit terrible over eavesdropping, no sir.

Used to be she would pick up the party line and make herself known, maybe join the conversation, but nowadays she wasn't so keen on Mary Claire.

That woman and her husband—the barber—carried more tales between them than all of Southwestern Bell. Her mama used to say, "Anyone who runs around carrying stories about others is bound to turn around and carry stories about you." Rebecca knew it was true.

"Well, you think maybe we should tell her?" There was a note of schadenfreude in the question, along with concern, which made Rebecca frown. She expected better of Dottie Shepherd.

"No way," Mary Claire said, and then she rescinded. "Well, you can tell her if you want, but not me. My mama taught me better'n to mind other folk's affairs."

Rebecca rolled her eyes, because that was as far from the truth as anyone could get. Mary Claire was all about minding other folk's affairs. And god knew, if she wasn't minding other people's affairs, she wouldn't know what to do with herself.

"Anyway," she continued, "I'm here to say . . . ain't no one wants to hear a thing like that. You might think you're friends now, but say one word about this to her, and I swear, Dottie, she'll turn on you just like that."

Rebecca heard the distant snap of fingers—at least that's what she imagined it to be. She could see Mary Claire doing it now. With her, everything was a snap of the fingers. "Hop to it," she would say to her kids. *Snap. Snap.* "Best you come here, right now." To her husband. *Snap. Snap.*

"But I feel terrible," said Dottie, sounding sad. "I like her, you know, and she would never tell a soul. She's having a real hard time."

"Well, who ain't nowadays?" There wasn't one bit of pity in her tone. "These are bad times, dear. You worry about yourself."

The two women lapsed into silence, and curiosity nearly slew Rebecca. She wanted to shout into the receiver for one of them to spill everything, right now, though she'd been listening far too long to carry it off as anything other than it was. She was eavesdropping, straight up.

Only now it seemed they were done talking about whatever it was that they were feeling sorry about. Or, more to the point,

Dottie was feeling sorry about; Mary Claire couldn't give two shakes nor a holler about anyone except herself.

"Well . . . I suppose you're right . . ."

Tell me! Rebecca wanted to scream. *Please, tell me!*

"Well, of course I'm right," Mary Claire said. And then, "Say, Dottie, maybe you should ask Billy about it? Maybe he knows what that no-good cheat is up to?"

Cheat? As in cards? Or cheating, cheating? As in . . . another woman?

There was a long pause on the telephone, and Rebecca pressed her palm more firmly against the receiver, hoping not to give herself away. She was in a quandary, for sure.

Any second the boys would be coming in from school, hollering at the top of their lungs for milk and cookies and she was torn between wanting to hang up now before the front door flew wide, and desperately wanting to know what these two old biddies were gossiping about.

What did Billy know?

Then again, Billy probably knew lots of things Rebecca didn't know because he and Joe were thick as thieves. Mary Claire had called Joe a cheat. *Was he cheating?*

It wouldn't surprise Rebecca much, but she'd be damned if she'd allow him to make a fool out of her—particularly when she had so much to lose. The ranch, for one. There was no way she was going to allow that man to walk away with her home, or hand it over to some other woman. Noble Ranch was hers, not his. Now that she had her plans in the works, she was going to pull their lives out of the dumps. Well, at least Dottie hadn't told Mary Claire about that.

But maybe it wasn't about a woman? Joe sometimes handled money for the Roadhouse. Maybe he was dipping into the pot? After all, he went and bought that blasted car. And before that, he'd spent most of their money at the Roadhouse on drinks and who knew what else. Oh, yeah, she knew they had girls in the back, not only poker tables. If those dirty old men were half so worried about their affairs at home rather than where to put their peckers, there wouldn't be half the hardship in this town. And Sheriff Taylor sure wasn't any help. She had wind he was knee-deep, himself.

It was a long time before anyone said another word, but when she spoke again, Dottie sounded downcast. "Well, you know I would ask, but Billy ain't been home for days."

"Oh no!" Mary Claire exclaimed. "You poor, poor thing!"

Rebecca scrunched her nose and squeezed her eyes tight, wishing Dottie hadn't confessed such a thing to Mary Claire. Now the entire world would hear of it.

"If you ask me, it's Joe Frazer's doing."

"No, no . . . it's not like that," Dottie demurred. "It's the mill. They let him go. He's out there trying to figure something out. 'Cept if he can't find a job, he says we'll have to move."

"Away from McKinney?"

"That's what he says."

"Lawd, woman! Why didn't you say something?" Rebecca knew better than to believe the concern in Mary Claire's voice. "Well, I hate to say it, but it might be for the best. There's plenty of work in Fort Worth."

"Maybe," allowed Dottie. "Maybe." Though she sounded as though she didn't believe it for a second, and the worry in her voice was tangible. It made Rebecca long to hug her. She desperately wanted to say, "Don't worry, Dottie, we'll fix everything." But she held her breath and her tongue, hoping Dottie wouldn't tell Mary Claire anything about her business affairs. That was the last thing she wanted Mary Claire to know about.

Outside, she heard the distant hullabaloo of boys at play, and she knew she had mere seconds remaining before she was found out.

Well, she could hang up now and let those two wonder who had been listening in, or she could make herself known and demand they tell her everything they knew. There were five more families on this line, she reasoned. Any one of them could have picked up at any time, overhearing everything said. It galled Rebecca that they would talk about her so easily, as though it weren't a thing. But at least Dottie seemed upset by it all.

"Well, I do feel like I should tell her," Dottie said, returning to the previous topic, and Rebecca nodded fervently behind her hand. *Yes, yes, please do!*

"Well, that's on you," Mary Claire said. "But don't say I didn't warn you," she added in a singsong tone.

There was a sudden click on the line and a male voice chimed in. "God dang it, how long you ladies gonna sit here gossiping. Ain't you got nothing better to do?"

"Mind your own business, Larry!" Mary Claire shouted. "We've got as much right to be on this line as you do."

"You're joking, right?" Larry asked snidely. "Long as you old windbags are sitting here sniping, ain't no one got any rights to this line."

"Well, I never!" exclaimed Dottie.

"Crazy coot! Nobody wants a thing to do with that man!" declared Mary Claire. "It's easy to see why."

"Dumb hags," Larry said.

Thereafter, the line erupted with curses that Rebecca had no business hearing. She slammed down the receiver, no longer caring whether anyone heard her or not.

Anyway, it wasn't as though they could possibly know it was her. Let them wonder who else had overheard. It would serve them right—Dottie as well, for not cutting off that mouthy gossip at once. Only now her hands were trembling and she was dying of curiosity . . . what the devil was Joe up to that she should know about?

The boys were coming up the drive now, quarreling over something—she didn't know what. It was always something with those two, but Rebecca had had more than enough bickering for one day, despite not having had any part in that argument on the phone. It was enough to have overheard it. Even if they could afford a television set, she wouldn't want one. Little by little, the moral fiber of this country was dwindling. It was all terrible news about Cuba, missiles, politics, and nonsense like *Bonanza*, with grown men shooting at each other over one thing or another.

Marching into the kitchen, she opened the fridge and took out the day's supply of milk. She set the bottle on the counter and opened the cupboard, reaching for two cups, still a little distracted. She placed the cups on the counter, then moved over to the stove where she'd set her batch of cookies out to cool. She placed the back of her hand against the tin foil, sighing when the front door opened and closed.

The boys were home.

"No, I didn't!"

"Yes, you did!"

"Did not!"

"Did too!"

The cookies were still warm. Hopefully they would shut the boys up. She rolled the tin foil back and plucked up a cookie for herself. Her pecan jumbles were perfectly decadent, just the way Silas used to bake 'em.

"Ma!" shouted Jeff.

"In the kitchen," Rebecca answered as best as she could with bits tumbling around her mouth. But even as she set the plate of cookies on the table and filled her sons' glasses with milk, the first thing she'd overhead Mary Claire say when she picked up the phone echoed in her ear.

"Oh, yes, ma'am. Harvey saw him, plain as day. It was him, alright."

"In broad daylight?"

"Yes, ma'am."

"Up on Anthony Street?"

"Oh, yes, ma'am!"

There were lots of folks those two could have been talking about, and any number of homes up on Anthony Street someone might disappear into, but that was where Leona Fox lived. Rebecca couldn't help but remember how Joe had watched her at the picnic by the creek.

Even her name sounded predatory, and God only knew, she was always out there watering her roses in some skinny, tight little skirt and high heels. Lawd, who in their right mind wore high heels to water their garden? *Leona Fox did, that's who.*

Women who were looking for attention did such things, and Leona sure got her share of that. She had half the town's men's tongues wagging, and if she ever deigned to attend church, she would no doubt raise male attendance at once. But no, there was no church going for Leona, who claimed she didn't appreciate the way other women treated her. Well, if she didn't stand around in those skimpy skirts and heels, thinking she was Greta Garbo or Elizabeth Taylor, maybe folks would like her much better.

The boys were no longer arguing. They dropped their book sacks at the kitchen door and made a dash for the table. Their murmurs of appreciation as they devoured her day's baking efforts were all the thanks Rebecca needed.

7

A PERFECT STORM

Just a few times in life one had the opportunity to witness a perfect storm, which was to say the chance combination of events wherein, experienced individually, might be far less impactful than their result altogether. Of course, the idiom was never used positively. Rather, if the chance combination turned out to be fortuitous, one could say "the stars aligned."

Precisely which of these two situations Gillian faced right now was not immediately discernable. But, to be sure, a cumulative dose—or doses—of blood-thinning aspirin, plus alcohol, which impeded clotting, plus alcohol-impaired judgment, were hardly a favorable combination.

She sat on the kitchen floor, watching as though in a trance as the red stain crept out over the fifty-year-old linoleum. *Arteries spurt, veins ooze,* she thought dimly.

But this . . . *this* was a steady flow, thicker than she might have supposed. But it wasn't spurting in waves with every beat of her heart. No, it couldn't be an artery. And if it weren't for the searing pain shooting up her leg, she might have sat longer, staring curiously as blood oozed out over the pale moonlit surface.

But here again, ooze wasn't the correct term either. Pus oozed, sores oozed. This was more a slow, steady warm stream, not unlike the trickling of the brook she and Kelly had picnicked near the summer they'd gone to Colorado. That stream had poured gently, but not stingily, out from cracks in the rocks. Thinking about that camping trip, Gillian stared at the color of her blood under the light of the moon—so dark it was nearly black.

The sole of her foot was numb, except that she reached down to feel about, she encountered something hard. She gritted her teeth, pulling it out, her heartbeat hammering a primal beat through her temples as she extracted the object and tossed it across the floor.

If this were a major artery, death would happen swiftly, she realized. Best as she could recall from her days in science class, adult hearts pumped blood at several liters per minute. The body contained four or five. She would be dead after two, three, four minutes tops if this were an artery. She'd already been sitting dumbly for at least two minutes, maybe more. So Gillian wasn't particularly alarmed.

Without any sense of hurry, she dragged herself up from the kitchen floor and hopped over to the counter to search for a rag —something, anything—to stop the blood flow. She found kitchen towels neatly folded in one of the kitchen drawers, but none were long enough to apply a tourniquet. Did she need one?

Probably not.

Grabbing the towel on top, Gillian snapped it out, unfolding it. She lifted her foot and pressed the clean rag against the bottom, putting pressure on the arch. Once again, pain shot up her leg.

The cloth turned a velvety black in less than a minute and Gillian marveled that so much blood could come from one tiny wound.

Or maybe it wasn't so tiny.

She could feel the open skin, wet and oily beneath her finger tips, but even then she wasn't precisely alarmed. No one had ever died from a cut on the bottom of their foot. *Had they?*

Grabbing another towel from the drawer, Gillian tossed the first one into the sink and pressed the second towel against her wound, then hopped over to the switch to turn on the overhead light...

Whatever surrealism she'd imagined under the glow of moonlight vanished at the sight of her own blood smeared all over the kitchen floor. A nasty shard of china—the curved lower edge, near the base, where the porcelain was necessarily thicker and sturdier—lay, turned upward, so that the sharp, long tooth was ready and waiting to bite into tender flesh.

Over the past few weeks, she had marched through his kitchen countless times without ever spotting that shard, so it must have slid under the step stool after her grandmother's fall, and tonight, in the dark, she had pushed out the stool, dislodging the shard from its hiding place.

"Damn it," she said, and then she grabbed another rag, surprised by the unstoppable flow. After the third rag soaked through, she went hopping toward the dining room to search for her purse, and keys, remembering only belatedly that she had left them both upstairs after returning from the grocery store. *Damn, damn.* She'd been so keen on diving into her book—and of course, let's face it, the bottle of tequila. She'd barely given herself time to pop open the jar of salsa and tear open the chips—both of which she'd had very little of—before turning to the bottle. In fact, if she were completely honest with herself, she'd only opened the book as an afterthought, exhausted after the long day in the barn with Baby.

But, hey, no worries; the keys were still in the El Dorado. So long as that car started, after sitting so long unused, it would do just fine.

There was a new ER barely a stone's throw away. Thankfully,

she wouldn't have to go all the way to Plano. But it didn't even occur to her that she might get pulled over on the way.

Even further from her mind was the fact that she might still be drunk. She *felt* sober. Hearing your father call you an ungrateful bitch had a way of sobering you immediately. And Joe was last person Gillian would reach out to now, even if she had nicked a stupid artery. She would lay down and die, right on the kitchen floor, before ever dialing Joe's number.

Of course, wouldn't you know it, the one time she might have called Kelly, he was too far away. At best, it would take him more than thirty minutes to reach her, and despite it not being an emergency, the cut wouldn't stop bleeding. It was pouring out of her wound, trailing a river of blood wherever she walked. Hobbling, Gillian left a wake through the dining room and all the way through the living room. It trickled between the floorboards, shining like black pearls along the darkened rooms.

As an afterthought, she grabbed a cotton T-shirt from a pile of laundry she'd left on the back of the couch, and then snagged a few more, knowing full well that anything she soaked with blood was going to remain forever stained. Even now, she was more concerned with which shirt to ruin than she was with bleeding out.

Annoyed at the turn of events, she stood, picking through T-shirts, and then she returned the ones she wanted to keep to the couch. She took the worst of the shirts—a threadbare Coons shirt nobody ever should have worn—and ripped it in half. She tore it again, rendering it into strips. Then she tied a piece around her ankle without really knowing why. It just seemed the right thing to do. And then, once that was done, she took another slice, shoving it into her cut—holy crap, was it deep—and then she tied that into place with another strip from the Coons shirt.

It was about time they'd changed the name of her high school mascot. Now they were the Raccoons, but the powers that be had waited until the last possible minute to change the name, until politically correct parents had called them out. Gillian had rediscovered the stupid shirt in her old bedroom—a relic from her past that she hadn't cared to take with her.

Once the makeshift bandage was secure, she hobbled out the front door, feeling a bit queasy.

Moving along on one foot, across the porch, down the front stairs, across the dirt driveway, she made her way to her grandmother's El Dorado, opened the door, and then slid into the driver's seat. Swallowing, she closed her eyes and turned the key, then sent a little thank you heavenward when the engine kicked into a purr. Still, she wasn't particularly alarmed.

Foremost on her mind was the mess she'd left behind, blood everywhere. All that blood, and she was going to have to clean it all up, all by herself. Damn that shard of glass.

She turned on the headlights, flooding the front porch with bright light, and then she proceeded to back up far enough so she could turn around and drive off the ranch.

It wasn't the easiest maneuver with one gimp foot. But she was fine. *Fine, fine, fine,* she reassured herself. It only looked like a lot of blood. Heads and feet, they bled more than it seemed they should, right? Unfortunately, the cut was on her right foot, and every time she pressed down on the gas pedal a sharp pain sprang up her leg.

Lifting her right foot up out of the way, onto the bench seat, she used her left leg as best she could. Outside the city lights, the night sky was a velvety blur, filled with tiny, haloed points of light. The drive down Old Mill Road was surreal, and so it seemed only par for the course when sirens went off and blue lights fell into view behind her.

"Damn," she said. Just her luck. All these months—no, years —*years* of walking and riding her bike and taking cabs, and this would be the night she got her first DWI.

"Damn, damn, damn," she said, smacking the El Dorado's steering wheel with the butt of her hand. "No, no, no," she whined, and she swerved to stay on the right side of the yellow line.

In her desperation, she had a thought. She could keep on driving, straight to the hospital—she did have an injury, after all. The minute she arrived, she would slide out of the driver's seat and he would plainly see she was covered in blood.

But it wasn't a life-threatening injury, just a cut—a very bad cut, but a cut nonetheless—and she had a disturbing mental image of her driving along Old Mill Road, OJ style, with police calling for backup, sirens wailing, and Glock 22s trained on her once she stepped out of the car.

Hadn't they recently shot some guy after a traffic violation? A white guy at that. She could see the papers now. White female, twenty-eight, shot by MPD.

It wasn't worth it, she told herself. With a sigh, she pulled over and stopped the car, feeling sick to her gut as she sat, waiting for the officer to show up.

He took his time. Feeling woozy, Gillian rolled down her window, waiting patiently, realizing with a start, as his face popped up beside her, that she'd left her purse, along with her wallet, back at the house. There was no one on the road except for the two of them. His cruiser lights were shining brightly into the driver's side mirror, half blinding her.

"Ma'am, do you know why I pulled you over?"

Gillian felt a bit like puking. "No, sir."

"Well, to begin with, you were speeding, and then once I got up behind you, you crossed the yellow line—more'n a few times." He took her measure, and then, turned up his nose and sniffed at the air. His brows furrowed. "Have you been drinking, ma'am?"

Gillian didn't want to answer.

Yes, she had.

How long ago?

How much had she had?

"Ma'am?"

By the time Gillian put that bottle up in the pantry, there was slightly over half left. Half of 750 ml, at forty proof . . . It didn't take all that much to disappear a bottle.

"Ma'am, I need to see your driver's license, please."

Gillian felt the rags at her feet become a sopping mess, and she smelled again the coppery scent of her own blood. She gagged suddenly, barely holding in her spew, but it was enough to alert the policeman to her condition. He stepped back, moving his hand midway to his holster.

"Ma'am, please step out of the car," he demanded.

And Gillian wondered, nonsensically, when in the world she'd become a ma'am.

With a sick groan, Gillian pushed open the car door, and stood, feeling woozier now than she had after the last drink. She put her foot down to stand and white-hot pain sliced through her right calf and up into her thigh, so far up it felt as though it stabbed her straight in the heart.

"Oh, God!" she said, and it was her last coherent thought. The last thing Gillian remembered was the smell and taste of baked Texas clay.

8

LUCKY LADY

"You're one lucky lady," the nurse said after examining Gillian's foot.

Gillian cracked a tired smile. It was difficult to say which had been the greater stroke of luck—the fact that she hadn't bled to death, that her liver hadn't failed from a cumulative effect of the aspirin, or that she hadn't been marched off to jail in handcuffs. Instead, she'd used her phone-a-friend option to ring Kelly. She'd barely gotten out the words, "I'm at the Frisco hospital," when he hung up, saying, "On my way."

He arrived in less than ten minutes. How this was possible, Gillian daren't ask, but the obvious answer was that he hadn't come from home. Judging by the mussed hair, the slightly swollen lips, and the hooded eyes, he had been asleep, though not alone. She recognized the attitude—that sated, after-sex swagger. And every muscle in his body was taut, because Kelly wasn't lazy in bed. Gillian imagined the acrobatics he must have performed for his new lover and felt a renewed gnawing at the pit of her gut.

She'd been right. He was seeing someone.

Of course, she wanted to be snide. She wanted to ask where

the other woman was, and maybe how she felt about him leaving her bed to rescue his ex-wife, but that was bound to piss him off, so she remained wearily silent, grateful at least that he'd come.

Besides, she was incredibly thirsty; talking only made the condition worse.

Her mouth felt as though it had been stuffed with rolls of toilet paper and then taped shut. Her lips were dry, but sticky, clamped as though with paste. She sent Kelly a desperate glance and found him studiously avoiding her gaze.

What did he know?

And where was the police officer?

Gone, Gillian hoped.

However, the nurse knew that she had arrived inebriated, and if the nurse knew, the cop knew it as well. Did Kelly know too? *Probably.* He knew her well.

Gillian had only vague memories of the officer calling for help. He'd examined the blood-soaked bandages around her foot, all the while talking to her gently, and then he spoke gibberish into his walkie-talkie up until EMS arrived.

The clock on the wall read 3:15 a.m.

What time did she leave the house?

It was probably a good sign that she'd been left to wait—without a uniformed guard—while the nurse saw to other patients. But she wasn't alone. Kelly stood nearby, arms crossed, waiting for the nurse to return. Once she did, he watched silently as the woman stitched Gillian's foot—a whopping twenty-four stitches in all.

The glass had managed to lacerate, but not sever, the plantar fascial ligament, that long ligament extending from the heel to the ball of the foot.

Fortunately, Gillian hadn't attempted to use the foot, because standing pulled the wound apart, which was why she'd experienced such godawful pain when she'd stepped out of the car. The pain alone had been enough to make her face-plant into the ground.

For the time being, the plan was to stitch her back together, but she had to make and keep an appointment with an orthopedic surgeon the following week, after which they would decide what course of action she should take. At the least, even without surgery, Gillian would be on crutches from four to six weeks. How she would manage to get the ranch in order and finalize the move from Dallas, she didn't want to consider.

Finally, they released her about 6:00 a.m.

The drive home was excruciating—far more so than the cut in her foot. The physical pain was easier to deal with than Kelly's disapproving silence. That thin, straight line of his mouth set over clenched teeth was painful to endure. Gillian didn't know what to say. "Thank you," she offered after a while, as they turned onto Old Mill Road.

Kelly gave her a begrudging nod and Gillian wanted to scream. "Don't worry about it," he said after a moment.

Gillian clenched her jaw. "If you need to lecture me, please get it over with. Go ahead; I deserve it."

He slid her a quick black-eyed glance. "I don't need to lecture you, Gillian."

"Of course you do . . . you're tense and ready to explode."

He opened his mouth to say something, but kept his eyes fixed on the road and simply breathed in, as though he were restraining himself.

And then, after all, he said nothing—just nothing—which only made Gillian feel a thousand times worse. She turned in her seat, resigned to his silence, staring out at the road ahead as they drove all the way to the ranch. Only once they'd turned into the driveway, he said, "Try not to drink while you're on pain meds, alright?"

Gillian had already decided she wasn't going to fill her prescription unless she had to, but his tone, so full of judgment, irked her. "I promise not to call you if I do. Go on now, run back to your girl and tell her I'm sorry for dragging you out of bed."

Without warning, Kelly stomped the break, bringing the car to an immediate, violent halt.

"Ouch!" Gillian said. She was ready for a fight. She needed tears today, needed to cry, but anger, and shame—yes, shame—kept her dry-eyed.

Kelly's eyes narrowed with fury. "What is wrong with you, Gillian?"

Silence stretched between them, like a taut rubber band.

"I don't know," she confessed. The front porch of her grandmother's house lay ahead, a sanctuary waiting for Gillian, but here, trapped in Kelly's car, she was a captive audience. And even if she agreed with everything he was thinking, she didn't want to admit it—not here and now.

I don't know seemed as much of a compromise as she could muster, because the truth was that something was wrong. And even if she had a suspicion she knew what it was, she didn't know how to fix it. She hadn't known how to fix it three years ago when Kelly left and she didn't know how to fix it now.

He was still glaring at her.

Did she owe him something for coming to get her? Gillian didn't know. Brutal honesty about her current state of affairs seemed to be fair payment for a ride home in the middle of the night, and yet—pardon the pun—she wasn't going to sit here and bleed for him.

"Look," she said. "I appreciate you coming to my rescue. You always do, and it's not fair of me to put you in that position any longer. I get it, Kelly. So I won't do it anymore."

The anger visible in his eyes didn't diminish with her promise. "You won't do what anymore?" he asked. "You won't call for help? You won't drink? What? What is it you won't do anymore, Gillian?"

Gillian turned her gaze toward the front porch, imagining

herself already there, waving goodbye. He made her feel like a scolded teenager, forcing her to acknowledge everything she'd done wrong. She wholly resented it. She resented him—nearly as much for coming to help her so readily as for putting her in this position. *Only what position was that?*

Gillian opened the car door, refusing to be bullied into emptying her heart.

This was not how or when it should be done. If and when she decided to bare her soul to him—or to anyone—it would be her decision to do so, on her own terms, not because someone harassed her into doing it.

"What are you doing?"

"What does it look like I'm doing? I'm getting out of your car."

"You can't do that," he said.

"Watch me." And, with some effort, Gillian shoved open the car door.

Refusing to look at him, she heard rather than saw the driver's side door open and Kelly getting out and running around the car to Gillian's side. He was already there by the time she managed to scoot herself into a position to put her right foot on the ground. Her new crutches were in his back seat and he opened the back door to retrieve them, anticipating her next brash move. "I don't need you," she said, hating herself for the lie.

"So you keep saying, but you do need somebody, Gillian." His tone was softer now, gentling enough so that she didn't refuse when he tried to help her out the door. He handed her the crutches, allowing her to lean on him as she scooted away from the car.

"This would have been easier for both of us if you were closer to the house," he said, supporting Gillian until she was able to move the crutch handles beneath her armpits and maneuver herself away from his car.

His headlights remained on as she made her way toward the front porch, with Kelly at her side, his arms out like a mother with a helpless toddler. The sight of him both relieved and aggrieved her because he wasn't going to stick around to support her. Soon enough he'd be gone.

Without another word, the two of them moved toward the front porch as the first tendrils of pink appeared on the horizon . . . sunrise. Another one with Kelly, only this one was unlike any other. Gillian's heart hurt as she allowed him to lead her up the front steps, one at a time, with the understanding that, once again, like the mother with her toddler, there would come a time when he would be forced to open his arms wide and stand by as she walked away.

"DON'T COMPLAIN IF HE'S LATE HOME FOR DINNER OR EVEN IF HE STAYS OUT ALL NIGHT. COUNT THIS AS MINOR COMPARED TO WHAT HE MIGHT HAVE GONE THROUGH THAT DAY."
—*THE GOOD WIFE'S GUIDE, HOUSEKEEPING MONTHLY*

8:00 P.M., Friday, July 8, 1960

IT WAS PAST DARK.

The boys were already in bed, having tired themselves out swimming in the creek. Rebecca had told them not to go there alone. Boys drowned there all the time. Neither of her children seemed to care. They were hunting cottonmouths, so they said— yet another pastime she would like to deter them from. More and more, they were impossible to govern, exactly like their father.

At this point, Rebecca had been waiting all day long for Joe to return, wanting to ask about what she'd heard, even though she knew full well it would start a new argument. She didn't care. She'd be damned if she would let him carry on with the town slut, shaming her to death.

His cold supper sat on the table, untouched. It was after eight now and there was still not the first sign of her husband, and she didn't have a clue where to look. But she sure had a mouthful to say when he walked through the door.

Right about the time she heard silence from the boys' room, there came a knock on the front door. It startled her out of her favorite sewing chair, and she went directly to the door. However, it wasn't Joe; it was the sheriff. He took off his hat when he saw her and smiled.

"Hey there, Becky, how you doin'?"

"Just fine," Rebecca assured. "I'm fine, Clarence. How about you?"

"Fine, ma'am. Mighty fine. Bertie says you ain't been around to see her in a while. She said to tell you hey."

"Well, you go on and tell her hey right back for me, please." She leaned against the door. "How can I help you, Sheriff?"

He shuffled his feet, peering down at his shoes as though he was loathe to speak. "Well, I'm looking for Joe."

Rebecca tried not to roll her eyes and it was all she could do to retain a hint of a smile. "He ain't been home, Clarence. Is everything alright?"

"Just fine, ma'am. Just fine."

But it wasn't just fine, Rebecca could tell. Clarence was nervous and jittery and there was something skulking at the tip of his tongue, even if he didn't mean to burden her with it.

When it was clear he wasn't going to leave, Rebecca opened the door a little wider. "Would you like to come in and wait?"

The sheriff seemed to think about it a minute, peering over his shoulder at his squad car.

"The boys are upstairs sleeping," she said. "I've got milk and cookies in the kitchen."

His eyes brightened. "Well, now, don't mind if I do," he said with a slow grin. "Ain't nobody in this whole town makes cookies the way you do, even Bertie says so." He wiped his boots on the mat and stepped inside, and Rebecca led him back to the kitchen to serve the man milk and cookies.

9

GRANDMOTHER'S GARDEN

They came to an agreement: if Gillian stayed away from alcohol—the drinking variety—Kelly would stop in once every day or so to check on her.

Of course, she let him leave without an actual confirmation. It galled her that he would set stipulations at a time like this, despite knowing she wasn't going to drink. Her life needed a change in direction, and the first thing she needed to do was forgo the liquor and get off the headache powders. Only, the second of these proved harder than the first. As it turned out, Gillian was addicted. Not so much to the alcohol but to the caffeine in the powders. And maybe there was also a psychological connection to the aspirin as a measure of her well-being.

The headaches were the worst, and despite the blood-thinning aspect having been a factor in her ordeal the night before, she couldn't stop herself from opening a packet and pouring the contents into her glass. Her foot hurt, she told herself. And anyway, she wasn't taking the heavy-duty ibuprofen they'd given her. The aspirin was mild comparatively. *Right?*

Right.

She convinced herself that was the case. Only then, after

having prepared a glass, she realized she had to begin somewhere, so she tossed the contents and grabbed a pair of kitchen
shears from the utensils drawer to cut a new packet in half,
placing one half on the sill and the contents of the other half into
her glass. Half a packet was okay to take, she decided—especially
since she intended to forgo the painkillers. Eventually she would
stop taking even that, but for now, with the pain in her foot, it was
an unthinkable prospect to cut out both alcohol and headache
powders together. Pain was not her favorite companion.

Antsy to get to work, she made her way around the house on
crutches, learning how to maneuver with them—not so easily as
one might have supposed. She needed them to walk, but it had
never occurred to her that putting all her weight onto the
crutches would dig into the pits of her arms, so when it was time
for bed at night, she had even more aches and pains to consider.

More powder wasn't the cure for that, and she longed for a
glass of wine. Wine might be fine, she thought. It wasn't nearly as
strong as tequila, but she'd promised Kelly—sort of.

At least she hadn't disagreed. However, there wasn't a question of compliance once she realized that the first time he showed
up while she was drinking, he'd leave again, never to return.
Something about that probability hurt far worse than the pain in
her foot.

Hoping to get ideas for the house from her grandmother's
magazines, getting excited about change, Gillian dragged the box
of vintage magazines into the living room and sat in Gigi's chair,
poring over the issues. She picked up a copy of *Life*, idly
wondering what year they'd stopped producing it. She'd have to
look that up.

A memory materialized from the ether—a silly ditty her
grandmother used to sing. "What's *Life*? A magazine. How much
does it cost? Ten cents. I've only got a nickel! That's life!"

The memory made Gillian smile, but really, what amused her
most was that Gigi had filed these issues away so meticulously, as

though she'd meant to use them for reference. And yes, Gillian had since determined the handwriting was Gigi's. Her humor, her love for the family, her presence, was in every issue in the box. Copy after copy, they were replete with advice for the dutiful housewife. Although the articles were shockingly dated, it gave Gillian insight into her grandmother's life and thoughts. Reading through them, it was almost as though Gigi were here in the house with her, and what she wouldn't give for that to be true. For one, she had so many questions. All her life, she'd presumed that she and Gigi were mostly cut from the same cloth, but now she could see that she was projecting. She placed a finger beneath every word in a line, as though doubting her eyes.

"Listen to him," it read. "You may have a dozen things to tell him, but the moment of his arrival is not the right time. Let him speak first—remember, his topics of conversation are more important than yours."

That's what it said. And it was triply underlined in pen—real pen, not print. Next to the article—beside that line—in the margins, Gigi had written. "You can do better."

Surely, it wasn't her grandmother who wrote that.

But yes, yes it was. Especially now, after sifting through her grandmother's bills and files, she recognized Gigi's handwriting better than she did her own. *Bizarre.*

Another ad, this one for . . . ties. *Really?* It depicted a man seated in bed with a woman on her knees holding up a tray in her hand. In bold letters above, it read, "Show her it's a man's world."

Gillian gulped as she moved to another ad, her expression one of horror as she flipped to a man seated in a chair, giving the camera his back. He actually had a woman bent over his knees and a hand poised to spank her backside. This ad read: "If your husband ever finds out you're not store-testing for fresher coffee . . ."

But at least there was this: The next ad was a picture of two women in swimsuits. "How do you look in your bathing suit?" A man's disembodied head inquired, "Skinny? Thousands gain 10 to 25 pounds this new, easy way." What was truly funny about this one, because otherwise it was simply ironic, was that her grandmother had scratched out the product name and written in the margin: "Eat more pie!"

Gillian closed the magazine and dropped it back into the box, peering at the collection with a disoriented stare. She raked her hair back from her face.

If those magazines were to be believed, her grandmother had spent her entire married life catering to a drunken bag of bones. *How was this possible?*

The Gigi she knew was not that woman. She was softhearted, to be sure, but more often than not she'd hid that fact behind an attitude of steel. It was hard to say if Gillian was disappointed by the discovery. More than anything, she was confused.

While she processed the new information, Gillian decided to clean out her grandmother's room. Gigi wasn't coming home, and despite having gone up and down the stairs half a dozen times already, she didn't want to have to traverse the stairs to go to bed every night. So then, realizing she must accept the inevitable, she made a few calls, and little by little, began emptying drawers and putting her grandmother's clothes into piles. Some she would take to the nursing home—only a few, because her grandmother's suite was too small. They had encouraged Gillian to bring in photos and gewgaws that would make Gigi feel at home, but the nurses wouldn't welcome a household full of junk. Nevertheless, some of the clothes could be donated to charity, and maybe Kelly would help her drag bags out to her car so she could haul them in when she could safely—and painlessly—drive again.

Every now and again, she glanced at her phone—like a child waiting for an ice cream truck. It was the prospect of seeing Kelly, she realized, and even though she was still slightly perturbed, she couldn't deny that she was looking forward to seeing him.

At the bottom of one of her grandmother's drawers, Gillian

discovered two small keys. One she suspected belonged to her grandmother's safe box, the other she had no idea. She set them both on the dresser, intending to put them somewhere safe.

Another drawer revealed a small box filled with personal letters that had never been mailed—all to some address in Maine. She set those aside on the dresser as well, and kept cleaning out drawers.

By the time Kelly arrived, around four, Gillian had the entire room emptied of Gigi's personal effects and had them all stowed away in packing boxes or contractor bags out in the living room. Kelly made his way through the maze of boxes, either horrified or amazed, judging by the sound of his voice. "Hey, you, what's going on?"

"Cleaning," Gillian said.

"Yeah, I can see that."

"I'm moving in," she told him.

"Here?" He stood in the doorway of the master bedroom, peering over short stacks of boxes. Gillian had had a hell of a time lifting them up and moving the lighter boxes onto the heavier ones beneath. She'd moved them around by setting her rear on the floor and shoving with her one good leg, sliding them around the slick wood floors. If it had been a brand-new floor, she might have worried about scratches. As it was, she couldn't remember the last time any of the floors had had a good polish. "Yes," she said. "I'm moving in here."

"So . . . you're actually leaving Turtle Creek?"

Annoyance wasn't a state of mind easily abandoned—especially with a jab like that, because Gillian knew what he was implying. "Yes," she said.

"Huh," he replied, and Gillian read the surprise in his tone. Evidently he hadn't believed she was capable of abandoning her proximity to nightlife and bars.

He shoved one hand into his pocket and stood, staring, as

Gillian kicked a particularly fat box in his direction, toward the door. "This would be a good job for hired help," he suggested.

"I have some guys coming tomorrow. I originally planned to take my old room upstairs but, for obvious reasons, I'm taking hers."

"Makes sense."

He stood there, surveying the room, and Gillian felt a tiny burst of pride for all that she'd managed to accomplish with one bad leg. Granted, she'd made a mess with the boxes, filling the house with low-lying stacks so you had to carve out walking space amidst them, like a miniature maze. Nevertheless, everything was packed—nearly every box she'd bought—and Gigi's room was cleared of everything her grandmother held dear.

The furniture would go tomorrow—some down to the basement, some to a storage unit Gillian procured before she'd so stupidly injured her foot.

In the meantime, there he was, her ex-husband and dubious savior, taking her measure. For some reason, Gillian took great satisfaction in the simple fact that she had already set all this in motion long before his ultimatums had been set.

Without Kelly's intervention, she'd already intended to move away from the bars. It was a foregone conclusion that she should stop drinking.

Except that, deep down, she knew full well that it would never have transpired without the unfortunate accident in the kitchen—with or without Kelly's ultimatums. What was it they said? You had to hit rock bottom before you could climb back up?

Kelly took the box she'd pushed in his direction and lifted it up, carrying it out into the living room without having to be asked. "How are you feeling?" he asked when he returned.

"Better," Gillian said, mindful to forgo the sarcasm. His question was genuine, and she had an obligation to answer in kind.

"Evidently."

Gillian grinned. "No telling what a woman can accomplish when she's told she can't, huh?"

"No man or woman in their right mind would ever tell Gillian Frazer what to do."

Gillian laughed, despite herself. "Right you are, sir."

Only left unsaid were the many, many times Kelly had, no doubt, wished to. Although in all fairness, he never had. Only maybe, Gillian realized in a moment of clarity, if he had, perhaps she might have taken it as a sign that he cared. Maybe then she would have tried a little harder? *Maybe.*

But that was neither here nor there. The time for complicated compromises was past.

Still, it was nice to see him smiling over something she'd said —not that demeaning little smirk he had, but a genuine smile that reached his eyes.

"Ya done great," he said, nodding with approval. And then again, without being asked to, he rolled up his sleeves to help. Gillian let him, tired of fighting, tired of everything. In fact, she was exhausted to her bones after a long day of physical labor. Every little thing took so much more effort when you were handicapped. "Have you gone to see Gigi today?" he asked.

"No."

"Good," he said. "I half expected you to defy doctor's orders and get behind the wheel, but I'm glad you didn't. I'll take you," he said.

Gillian stopped what she was doing, which was essentially nothing from the instant Kelly arrived, merely pushing boxes around until he took them away. "You will?"

"Yeah," he said. "I'd like to see her."

Feeling the world rock beneath her, Gillian scooted backward across the floor to rest her back against the foot of the bed. Somewhere, deep down, a torrent of tears threatened to burst up and out of a bottomless well, but she trapped them before they could escape. "You won't like what you see," she warned once she composed herself.

He held her gaze, the warmth in his eyes forcing her to swallow. "I want to go," he said.

"Okay."

~

GILLIAN GASPED as she entered her grandmother's suite at the nursing home. If Kelly hadn't been behind her, she might have toppled onto her rear.

The bed was frighteningly empty. A nurse stood, changing sheets, and smiled as she spied Gillian. Only then, correctly interpreting Gillian's expression, she said with a reassuring smile, "Ms. Frazer is enjoying the sunshine. Out in the garden."

"Oh," Gillian said, as confused as she was relieved.

Only two days ago the prognosis had been so bleak that the notion of taking Gigi out to enjoy anything was inconceivable. *Was she better now?* Had she made some miraculous recovery during the time Gillian had been nursing her own wounds?

"Do you need a chair?" the nurse asked politely.

A wheelchair? For her foot. Gillian shook her head. "No, thank you."

Kelly offered a gentle touch at the back of her arm, reminding her of his presence. He smiled at the nurse. She could hear it in his tone. "I've got her," he said, and judging by the woman's blush, he likely winked at her as well.

"Lucky lady," the woman said, and Gillian grit her teeth as she turned around. Already, life was too complicated. At the moment, all she cared about was locating her missing grandmother and finding out if there was a change in her prognosis.

It took a few inquiries to ferret out where the garden might be. It wasn't clear from the exterior of the building that there was a garden at all. There was no yard outside; it was a nursing home that looked like a hospital, surrounded by hot, steaming asphalt. But the garden, as it turned out, was no more than an indoor court-yard with a domed sunroof. Small raised beds with hassle-free marigolds and red geraniums bordered the room in flower boxes. There was nothing in the center to catch the wheels of chairs—or a wayward crutch. A nurse sat on a nearby bench with a book, watching her charges. She smiled as Gillian and Kelly entered, and Gillian nodded toward her grandmother, who was seated in a wheelchair in the center of the room . . . her expression unchanged.

Swallowing, Gillian glanced back at Kelly, and her heart twisted at the fluttering of his brows—an indication that he clearly hadn't anticipated Gigi's condition, even in spite of Gillian's warning. Taking baby steps, careful not to put too much weight on her injured foot, Gillian maneuvered her way across the room with Kelly close behind her.

"Lovely garden," he said to the nurse. But it was a lie. It was the coldest, most uninspired garden Gillian had ever seen. Nothing about it brought to mind any of the gardens her grand-mother had nurtured—not the pretty pine-strewn garden out in front of the house, nor the vegetable garden she had tended, surrounded by a white picket fence—a fence Geeg had built herself, with only marginal help from ten-year-old Gilly.

"Yes," the woman said. "Lovely."

It's not! Gillian screamed inside. It was a box without windows. Only a sunroof offered any means for a raging sun to glare into the white, sterile room.

Small talk was more Kelly's forte, so Gillian left it to him.

Maneuvering with her crutches, she made her way across the room toward Gigi. Only realizing she might need his help, Kelly hurried ahead of her, anticipating her need for a chair. He gently pushed one closer to Geeg, taking care not to inflict any harsh noises into the deafening quiet.

Not once during all this time did Gigi meet either of their

gazes, or even acknowledge that she sensed anyone was near. Any hope Gillian had that she might be improving was lost as she sat down in the chair beside her grandmother.

Kelly grabbed another chair, lifting it up and moving it to the other side of Gigi's wheelchair; all the while Gigi sat with her eyes wide and her lips twisted into a horrific *O*.

"There's a spray bottle in the pouch on the side of her chair," the woman said to Gillian. "To moisturize her mouth," she explained when Gillian gave her a perplexed look.

Gillian nodded, her stomach roiling.

She wanted to ask if Geeg ever closed her mouth, but she must. *How else would she eat?* They'd taken her off the feeding tube and, for that matter, her IVs as well. All that remained to evidence the use of intravenous care was the bone-deep bruises on the skin of her arms.

Gillian reached down, grabbing the spray bottle from the pouch, peering at the label. It read: "advanced oral moisturizer with hyaluronic acid." *Spearmint.*

Her grandmother hated the taste of spearmint. *Was this hell?* Unable to bring herself to use it, Gillian dropped the spray back into the pouch. There had to be another flavor they could use, and she must stop by the receptionist's desk to inquire. If they didn't have any here, she would track some down and buy it and give it to them. Even if Gigi didn't understand on a conscious level, subconsciously, she must feel the loathing.

Kelly sat down, taking Gigi by the hand. He placed his long fingers over hers. "Hi, Geeg," he said. Gigi didn't respond.

Gillian placed her own fingers over Kelly's, partly to thank him, and partly because the feel of his warm hand promised to renew her strength. It was crazy how ambivalent she felt toward the man she'd married, and divorced.

Their gazes met and held, and Gillian felt anew the sting of tears in her eyes. Kelly was the only person on the face of the earth who could level her barriers with nothing but a look. It gave her an inexplicable jolt of dread, and she felt the panic acutely in the closing of her throat.

Gillian tore her gaze away. "Hey, Geeg," she said softly. "I cleaned Baby's stall." She waited only a few seconds before continuing, resigned to the fact that Gigi wouldn't respond. "She's great," she said, daring to meet Kelly's sympathetic gaze. He shifted his hand, placing it atop hers, sandwiching Gillian's hand between his and Gigi's, giving her the strength to go on. "She misses you, Geeg—but, you know, she's spunky as ever. She waits so patiently until I'm done and then goes back into her stall on her own. Smart horse, like you said."

Gigi didn't answer.

Gillian's eyes stung again. "So . . . um . . . are they treating you well?"

Again, no response. But the nurse on the bench peered up from her book and smiled.

Gillian's throat closed, and the silence stretched on until she could barely stand it. How was she going to get through this? Gigi was everything to her. Was she supposed to sit here each and every day, making idle chatter, with no clear indication Gigi understood?

This is painful.

If only Gigi would close her mouth—lift a brow. Or even if she would twitch a finger, instead of leaving her hand flopped on her lap like a discarded rag doll.

Kelly squeezed her hand and Gigi's beneath hers. "Hey, Geeg," he said, breaching the silence, speaking conversationally as if it were the natural thing to do, just like Gillian had done. "I went by the house today. Looks great. You kept it so well. I don't know how you do it . . ."

Neither did Gillian. Even before the crutches, she had been overwhelmed by the laundry list of things to do. And it wasn't as though Geeg were twenty anymore.

"But . . . I couldn't help but notice the barn doors are wonky."

His voice was gruff, and Gillian could hear him swallow after the pause. "I'll fix them for you."

Gillian's gaze shot up to meet Kelly's. She frowned in response to the pity she saw his eyes. It wasn't his job to repair her household and, let's face it, it wouldn't be for Gigi, because Gigi was never going to know. The house was Gillian's now, and she felt a deep and abiding need to fix it on her own. Nor did she want to get used to having Kelly around—especially if he was seeing somebody else. "You *don't* have to do that."

He smiled indulgently. "What if I do?"

"But you don't."

His lips curved slightly. "I see your granddaughter's proud as ever," he said to Geeg without looking at her. Gillian frowned and slid her hand out from beneath his.

"That's alright," he said. "I'm used to it by now." To Gillian, he said, "What else do you expect me to do when I come around checking on you?"

Just in case Gigi could hear and understand, Gillian kept her voice low. "You don't need to do that either."

"But I'm going to," he argued. "And if I'm going to, I'm going to fix the damned barn. It's my gift to your grandmother."

"It's not necessary," Gillian maintained. "She can't pay you, and I won't. We—*you* have a business to run, or maybe you've forgotten? We can't both be gone at once."

Kelly's smile persisted. "I forget nothing," he assured her. "And anyway, if you paid me, Gillian, it wouldn't be a gift, now wouldn't it?"

As always, his unflappable temperament annoyed Gillian to no end. He claimed she was cold, but it simply wasn't true. Not far beneath the surface, her anger sizzled like burning coals. He, on the other hand, showed little emotion, no matter the provocation.

God help her—no matter how strong she tried to be, Kelly

was like kryptonite. All he had to do was be present, and she turned into a puddle of mush.

The culmination of the past few weeks' events had taken their toll. She was a kettle of bad temper, ready to blow. Still, she spoke calmly. "It's not like she'll ever know. She won't ever know, Kelly, so what's the point? She can't even thank you."

Kelly held her gaze, nailing her to a crucifix formed of her own words. "Wasn't it you who said the best gifts were those given without a promise of reward?"

Gillian started to gather up her crutches to pull herself out of the chair. "Yeah . . . that was a lifetime ago. Things were different."

"Not so much," he argued, and Gillian's eyes burned. Anger surged like a wildfire into her breast—anger over Gigi's condition and anger over not being able to get up and run away—anger because the biggest part of her wanted and needed Kelly's help but she couldn't and shouldn't get used to having him around.

"Are you so sure your new girlfriend won't mind?" she asked sourly, pulling herself up awkwardly and stabbing the crutches beneath her arms. All the while Gigi sat, oblivious. "I'm ready to go," she snapped.

She turned then and hobbled across the room, acutely aware of the fact that Kelly remained seated, chatting with Gigi as though she understood every single word.

"At least she's not holding it in," he said. "You see that look she gave me? Damned if I don't feel like bursting into flames."

Barely holding it together, Gillian didn't dare look back, because as furious as she was with Kelly—justifiably or not— she'd rather pretend, if only for an instant, Gigi was looking him in the eye, nodding away in agreement.

10

PECAN JUMBLES

"GREET HIM WITH A WARM SMILE AND SHOW SINCERITY IN YOUR
DESIRE TO PLEASE HIM."
—THE GOOD WIFE'S GUIDE, HOUSEKEEPING MONTHLY

8:59 p.m., Friday, July 8, 1960

SHERIFF TAYLOR SAT across the table, stuffing pecan jumbles into his mouth. He was eating them as fast as she set them down on his plate. "More milk?"

He pushed his glass forward. "Don't mind if I do," he said without waiting to swallow. He talked around cookie crumbs, spraying some onto her table, and Rebecca noted where they landed. She got up, restraining herself from grabbing a rag instead of the milk.

Ants would have a field day with those crumbs. The last thing Rebecca needed was to have her kitchen overrun. They'd been waiting patiently for Joe for nearly an hour and that mean old coot had yet to return home. Approaching the table with the milk jug in hand, she turned the lip over Clarence's cup, filling it to the brim.

He set his cup down and went for another cookie, the last of the batch. Watching him, Rebecca considered the fact that she hadn't had even one. *Not one.* She'd labored over that last bunch a good, long hour, chopping pecans. But that was fine, she told herself, because it was time to start watching her figure if Joe was out there turning his gaze toward Leona Fox.

Fickle, fickle man.

Then again, maybe it would be the best thing for everyone if he up and ran away with the two-bit whore. She had her own house to keep, and maybe that was more than enough impetus for Joe to leave her Noble Ranch.

Wondering how she would feel about her husband taking up with Leona over on Anthony Street, she sat again at the kitchen table, leaning forward and resting her chin on the back of one hand as she'd seen them do in the magazines—all dainty like, listening intently, the way men preferred. But, in fact, she wasn't listening to a word Clarence was saying—something about trouble up at the Roadhouse, although he was careful not to implicate Joe.

Nevertheless, Rebecca sensed why he was here. Joe ran errands for the Roadhouse—what those errands entailed, she didn't know. Whatever it was, Clarence Taylor was hardly an innocent. If he had come here looking for Joe, Rebecca had an inkling it must be because he had an interest in finding her husband before anyone else did. As she sat listening, she came up with an entire scenario in her head. Maybe Joe stole some money? Maybe Clarence was aiming to get himself a cut? Or maybe Joe was into something else . . .

Rebecca didn't know much about anything but she wasn't stupid. The Mill was barely hanging on. Folks were feeling like it was time to pack up and leave, or find another means to get by.

Take Dottie for example. Hadn't she said she was moving to Fort Worth?

No. That was Mary Claire saying there might be work there. Dottie was only saying Billy hadn't come home...

Times were so hard, good folks found honest ways to sustain themselves. Bad folks glommed on to bad things. Joe wasn't any paragon of virtue, and it was no hard stretch to imagine her husband getting into illicit acts.

Wasn't that what they called them?

Illicit acts?

As for Sheriff Taylor... She paid attention to his tone more than she did his words. He might or might not be corrupt, but he sure had a mighty fine house to keep. And he did it on a municipal salary. His wife Roberta always showed up to church with a nice, new dress, and their girls were always wearing the latest fads—those short, short skirts, though thankfully Bertie would never let them wear those hip-hugging cigarette pants. Downright shameful was what that was. And, in the meantime, her boys were clad in gamey old rags. Jeff wore nothing but hand-me-downs. And while it didn't bother her so much that other people had nice things, it did bother her that she couldn't control what she had. Every day she had to watch Joe waste money and it really made her mad. After all, it wasn't everyone who had a nice home, paid free and clear. They had the means to do so much more with their land. Instead, he up and bought himself that stupid new car.

Four thousand eight hundred and ninety-two hard-earned dollars for that hardtop coupe. It was nearly every penny that was left from her father's savings—money she should never have allowed Joe access to, but then, how could she refuse?

Rebecca studied Sheriff Taylor's face—the hard lines of his jaw. After all was said and done, even Clarence, who had never excelled at much in school, was a far better catch than Joe. Her papa warned her . . .

"Well, Mrs. Frazer—Becky—it's been a while now, so I guess I should be going . . ."

Rebecca shook herself free of her reverie. That dumb little crumb on the table was still driving her insane. Hopefully Clarence was fixing to leave so she could clean that up.

"You'll have to give Bertie your recipe," he said, stirring in his chair and eyeing the tin-covered plate Rebecca had left sitting before Joe's chair.

"Well, yes, I sure will," Rebecca said, reanimating herself.

Sheriff Taylor glanced up at the kitchen clock and then again at the cold dinner waiting beneath the tin. "Seems like Joe's . . . uh, otherwise occupied," he said. And Rebecca smiled. Even now, those good old boys looked out for one another, didn't they? It irked her that everyone in town should know what she didn't.

"Seems so," she agreed. But she wanted him to understand she wasn't without her little birds. "Have you checked for Joe's new car up on Anthony Street?"

"Anthony Street?" Clarence blinked, cocking his head and narrowing his gaze.

Rebecca smiled faintly. "Yes, well, to hear, Joe's been spending time up there."

With some effort, Sheriff Taylor pushed himself up from the table. He couldn't retrieve his hat any quicker. "You mean up at the Roadhouse?"

"Oh, is that up on Anthony Street?" she asked innocently, knowing full well it wasn't, even though she'd never put a foot inside that establishment. Everyone in town—even the young'uns who'd been warned away from the place—knew where it was.

"No, ma'am."

"Well, I suppose he could be there," Rebecca said pleasantly.

"Alright then, I'll drive on by," he said as he moved out of the kitchen and through the dining room.

"Thank you, Clarence."

He peered over his shoulder. "New car, you say? What's Joe driving now, if you don't mind me asking? I noticed the Studebaker out front."

Rebecca lifted her brows to feign a little excitement. "We got a brand-new car."

"Really?" he said, stopping. "Must be why I keep missing him. What'd you get?"

"An El Dorado."

The sheriff whistled. "Oooh, baby," he said. "What color?"

"Gold."

He nodded. "Must be nice!"

Rebecca forced a smile. "Yes, well, if you see Joe before I do, Clarence, please tell him I'm keeping his supper warm." *Like a good wife should.*

"Will do," he said, then winked, and once again moved toward the door, but not before giving Rebecca a once over that warmed her cheeks. "Joe's one lucky man," he said.

Rebecca crossed her arms over her breasts, ashamed that her nipples tightened over the compliment. "Thank you, Sheriff."

"Any woman who can bake like you is a real gem." His eyes remained on the region of her bosom another brief moment before he lifted his gaze. "Tell him I said so, ya hear?"

"I will," Rebecca said, following him to the door.

He doffed his hat before walking outside. "Well . . . I'll be seeing you," he said. "You and the kids have a lovely weekend. And if that man of yours comes around before I run across him, tell him I'm aiming to speak with him."

"Certainly," Rebecca said. "Good night, Sheriff."

"Good night," he said, and Rebecca waved, fluttering her fingers, as he moved off the porch toward his squad car.

As she watched him go, she moved onto the porch, wondering

what it could be that her husband had gotten into. She knew Clarence well enough to know he'd never burden her with details. But whatever it was, Rebecca hoped Joe hadn't put the ranch at risk—like gambling it away or something stupid like that.

She watched the squad car turn in the yard. Clarence made a three-point turn and headed out over the long dusty drive, his red tail lights illuminating streams of dust.

But then she smirked, thinking about his destination.

Sometimes Joe claimed she had a mean streak, and perhaps she did, because right about now she was perfectly amused by the thought of Sheriff Taylor catching him at Leona's and then discovering it was Rebecca who'd sent him there.

Of course he would never admit it, and neither would Rebecca, because if they dared to do such a thing, it would turn into a knock-down-drag-out fight, and Rebecca wasn't ready for that . . . not yet. Nevertheless, it would do him good to wonder what else she knew.

Only after a while, when she didn't speak up, he would convince himself she didn't know a thing. But of course she knew. Oh, she knew. Women had an intuition for such things, and someday, when she had all her ducks in a row and was ready to go toe-to-toe with Joe, she'd stand right up to that man. Until that time, she was going to be a good, obedient wife.

She made her way over to the phone and gently lifted the receiver.

Tonight, there was only a dial tone, so she set the receiver back down into its cradle and went over to the record player to put on a song. She put on a forty-five and set it to repeat, then went back into the kitchen, listening to Elvis croon on:

WELL, *that's all right now mama*
That's all right with you,

That's all right now mama, just anyway you do.
That's all right, that's all right.
That's all right now mama, anyway you do.

SHE GRABBED HER RAG, returning to the table to sweep up crumbs as the record player carried on:

MY MAMA, *she done told me,*
  papa done told me too,
  Son, that gal you're foolin' with,
  She ain't no good for you.

∼

PRESENT DAY

GIGI WASN'T SERVED by Gillian's visits, nor was she soothed by Gillian's presence. Her blood pressure rose when Gillian came around, but not enough to indicate she was aware of Gillian or that she might be frustrated by her inability to communicate. She was merely agitated, as an infant might be when faced with a stranger. On the other hand, Gillian was incredibly frustrated by the visits. Her desire for alcohol increased tenfold on the days she made the trip to Frisco. At this point, staying away seemed the best thing to do.

On the bright side, she never even once ran into her father or her uncle. Neither seemed to have any interest in seeing their mother, only in what Gigi could do for them, and since Gigi could no longer do anything for herself, much less for either of them, it put an immediate embargo on nursing home visits for the gruesome twosome.

In fact, not since the night of Gillian's accident had she even heard from her father. Whatever Little Joe was doing, he was blissfully unaware that Gillian had nearly severed a tendon and bled all over the kitchen floor, or that she'd face-planted, half-sotted, at the feet of a Texas trooper. No doubt realizing she was a stone wall regarding Gigi's will, Joe and Jeff were perfectly content to avoid Gillian altogether.

That was fine. It suited Gillian fine. She didn't want her dad to realize she was handicapped, because, well, she didn't want him to seize the opportunity to grab what he desired and walk away with it simply because Gillian was helpless to chase after him. Really, she wouldn't put it past him to haul away anything that would make him a buck, or even to put up estate sale signs all along Old Mill Road, allowing strangers to come haggle over Gigi's stuff. It was certain that he wouldn't have the first sense of compassion or obligation toward his only daughter, so it was better he didn't know.

Left to her own devices, Gillian learned to make her way around. By the second or third day on her own, she had already discarded one of the crutches and was using one to move about the house. She had discovered that if she kept the weight off her right foot, she barely felt any pain. Half a headache powder in the morning and half at night kept the edge off as well. Occasionally, she'd slip in a third. It was better to break it up that way, rather than take them all at once, and since she wasn't drinking anymore, it shouldn't be so hard on her stomach.

Right?

Right.

Eventually, she'd stop taking them altogether, but not now.

As for Kelly, all his good intentions went off the rails after the movers came. That day, he brought Gillian a burger and kept mostly out of the way, watching as she ordered the movers around. He left before they did, with a clear sense that Gillian was in control, and maybe that was a purposeful exercise on

Gillian's part because she didn't want Kelly feeling sorry for her. She realized he had a life to live, and she only wanted him to hang around if he wanted to be there. So much of his body language said otherwise. He was the ever-present, long-suffering caretaker, giving freely of his time, but not without resentment, if his silence and dour glances were any indication. Just for good measure, after she woofed down her burger—hungrier than she'd realized—she directed him to the top cupboard where she'd stashed her tequila bottle and instructed him to take it with him when he left. Gillian hadn't touched a drop since returning home, and she didn't intend to ever again. He went after it the minute she brought it up, as though he were waiting for the chance to bolt. And then he stood there, eyeing the bottle in his hand with disgust, not quite able to make eye contact. "So how's Dana doing with Burke?" she asked.

"Great," he said. "Great." He slid one hand into his pockets, all the while dangling the tequila bottle from the other. He was uncomfortable in her presence, eager to be away. The conversation was as painful as the last "talk" they'd had before the divorce. "She's got his number. She knows how to play him," he said, smiling, though not at Gillian. "He's already called twice to say how thrilled he is with the job she's doing."

Something about the praise sat uneasily with Gilly.

"You taught her well," he said, breaching a long moment of awkward silence.

"Great," Gillian said. "Great." And she meant it, although it stung that he seemed to be saying they didn't need her. Only rather than make her long to get back to work in order to prove herself, it strengthened her resolve to part ways with Kelly and the company once and for all—for both their sakes. He left immediately after that painful exchange, taking the tequila bottle with him, and the following day, he called instead of coming by. The phone rang as she was perusing her Grandmother's vintage magazines at the kitchen table.

"How's it going?"

"Fine."

"Good. You seem to have everything under control."

"Yep."

"Good."

"Yeah," she agreed. "Thanks for everything," she said, absolving him from all future visits and/or phone calls.

"No problem, Gillian. Take care. You know where to find me if you need me."

"Yeah," she said. "I do." And she hung up with tears in her eyes, swearing to God she wouldn't call him again unless she absolutely had to. Kelly was her past, she told herself, not her future. But the truth of that matter hurt more than she figured it should after three long years.

After that last phone call, he resorted to quick, short texts rather than calling or making a trip out to the ranch, and Gillian likened his move to her own in regard to nursing home visits.

Certainly, he was doing it for the same reason. It stressed them out to be in close proximity; why put each other through it?

Gillian couldn't bear the thought of sitting across a table from him, making idle talk, wondering all the while who he was sleeping with. Whatever they'd once meant to each other, it didn't seem to be enough to hold on to anymore. Unfortunately, there was a small hollow in her heart she suspected would be impossible to fill. Even so, she daren't inspect it too closely because she was afraid it wasn't so tiny as she liked to believe.

Going back to her grandmother's magazines, she marveled over the cultural changes that had occurred between Gigi's time and now. Gillian was obsessed with them, diving for the box of magazines any time she had a few quiet moments. Her grandmother's notes were such complete dichotomies to the woman Gillian knew, but speaking as someone with a career in marketing, the ads were perfectly horrific.

For example, she stopped to read an ad for a postage meter.

The headline read—no kidding—"Is it always illegal to kill a woman?"

Couched as an article, it was a man's rant about his redheaded stenographer. He's begged his home office for a postage meter for weeks and once it arrives, the stenographer says, "Oh, but I have no mechanical aptitude. Machines mix me up." It's not as though he's asked her to fly a jet, the man retorts, admitting he's about to blow his top. So he begs the stenographer to use the meter for two weeks, couching the request as a bid for diplomacy with thinly veiled derision. After two weeks, the stenographer puts a stupid pink bow on the meter as a symbol of her approval, then raves about how the mail goes out early now, giving her ample time to dash into the girl's room to "hear all the dirt." The man now wonders if it's always illegal to kill a woman. Worse than blatant sexism, it was easy enough to see why men had to unlearn this deep-seated behavior. Clearly, they needed Twitter back in the day, and #Metoo hashtags. There was little wonder Gigi had opted never to marry again.

Gillian was too young to swear off men, but she could say with a certain conviction that Kelly Ruby would be the bar by which she would measure every man who would ever enter her life. That should probably make her sad, but what was it they said? It was better to have loved and lost than to never have loved at all. If she clung to that as a maxim, she could nurture a little gratitude for the time she and Kelly had shared together.

She might even be okay with the notion that everyone who came after him would necessarily be second best. And then she could even be happy with second best, so long as she didn't have to face No. 1 on a daily basis. "Good luck with that," she said to herself.

Maybe it was time to get a cat?

11

ELIJAH FOX

Though Gillian had once claimed she'd never known boredom or loneliness, both were now her indisputable companions.

Stuck on the ranch and unable to drive, she didn't want to call Dana or Shannon. Only now, she realized how shallow their relationships were, and how seldom she'd ever bared her soul to either woman. They were bar buddies, nothing more. Except in Dana's case, she was also Gillian's employee, which necessarily kept some barriers firmly in place.

Aside from Gigi, Kelly had been the one person she'd felt comfortable sharing her deepest thoughts with, but she was too hurt and irritated to call him.

In the absence of any true confidant, she was drawn, as though to a lodestone, to Gigi's vintage magazines. Despite the fact that there was nothing in the issues that represented the woman who'd raised her, it was Gillian's closest link to her grandmother. Whether that was because she felt her grandmother speaking to her through the pages—through her copious notes—or whether it was in fascination over the indisputable change in her grandmother's personality, she was driven to the magazines time and again. Literally every time she felt like picking up the phone to ring Kelly, she picked up a magazine.

Now as she turned the pages, she thought about the woman who'd so easily closed the door on her delinquent sons. Gigi wasn't a doormat. She had very clear ideas about what it took to be a good person, and she didn't bend the rules to keep people in her life. In short, she was nothing like this biddable, "just take it" sort of housewife who arose from her subordinate notes.

Furthermore, it would seem that if Rebecca Lee Frazer had truly aspired to be the person depicted in these pages, she would have been an extremely miserable person without a husband to care for. And she wasn't. She never was. If Gillian could say anything about Geeg, it's that she was truly contented—in a way, that would only be possible for a woman who'd lived her life exactly as she'd pleased, and without regrets.

Whatever nurture she'd had, she must have gotten it out of her system with her boys.

Okay, so she'd doted on Gillian as well, but nevertheless, she'd never coddled her granddaughter. She'd taught her to be an independent spirit and told her repeatedly never to count on a man. "Keep separate bank accounts," she'd said. "Never ask someone to do anything you can do for yourself." And, "Don't drink the Kool-Aid, Gillian: There are no rules. Riding sidesaddle is a good way to crack your skull." But if all these magazines were to be believed, Gigi had lived a lie. She'd allowed the prevailing wisdom of her time to undermine who she was.

So then, what was her catalyst for change? Her husband's abandonment? Was she then forced to live up to her own standards instead of the dictums of her time? Had her bratty sons cured her of the need to please?

Gillian turned to an article with a headline that read: "Successful marriages start in the kitchen!" Or maybe it was an ad for cookware. It was difficult to tell at first glance. So many of the

articles seemed to wage psychological warfare against the average
housewife.

The article read: "Now the new mistress of the house can go
ahead with some of those girlhood dreams—planning lovely
meals for her man."

Sheesh. Living with Kelly had been nothing like that. *Thank
God.* He'd loved to cook, and Gillian was terrible, so she'd gladly
left the task for him. If, for some reason, he'd come home late,
she'd happily give it a shot, but ultimately, their stomachs were
happier when Kelly was in command of the kitchen. In fact,
Gillian knew a lot of men who were more comfortable in the
kitchen than their partners. But, for the first time in her life, she
wondered if she too had fallen prey to some reverse order of
social pressure. The fact that Kelly seemed to enjoy cooking, and
did so not because it was mandated but because he wished to,
was telling. Gillian had no doubt that Gigi had been taught to
serve, just as Gillian had been taught to value her independence.
But maybe she had learned her lessons too well, because she'd
deprived herself of the pleasure of doing something nice for
someone else—not because she had to, but because she
wanted to.

She went to bed that night wishing for a do-over.

THE FOLLOWING MONDAY, Gillian got up and, wearing only a T-
shirt, shuffled around the house, going from room to room, trying
to decide what else she could do to make the house her own. It
wasn't that she was in a hurry to be rid of her grandmother's presence. To the contrary, some part of her wanted to hang on tight.
But she wasn't a pretender by nature, and the notion of waiting
for something that would never happen was, well, it was
depressing.

She was also coming to terms with the fact that her addiction

—emotional or otherwise—was very real. Okay, so no, she wasn't having physical withdrawals, which might indicate a more serious dependency, but she nevertheless needed a drink and that need was an intense physical desire. Her heart raced all morning long, and she felt hung over despite her lack of consumption.

She had given the bottle to Kelly as an afterthought, and rather vindictively, as though she were hoping to prove to him—and herself—once and for all that she didn't need it. But now that the bottle was gone, she could feel the empty cupboard in much the same way she felt her grandmother's absence. The space it once occupied was filled with the ghostly apparition of its form, so that Gillian had the uncanny notion it might still be there.

More than once, she opened the cupboard just to be sure. But nope, the bottle was gone.

Like her grandmother's furnishings.

Everything had been moved to a storage facility out in Frisco, but their presence in the house was like a pentimento—an artist's term for regret. Gillian had become acquainted with the word, mostly in respect to physical renditions, but pentimenti existed digitally as well.

On canvas, when you started a painting and then abandoned it for another, the older iteration sometimes remained visible as an under drawing. Sometimes these could be viewed with the naked eye. Other times, it took X-Rays to reveal them. For example, in the case of "The Old Guitarist" by Picasso, the subject was completely changed, but you could still see a woman's face behind the white-haired old man—layered in new paint. Like the ghosts that lingered in this old house, the woman was still there, ready to reveal herself if you looked hard.

In Gillian's present state, there was little hope of looking past her grandmother's ghost, but she realized that if she was ever going to straighten her life out, she needed to paint new, more indelible layers on the canvas of this house—and her life. At the moment, her grandmother's face loomed everywhere—in the kitchen, in her chair, ambling up the stairwell, peering back over her shoulder to warn Gillian not to stay up too late. "Early to bed, early to rise," she would say.

Gillian wasn't an early riser, although she'd managed to be moderately healthy and wise. But like most Americans—even those who succeeded in waking before the rooster's crow—she was still pursuing wealthy. Money wasn't everything and it couldn't buy happiness, but she'd had an up-close perspective of the misery to be wrought without it and she didn't intend to end up in a long-stay motel, where the concept of pentimenti took on a whole new meaning.

She could never bear sitting on her mother's bed, imagining how many times the sheets had been abused. All these years later, she cringed over the thought of the mess a black light might have revealed. Only thanks to Gigi, that life was not hers. But now that Gigi was gone, Gillian had to find a way forward in this place where there was no touchstone. Rather, the house itself must become her touchstone, and the trick would be in making it all her own without exorcising all of Gigi's ghosts.

Day by day, little by little, the house began to take on a more minimalistic character. Fewer things to dust meant less time spent keeping house, and Gillian briefly logged into the work server to peek at Dana's progress. She felt odd doing so; it felt invasive. Barely a few weeks removed, and already it felt like a faraway life, not entirely her own. Afterward, she sent Dana an email with an open invitation to brainstorm. The email that came back was a lukewarm seven-word response. "Thanks, Gilly. I'm good. Feel better, okay?"

Another email to Kelly went unanswered until the wee hours of the morning. "You need to heal," he wrote back, as though Gillian were a child. "Work can wait. Dana is doing fine."

Along with the immediate rush of relief, she felt a surge of resentment. Why did it always feel as though she were dancing to somebody else's tune?

With nothing left to do, Gillian began searching for projects at home. She didn't have to look far. As Kelly pointed out, the barn doors needed fixing. The entire structure also needed repainting. For that matter, so did the house. Unfortunately, in her present condition, she couldn't accomplish any of these tasks on her own. She searched for and found the ad her grandmother had placed a few weeks before her event, and ran a new ad in the *McKinney Courier-Gazette* for hired help. In a short matter of time, Gillian was inundated with applicants. Most were over- or under-qualified, or they didn't speak much English, but one man stood out. It was a no-brainer to hire him: Elijah Fox was his name. Eli for short, he said.

Presumably, Eli was older than Gillian, by maybe five or ten years. It was difficult to say. But since the question wasn't legal to ask a potential hireling, Gillian didn't inquire.

Tall and lean, Eli had the shape of a man who was accustomed to hard labor, and the complexion of someone who either enjoyed time on a boat or who spent his days working outdoors —except that his hands appeared manicured. *Whatever.* So long as he could do the job, Gillian didn't care if he spent his money on mani-pedis all day long.

As for Baby, she intended to continue taking care of the horse to the best of her ability. Somehow, this was a connection she needed as much as Baby needed care. It was a lifeline to Gigi. Eli could help with the heavy lifting, but Gillian was inclined to do the rest.

On Eli's first morning, while he was outside doing prep work, Baby reached over the stall to nip at the collar of Gillian's blouse. Gently but firmly, the old mare pulled Gillian closer, refusing to let go until she was sure Gillian wouldn't leave. Then, the horse cradled her muzzle into the crook of Gillian's neck, pressing firmly, as though to embrace her. The simple act of communion brought a powerful sting to Gillian's eyes. The gesture said, "Don't go. Please don't go."

Understanding the horse's plight, Gillian lifted a hand to the animal's forehead, brushing the hair from her eyes, acknowledging Baby's loss, allowing herself to be needed.

It was easier than she might have supposed. And she realized that come tomorrow's sunrise, she'd be back again, and would do so without discontentment, or resentment, or any sense of obligation. She would come, because she and Baby shared a bond.

Like Gigi, the horse was old. Gillian could smell the rot of age in her breath, and maybe one morning she would come out and find her "gone." But here, now, there was something entirely satisfying in the bittersweet knowledge that she willingly crossed this line: to love a dying animal.

Long life was not a certainty; all things existed on borrowed time.

"I'll be back," she promised the horse. And then, sounding more like Gigi than she ever intended, "Don't worry, Baby Girl. Ain't no bad leg gonna keep me from you."

The horse sneezed, and Gillian smiled, patting the mare lovingly before turning away. She hobbled out to watch Eli work, taking care to stay out of his way.

Already, he had begun with the barn door, pulling it off its hinges and removing the hardware. His first task was to shore up the frame and replace rotten wood.

On a paint-splattered tarp lay one saw, a number of two-by-fours, an orbital sander with the cord still bound, a few sheets of sand paper, a bucket of white primer—leftover from another project, he'd said—and a carpenter's box with the lid open wide. The barn door hardware lay together in the middle of the tarp, the screws huddled together like large black ants on an ice cream stain. "So, how long you been doing this sort of work?" she asked after a while.

Eli peered beneath the door sash, through the rungs of his

ladder, meeting Gillian's gaze. "It's not my primary skillset," he admitted.

Gillian nodded, surprised. So far, he hadn't needed much direction. He appeared to be an old hand at ranch work, finding his way around without any effort.

Squinting her eyes against the sun, she tried to remember where else he'd said he'd worked. Most of what he'd talked about were repairs to an old house up on Anthony Street. Best as she could recall, it was one of those houses on the historic register. It stood out in Gillian's memory only because she remembered Kelly's sister, Jennifer, ranting about notices that had been sent to its absent owner, threatening liens for the upkeep. A few years past, Jennifer had represented one of the homes nearby, and it pissed off her client that the house was always a year or two late making necessary repairs. Eventually, the homeowners had complied, but not until everyone had their panties in a wad. Never as pristine as its neighbors, but not precisely dilapidated, it sat unoccupied, as though waiting patiently for its owner to return. Only now she realized, Eli Fox must be the delinquent homeowner. "So," she said, prying, "Do I detect an accent? Where you from, Eli?"

"Maine," he replied.

Gillian shifted her weight, readjusting her crutches. "Hmm," she said. "That's one place I've never been, but I always wanted to go. I hear it's beautiful."

"Yeah?"

"Yeah."

The muscles in his forearm tightened as he formed a fist then smacked the sash with the butt of his hand. The quiet strength of the man was intimidating. "You should go sometime," he said without looking at her. "It's God's Country."

Gillian lifted a brow. How many times had she heard that exact phrase regarding Texas? "As in, God was your neighbor?" she asked, teasing.

He made a halfhearted attempt at laughter, his chest puffing as he snorted. But that was all. He looked down again, eyeing Gillian's crutches. "You're a real funny girl," he said, wresting a rueful grin from her. But it was difficult to tell if he'd actually meant that or if he was being facetious.

Certainly, Kelly no longer thought Gillian was funny. Her ex-husband used to laugh at nearly everything she said, funny or not, but these days, if Kelly ever smiled, it was that signature smirk that made her long to beat the hot wind from his lungs. The crutches dug into her armpits. "So, what brings you to Texas, Eli?"

He jumped down from the ladder, landing like a green-eyed cat, with an agile little bounce. "Family home. I came back to fix it up and put it on the market."

He continued working, and Gillian decided that talking to the man was like pulling teeth. While he seemed forthcoming enough, he didn't appear to wish to say more than was required. Gillian watched him work for a few minutes longer, then asked, "This would be the house up on Anthony Street?"

"That's right. There's a bit more to be done before we can hire a realtor."

Gillian wasn't normally so intrusive, but, after all, he was working on her property. She thought it prudent to discover as much as she could. "A house like that can be expensive to restore. I imagine it takes a lot of time and money."

He gave Gillian a little smile and, once again, Gillian couldn't tell if it was genuine or merely tolerant. "There's enough to get the job done," he said, and then picked up a level from the ground to check the straightness of his new sash. He lifted it up and pressed it high against the exposed wood overhead, every so often, butting the board with his hand until it sat precisely where he meant for it to sit. He fell silent and Gillian shifted her weight, once again watching him work.

Only something about his answer bugged her. She wasn't sure

why. It would be in her own best interest to go back inside and leave him to work, yet still she lingered. "I know a good realtor if you don't have one yet," she said, rambling.

Silence met her offer.

"Jennifer's from McKinney. She knows the area well. I went to school with her." It just so happened that she was also Kelly's younger sister, although the two rarely spoke. By no means was it a way to keep in contact with Kelly. She was merely offering. That was all.

"Thanks," he said. "I have one."

"Hmm," she said. "So, you're staying at the house? I mean . . . is it livable?" He shot her a questioning glance. "What I mean is . . . I have a guest house on the property if you should need it."

Only after she said it, Gillian frowned. What in God's name was she saying? Generally, she wasn't in the habit of inviting strangers to live with her. God only knew, if she couldn't have a pet, she wasn't ready for a man. Had the prospect of splitting with Kelly unsettled her so much that she had to have someone waiting in the wings? It boggled the mind to think she would open herself up to such a mess. She was relieved when he said, "Thanks. I'm good."

Gillian inhaled as she watched him run his fingers across the raw wood of the sash, presumably feeling for splinters. It was only then that it hit her—the thing that bothered her. "So . . . why take a job if you have stuff to do on your own house?"

Eli stopped what he was doing. He eyed her squarely, setting down the level. "I knew your grandmother," he said. "I guess she was having trouble getting good help. She came by the house to see if I would be interested in a job."

The revelation shocked Gillian. "Rebecca Frazer? She offered you a job?"

He nodded without bothering to look at her. And once again, he was adjusting his sash. He took the hammer he'd placed on a lower rung and tapped the flat nose against the wood, moving it over.

Gigi hadn't said a word about offering a job to someone in town. But she was inclined to be forthright. Her grandmother was quite direct and didn't rest much on her laurels. If something needed to be done, she went after it. It was true: she'd said she wasn't having much luck finding good help, so maybe she'd decided to ask someone she trusted . . . except . . .

Gillian had never heard of this man standing in front of her.

She'd lived with her grandmother most of her life, up until she'd married Kelly. So, it would stand to reason that she should have at least heard Eli's name. But she hadn't. Not until he applied for the job. And just to make matters more confusing, Eli was a transient, or so he would have her believe. So, then, when had Gigi gotten to know him? Had he done work for her before? Had they run into each other at the hardware store? Did Gigi up and take a chance on some guy who was working on a house in town? Where and when had their paths crossed?

Not for the first time, the fact that she could no longer ask her grandmother any such questions brought her down. Faced with questions, Gigi's face remained a blank slate.

"Do you need water, Geeg?"

No nod. Nothing. There wasn't even a glimmer of anything resembling a thought behind the cloudy, blue-green-flecked eyes.

"Hey, Geeg, want me to paint your nails?"

No answer. And God knew, Gigi wasn't a nail-painter, although Gillian had only asked the question in hopes of getting her grandmother's usually sassy response.

"Why would you ask me that?" she might say. "I got work to do, Gilly Pie. Nail paint would be off my fingers in the blink of an eye. It's a waste of time."

And yet, now that Gigi was vegetative, it was all Gillian had left to do in her presence—paint nails and talk, never getting any response.

To date, they'd tried Hot Pink and Cherry Chocolate, and even Sorbet and Very Berry. All the while, Gigi sat, staring ahead, wobbling her head like a dashboard Chihuahua.

It was a long, long time before Gillian uncrossed her arms to speak again, thinking about her grandmother. Gigi had given up so much of her life to raise Gillian, but really, how much did Gillian know about Rebecca Frazer? Maybe not as much as she'd like to believe.

Suddenly, she had a thought. Could Eli have been the proprietor of that extra cup in her grandmother's kitchen on the day of her event? If so, was he the one who'd called EMS? And if so, why hadn't he already said so?

Standing there watching him, Gillian ground the rubber tip of her crutch into the hard Texas clay. "So," she began, trying to sound casual. "When was the last time you saw Geeg?"

He lifted a blond brow. "Geeg?" And then he seemed to figure it out. "Oh, you mean Rebecca?"

"Yeah . . . Rebecca."

He tossed his hammer down onto the tarp, eyeing Gillian curiously. "Few weeks ago, maybe?"

"So . . . before her accident?"

He tipped Gillian a look of ill-concealed amusement. "Certainly not after."

"Right," Gillian said, looking him in the eyes, trying to determine how best to ask: *Were you present the day my grandmother had her stroke?* Except she found herself tongue-tied, because, ultimately, what she would be asking was so much more than that. Because if he were here that day—if Eli had been present when Gigi had her stroke—it would imply he'd left without waiting for EMS to arrive . . . and more importantly, if he'd left the scene, then why?

Gillian didn't get a sense that the man was dangerous. Formidable perhaps, but his demeanor was far too easy. Gillian had good intuition, and nothing about him raised any red flags.

He was just a guy . . . a guy who, for all that he seemed guarded, had answered all her questions openly and without any subterfuge. The last thing she wished to do was offend him, particularly when she needed him. Their gazes held a long moment, and Gillian felt the onset of a new headache. Inside the house, there was half a powder calling her name. She'd cut it in half and leaned it against the bathroom mirror to use later. She lingered just a moment longer, if only so Eli wouldn't take offense by her sudden departure. "Well," she said. "I'll let you get back to work."

"Alrighty," he said. "Catch you after a while."

Gillian turned and hobbled away, stopping once to peer back at him. Already, he had dismissed her and was back to work, his manner completely at ease, as though he hadn't sensed any tension. But Gillian did feel tense. Sighing, she turned back around and made her way up to the porch, thinking again about the cat she'd like to adopt. Maybe tomorrow she would be ready.

"NEVER COMPLAIN IF HE COMES HOME LATE OR GOES OUT TO DINNER, OR OTHER PLACES OF ENTERTAINMENT WITHOUT YOU. INSTEAD, TRY TO UNDERSTAND HIS WORLD OF STRAIN AND PRESSURE . . . "
—*THE GOOD WIFE'S GUIDE, HOUSEKEEPING MONTHLY*

1:00 A.M., Saturday, July 9, 1960

BUT THAT'S ALL RIGHT NOW, *that's all right*
    That's all right now mama, anyway you do

. . .

ELVIS WAS STILL CROONING when Rebecca heard the engine idle outside. She moved to the window, parting the curtain.

Joe was seated in that car, staring ahead, hand to his chin, elbow on the door. It was difficult to say what his mood could be, but the loitering didn't bode well.

The car was good-looking. Shiny and gold, like a new bar of Fort Knox gold. The rooftop glistened under a sliver of moon. In the short time he'd had it, Joe had waxed it and washed it, and doted on it more than he ever did Rebecca or either of their children. Certainly, it was a fine car, but they hadn't needed it. That old Studebaker her father left them ran fine, and ... well, she had a terrible foreboding—a choke of apprehension.

Joe had wanted something of his own to drive, not some rusty hand-me-down of her dad's. He'd come home in that ... thing ... with a toothy grin that made her heart skip a beat because it was the first smile he'd given her in years. Now, if Mary Claire was to be believed, he was flashing his smile for someone else and giving rides in that buttery soft leather seat.

Were they wearing out the rear seat as well?

Rebecca didn't want to think about that.

Not tonight.

Simply because she knew it would put him in a better mood, she'd made more cookies ... all the while she'd waited for him to come home. Sweating like a butcher, she'd toiled over a new batch, and then she'd cleaned up the kitchen, leaving it spotless.

At this point, she wasn't at her best. Her makeup had long worn away. On the table remained his dinner, covered in tin foil. She'd made good and sure the table was clean so he wouldn't find anything to criticize once he sat down. She'd even burned a bit of lavender in a dish to rid the kitchen of the smell of bleach. She would have put his dish in the oven to warm as well, but there was no telling how long he'd be, and she didn't want to dry out his pork chop. She toyed with the idea of running into the kitchen now, firing up the stove, but it was difficult to say which would make him angrier—a cold dinner, or finding an empty table.

At her back, Elvis sang:

I'M LEAVING TOWN, *baby*
   I'm leaving town for sure . . .

A HEAVY, heavy weight settled in Rebecca's breast as finally, after a long, drawn-out moment, Joe opened the door and slid out of the car. He came marching toward the house, the look on his face as sour as an unripe peach.

Very gently, so he wouldn't see the curtain flutter, she set it back into place and hurried into the kitchen, seating herself at the table, where she'd begun to write down her recipe for Roberta Taylor. At six feet three inches and more than two hundred pounds, Big Joe's footsteps were heavy on the front porch. She could hear him clear back to the kitchen, and the door slammed shut when he came inside. Rebecca grimaced over the sound. He went and slapped the needle off the record, and Elvis's singing screeched to a halt.

Clearly, he was in a foul mood.

She wondered if Sheriff Taylor had found him. She wondered too if he'd said what she'd told him to say. Only now, she feared it had been a mistake . . . especially if Joe had been drinking . . .

She listened as he made his way through the dining room, the tip of her pen burrowing deeper into the notebook paper. And then his shadow fell over the room.

"What are you doing?"

Rebecca turned to face her husband, forcing a smile. "Waiting for you, dear."

He was leaning on the doorframe with one hand. "No," he said. "I mean what are you doing?" He pointed at the notebook.

"What the hell's got your attention so you cain't get up off your fat ass and greet your husband like a proper wife?"

With a shuddering breath, Rebecca set her pen down. At once, she raked her chair back and rose to greet Joe, hurrying over to peck him on the cheek. "I was writing down a recipe for Roberta, that's all. I have your dinner waiting—oh, and look!" She turned around, darting back to the counter to sweep up a new platter of cookies. "I made you a fresh batch of pecan jumbles!"

He eyed the platter of cookies with annoyance and brushed past her. "I'm hungry enough to eat the ass out of a skunk," he said, and Rebecca held her breath over the intense alcohol scent that accosted her. She stood with the platter in hand, searching her brain for a proper response—one that would get them through the night, unscathed.

Certainly, it wasn't necessary to speak about Sheriff Taylor—not tonight.

Nor did she have to broach the subject of work, or money, or the mill.

And she wasn't going to ask him about Leona.

The boys seemed a safe topic, so she carried the platter of jumbles over to the table and set it down gingerly as he took his seat behind the tin-covered plate. "Jeff and Joe said to tell you they love you—here, let me get that for you," she said, diving for the tin on top. She peeled it back to reveal his favorite meal—pork chops with macaroni and cheese and perfectly browned drop biscuits, just the way he liked them, with a butter-crisped bottom.

"Sheriff Taylor been here?"

Wincing over his tone, Rebecca sat down at the table with some trepidation, choosing a seat at the opposite end, where she couldn't smell the alcohol wafting off his breath. "Yes, he was here."

She folded her hands in front of her, glancing at the paper

with the recipe. The scent of alcohol wafting off Joe tonight was pharmaceutical grade—like the rubbing alcohol she used to swathe her sons' scraped knees. But he wasn't slurring his words. More and more often, it took more and more to get him drunk. Aside from the mean gleam in his glassy eyes, you'd never even guess he'd been drinking. "It's cold," he said, lifting a pork chop by the bone.

Instinctively, Rebecca reached for her pen, pulling it close. "I know. I'm sorry. I was afraid it would dry up if I left it in the oven too long. Should I warm it for you now?" She depressed the pen's little silver clicker. "I don't mind."

"No," he said.

Tense now, she clicked the pen a few more times. "How was your day?"

"What?"

"I was asking you how your day went."

"Same as any other day, Becky. What's with all the damned questions?"

Her voice grew smaller, but her brow furrowed defiantly. "I merely asked how your day went."

All the while glaring at her, he tore a bite out of his pork chop, violently, like a lion might his devour prey. *Alive, and still struggling as he chewed, ruthlessly ripping the life out of it.*

Nervously, Rebecca pushed a strand of hair behind her ear, hoping she didn't look so disheveled as she felt. After a long, tense moment, he went back to looking at his plate, finally tearing his gaze away from Rebecca, leaving her enervated.

He hadn't been home five minutes and already she was wishing she could put her head down on a pillow and wake up to a new day.

Now, for sure she wasn't about to tell him about the phone call she'd overheard between Mary Claire and Dottie Shepherd —or about Dottie's husband Bill. Nor would it be wise to discuss Leona Fox, or his alleged visits to Anthony Street.

Furthermore, she didn't think she was up to discussing the visit with Clarence tonight, or the fact that the boys had nearly caught the barn on fire, yet again. If they had succeeded in striking up a flame with those stones, as dry as it was, everything would have gone up in smoke. Especially there, near that store of cottonseed. The boys needed their father's direction, but they were never going to get it, and Rebecca was beginning to feel a sense of overall futility. She clicked the pen a few more times, working up the nerve to speak, watching Joe eat.

"I was thinking, Joe. Now that summer's here. What do you think about sending the boys out to Farwell to spend time with their cousins?" Maybe then, while the boys were gone, she could muster up the nerve to ask Joe to leave.

He glanced up, furrowing his brow, but merely grimaced—as though the sound of her voice were the same as fingers across a chalkboard.

"I was thinking it could give me a chance to get some work done."

Maybe get ready to have the girls begin work, though she wasn't going to tell Joe that part either. She needed the boys out of the way for that. If they stuck around, they would run their mouths to their father, and it wasn't as though either of them would be much help. Watching over them would be a hindrance —at least until she got the girls settled.

"You trying to shuffle off responsibility?"

"No. I was thinking maybe it would give us some time to ourselves—and maybe while you're out . . . working . . . I could straighten up a bit."

"I don't give a damn," he said.

Rebecca exhaled in relief, but then second-guessed him and meant to ask for clarification. Did he mean . . . he didn't care if she sent the boys away . . . or he didn't care to spend more time together?

Rebecca clicked the pen a few more times, and then froze as

Joe's gaze moved up from his plate to her face, meeting her gaze directly. He chewed slowly, as though he'd discovered a piece of gristle in his mouth. He swallowed and asked, "You offered cookies to Clarence?"

The question surprised her. "Only a few."

"Only a few?"

"Well, I suppose he ate quite a few, but I made more."

"You made more?"

Rebecca gave him a halting smile. "For you," she said. And then, out of nervousness, she rambled on. "He said he wanted me to give Bertie my recipe because he loved them so much." She reached out to put her hand on the notebook paper. "So, well, here it is." The recipe sat like an eyesore between them, and Rebecca continued nervously, "He said Bertie ain't much of a baker, so I was writing down my recipe for her." He glared at her and she added, uneasily, "Anyway, that's what I was doing when you came in."

"So, let me get this straight . . . You been sitting here writing up that crap when you shoulda been heating my supper?" He dropped his fork onto his place with a clatter. "What else you been giving Clarence Taylor?"

Rebecca frowned, not understanding his question. She clicked the pen again. It was far too quiet, and she wished he had left Elvis crooning in the living room.

"Damn it!" he exploded. Suddenly, he hurled his plate toward the sink. It crashed against the cupboard and shattered into pieces, raining food bits all over the floor. His pork chop, half eaten, ricocheted off the counter. The bone bounced a few times before landing at Rebecca's feet. "What are you so nervous about? I know you, Becky. What else you been handing out to Clarence besides your goddamned cookies? You been spreading your legs for him, too?"

Rebecca's breath caught. She clutched the pen like a weapon, leaping up from the table and moving away, toward the back door. Joe lurched after her, catching her by the hair before she could turn and open the back door. He jerked her back, flinging her toward the opposite wall.

Rebecca's left eyebrow smacked the dining room door frame and she bounced like his pork chop bone, landing in a heap on the kitchen floor amidst broken shards of porcelain and sticky bits of macaroni and cheese. A piece of macaroni stuck to the bottom of her palm as she lifted it, instinctively putting a hand in front of her face to ward off blows.

But Joe didn't move in on her. He stood across the room, looking at her as though she were a pile of horse dung. Something warm trickled down her brow, through her lashes, and she realized before she saw the first drip on her dress that it would be red.

For a long, long moment, nothing more was said. She hoped it was over, but in his present mood, there was no telling.

Sometimes he apologized, realizing what he'd done.

Sometimes he got angrier still, as though he blamed Rebecca for his lapse in temper, as though she were somehow responsible for it all.

She was getting good at staving off additional blows. Look too sheepish and it got his goat. Look too furious and he would attempt to teach her more humility. So Rebecca avoided eye contact, as you were supposed to do with wolves, coyotes, and wild dogs—never daring to challenge them, though never really cowering either. You simply kept your face to them, backing away slowly, never meeting their gaze. Though you didn't turn your back to them either, or you'd find a set of fangs in your nape. She got up as best she could, avoiding all the little slivers of glass.

"You're a sorry piece of shit," he said. "Look at you. Cain't even dress properly. Ain't nobody ever told you that you cain't keep a man looking like that? What makes you think I'd put my pecker anywhere near you?"

Rebecca swallowed any response she might have uttered as

blood from her eyebrow found her pursed lips, then trickled to the floor.

"Waste of time," he said, turning around and making for the same door Rebecca had lunged for. He walked out into the night, cursing up a storm, and let the screen door slam shut behind him. Only then did Rebecca dare look up from the mess he'd made on the floor. She found her gaze settled on the screen door and she continued to stare, half dazed, until she heard the car engine fire up out front. She waited until he was gone. Then she got up and, one by one, yet again, she picked up the pieces of another china plate, realizing what she must do.

They simply couldn't go on this way.

First thing come morning, she'd arrange to send the boys to Farwell.

12

BLEU

For most women, the prospect of independence was a double-edged sword. On the one hand, fostering an attitude of dependency was an archaic and subservient concept that should be discouraged in mothers raising a new dynasty of daughters. The good wives of the sixties had gone the way of the dodo bird, and much rejoicing was heard. On the other hand, gone, too, was chivalry—the opening of doors, particularly car doors, the offering of coats on a brisk evening, and the sharing of umbrellas. These were rarities for women of the new millennium, and, in fact, most millennials probably didn't know what it felt like to have a guy shrug off his coat in twenty-degree weather and hand it over, because, "WTF, girlfriend? Why didn't you bring a coat?"

Chances were, you might get lucky and have someone open a building door for you, but that was no longer a gender-specific consideration. Some people were more polite than others, and even so, nine times out of ten, if you were lucky enough to have a door held open for you, it was more likely because the person who went in ahead was at least considerate enough not to want to shut the door in your face. Every now and again, you might run into a guy whose mom taught him better, who rushed to get a door for you. But forget that car door, baby. You'll get a honk from the curb instead of a knock on the front door, and there's no way he's getting out to open the passenger side door. Flowers? Plant your own garden. All this was fine to lament the passing of, but whether there was a mean-spirited "so there" attached to these gender-social casualties, or a natural passing of the knight errant as a consequence of watching your female sparring partner bench press more than you can, these were the indisputable tradeoffs for things like equal pay, the right to fight for your country, and the right to not only vote but to run for and lose the office of the presidency. Gigi used to say, "Be careful what you wish for, Gilly; or, at least know the consequences."

But consequences weren't normally deterrents for decisions that were made in the heat of the moment. You didn't think about consequences until later.

Take divorce, for example. You didn't refuse to marry the man you loved because you loathed the thought of your potential ex dating someone else. But this was a consequence of divorce. Exes dated. That's what they did.

Gillian considered herself an independent woman—perhaps too much so. She'd come by that trait honestly as the daughter of a drunk and a bad-tempered mooch—who, by the way, also happened to be a drunk as well. Neither parent ever encouraged her to count on them, because counting on them meant that lunches didn't get made or you didn't get picked up from school —not merely late, but period. Still, you didn't weigh the pros and cons of not counting on others. You simply did what you had to do. Gillian brought this baggage into her marriage. No doubt it was part of the reason she couldn't properly commit. In so many ways she was as broken as her parents, but with one major difference. She didn't have a child counting on her to do the right thing. She didn't have anyone, in fact, and that was never more apparent than it was at the moment, as she sat in her car, positioning herself to simulate a trip to the store. It was awkward at best. The little boot brace kept her from bending her foot and subjecting herself to more pain, but it was in her way and it simply prevented her from getting a proper feel for the pedal. Putting her right foot up on the seat and depressing with her left foot also wasn't ideal. Plus, her crutch took up so much of the passenger seat in her two-seater that, subsequently, a kennel wouldn't fit.

Already, at two minutes past ten, the sun was blazing hot, kicking her sweat glands into overdrive. She sat in the driver's seat with a mean Texas sun glaring down through her front windshield, a thin sheen of perspiration building on her upper lip. Mind you, she wasn't normally a sweater, but enclosed inside a black Z-3 was tantamount to sweltering inside a sauna, even with the driver's side window down.

Contemplating turning the key and putting on the AC, Gillian glared at the front porch, knowing instinctively that this—driving herself to the store—wasn't the right thing to do.

Already, her foot was better. She was making her way around easier. By next week, she might be fine to drive, but not yet. The thing was, the more she thought about that cat, the more she needed to get herself to a shelter. He was out there, somewhere— her little fur baby soulmate. She only needed to find him and save him. At least that's how she imagined it in her fantasy.

Charlie.

He and Baby would get along famously, and the more she thought about it, the more she needed to do this. Although, in reality, if she did manage to get going, what she really needed to do was go buy groceries, get to the feed store, and stop by the nursing home to see her grandmother. It was difficult depending on others. Gillian didn't like it. Especially since the one person she felt most confident counting on was, for all practical purposes, a vegetable right now.

Feeling uncharacteristically emotional, Gillian blinked away tears and sat staring at the house, feeling like a saucer-eyed waif in a Margaret Keane painting. She was alone in this world. Completely and utterly alone.

Unfortunately, feeling sorry for herself wasn't going to accomplish anything, so she sat stubbornly in the hot car, dampening her blouse, trying to figure out a workaround.

She could call a cab, though cabs in Dallas were notoriously expensive and they took for-freaking-ever. Besides, she wasn't exactly Warren Buffet. She had enough money to get by until she could figure something out, but daily cab rides weren't an option.

The last time she took a cab from downtown to McKinney it was something like sixty bucks—and that was a straight shot, one way. She couldn't see it being less than that, even if she kept the trip short, especially with two or three stops—not to mention a predilection for indecision where adoptions were concerned. She could imagine it now—the cab waiting outside all the while she contemplated the pros and cons of going through with the adoption. The fare ticking up and up and up as she filled out papers. Of course, she could always have the cabbie drop her off, but then she'd have to wait a decade for another one to show up, all the while simultaneously holding a cat kennel in her hand and manipulating her crutches. None of that appealed to her.

If only she were living downtown, she could walk anywhere she needed to go—even with a bad foot. But no, here she was, so far removed from her everyday life that she was literally stuck.

She realized both Dana and Shannon were giving her space, but it was funny how silent her phone had grown since hopping off the happy-hour circuit.

Out in the distance, beyond the house, Eli Fox was hard at work on the barn doors. Every so often, he cast a glance in Gillian's direction, but otherwise, he didn't dawdle.

In barely two days' time, he'd gotten the wood on the barn door replaced, sanded it, primed it, and was getting ready to paint. She'd handed him a check yesterday afternoon for five hundred dollars—enough to cover paint and supplies. She supposed she could ask him to take her to the store, but he hadn't signed on to be her driver.

Nor did she know him well enough to ask for favors.

Sighing, resigned, she dragged her purse out of the passenger seat and into her lap. Then she fished out her cellphone and started to dial Kelly's number, only reconsidering at the last minute and dialing Dana instead.

"Dana Salvo."

Clearly, Dana didn't look at her caller ID.

"Hi, it's Gillian."

"Gilly!"

"How's it going?"

Dana didn't answer for a minute. She covered her receiver with a palm—or so it seemed—and then returned. "Good, good," she said. "I was about to go into a meeting."

"With Burke?"

"No . . . um . . . with Kelly."

"Oh," she said. "Anything I should know about?"

"No."

It was a firm no, not the least bit uncertain. "Okay . . . well, I was wondering what your day looked like," Gillian said. "I was hoping for a ride to PetSafe."

Silence. And then, with some confusion, "You got a dog?"

"No."

"What then?"

Frowning, Gillian fingered the glass on her dash, tracing the circles of her speedometer. "Well . . . I was thinking about getting a cat."

"Ah."

"Because . . . well, I think there's a mouse in the house." Gillian rolled her eyes, disgusted with herself. Why couldn't she simply say, "I'm lonely; I need and want a cat"?

"Actually, it's a bad day for that," Dana said with a sigh. "How's Geeg?"

"Same," Gillian replied. "Same. But, well . . . that's another place I need to go today. But don't worry, I'll ring Kelly. Is he in his office?"

"Hold on now. I didn't say I wouldn't do it," Dana said, sounding annoyed.

The irritation in her voice took Gillian aback. Was she annoyed because Gilly intended to ask Kelly? Did she not wish for them to talk? Or was she simply vexed because someone was bugging her at her desk? "Are you sure?"

"Yes, I'm sure." Still distracted, Dana spoke softly beneath her breath, giving instructions to someone. "Yes," she said, covering the phone again. "Angle the cask like that. But try a different font," she said, and then her voice returned to its full octave, without a trace of ire. "I can swing by at noon," she said formally. "Is that too late for you?"

Beads of sweat dripped from Gillian's left temple and the material beneath her armpits was swampy. If she went into the house, she would be tempted to nap. And then, goodbye kitty-cat. Only this was the downside about being reliant upon others, she couldn't call the shots. "Yeah," she said. "Noon is fine."

"Great," said Dana. "I'll see you then." And then far more exuberantly, she said, "Got to get into that meeting now."

"Right," Gillian said. "See you at noon." And she hung up, though not before Dana did.

Sighing, she got out of the car, dragging her oversized Coach purse out with her and tossing it on the dusty ground before returning to jiggle her crutch free from the passenger seat, and then cursing when it wouldn't immediately come out. She'd had to angle it just so. And then, after she was out of the car with her purse and her crutch, she slammed the door, jabbing the crutch beneath her damp armpit, suddenly in a cranky mood.

"Need help?"

Gillian practically jumped out of her shoe. "Holy cow," she said. "Where did you come from?"

"You were distracted."

She must have been quite distracted to have missed Eli's approach. He was standing right behind her. "You looked like you were having a time of it," he said.

"A little," Gillian confessed.

He flicked a glance at her booted foot, then at the crutch in her hand, and then back to her face. "I'm guessing you shouldn't be behind the wheel yet?"

"I'm . . . I wasn't," she said.

He grinned. "You were."

"Well, so I was . . . but I was only pretending," Gillian reassured. "I came to my senses the instant I sat down in the driver's seat."

Eli smiled at her, a knowing smirk that reminded Gillian of Kelly. "Well, you're in luck," he said. "I need to get to the hardware store. So, how about I give you a lift? I'll take you wherever you need to go."

Gillian furrowed her brow. "Are you sure?"

His grin widened. "Sure as shit, as my pop used to say."

Gillian lifted her brows. She laughed, then asked, "On the clock or off?" She was fully prepared to pay for his time.

"Depends on which makes you say yes."

Gillian laughed again. "Either one," she confessed. "Though, in case you haven't noticed, I'm not in a position to negotiate." She half lifted her crutch. "However . . . before you commit, I should warn you that I need to stop by and see my grandmother, and then afterward . . ." She winced. "You might be carting back a fur baby in your nice clean truck."

"Cat or dog?

"Cat," Gillian said.

Eli studied Gillian a long moment, tilting her a curious glance. "Tell you what," he said finally, bending to grab her purse from the ground. He handed it to her, dangling the leather bag from the tips of his fingers. "You buy me lunch and we'll call it even. We'll swing by the hardware store first, then go feed my face, then afterward we can go see to your Gigi and wherever else it is you've got to go."

Gillian took the purse, shrugging it over her shoulder, offering Eli a genuine smile. "It's a deal. You want burgers or tacos?"

"Tacos," he replied. "What about that new place on the other side of the tollway?"

"Perfect." She dug her cell phone out of her purse to call Dana back, fully expecting to leave a message since Dana had been in such a hurry to get to her meeting. "Let me just call off my taxi," she said, and Eli winked as he walked away, giving Gillian privacy to talk.

"I'll grab my purse and meet you by the truck," Eli said, and once again Gillian laughed, only realizing it as Dana answered the phone. "What's so funny?" Dana asked.

"Nothing," Gillian replied, surprised Dana answered. Since when did she ever feel in so much of a hurry to get off the phone? "Hey, listen, I don't need a ride after all."

"Great!" Dana sounded enthusiastic now. "You'd never believe how much work I've got. Already, Burke has asked for ten million revisions. We're nowhere near being done. So far, we haven't started charging for iterations, but he's so happy with the work we've done that I haven't had the heart to add more to his invoice. Don't worry, I okayed everything with Kelly."

He couldn't be too pleased if they were doing so many revisions, but then again, that man seemed overjoyed by the entire process. Making Burke happy was going to necessitate dumping the next project into someone else's lap, and skim money of their profit. But if Kelly was onboard and no one minded the extra work, Gillian was fine with it. Smiling still, only a little less genuinely, she offered, "Alright, well, good luck with your meeting."

The jab went over Dana's head. "Oh, yeah. Thanks! Bye!"

"Bye."

They hung up together, both clearly eager to end the call. That was to say, Gillian knew why she wanted to get off the phone; she didn't want to explain about Eli. But on the other hand, Dana's curt, then suddenly jubilant mood was odd.

A worm of an idea slithered through her brain. Gillian squashed it before it could bore a permanent place into her thoughts.

Those two, Dana and Kelly, had never once flirted with each other. Kelly barely noticed Dana. If anything, he'd resented her because it was usually Dana who'd tempted Gillian into bars—nine times out of ten because she was crushing on some new bartender.

She probably was going into a meeting, even though meetings at the office were laid back enough that no one would question her tardiness—especially since the phone call happened to be with one of her bosses. It was more her awkwardness toward Gillian that unsettled her.

Gillian tried to recall the last time she and Dana had had a good chat. Aside from the phone call the morning she'd given Dana instructions for the Burke account, they hadn't had one in more than three weeks. That alone was strange, considering they usually talked more than once a day. Until now, Gillian hadn't questioned it because she'd had so much on her mind, but really, shouldn't good friends be around even in bad times, even if you didn't want them to be?

Pushing thoughts of Dana and Kelly out of her head, Gillian dropped her cell phone back into her purse and hobbled over to Eli's truck, wondering why anyone would buy a black car in this brutal heat—herself included.

"Ready?" he asked.

"Ready," she said. "I appreciate this so much, Eli."

He rushed around the truck, grabbing the handle before Gillian could pull it, and tugged the door open for her. And then he took her by the hand and gave her a boost up into the truck, waiting patiently as she situated herself comfortably into the hot leather seat.

Grateful she was wearing long pants, Gillian closed the door, inhaling the sweet scent of hot leather, and watched him walk around the front of the truck.

He was hotter than she'd first supposed. His shoulder-length, sandy blond hair framed a face that was prettier than it was handsome, and his stark green eyes were piercing. He and Kelly were both about the same height—six three. But there was something more imposing about Eli.

For one, his shoulders were wider than Kelly's and his chest was thicker. He looked like a man who worked out, though he couldn't be all that attached to a gym when he spent so many hours at work. He came in early and left only after he was finished at the end of the day. He had the vehicle and the know-how of a construction worker, but there was something more . . . refined about him . . . something that went beyond the manicured nails and perfectly trimmed goatee.

He got in, and Gillian realized only belatedly she was staring. He lifted a brow and Gillian's face warmed as she turned away, pretending an interest in his soft, buttery seats—not a single crack in the leather, despite the heat. Like the man himself, the truck seemed new to the area.

She peered into the backseat of his cab, finding all the expected accoutrements for a man in his line of work—a heavy-duty toolbox among other tools.

"So," she said, turning back around, "What is it you do back home?"

He started the engine. "I'm an architect. I design homes for people who don't live in them more than half a year."

Gillian furrowed her brow.

"Second homes," he said. "Takes more fortitude than most people have to stick around through a winter."

"Ah," she said. "Makes sense. Maine seems cold."

He didn't bother with a three-point turn, he swung around in the yard, kicking up dust as he made for the road. He eyed Gillian across the seat, smiling as though it amused him that she had scooted over as far as she could go. His posture behind the wheel was that of a man in control. "If you don't mind my asking, how'd you hurt your foot?"

"Stupidity," Gillian said, bouncing like popcorn as he climbed onto Old Mill Road.

"Most accidents can be attributed to that," he allowed.

"I stepped on a piece of glass . . . in the kitchen."

He flicked Gillian a glance, his gaze canny. "Here . . . at the house?"

Gillian nodded.

"Hmm," he said, giving her a thoughtful nod as he returned his attention to the road.

But Gillian's revelation didn't prompt any further questions, and she was relieved not to have to tell him that she'd done so while drunk and full of aspirin and then had stupidly climbed behind the wheel of her car. As a matter of habit, she reached back, patting her right back pocket where she kept an extra powder.

One-way conversations sucked.

Gigi's condition remained unchanged. She didn't appear to recognize Gillian, or anyone else for that matter, and despite the futility Gillian felt during her visits, she couldn't spare herself the grief. A caregiver filtered in and out of the room without her grandmother's acknowledgment. Offering Gillian an obligatory smile, the woman checked the position of Gigi's bed, fluffed her pillow, then took a manual heartbeat, laying two fingers across the bulging vein at Gigi's wrist. She closed her eyes, counting, then opened them again and walked out of the room without a word.

This had become routine—this coming and going of care-givers. But there were no monitors in Gigi's room. Her condition was no longer critical. Nearly two months after her event, it simply was what it was. Hope for recovery diminished by the day.

In some cases of global aphasia, patients benefited from ther-apies—a speech/language pathologist, for example. But according to her doctors, Gigi's aphasia extended beyond Wernicke's and Broca's areas—the cortical areas responsible for the production and comprehension of human language. She also suffered a condition called hemiplegia, which was a sort of paral-ysis on one side of the body, as well as facial apraxia, which was the inability to coordinate facial and lip movements.

Sometimes, now and again, Gillian thought she detected something—if not recognition, perhaps a spark of cognition—like a fried lightbulb that somehow flickered on and off, not precisely burnt out, though somewhere along the path was a faulty connection. Occasionally, if the wire were readjusted a Planck length, the light flickered on for the briefest instant. As Gillian viewed it, if a connection existed, no matter how faulty, there must be hope.

This was the reason for her continued visits, and it was also why she didn't share her own recent visit to the hospital with Gigi. It was Gillian's worst idea of hell—the visceral image of a working brain behind the paralytic face, one that could hear and understand, and therefore worry, but never quite able to assuage its torment by asking a single question.

It was inherently the same as being trapped alive in a coffin, but this coffin was flesh and blood and bone, and nevertheless deteriorating day by day.

She reached out to take Gigi's left hand, caressing the delicate skin with the tips of her fingers—very gently, because the skin appeared so fragile that it felt as though it would tear.

The physical contact didn't elicit so much as a blink from Gigi.

"Remember Baby?" Gillian asked, getting no response. "She's doing great," she continued. "She misses you, Geeg." *I miss you.* She swallowed an immense wave of grief that threatened to bring tears. "I hired some help," she said, free to ramble, because although Eli had been so kind as to drive her around, he'd insisted upon staying outside.

Who could blame him? Gigi wasn't his grandmother. Nobody in their right mind wanted to wallow in other people's misery.

"Hey, so, Geeg, do you remember that guy you tried to hire . . . the one on Anthony Street . . ."

Gigi's hand twitched and Gillian gasped. She continued, watching Gigi's expression closely.

"He seems nice enough," Gillian said. "But I guess you already knew that since you tried to hire him. Anyway, he took the job. He's painting the pole barn—there's no way I could have let Kelly do that. The last thing I need is for him to hang around —you know he's dating someone, right?" *Not a blink.* The twitch had been no more than a coincidence. Swallowing, she continued, "Of course, he won't admit it, but, well . . ."

She wasn't going to explain that she'd awakened him in the middle of the night and that he'd arrived at the hospital within minutes, looking as though he'd just gotten out of somebody else's bed. Because then she would have to explain the face-plant, and the accident . . .

Gigi's gaze appeared to be fixed on a pinpoint on the wall. Gillian turned to assess the view. Aside from a dark scuff that was probably made by moving around beds or other elder-care equipment, the pale gray walls were nondescript.

Frustrated, she wanted to wave a hand in front of Gigi's face and shout at the top of her lungs: "I'm here, Geeg! Goddamn it! I'm here! Where are you?"

With a pang in her heart, Gillian got up out of her chair and gave Gigi a kiss on the forehead, then walked out of the nursing home, feeling tired and melancholy.

Eli was seated in his car in the parking lot with the engine running. She climbed back into the truck and thanked him for waiting, then stared at him, trying to imagine making love to him instead of Kelly. He was good looking, no doubt about it. Dana and Shannon would be drooling over him. He had the looks, as well as the body and attitude. In fact, there was nothing about him that would rule him out as a potential bed partner, but Gillian couldn't picture herself lying naked with him—or anyone else for that matter. Clearly, that was something she needed to get over.

"All good?" he asked, pulling out into traffic.

Gillian turned to look out the passenger-side window. "As good as can be expected," she said, and fell silent. There was a man two cars over picking his nose, oblivious to the fact that everyone could see. Terrified that he might do something horrific, Gillian turned to stare out the front window instead.

"I'm a good listener," Eli said.

"Thanks. I'll keep that in mind."

She'd rather talk to a cat—a sentient beast who could give her loving glances, but who couldn't lecture her about the evils of alcohol or the dangers of taking too much aspirin.

Or remind her that she was broken and unable to love.

Or feel the senselessness of loving someone and allowing him to walk out of your life.

Or the illogical prospect of bowing out of a thriving business, only because she couldn't bear to be connected to a man who was slowly but inexorably drifting away—especially when she'd had every chance to mend things and had, time after time, eschewed every one.

What's wrong with you, Gillian?

Only now that Kelly seemed to be drifting out of her reach did she dare acknowledge all the lost opportunities—as though she needed more reasons to drink.

She was glad now that she wasn't up to driving herself, because she would—let's face it—eventually be tempted to go by the liquor store, and nevertheless, she felt the presence of the powder in her back pocket, as though she were seated on a hot coal.

Somehow she'd talked herself out of dumping it into her iced tea during lunch, because really, what was she looking to medicate? The only ache she had right now was in the vicinity of her heart, and no headache powder could dull that one.

"Where to?"

"PetSafe."

It was the final destination on their rounds. Once there, Eli insisted on coming inside—why, Gillian couldn't imagine. She bristled over his insistence without any good cause.

It was so hot, they'd taken the animals inside today, and the selection was good—or bad, depending on how you looked at it. On the one hand, there were too many fur babies without homes. Conversely, Gillian had her pick of a few gorgeous cats. There was a blue point Siamese, a calico, a long-haired tortie, a sweet black little kitty with white boots, and one called a Ragdoll. In fact, the Ragdoll was the one she was most drawn to, only because it was the youngest of the bunch. However, it was the blue point Siamese who seemed most interested in her.

"His name is Bleu," the handler said, smiling as the cat thrust a paw outside the cage. "French for blue."

"Cute." The friendly animal rubbed its face against Gillian's finger. His cerulean blue eyes peered out at her with a perpetually mournful look.

If she brought this cat home, she couldn't change his name.

He was too old. The name tag she'd bought would have to be thrown away. She'd have to buy another.

"True fact," said Eli. "Blue points will fetch like dogs. Plus, they're great with kids."

"I don't have kids," Gillian reminded him, as she let the cat lick her finger.

In fact, the way she was going, she would never have children. She let Bleu lick at her finger while she stared longingly at the Ragdoll, imagining her name tag on a collar around his neck.

"He's beautiful," he said, noting the direction of her gaze. "But trust me, he's going to be high-maintenance."

"How so?"

"Well, for one, his hair will get longer and you'll have to brush turds out of his coat."

Gillian made a face, twisting her lips. *Was she so obvious?* Had he guessed by looking at her that she couldn't handle needy people or pets? The fact that she had been catering to Baby's every need somehow didn't change her view of herself. One dependent changed nothing—particularly one that was inherited —but two . . . two began a pattern.

"Have you got another kitty at home?" asked the handler, looking back and forth between Eli and Gillian, perhaps mistaking Eli for her significant other.

Gillian was quick to answer to save him an explanation. "No," she said, as she removed her finger from the blue point's cage.

Eli answered anyway. "No," he said, and Gillian leveled him a glance.

"You know a lot about cats for a guy who doesn't have any cats."

"My mother took in every stray she encountered."

"Ah," Gillian said.

The blue point peered up at Gillian, as though willing her to want him. And she did want him. He rubbed himself across the metal bars. His coat varied from pale gray to soft beige, with darker gray areas around his face and upper back. He was lovely, but like her, he probably came with baggage. Nevertheless, Gillian was warming to the prospect.

"Do you want to hold him?" asked the handler.

Gillian flicked a glance at the Ragdoll. Aside from a passing interest, the kitty couldn't care less that Gillian was there. It pawed contentedly at a feather-tailed toy in the cage.

Why can't you love the one who loves you? Kelly's voice pleaded in her ear.

The memory was bittersweet. One of the final times they had made love before splitting. He'd held her desperately, rubbing his whiskered jaw against her shoulder, offering baby kisses as he locked his legs around hers.

"Nah, I don't need to hold him," Gillian said, feeling her throat tighten with emotion. "I'll take the blue point."

"Great choice," said the handler. "He's older, but so sweet. His 'mommy' passed away and her entire family is allergic to cats. This guy's going to need a lot of love. He had one more month with us before—well, you know . . ."

Gillian did know. That was all she needed to hear. She had no more hesitation over taking the cat home. He needed her; she needed him. Together, they would get through whatever life chucked their way. Once the adoption papers were signed, they rode all the way home with the cat kennel in Gillian's lap, despite there being room in the back, because every time she tried to put the kennel down, the cat yowled. He seemed a bit more mollified in closer proximity.

"He's already attached to you," Eli said as she stuck her finger back into the cage to stroke the folds of skin around Bleu's thick neck.

Gillian smiled. "Looks that way."

Once home, Eli helped her carry the cat supplies into the house and offered to haul Baby's feed to the barn. However, the cat she stubbornly refused to give him. She hobbled along behind him, wincing in pain as she put too much weight on her foot, nevertheless thanking him profusely while somehow managing to carry her purse, the kennel, and one of her crutches inside.

He unloaded his burden, then passed her on the way back out to get her groceries. He returned a few moments later with a bag and Gillian's remaining crutch.

"Hey," she said, before he could head back out the door. "Why don't you stick around? Let me thank you by making dinner?"

"You're going to feed me twice in one day?"

Gillian shrugged. "I make a mean lasagna."

He lifted a brow. "Lasagna's my favorite. How did you know?"

Gillian smiled. "Nah uh."

He winked at her. "Why would I lie?"

At that, Gillian lifted both brows. "Why would anyone lie?"

"Good point," he said. And nevertheless, he came back in, closing the kitchen door behind him. Once the door was shut, Gillian walked over to open the cat kennel and then stood back to see what Bleu would do.

Whereas he had been friendly enough before, trapped behind closed doors, the instant he realized there was a clear path to freedom, he bolted from the kennel and scurried away. Slipping and sliding on the transition from vinyl to hardwood, he turned the corner, fled into the hall, and disappeared.

"He'll come back when he's hungry," Eli reassured.

"Unless he finds a stash of mice somewhere. There's no telling what's in this old house."

Eli smiled faintly. "True. Still, he'll be back . . . seems like a smart cat. It's not everywhere you can get dinner and a free massage. Hell, I'd forgo dinner for a good massage," he told her.

It was Gillian's turn to laugh. "Well, I won't promise *you* a massage, but please do sit down. Let me get you a glass of tea," she offered.

Eli pulled out a chair from the dinette—one of the few pieces of her grandmother's furniture Gillian had kept. "I'll settle for tea," he said. "I'm thirsty as a shaggy dog after a mile-long run," he said with a drawl.

Gillian tilted him a glance. "You sure you aren't Texan?"

"Hey," he said with a shrug. "I can be whatever you want me to be." But as come-ons went, it was lame, because his tone didn't match his words. He was examining the table now. "Looks like original hardware," he remarked.

"It was my grandmother's," Gillian said, studying him—the hard lines of his shoulders, the strong jaw. The full lips. And consequently, for the first time in a while—maybe the first time since she and Kelly split—she wondered what it might be like to taste another man's kiss . . . this man's.

Their gazes met and held. Gillian blushed and turned away, giving Eli her back while she quietly emptied the bags and put away groceries.

Her phone rang inside her purse and she fished it out, glancing at the screen. It was Kelly. Her heart jumped. Guiltily, she set the phone down on the counter, pushing it away, letting it ring out. Only after she was sure her wayward thoughts were corralled, she opened the cupboard, and took out a glass.

13

THE SLEEPING PORCH

"Minimize all noise. At the time of his arrival, eliminate all noise of the washer, dryer or vacuum. Try to encourage the children to be quiet."
—*The Good Wife's guide, Housekeeping Monthly*

3 :*00 p.m., Friday, July 15, 1960*

The bus arrived on time—a silver, white, and red shuttle from Continental Trailways. On the side of the dusty vehicle, displayed prominently on galvanized steel, a red, white, and blue sash carried in the beak of a golden eagle flew through a logo that read: "Silver Eagle." It looked exactly like the die-cast bus commemorating the new fleet that the boys had back home, a last-minute gift from their father on Christmas, when he'd returned from Houston empty-handed. He'd stopped for gas and bought one for the boys to share—one, mind you, only one, a single seven-inch die-cast toy that easily doubled as a weapon when the boys couldn't decide whose turn it was to play with it. Even now, the thoughtlessness made Rebecca long to thump it upside Joe's head.

"Hey, it's just like ours," said Joe Jr. "Boss!"

Jeff shook his head, not quite having warmed up to the fact that he and his brother would be traveling so far from home, all alone. "It's not boss," he said, rubbing his eyes. "I don't like it."

Today, it was only the three of them at the bus stop. Rebecca picked up the suitcase at her feet and took Jeff by the hand, crossing the road as the bus door unfolded.

"Wait just a minute," she said to the driver. She held up a finger once she got his attention. "Wait a minute, please."

He gave her a nod, and Rebecca returned a grateful smile, setting the suitcase down in the middle of the road so she could position the boys in front of the open bus door. She straightened both their collars, and once they were posed, she took her new Kodak Brownie Starmatic out of her purse to snap a photo. The camera had an electric eye, so the advertisement said. "Just aim and shoot." And so she did.

Thinking of her dad—the priceless moments he'd captured on film the day they'd left Farwell—Rebecca had bought the midget camera at the drug store when she'd gone to pick up bleach and supplies for the boys. It was her one and only guilty purchase, but at $34.95, the camera was far less extravagant than Joe's damnable car.

The flash popped. The boys blinked. The bus driver nodded and smiled.

Amazed by the technology, Rebecca took yet another photo for good measure—and then one of the bus driver. The man hoisted up a thumb and gave her a toothy grin that made her feel better about entrusting him with the boys.

Chances were she wouldn't get by the drug store to get the

pictures developed before the boys returned home, but at least she would have a memento of today.

For once, the boys stood quietly. For the most part, Joe seemed unfazed by the journey to come. He'd taken to heart that he was a growing boy, and he had developed a new swagger Rebecca couldn't help but notice on the way to the bus stop. "You are so grown up," she said, admiring them both.

"But I don't want to go," complained Jeff.

"You'll have a great time," Rebecca coaxed. "Come, now." She put the camera away, and then, bracing herself for a tearful farewell, she carried the boys' suitcase aboard the bus and tucked it neatly beneath their seat. They followed her onboard, standing behind her as she settled the bag.

As buses went, this one was clean, but of course, it was new. She only knew that because of the toy Joe had brought home that was meant to commemorate a new, uniform look. They were trying hard to compete with Greyhound Lines.

An old black woman sat in the back, clutching a set of knitting needles, and a handsome young man who reminded Rebecca of James Dean—a throwback to the fifties, with his neat pompadour and clean white T-shirt—sat in the middle. The sweat stains beneath his armpits spoiled his look. It was too hot for a jacket today, so he'd placed his leather coat on the seat beside him and sat back with his arms spread across the back of his chair. He gave Rebecca a polite nod as she brushed off the boys' seat and pulled a still-damp cloth out of her pocketbook to swipe over the leather. A tear slid past her lashes.

"Why, Mama? Why do we need to go?" Jeff asked once she turned to face him.

"Don't ask so many questions, retardo," Joe demanded of his brother. "Cain't you see mama's bawling?"

Jeff rubbed his eyes again, peering up at Rebecca with trembling lips as she lifted him onto the seat. "Is it because we been bad, Mama?"

She cupped him gently beneath the chin. "No, baby, no. You ain't been bad." She turned to Joe and said, "Joe, please don't call your brother names. Be good to each other, okay?"

Smiling a little queerly, Joe climbed onto the seat, next to his brother, and said, "Yes, Mama."

"I don't want to leave you," sobbed Jeff.

"Don't worry, baby. You're gonna have so much fun. Do you remember Cousin Elliott? He can't wait to see you." She wiped a dirty tear from his left eye—remnants of the long, dusty walk to the bus stop.

Jeff crossed his arms. "He's weird," he said plaintively.

"You're weird," said Joe, giving his brother a lowering glance.

"Now, now, boys," Rebecca said. "Be good. Please. Don't fight. And do not get off this bus until the driver says so. Also, please don't stand in your chair. And don't leave your seat. If you need to stretch your legs, stand right here."

"What if I have to pee?" asked Jeff.

Rebecca smoothed the bangs from her youngest son's face. "Then you tell the bus driver, okay?"

Jeff nodded, tears sliding from the corners of his eyes.

"Ha, ha! I'm gonna wait until he's in the bathroom and tell the bus driver to drive away fast," said Joe with a mean little laugh.

Jeff turned his face up to Rebecca with wide, frightened eyes.

In response, she seized her eldest son by the wrist. "You will not," she told him firmly. "You will go with your brother, and you will stay together at all times. Do you hear me? It's an eight-hour drive. The bus people said this bus will stop for a restroom break and the driver will take you to the toilet. Try to wait, okay?"

Jeff nodded, his lips quivering still.

"Be a big boy," she demanded of them both. "Your Aunt Lucinda will give you treats when you arrive—but only if you are good."

Joe's expression was a mirror image of his father's, devious and scheming. "How will she know?"

Rebecca lifted her brows. "The bus driver will tell her every-thing," she said, and then stood, wiping both their cheeks as she rose. She said one last goodbye, and then left before there could be more tears. On the way out, she had a good chat with the driver before paying him the fare from the money she'd been saving in a tin on the sleeping porch. And then, once the fare was paid, she returned to the boys for one last kiss.

With sullen faces, her two boys sat huddled in the same brown leather chair, quiet as she had ever seen them. Even Joe, faced with the inevitable truth—that they were leaving—looked fearful. She gave them each a hug and got off the bus. Both boys stared straight ahead like mannequins as she moved along the side of the bus to tap at their window.

At once, they swiveled in their seat, pressing their little noses against the dusty window—Jeff down below, with only the top of his nose and his woebegone eyes peeking from behind the metal flank, and Joe directly above him, with an elbow boring into the pate of Jeff's head.

In that moment, they looked so innocent—even Joe—so desperate for their mama that Rebecca had a pang and nearly banged on the side of the bus to demand they be taken off.

Before she could finish the thought, the bus engine revved and the driver pulled away, carrying off her boys, leaving her standing in a billow of dust. She swallowed her grief as she waved at the back end of the bus.

Kneeling in their chair, both boys turned to wave back, and kept on waving until Rebecca could no longer see them through the dirty back window.

Only as they moved on down the road, a rush of terror threat-ened to overwhelm her. Every bad thought and every horrible scenario accosted her, but she managed to tamp down her fears, reminding herself of the days to come. It wasn't going to be easy, she told herself. It was so much better that they go. *Now.* Before she changed her mind. Her eyes welled with tears as she lifted her shoulders and raised her head, tasting grit at the back of her throat.

It seemed so surreal that she would be sending her boys back to the place her family fled twenty-five years ago. She'd left Farwell at the age of five, and her youngest was now returning at the same age. They would be fine, she told herself. Fine. *They will be fine.*

In fact, two summers ago, her cousin Lucinda had sent her eldest son to spend the summer at Noble Ranch; he was only nine at the time. At eight, Little Joe was twice the size Elliott had been at nine. He was perfectly capable of seeing to his brother. In any case, they were already gone.

Smacking the road dust from her yellow dress, she turned back toward the house. It was a good mile's walk from the bus stop, too close to take the car. Besides, she'd needed a proper amount of time to say goodbye before putting the boys on the bus.

She wondered now if Lucinda would take them to the same ice cream parlor she'd frequented as a child. She wondered, too, if the boys would visit her grandfather's grave.

Lucinda's mama—her father's sister—had refused to abandon the family home. As a result, those two had never spoken again for the remainder of their days. It was Rebecca who'd reached out to Lucinda, against her father's wishes, inviting her long-lost cousin to her wedding. Only after she'd arrived, her father had been so pleased with the visit, and he thanked Rebecca for bringing them together. Looking back on it now, it was the single bright spot of Rebecca's wedding, because her papa sure hadn't been pleased about Rebecca's choice of husband—or the fact that they would be living together at Noble Ranch.

"A man ain't a man until he leaves home," her father said.

Rebecca was quick to defend Joe. "It's not like that, Papa. It's not like we're gonna go crash his mama's basement or something."

"No," he'd argued. "It's worse than that. The spineless ditz is mooching off his woman. What kind of dipshit does a thing like that?"

"He's a cool cat, Pop. You'll see."

"Hang it up, Becky. He's a ne'er-do-well, and you know what I think about that."

"Yes, Papa."

"It's just a matter of time before he shows his true colors, you hear me?" It was a losing proposition, trying to win him over to Joe, so Rebecca gave up. And then he said, "The first time I see him disrespect you, I'll put my fingers around his neck and choke him off. Do you understand me?"

"Yes, Pop. Don't worry, Pop. Hang loose."

"Don't tell me to hang loose! That's another thing, young lady. Don't care to hear no more of that jive talk in my house, do you hear me? Ain't a thing wrong with the words we already got."

"Yes, Papa. Don't worry."

Don't worry.

Those were the same words Rebecca had said to him the day he'd died, as they drove away. The same day her mother died. Both at once.

Don't worry, Daddy.

Well, he'd been right all along. Now Rebecca had a nice little cut on her brow that probably should have been stitched. Luckily, her eye wasn't bruised. Unfortunately, it wasn't the first time Joe had raised a hand to her, but it most certainly was the most frightening. She didn't want her boys growing up with an example like that.

Behind her, a car horn bopped. Rebecca started. Her hand flew to her breast as she turned to face the vehicle. Clarence Taylor pulled up alongside her. "Evening," he said, speaking through his passenger-side window.

"Sheriff Taylor! You scared the devil outta me."

He shook his head, with a faint smile. "Ain't no devil ever been near you, Becky Lee."

Rebecca feared it wasn't true. She felt a devil inside her right now.

"You needin' a ride to the house?"

Fearing the argument she and Joe had had, Rebecca shook her head. A ride was the last thing she needed. After all that, if her husband ever found out she was in Clarence's car, she loathed to think what he might do. As it was, he'd begun taunting her with silly jibes about Clarence—as though she'd ever had a thing to do with him in school. They'd barely spoken to one another back then. She barely spoke to him now. In truth, Joe knew him better than she did.

Clarence tilted his head, as though studying her, and Rebecca smiled tightly. "Really, no—thank you, Sheriff. I'm enjoying my walk." She lifted the collar of her dress, hiding the tiny bruise on her collarbone that was turning green. The cut on her eye was covered with makeup, though she hadn't bothered with the bruise.

"You know if Joe's back at the house," he asked.

Self-consciously, Rebecca pulled a loose curl across her brow. "No, sir. I've not seen him."

He leveled Rebecca a curious look. "What do you mean you ain't seen him? Since when?"

She forced a smile. "Since this morning."

The sheriff sat back in his black leather seat, leaving off with the staring. "Ah, well . . . alright," he said, but then he tilted Rebecca another look, one she couldn't read. "You tell him about my visit the other night?"

"Well, yes, sir, I did."

He nodded, pursing his lips.

Rebecca stood silently, hoping he would leave. She didn't know what to do if he was fixing to come by the house. What if

Joe came home? It would be better if he left now and came back later.

"You know, I told Bertie about those cookies you made. They were so good."

Rebecca's smile persevered, thinking about the recipe sitting in her trash. "Thank you," she said. "I'll be sure to get her that recipe . . . soon as I have some time."

"Thank you, I'd be much obliged. You sure you ain't needin' a ride?"

"Quite sure, Sheriff. I'm fine to walk. My legs have been needing a good stretch."

He turned to face the road then. A bead of sweat swelled at his temple and rolled down the side of his face, into his sideburns. He sat so long that Rebecca wondered what he was building up to say. But he nodded finally and said, "Alrighty." Only instead of leaving, he turned again to ask, "Say, you headin' home from the bus stop?"

Feeling the intensity of the sun atop her head, Rebecca nodded.

"Coming home or thinking of leaving?"

Rebecca blinked.

"I only ask 'cause Bertie said you wasn't in church."

Rebecca hadn't been to church for weeks, but she said, with a long-suffering smile, "Neither, Sheriff. I put the boys on the bus to Farwell, is all."

He narrowed his eyes. "Yeah?"

"Yes, sir. They've gone to visit a spell with cousins."

"How long?"

Rebecca was wholly uncomfortable now, hoping to God Clarence wouldn't run into Joe before she had the chance to tell him about the boys. She screwed her face. "A few weeks, maybe?"

"Yeah, okay, it's a fine thing for young'uns to do in the summer—visit with cousins. They doin' alright?"

Rebecca's lips were getting tired of smiling. "For the most part. You know how boys do when they get bored."

"Oh, yes, ma'am, I do." He nodded. "Boys'll be boys, you know. Makes me real glad Bertie only gave me a split tail."

Rebecca gasped softly. Although she'd heard the term before, it took her aback. "Yes, well . . . I . . . well, she sure is lovely," she offered.

"Thank you," he allowed, oblivious to her discomfort. "Thank you. I suppose I should be going, ma'am. Tell that man of yours I'm still needing to hear from him, alright?"

"I sure will."

"See you later, Rebecca," he said, giving her a nod as he pulled back onto Old Mill Road, taking care not to shower her with dirt as he drove away. As soon as he was gone, Rebecca exhaled in relief and once again started home.

Something about the entire conversation left her feeling gut-sick—not merely Clarence's intense scrutiny, or his inappropriate reference to his daughter, but there was a look in his eyes she couldn't quite decipher. Worrying the tender spot at her brow, she wondered if he'd seen through her makeup. The thought disheartened her. She'd worked so hard to make a good home. *Perfect. Clean.* But like a glass house full of cracks, she felt in danger of shattering, only with one good scream.

PRESENT DAY

GILLIAN LOGGED into the work server to peek at works in progress.

She found Dana's folder—Burke's files—and poked around, holding her breath as she clicked open each one, fearing it would already be open. However, fear of discovery didn't stop her. After all, she was Dana's boss, and Nick Burke was her account. Just so long as she didn't save the files and closed out quickly, no one would be the wiser.

It was good work, she thought after a cursory glance. *Very good work.*

Dana had risen to the task, finding a unique way to give Nick Burke what he wanted without the logo looking hugely derivative. In fact, it was downright clever. She'd placed an oak barrel with the rocket logo into a party helmet, with a long, whimsical straw that wound its way around the dog's head and finished between his lips. One of the dog's eyes were closed in a lazy wink, and his jowls turned into a bit of a Cheshire grin. She couldn't have done any better herself. Glancing through the files, she was both annoyed and proud—like a big sister who'd taught her little sister how to kiss, only to have her steal her boyfriend. She was looking over the last file when she heard Bleu yowl. Startled by the feral cry, she bounded up from the chair.

All day long, stalking the house like a tiny panther, she'd watched him sniff beneath every door, mewing as he pawed the space between. He stalked each room with measured steps, looking for danger in unexpected places. It was as though he expected that something treacherous lurked behind every closed door.

Once upon a time Gillian could have related. At six, she'd come to the Noble house to stay, already a jaded child after too many instances of her mom yelling out from the bathroom, "No, Gillian! Don't answer the door!"

What lurked behind that door, Gillian couldn't say, but she hadn't missed the fear in her mother's voice. It could have been the police. It could have been a robber. It might even have been Joe, except that whenever Joe showed up, there was never any doubt.

Caught between two closed doors—the one to the bathroom and the one barring entrance to the 450 square-foot room where they'd lived—Gillian was never too sure which door was the most frightening. Inside the bathroom, she'd heard ungodly sounds—sounds she presumed were her mother puking out her guts. Now and again, when she thought back to those days at King's Crown Hotel, she imagined Maria seated on the toilet, wrapping a rubber band around her arm. Or, alternately, kneeling on the floor, head hanging into the toilet, with crusted puke and toilet water dampening the frizzled ends of her hair.

Most likely, whoever it was that had come knocking was the hotel manager, trying in vain to score rent. But as a child, Gillian could never be certain, and the knocks on the door always went away . . . while the sounds inside the bathroom remained.

Upon her arrival at the Noble house—a place she'd rarely visited before—she'd been wholly terrified by so many doors. The door to the basement had bedeviled her most, probably because her grandmother had immediately placed it out of bounds. And yet, that door aside, there were a dozen more Gillian had been forced to navigate, all leading to cluttered, dusty rooms that were like parlors in a spooky museum to a six-year-old who until that point had lived in a single, mostly barren room. Every room housed a story, not her own. Every item in the house had been foreign to her, until one day she'd happened upon an old die-cast car in the closet of her bedroom. She'd asked Gigi whose it was. "It was your papa's," Gigi had said.

Gillian looked up, blinking in surprise. It wasn't so much that she couldn't imagine her father having been little once. It was more that she couldn't imagine Joe playing with toys. To her, Joe had always been a fully formed, screaming maniac, a wild ape beating his chest.

"Do you like it?"

Gillian had given a tentative nod that could easily have swiveled into a shake of the head.

Rebecca Lee Frazer smiled. "Well, it's yours now." And then, just when Gillian meant to put it down for fear that Joe would discover it in her hands, Gigi had knelt beside her and petted her hair. "Do you know what it is?"

Gillian shook her head.

Her grandmother's voice was soothing, like the tinkling of a brook. "It's a replica of the Continental Trailways. Your father rode one once." She tapped the side of the bus, die-cast steel that was scratched and dented after so many years. "When he was not much older than you."

Later, much later, Gillian would hear Gigi's impression of her new ward: dirty, hair knotted in tangles so thick a rat couldn't find its way in or out, too-tight stained shirt, too-short pants that had been snipped in the waist to make room for a protruding belly. And nevertheless, Gigi had looked at Gillian with such adoration that, even at the tender age of six, she'd understood it to be precious and rare. Her grandmother had loved her unconditionally. She had welcomed her into her home without reservation. Everything in the house was Gillian's to share.

That day, with the truck in her hand, Gigi had sunk down onto the floor, crossing her legs as she tapped the third window on the bus. "That's where they sat—your pop and uncle. Right here."

Gillian remembered being slack jawed, though whether it was the story about her father, or the fact that Gigi was so good-natured, she wasn't sure. "Where did they go?"

Gigi's smile was infectious. "Farwell, Texas."

"How come?"

"Well, my dear, that's a story for another day, but we'll have plenty of time for stories. Do you like cookies, Gillian?"

Gillian had nodded enthusiastically.

The demons of her past had faded over time, but, even now, Gillian held on to a bit of wariness over the sight of a closed door. Realizing Bleu probably wouldn't relax until he discovered what lurked behind every door in the house, she struggled up the stairs to find him pawing at the door to the sleeping porch—an upstairs deck that had been screened in for sleeping in warmer months, except that no one had ever used it for anything like that during Gillian's lifetime.

Back in the day, during the heat of summer, Gigi's family used to sleep out on the porch in a single bed, on the off-chance they would catch a breeze—mind you, three kids and two adults in one bed. The thought alone made Gillian sweat—or maybe it was two kids, or one, depending on the year. Gigi's sister Margaret died at nine, worsening after their move from Farwell. Her brother was gone soon after. He drowned at Bush Springs. Apparently, he had jumped off a trellis on a dare and hit his head on a piling. His friends were so terrified to admit their part in his death that they ran home and left poor Henry Jr.'s body in the creek to bloat. They found him days later, only after one of the boys tearfully confessed.

Nowadays, the sleeping porch was more of a storeroom, filled with chests, trinkets, and old furniture Gigi didn't wish to part with. Instead of carting everything down to the basement, which was already full to the rafters, or moving any of it to her storage unit, Gillian had simply closed the door. The ample-sized room was no longer screened in. Windows had been installed, but they were not weatherproof. Therefore, if the door were left ajar, it would be like cooling the great outdoors—a losing proposition from the get-go. Eventually, she would have to go through everything on the porch—as well as the basement—but for the time being, they were out of sight, out of mind . . . except that for some reason, Bleu was drawn to the door—likely because it was the only one upstairs that remained closed. She opened the door, peering into the jumble. Meanwhile, Bleu took the opportunity to bolt inside. He disappeared behind a box. "Holy cow," she said, looking at the mess. And then something caught her eye . . .

In the left-hand corner of the room, she spotted her great-grandfather's walking canes; five or six of them were wedged between two dressers. Now that she was transitioning off her crutches, she needed something light for support. One of his canes might do. She wandered over to inspect them, momentarily forgetting about the cat.

They were lovely. All of the canes were hand-carved, some polished to a shine, others left *au naturale*. One looked a lot like Gandalf's staff—old and gnarled, made of ash wood with an elaborately carved handle. Another had a handle shaped like a hammer, only styled like the curved back of a Victorian chair. She couldn't imagine anyone walking around with it. It was a heavy, solid piece of wood, thicker at one end than a baseball bat. Another cane was made of wood, in the simplest of forms, as though Henry had discovered a stick he'd liked the shape of and simply carved off the bark and painted it with shellac.

Gillian held onto the last one and put the others back, testing its height by tapping it along the floor in front of her, feeling ridges beneath the handle. She lifted the cane again to look closer and found a set of initials carved there: HHN. *Henry Hayden Noble.*

Smiling, she gave the empty room a nod. She'd only suspected they were his because he was never without one in photos. But as far as Gillian could recall, they hadn't lived in this room during her childhood, which only made her wonder what else had made it upstairs from the basement. One of these days, she'd go through the boxes.

Taking the cane along with her, she moved through the room, stopping to poke around in an old jewelry chest while Bleu crept around underneath an old dresser, slapping at something beneath—cobwebs most likely, as some of the pieces had been sitting in the room for thirty years or more. The sound of cat claws rang against tin. Gillian furrowed her brow.

Curious over what Bleu might have discovered, she closed the jewelry box and got down on all fours to peer beneath the dresser, spotting an old tin can. Flattening herself onto the floor, she reached underneath to pull out the can. Once she had it in her hands, she sat on the floor and proceeded to look inside, discovering two quarters and a few nails, along with five photos, two colored and three black-and-white. She took the money and put it in her pocket, intending to look at the dates when she had a chance, then fished out the photos.

The first photo was an old black-and-white of a carload of kids seated atop a mountain of furniture in the back of a truck. They looked to be a well-dressed version of the *Beverly Hillbillies,* only wearing bank-robber styled bandanas around their noses and mouths. A blonde woman stood by the car—a roadster-bodied half-ton pickup. Dressed in black, she wore a Peter Pan looking hat and held a hand pressed against her nose. All you could see were her eyes. Behind the car, the sky was overcast. But the thing that struck Gillian most was the look of wild excitement in the four pairs of eyes. Scribbled on the back of the photo was a month and year: April 1935.

The second photo—also black-and-white, was of an old black man with prominent freckles. He had short cropped hair and a beard. He was smiling at the photographer—no telling who that could be, but Gillian had a sense it must be Gigi. On the back of that photo, in Gigi's handwriting, was written just one word: Silas.

Gillian had never met the man, but she felt as though she knew him. Silas Wright had, for all intents and purposes, been part of the Noble family. He'd lived on Noble Ranch, and died here as well. Gigi had loved him as much as she had her own parents.

The third photo was of a man—youngish. Despite the lack of a cane, Gillian thought it could be Henry Noble. He was perhaps nineteen and wore a white collared shirt with a dark vest and a light-colored fedora—some shade of tan by the tint. There was no date on that photograph, but there was a scribble on the back she couldn't quite make out. He looked happy and dapper. Wasn't that a word they used back then? *Dapper.*

What year might this have been? Gigi was two when they left

Farwell. Her brother had been—what? Ten? No, because her sister was ten the year she'd died, which meant she must have been nine the year they moved. In turn, that would make the brother something like six or seven?

Gigi had been the youngest of the bunch. She'd barely recalled anything about them. Understandably; she would have been three when Margaret died, and barely older than that when her brother drowned.

Gillian sighed. Life could be so hard. Even with her screwed up past, she couldn't hope to compare her own hardships to Gigi's. Only one thing was certain: Gigi had been loved, and she knew how to love in return. That was perfectly evident by the looks on the faces of her parents and siblings.

The next photo was in color—a man driving a bus. He smiled amenably. The final photo was a small square colored photograph of two little boys, probably eight and six. Clearly—not just for the color film, but for the clothing as well—the picture was not as old as the other two. In this one, she recognized the faces only too well. Jeff and Joe, presumably sometime before they'd turned into full-fledged demons. On the back of the photo, the date was July 15, 1960. Gillian stared at the faces she had grown to dislike so much. They must have been—she counted on her hands—eight and six. Joe was fifty-seven now and Jeff was fifty-five. It was difficult to think of them as sweet, but that's exactly the way she would describe them in the picture.

Returning all the photos to the tin, she abandoned it on the floor and got up, grabbing the ash cane and ambling over to the door. "C'mon Bleu," she demanded. "Here boy."

There was no point in wishing things could be different. People were what they were. Her father was an evil bastard, and Jeff was a lackey without a spine.

The cat shuffled around beneath the dresser, as though suddenly excited by the sound of his name, and then he poked his head out, looking surprised.

"Let's go," Gillian said with a hand on the knob. There was only so much of the past she could digest without getting full-scale indigestion.

Like a nice puppy cat, Bleu shimmied out from beneath the dresser, trotting toward the door, making Gillian smile. "Good boy," she said, "Good boy."

Smart cat, she thought as she closed the door to the sleeping porch and started for the steps. Only then, remembering to check the litter box, she turned around and made her way back into her old bedroom to have a look around.

The room was empty except for the litter box, which was clean right now. Funny how the cat's bathroom was ten times the size of her own. The hardwood in this room was already ruined, so it seemed the appropriate place to put it. While Gillian had occupied the room, Gigi had covered the floor with a braided rug, large enough to conceal the withered, dried-up wood beneath. Gillian had never realized how ruined it was because so long as she'd occupied the room, Gigi had never moved the carpet. It was so disgusting she'd tossed it before the movers arrived.

At this point, the upstairs rooms were all devoid of furniture, except for the sleeping porch. Her furnishings fit neatly in her apartment, but here they were dwarfed by the size of the house. Most of her furniture remained downstairs, and she was accustomed to living in half the space.

Truth to tell, Gillian didn't have a clue what to do with so much space.

Maybe she could start a B&B. Or a working ranch, where she could continue her grandmother's legacy with the mares. The idea excited her. The B&B could fund the horse rescue, and she could allow visitations with the mares—a cool way to bring a little love to the animals. It was entirely doable. There were three bedrooms upstairs, if you counted the sleeping porch. Eventually, she could sell her share of the business, then buy all new beds for the bedrooms. She could hire a full-time ranch hand—someone besides Eli since she sensed he would eventually go back to Maine.

As Gillian contemplated the possibilities, Bleu slunk in from the hall, sniffing ardently at the floor. Gillian tried not to imagine what he could be smelling after all these years. Removing the carpet had revealed an odd, light-hued discoloration. Gigi had spilled some kind of cleaner there, leaving it to soak into the wood a long while before ever mopping it up. As soon as Gillian had things squared away, she'd have it repaired. In the meantime, if Bleu missed his box, who cared?

In the very spot where the stain appeared lightest, Bleu sniffed about, then tumbled onto his back, flipping back and forth, from side to side. The sight of him wallowing made Gillian smile, because he was clearly getting comfortable with his surroundings. Leaving him to whatever he was doing, she crossed the room to the window to look outside.

She'd forgotten how much of the ranch could be viewed from up here.

Over by the barn, Eli was hard at work. Already, he was finishing up the stable doors. Way out in the field, Baby Girl was enjoying her freedom.

Farther out, way out in the back forty but still visible over the fallow fields, stood the old pecan tree Gillian used to climb, with its massive canopy of branches and rich green leaves.

Gillian had always loved that tree. She and Gigi used to walk out there to collect pecans for pies and jumbles. To make the jumbles, Gigi used an old recipe she'd gotten from Silas. Together she and Gigi would pile up baskets and baskets of pecans to haul back to the house, three and four at a time. Crossing her arms, she returned to watching Eli work, her thoughts on Silas. She wished she knew more about how he'd died. If ever she'd heard that story, she couldn't recall it anymore. And now, unfortunately, anything that hadn't already found a foothold in her brain was lost forever, because there was no one left to ask. Not Gigi, and not her father.

The only thing Joe Frazer cared about was himself, and Gillian doubted he knew anything about Gigi that he hadn't witnessed for himself.

Certainly, he would never ask about anything that didn't immediately concern him. Sighing, she turned around to find Bleu crouching in his box, so she left him to his business.

Feeling peckish, and realizing how much time she'd let slip away, she headed downstairs to the kitchen to make herself a sandwich. It must be close to three, and Eli was probably hungry as well. As far as she knew, he'd never stopped for lunch.

By now, they'd settled into a routine. He showed up for work, never bothering to ring the bell. He went straight to it, then around one or two, Gillian took him a snack. Afterward, she sat and talked awhile as he worked, and then left him to his business. Every day, he left around four. He was a decent guy, she'd decided after a while, and if in fact he'd been around the day of Gigi's event, he'd never let on, so Gillian let it go. It was an awkward question at best. And what should it matter anyway? For all she knew, whoever was here that day could have been long gone by the time Gigi had her stroke. *But who called EMS?* That was the one question that wormed its way through her brain, and Gillian kept shoving it out again, because really, it was possible Gigi had called EMS, herself, before she lost consciousness. Only now that her grandmother couldn't communicate, it was bound to remain as much a mystery as the story of Silas Wright, and Gillian was grateful someone had called.

But why was she grateful? Two months out and Gigi's prognosis wasn't any better than it was the day of her event. In the meantime, Gillian was a wreck—less so now, thanks to Eli, but a wreck, nonetheless. And throughout it all, Kelly was MIA. His phone calls were fewer and farther between. He didn't come around anymore. And work was less and less appealing by the day. Evidently, they didn't need her at the office, so what was she holding on to?

Unfortunately for Gillian, time away hadn't forged an "out of sight out of mind" attitude. Rather, it was more an "absence makes the heart grow fonder" frame of mind, which was entirely depressing, because what had begun as a test of wills—let's see who calls who first—now felt like a wide and yawning chasm. Days went by without a word from Kelly, not even a phone call to check in or to tell her what was up at work. For the time being, Gillian was drawing a paycheck, but with every unearned check that was deposited into her account, she felt less and less comfortable with it. It was enough to give her a headache.

Back in the kitchen, Gillian took two sets of bread slices out of the bag and set them on the cutting board. She went to the fridge and pulled out jars of mayo and mustard, along with prosciutto, lettuce, tomato, and cheese. She carted everything back to the counter and set it all down. Then she took a butter knife out of the drawer. But first, before putting the sandwich together, she pulled out a packet of powder from the kitchen drawer, grabbed a glass, filled it with water, and dumped the full packet of headache powder into the glass.

Yep, home sweet home.

Old habits die hard.

By now, there were headache powders in nearly every drawer of the house. Pushing that thought out of her head, she downed the glass, feeling it burn on the way down, wondering when she'd begun using aspirin as a preventative rather than a treatment.

Meanwhile, she hadn't touched a glass of wine, or even one shot of tequila, but here she was, downing hangover packets as though her health depended on it—and it didn't.

Disgusted with herself, Gillian went back to the sandwiches, piecing them together, one for her and one for Eli. She was nearly finished when she felt a cold trickle beneath her nose.

Reaching up with a finger, she felt something wet and pulled it away to reveal blood.

Nosebleed?

Hurrying to snatch a paper towel, she dabbed it beneath her nose.

Good God, in all her life she had never had a single nosebleed. But then it stopped, so shook it off. She wiped her nose and tossed the paper towel into the trash, intending to wipe up the spot on the floor. Except she forgot whilst finishing the sandwiches. And once she was finished, she grabbed two glasses from the cupboard, filled them with tea, and placed them on a tray, then she carted everything out to the yard. She was already to the back porch when she realized she was managing without a cane.

14

JUST STOP

There was still pain in Gillian's right foot, but it was easier now to walk without putting pressure on the injury. "Ready for a break?" she called out.

Even at this distance she could see Eli was sweating profusely. At this hour of the day there was no respite from the sun—especially on a property with so few trees. Red-faced from the heat, Eli turned to her. He didn't say a word, but he threw down his hammer and swiped a hand across his face, mopping away sweat. Then he shook the hand, dispelling moisture like rain.

"You know, I don't have a problem with you working half days. It's too hot to work through the heat of the day."

"I'll keep that in mind," he said, walking over to a bale of hay and planting his rear on it, watching Gillian approach. She shook her leg, showing him that she was walking without help—and most importantly, that she was balancing a full tray. She held the tray higher.

Eli grinned as she laid down her tray on the bale of hay beside him, revealing two fat sandwiches and two mostly filled glasses of tea. She wasn't brave enough to fill them higher.

"There's a full pitcher inside on the counter," she said. "Freshly made."

"Great," he said, going for the tea. "I'll grab it as soon I down this one."

Gillian didn't argue, realizing he would accomplish the task faster and easier than she could. He lifted his glass, downing the tea in one long pull, and then set the glass down again, reaching over to choose a sandwich, lifting one corner of the bread to check beneath. "You can drink mine too," she said jokingly.

He regarded her out of the corner of his eyes. "You're not afraid of cooties?"

Gillian chuckled. "Nope. Wow. What a word! I haven't heard it in so long."

"Yeah," he said. "Well, my mother was a germaphobe." He tore into his sandwich and then said with a mouth full, "I'm of the mind that she, and she alone, put bleach and Lysol on the consumer map."

Gillian reached over to grab her sandwich. "Man, Gigi too," she said. "I swear, she uses it for everything." *Used.* Not *uses*, she mentally corrected herself, and tried not to betray her sudden funk. She bit into her sandwich, thinking about Gigi with that washrag . . . whipping it about the kitchen, wishing she could see that sight just once more. She sighed then, no longer hungry.

Eli was watching her. "I'd place bets on it," he said. "If you walk into any Boomer household, you'll find six things—Pepto-Bismol, witch hazel, Clorox bleach, Vicks VapoRub, Lysol, and Robitussin."

"You forgot Noxzema and Vaseline," Gillian said, appreciating Eli's effort to cheer her.

"Yep. Those too." He made short work of his sandwich, watching Gillian as she ate. "Thanks for this," he said, showing her his last bite.

Gillian smiled. "Yeah, well . . . it's the least I can do."

"Actually, the least you could do is nothing," he countered with a wink.

Gillian nibbled at her crust. The sandwich tasted like cardboard suddenly—especially once she recalled the goop they were shoveling down Gigi's throat. You couldn't prompt her to swallow, or warn her it was coming. She ate instinctively now—like a baby, responding to a spoon between her lips. "Honestly, if it weren't for you, I'd have gone loopy by now." She picked off a piece of her crust and tossed it to the ground. It was particularly depressing if she stopped to think about Kelly and his absence. Or Dana. Or even Shannon. Though at least Shannon wasn't screwing her ex-husband. It was true. At times like these you really learned who your true friends were . . . except . . .

Kelly had always been there for Gillian. She'd been working on pushing him away for so long now, and finally, after all this time, he was responding the way normal people did. Except Gillian missed him. Even as sweet as Eli seemed . . . he wasn't Kelly.

Finished with his sandwich, Eli brushed off his hands and sat while Gillian ate—or rather, while she picked at her sandwich.

"No friends or family?" Eli asked, as though he'd read her mind.

"Nope. Just Geeg." It wasn't exactly a lie. Her father was a liability more than a help. Certainly, Gillian had ceased to think of Joe Frazer as anything but a parasite—like some leech you picked up walking through a swamp. You had to know what to expect before wading in, and then purposely search for and remove them once you got to the other side. If you didn't, they'd suck you dry.

He tilted Gillian a long glance. "Friends?"

"What about them?"

"When you need them most . . . that's when you find out who your people are."

What was he, psychic?

Gillian rolled her eyes. "Funny you should say that . . . I was just thinking the same."

"So what about that guy?"

"What guy?" Gillian knew she was being purposely obtuse.

"The one who came by the other day."

"You mean, like, weeks ago? That one?"

"Yeah, that guy."

Kelly. He was here on Eli's first day at work and hadn't been back since.

"My ex-husband," she said. "He took me to the hospital after my . . . ah, accident. I'm guessing it took him over the edge."

Gillian had never been more ambivalent. On the one hand, she couldn't blame him, and on the other, she wished he'd stuck around—especially now that she was beginning to see things a little more clearly.

Eli frowned. "Over the edge?"

"I mean . . . well, it's a long story, Eli. But I would say he's a little pissed at me."

Eli crossed his arms, undeterred. "Yeah? Why it that? You leave him or something?"

"Or something."

He gave her a little smirk. "Sounds like a yes."

"Well," Gillian said. "It's complicated."

"Like Facebook complicated?"

Gillian screwed her face. "Yeah, what is that anyway?" She took another bite of her sandwich, hoping the question would throw him off, but he was like a pit bull with a bone.

"So . . . how long you been exes?"

Gillian heaved a sigh. "Three years." *Plus fifteen days.* She thought back to the last time she saw Kelly—physically, not just a phone call—and realized belatedly, and with a start, that he hadn't been by in exactly fifteen days, since the day of their would-be anniversary.

"Hmmm," Eli said.

"Hmmm what?"

"Personally, I never talk to my exes."

Gillian turned her palm up. "Apparently, I don't either," she countered. "But it's hard not to when we own a business together."

"Hmmm," he said again.

"It's not like it sounds. Our phone calls are short and to the point," she said defensively. "We don't discuss anything personal. It just so happens that we have a thriving client list, and neither one of us is willing to let that go." Except that she was. And why she didn't do it was beginning to be less of a mystery.

"Hmm," he said again, narrowing his eyes.

They were skirting close to "none of your business" territory. The last thing Gillian wanted to do was offend Eli when she still needed him. But she wasn't inclined to explain her business arrangement—or the fact that, until her grandmother's event, she had worked twice the hours Kelly had. Her ex-husband put in eight hours and left for the day, every day. It was Gillian who rang up the overtime. It was Gillian who'd managed every project as well as the client list while Kelly managed the office. He had a few favorite clients, but nearly always, even so, he came to Gillian for help. *Who was he going to now?*

Dana?

The idea left Gillian feeling sour. And the good mood she'd fostered for having made it outside while balancing a tray quickly dissipated. Nevertheless, she didn't blame Eli for calling it the way he saw it. He was nosy, for sure, but as straightforward as he was, she sensed he didn't intend to offend her. Still, she wasn't accustomed to being questioned or made to answer for her decisions.

Eli was undaunted by her silence. "Let me put it this way . . . if that were me—whatever the reason for the divorce—I'd have moved heaven and earth to separate my life from yours."

Gillian finished the last of her sandwich—holding back the urge to tell him to go fly a proverbial kite.

"The fact he's not done so is rather telling . . . and you say your finances are still linked?"

Gillian flicked Eli a glance. She opened her mouth to argue that they had separate bank accounts and separate finances—and they had always kept them separate, even during their marriage—but the argument seemed moot, because most of their assets were in fact linked through the business.

"My point is . . . I suspect that if he didn't care about you, Gillian, he wouldn't be so pissed."

"He's dating someone else," Gillian blurted, as though it were proof of Kelly's detachment.

"Why shouldn't he? You left the guy."

"Actually, I walked out in anger; he's the one who shut me out."

It wasn't precisely true, she acknowledged to herself. She'd told Kelly to file for divorce. She had been the one to leave—both physically and emotionally.

He looked at her dubiously. "So you stuck around to work things out?"

Gillian averted her gaze. "No."

"Just calling a spade a spade . . ."

Gillian fell silent, wishing now that she hadn't opened the door to this discussion.

Deep down, she realized that everything Eli was saying must be true. It would have been simple enough to separate their business interests. *Really.* Who was she kidding?

"You still love him, don't you?"

Leave it to a stranger to see the truth.

"No," she lied. It was too late to put their marriage back together. In her heart, she feared Kelly had moved on. She should too. In fact, she should sleep with Eli—except that not only was she annoyed with him now, she sensed he wasn't into her.

There was nothing in Eli's demeanor that hinted at flirtation. Sure, he was polite. And sure, yes, he was helpful, but she had thrown out several advances since her suspicions had arisen about Kelly and Dana—and Eli never took the bait. Not once.

It wasn't that Gillian wasn't attractive, she realized. She was objective enough to know her faults—and they were many—but Kelly had always said she had a body that wouldn't quit. She had a good smile and nice eyes. There was nothing about her that should put a guy off, unless they found themselves on her bad side.

For a while, she and Eli sat in silence—mercifully—and then, finally busting up the hush and the tension, Eli eyed Gillian's empty glass and said, "I'll be right back."

Gillian watched him head over to the house, mulling over their conversation and, more to the point, her own feelings about Kelly. She sat for a time, confused by her emotions.

She was grateful Eli took the job. Really, she hadn't been joking. If it hadn't been for him, she'd have weathered these past weeks a lot worse . . .

In fact, she'd almost hated to come traipsing out with the tray in her hand, because as soon as she was back to normal, she half expected him to quit and go back to restoring his house.

Gillian didn't have a clue why he was doing this anyhow—not when he had so much work to do to the house on Anthony Street.

And besides, as much as she would like to jump on her high horse and get all pissy about his "calling a spade a spade," she realized that every word of what he'd said was true.

So, then . . . what was she supposed to do?

Already she'd been considering the consequences of dissolving the partnership with Kelly. After all this time, she had zero interest in returning to work—and less now when she considered the possibility of his dating. Why would she put herself through that? Going to the office every day, watching him fall in love . . . with someone else.

Dana?

Screw Dana.

But it wasn't only that . . . Gillian wasn't fulfilled by the job any longer, and, really, when she thought about it, the only aspect of her job that had ever fulfilled her was the notion that she was making Kelly happy. It was all for Kelly that she'd opted in to that deal—never for herself.

For all she cared, she'd get a whole lot more contentment figuring out something to do with the ranch . . .

Even if the B&B didn't work out, there was enough land to grow something, even if it offered only a marginal profit. Locally sourced food was all the rage now, and if she wanted to, she could put up a small farm stand. *Why not?* The house was paid off. The land as well. Every inch of it was bound to be hers someday. The overhead would be minimal, and Gillian would have enough capital to invest from her part in the business if she opted for a buyout.

Or if Kelly couldn't afford an immediate buyout with his current state of finances, she was in a position to allow him some leeway. There was nothing tying them to one another . . . except, their own stubborn unwillingness to let go . . .

Somehow, she managed to swallow the rest of her sandwich while Eli was gone. Lost in thought, she waited—and waited and waited—for Eli to come back, not quite realizing how long he'd been gone until she grew thirsty. She wondered what time it was as the sun beat down on her head.

He was probably in there petting Bleu, she decided. It was hard to resist that cat. He was so damned sweet. She considered following Eli inside. Except that . . . it might seem weird now, because he would think she didn't trust him . . . as he clearly didn't trust her, judging by the little gesture of checking beneath the bread of his sandwich—as though he might be worried she would spit on it. In reality, he was probably merely curious. But really, she didn't know him, did she?

Aside from the fact that he was super straightforward—disarmingly so—and that he knew his way around a ranch and how to use carpenter tools, she knew next to nothing about Eli Fox. She'd taken him at his word, hiring him on, because why not? He was cute, for one. And she was lonely. And more to the point, if he sucked at the job, she could easily fire him. It was somehow comforting to know that he had known Gigi . . . and maybe that Gigi would have approved.

Staring at the back door, Gillian waited for it to open—half dreading it, mostly because of the cat. She didn't believe she'd ever open or close an exterior door again without fearing Bleu would dart out. But surely Eli would think of that . . .

Just when she'd made to get up and go check on him, the back door swung open, and out came Eli with the pitcher of tea in his hand. Gillian watched as he approached.

"Sorry," he said. "I had to use the little boy's room."

Gillian nodded. "Did you run into Bleu?"

"Yep. Cute little bugger, ain't he?"

"Yep. Sure is."

He filled Gillian's glass before refilling his own. Afterward, the two of them sat without talking until Gillian's curiosity got the better of her. "So, I guess you got things to do at your own house up on Anthony Street?"

"Sure do."

Gillian inhaled a breath. "I expected you'd get done here quick and be on your way."

He lifted his brows. "You ready for me to leave?"

"No—really, no. It's just that . . . it's hot here for a Northern boy. I'd have guessed you'd be in a hurry to get back to . . ."

He narrowed his gaze. "What?"

Gillian blinked at the unexpected challenge, thinking she must have stumbled onto a private matter and hungry for more information, she asked, "Well, yeah . . . I guess you have your own reasons for being here, right?"

"You mean . . . aside from fixing up an old house?"

Gillian nodded.

"Yeah," he said, and gave her an exaggerated wink.

Gillian averted her gaze, wondering if that were his way of saying he was sticking around for her—but really, he was a no-nonsense kind of guy. If he wanted to ask her out, he would do it instead of working for weeks on end in this miserable heat. *No, it wasn't that.* Already, she'd determined he wasn't interested in her that way.

Again, he was watching her, Gillian realized. She could feel his gaze on her. "Did I ever tell you my grandmother disappeared?"

Gillian blinked, looking up. "Huh?"

He was watching her intently. "Yeah. She vanished one day."

"Weird," Gillian said, blinking, then she frowned, but not because he had a grandmother who'd disappeared. It was strange because Gillian also had a grandparent who'd skipped out. Confused, she blinked again, marveling at the coincidence, and as she sat there staring into his bold green eyes, she had a crazy epiphany . . .

Had those two skipped out together? His grandmother and her grandfather? Had her grandfather run off with Eli's grandmother and leave his mother to be raised—as Gillian was—by grandparents? The thought gave Gillian a sick feeling in the pit of her gut . . .

For an instant, it seemed as though Eli might already know the answer to all her questions, and more. It was something about the way he was looking at her that made her skin crawl. Gillian tried for a casual tone. "So . . . when did she . . . disappear?"

"Not sure, exactly. The last time anyone spoke to her was sometime in July 1960."

Gillian lifted her chin, half opening her mouth . . . and then she closed it again. "Hmm, 1960?" It no longer felt like a coincidence—none of this did—but she wasn't quite ready to share her grandfather's story—not yet. He'd gotten enough personal information out of her for one day. It wasn't as though he was a fount of info himself, and anyway, he was only now spilling his beans after three weeks in her company. *Well, two could play at that game.*

"Crazy thing is . . . that house looked like it must have the day she walked out. Everyone expected that she was out here in Texas living it up. She had a selfish streak a mile long, or so I'm told."

Gillian sat, listening, perfectly stunned by the revelation, letting him speak.

"She had my mother at seventeen. Her dad—my grandfather—bought her the house on Anthony Street so she could take her kid and start a new life. But she came to Texas by herself, and left her little girl to be raised by her parents."

"So, then . . . your mother . . . she was raised by your grandparents?"

"Uh huh."

Gillian averted her gaze. "Ouch," she said, and meant it. "I know what that feels like. My mom dropped me off with Geeg when I was six and never came back. She's dead now."

"What about your father?"

Gillian wanted to say dead, as well, but instead she shook her head, inadvertently misleading him.

"Sorry about that," he said.

"Trust me, it's better that way."

"My mother as well," he said. "She was raised right, married a great man. She was much better off without her mother, that's for sure—or at least that's the consensus. My dad took good care of her, and her father before him. Good man—big heart, forgiving as hell. His worst sin was that he had too much money, and there's a thing that happens to people who have too much."

"What's that?"

"They're sometimes too busy to handle things at home."

Gillian interrupted, thinking of the house on Anthony Street. "He must have been a very generous man. That's an awful nice house to be gifted."

"Yeah, it is."

Nineteen sixty. Her grandfather took off the very same year. Gillian had no idea what month, but it shouldn't be too difficult to find out. "You said no one talked to her after July?"

"Of 1960," he reiterated, and the words grated on Gillian's nerves, like an out-of-tune guitar. "One day, she just stopped answering letters and phone calls. It wasn't until much later that my granddad came out to reason with her."

"Reason with her?"

"My mom was having a bad time, health wise. She got stuck in the leg with a rusty bobby pin. Her wound festered, nearly gave her gangrene."

"Yeesh."

"So, they came looking for Leona and found that house empty as a buzzard's nest except for that . . ." Gillian looked up at him, holding his gaze. His green eyes glinted with something she couldn't name. "Her belongings were all exactly where she'd left them. She even had a stash of unused valium tucked under the bathroom sink."

"No kidding," Gillian said, distracted, wondering if there was anything in Gigi's safe that would answer arising questions. "It's a wonder no one broke in and stole them."

He was staring at her again. "That house sits on a busy street, smack in the middle of town. I'm guessing the location kept it out of thieves' crosshairs. Later, once it deteriorated, they probably weren't all that interested. The city stayed on my grandfather to paint it, put a new roof on, whatever. And then, when he died, the task fell to me."

"Crazy," Gillian said.

"But seems there was something missing," he ventured.

Once again, Gillian met his gaze. "What?"

"A Smith & Wesson twenty-two caliber handgun."

A shudder passed through Gillian.

"My grandfather gave it to Leona for her protection, taught her how to use it."

"I hate guns," Gillian said, changing the subject. The entire conversation was giving her the heebie-jeebies. "Seems he should have been tempted to get rid of the house long before now?"

"Seems so," Eli allowed with a shrug. "But life has a way of getting in the way. And," he continued, "I think he thought my mother would want it someday—or me."

"And you don't?"

Eli shook his head. "Texas ain't my idea of paradise—far from it."

"So, what happened to your mom?"

"The leg?" Gillian nodded, and he smiled. "She recovered."

"That's great." Gillian lifted her glass, raising it to her lips, uncertain what more to say. The conversation had taken a decidedly morose turn.

So, was this how Gigi knew Eli? Did she know him because she knew her husband messed up a little girl's life? Had Gigi gone searching for Eli because she'd wanted to—what? Make it up to him? *Why?* What part did Gigi have in her husband's affair? After all, it wasn't her fault her husband was a cheat and a—what? And where did he and Leona go? Why would she leave a house and all her belongings? And then, suddenly, Gillian had an idea that Eli hadn't applied for this job out of any sense of altruism or any desire for quick cash. She had the impression he already knew her story, but she told it anyway. "You know my grandfather disappeared, right?"

He nodded slowly. "In 1960, right?"

Her suspicions confirmed, Gillian gulped back a swallow of tea and set her glass down, contemplating all the things she had discovered today during the course of this bizarre conversation.

"Amazing coincidence, wouldn't you say?"

"Yeah," Gillian agreed. "Amazing."

He tilted his head, gave Gillian a squinty-eyed look, and said softly, "Gillian . . . your nose is bleeding."

"Gather up schoolbooks, toys, paper, etc. and then run a dust cloth over the tables."
—*The Good Wife's guide, Housekeeping Monthly*

8:33 p.m., Friday, July 15, 1960

The air was stifling.

Slowly, like a growing plague, the chirping of crickets increased in frequency. Hoppers smacked the back screen door, as though trying to escape the unbearable heat. Only it was hotter inside the house than it was outside, despite the fact that the oven hadn't run all day.

That was the thing about mistreating someone the way Joe did: it didn't inspire anyone to do anything for him. To the contrary, now that the boys were gone, Rebecca didn't feel obliged to cook. She'd pushed a spoonful of homemade yogurt into her mouth, but otherwise hadn't eaten a bit because her stomach was tied in knots. For once, there wasn't a dinner plate covered with tin waiting before his seat at the table. No sweaty jug of tea. No lights were on in the kitchen, only the tinny glow from a sliver of moon. Out in the distance, somewhere in the back forty, the howl of a coyote sounded closer than she was comfortable with. Rebecca sat at the kitchen table, worrying a thumbnail, fretting over the chickens, and wondering why Joe hadn't come home.

The house was all too quiet with the boys gone. Usually at this hour, while they were supposed to be asleep in their beds, she could hear them whispering beneath the covers—and of course she could hear them. Like their papa, those two boys didn't know how to use an inside voice. Only Rebecca liked hearing them conspire together, even if it meant they were defying her wishes, so she let them carry on until they fell asleep on their own.

It was now 8:47 p.m. She hoped they were doing okay. It'd be another two or three hours before they arrived in Farwell—maybe somewhere closer to midnight. Hopefully they would be fast asleep in their seat, leaving the driver to his business. Yet again, she glanced at the clock: 8:53 p.m.

Where was that man?

Rising from her chair, she noticed a spot on the table where a bit of cheese had crusted. Old habits die hard, so she scraped it up with a thumbnail. How was it she hadn't noticed it before? Food brought ants, and ants brought fights. At last, after working at the crust, it chipped and flew away, landing somewhere she couldn't see. It didn't matter. She was ready to face him now.

If he didn't leave this house at once, she would get on the phone and ring Sheriff Taylor. No man was ever going to get away with a thing like that—not with her.

If Joe thought for one second she was one of those milquetoast ladies, he had another thing coming. She was made of sterner stuff than that—thanks to her mom and pop.

9:02 p.m.

Rebecca began to pace, and the longer she paced, the more settled she was in her decision. This was not what she'd married for. She wasn't going to be that girl. *No, sir.*

She went to the fridge to look at the drawing her son had made for her. She'd put it here, held fast by a Piggly Wiggly magnet, so she could remind herself to stay strong. It was a drawing torn from a composition notebook, colored by a six-year-old's hand. The surprisingly well-drawn house was bright red, with flames licking out from the rooftop and two stick figures peering out from the upstairs window. Green flowers in the yard wept blue tears. Rebecca shook her head, because she didn't know what it meant, but she knew this much: her boys were unsettled—Jeff, in particular.

She wished she had the nerve to climb into her papa's old Studebaker and drive over to Leona Fox's house. But of course she wouldn't do that. What would be the point? She didn't care if those two were carrying on. She only needed to know. And even more than that, she wanted him to leave. If anything bothered her at all about Joe and Leona, it was simply the fact that everyone in town knew about it except Rebecca. "Poor Becky," they were saying. "Poor, dumb Becky."

But she wasn't dumb. She'd been stupid to believe a word that man ever said, but she wasn't dumb. Curiosity drove her from the kitchen. At exactly 9:16 p.m., she went into the living room to pick up the phone. Slowly, she put her hand down, touching the receiver, and then quietly lifted it up to set it to her ear. A female voice left off mid-sentence. "Did you hear that?"

"Larry?" said Mary Claire. "Larry, is that you again?"

Rebecca pressed her palm over the receiver.

"That nasty old coot. Just ignore him," demanded Mary Claire. "He'll go away."

The other party wasn't Dottie Shepherd. It was Julia Hart. There were six families on this line: Rebecca and Joe, the Shepherds, the Harts, Larry Fine, Mary Claire and her brood, and an old man down the road, who never even used his phone.

"I'm so worried about her," said Julia. It was so like her to be fretting about somebody, but Rebecca couldn't remember the last time Julia ever got off her fat duff and offered to help.

"Really, with just cause, dear. It's not every day you lose a husband." She sighed so deeply it ended with a shudder. "Especially like that."

Like what? Good grief, were they talking about her again? Had Joe finally gone and left her? Did the whole town already know her personal affairs?

"What I heard tell is they found him ... floating facedown in the creek, out by the trellis—so sad," said Mary Claire. "All bloated up, and—well, I don't want to repeat the things I heard."

Rebecca blinked.

Found him? Facedown. Someone died. Who?

For a moment, Rebecca almost forgot herself and asked, but then she caught herself and managed to hold her tongue, listening intently. Already, they'd forgotten about Larry and were too engrossed by the unfolding drama—but so, too, was Rebecca.

"She's crying her eyes out, but I'm here to say ... that man was bound to break her heart."

A tsk of disapproval. "I'll say," said Mary Claire. "You cain't go 'round threatening colored people and not expect to find yourself in a mess of trouble."

Rebecca furrowed her brow. *Joe was harassing colored folk?*

She knew there was strife in the old neighborhood, but why should Joe care what was going on down there? It's not like he was worried about losing his job. He didn't even have a job—at least none that Rebecca could put a finger on, though clearly he was getting money from somewhere because he'd bought that damnable car. Only they mustn't be talking about Joe, because Rebecca was not sitting around crying, and even if she were, she hadn't talked to Julia in weeks. How would she know?

"How awful," said Julia. "I didn't realize he was doing that."

"Yes, ma'am; that's what I heard. He and that dirtbag Joe Frazer—" She stopped abruptly and it sounded like she closed a door. "Hey, what's with all these hoppers tonight? You see 'em out there. It's like a plague. Annoying!"

It was Mary Claire that was annoying. Frustrated, Rebecca wanted to slam down the phone, but she held on, waiting to hear more.

"Are you seeing this, Julia? I declare!"

"So what about Sheriff Taylor?" Julia said, staying on topic.

Bless you. Bless you, Julia.

"What about him? My God, I have never seen so many crickets in all my life!"

"Well, if it's true those men have been down there, I'm sure it's Sheriff Taylor who put 'em on those poor folks."

Mary Claire's tone sounded incredulous. "Poor folks?"

"Well, you know what I mean, Mary Claire. For the most part, ain't none of them hurtin' no one. They gotta eat too, same as us. Alls they're doing is the best they can, like you and me."

"Hmmph!" Mary Claire's voice was angry now. "Says who? Don't you tell me you're gonna turn into one of them bleeding hearts! Those people are up there taking jobs when no jobs can be found. Look at Billy—God rest his soul—I guarantee you that man would've had nothing to do with any such business unless he were desperate. They laid him off last week, you know. They gave him his papers when they could just as well have let one of those other people go."

"I didn't know," said Julia, and Mary Claire's tone was smug.

"Sure did. Last week. Dottie was so sure he was out in Fort Worth, looking for work, but no, ma'am, all this time he was out there floating in the creek—awful business."

"Terrible, terrible."

"We'll have to bake some cookies tomorrow."

"Oh, yes. Let's! I have a wonderful new recipe for jumbles."

Mary Claire sounded skeptical. "Not the one you got from Rebecca? 'Cause I hear it ain't all that great. Roberta said Clarence came home ranting about them last week, but I have eaten that woman's jumbles and I cain't say as they're any good. God only knows, if she would spend more time learning how be a proper wife, instead of trying to rope us into saving her stupid ranch, that man of hers wouldn't spend so much time up on Anthony Street."

"Yeah . . . yeah . . . you're right," agreed Julia, and anger stoked a brand-new flame in Rebecca's breast.

"Well, of course I'm right," said Mary Claire, and Rebecca's throat tightened. Her chest did as well—but not because those two old biddies had confirmed her suspicions that Joe was out there cheating—but because Billy Shepherd was dead and Dottie was home crying. It sickened her that Mary Claire and Julia wanted to bake cookies—like somehow pecans and sugar were supposed to make everything alright. Having heard more than enough, she put the phone receiver into its cradle, no longer concerned with being found out. Let them wonder who was listening. Better yet, let them know it was her. And, in fact, she had half a mind to pick up the phone and scold them both on the spot. Only now she didn't have the gumption.

Her husband and Billy Shepherd were out there harassing honest men into leaving good-paying jobs. How could she love a man whose conscience ran so low?

It wasn't so much that she was surprised to hear about the persecution going on in this town. She'd known this sort of thing transpired, even on Sundays, behind all the smiles and pretty little dresses, but the notion that she had sat with Sheriff Taylor just a few nights earlier, feeding him cookies . . . and all the while he was coming here to—what? Hire Joe to do his dirty work? Something like nasty vipers squirmed about the pit of her belly, making her nauseous.

Billy Shepherd was dead.

Dead.

And where was Joe?

Nevertheless, it wasn't her husband's whereabouts or his well-being that preoccupied her right now; it was the memory of a sweet old man she'd long ago put out of her mind. Silas Wright. And with the sudden disinterment of his memory from the depths of her regret, all that was potentially shiny in the world was suddenly cast in a gray, putrid light. She stood a moment, thinking of all those sweet black babies put onto the road, and then she rushed into the bathroom and vomited into the commode.

PINCHING her nose and holding a hand beneath her chin, Gillian rushed into the house, tasting the tang of her own blood at the back of her throat. A warm trickle dripped past the pads of her hand and onto her T-shirt.

Feeling lightheaded, she tugged open the screen door, hoping the cat wasn't around, and felt a rush of relief when nothing shot past her ankles. Once inside, she ran straight for the sink, leaning over it and turning on the faucet.

Filling her palm with water, she splashed it onto her face, horrified by the sight of so much red. Her nose was bleeding profusely, so she pinched it again, trying to get it to stop, all the while leaning over the sink. After a while, it seemed to lessen and she rinsed her face again, clearing her throat to spit up a bit of bloody phlegm.

It was the aspirin, she realized.

You have to stop.

Nosebleeds weren't a thing she'd ever had to deal with before, so it must be the aspirin thinning her blood. The nurse had warned as much in the ER, but Gillian hadn't listened. She'd assured herself that the real issue was her drinking, and so she'd stopped that. Since then, despite her foot healing, she'd begun ramping up her aspirin intake, little by little, half a packet here, half there, a whole one later. *Good God, just stop.*

Do you have a death wish, Gillian?

Finally, at last, the bleeding seemed to stop. But Gillian's legs were wobbly and her stomach burned—and that, she realized, must be an effect of the aspirin as well.

People died of this sort of thing—old people mostly, but it happened. A friend of hers had a grandmother who'd passed out one day after complaining about ulcers for decades. They took her to the ER and found she had been bleeding internally. Despite intervention, she died within hours.

So what the hell are you doing?

The scare in the ER wasn't enough?

Peering down at the blood trail on her T-shirt, and the one she'd trailed all the way from the door, Gillian moved to the kitchen table to sit and regain her bearings. After today, no more. This was it. She was through. After a while, she heard Eli's voice outside the screen door. He was looking in. "You alright?"

"Yeah," Gillian replied. "I'm fine." But she didn't invite him inside. More conversation was the last thing she needed now.

"Alrighty, well, I'm going to take off . . . unless you need something?"

"No, no . . . I'm fine," Gillian said. "I'll see you tomorrow, okay?"

"Sure," he said, though he could hardly have missed that it was a question, and still he walked away.

Something had changed out there, although Gillian couldn't put a finger on what or how. It's not as though they had been close before that conversation, but a wide chasm had parted in the landscape of their budding friendship.

As soon as Eli left, the first thing she did was find and throw away every last headache powder in the house—out of the kitchen drawers, out of the bathroom drawers, out of her pockets, out of her purse. She opened each one and sprinkled the white powder into the sink, then ran the faucet and washed it all down.

Then, afterward, she went straight for her laptop to Google Eli Fox. She found him easily enough, and was relieved to discover he wasn't lying about his chosen profession. Eli Fox was a rather celebrated architect with prominent websites and clients from Maine to California.

She spent about an hour browsing his personal and business pages, clicking through photos of homes he had designed. Eventually, she grew bored with that and went to change her T-shirt. It was only then, as the house grew dark, that she realized she hadn't seen Bleu.

15

CRICKETS

"Bleu! Here boy!"

Gillian searched everywhere—upstairs, downstairs. When she couldn't find the cat inside, she went outside, on the off-chance he'd gotten out. He was new to the ranch. If he'd made it outside, there was hardly any chance he would stick around. Damn it. She'd finally gotten herself a cat and her worst fear would come true; she'd failed him. The thought of coyotes getting hold of him made her stomach turn.

Hands on her hips, she stood on the back porch, gazing over the expanse of property, listening for any sound to indicate Bleu had gotten out.

Crickets.

That's all she heard.

There had been a rash of bobcat sightings lately, although Gillian had never actually seen one with her own two eyes. However, bobcats were cats too, she reasoned, and she doubted they had other cats on their radar. Then again, what did she know?

A lot.

There was a lot she didn't know these days—like, for example, what was Eli Fox doing hanging around McKinney, Texas? And why would a celebrated architect bother with a crap job? And didn't he say he'd run into Bleu inside?

Bemused, Gillian turned around and walked back into the house, closing the screen door behind her. "Bleu!" she called again. "Here boy!"

With the sound of crickets rising in frequency and the moon riding high in the sky, she stood stock-still in her kitchen, listening for cat sounds in the bowels of the house. *Scratching. Mewling. Anything.* Only when she was afraid he was gone, she heard a distant *mew* . . . as though he might be stuffed inside a box. Listening intently, Gillian followed the sound . . . all the way to the basement door, which was firmly shut. Confused, she placed her hand on the doorknob and tugged it, expecting to find it unlatched, but it was firmly closed.

Someone had opened, then closed the door again, shutting Bleu inside. For all his pawing beneath the door, there was no way he could have opened it, and Gillian hadn't opened it since the movers were here. With a furrowed brow, she turned the knob and pulled opened the basement door. Much as he had done on his first day, the cat shot past her ankles, into the main part of the house, and Gillian stared after him, listening to him lope up the stairs, sounding like a panther rather than a housecat. She was relieved but confused, thinking Eli must have mistaken the basement door for the door to the bathroom. Though quickly on the heels of that thought came annoyance that Eli hadn't thought to be sure Bleu wasn't trapped downstairs. Frowning, she closed the door again, making sure it latched, and then made her way upstairs to check on Bleu.

"PREPARE YOURSELF. TAKE FIFTEEN MINUTES TO REST SO YOU'LL BE

REFRESHED WHEN HE ARRIVES. TOUCH UP YOUR MAKEUP, PUT A
RIBBON IN YOUR HAIR, AND BE FRESH LOOKING."
—*THE GOOD WIFE'S GUIDE, HOUSEKEEPING MONTHLY*

12: 03 a.m., Saturday, July 16, 1960

THE MIRROR REVEALED A HAGGARD WOMAN.

Considering this truth, Rebecca studied herself in the glass her mother once used to fix her own hair. As a matter of fact, she looked older now over the course of a single day than her mama did the day she'd died.

How was this possible?

Already, crow's feet were forming at the corners of her red-rimmed eyes, and she could spy fine lines etching their way into her brow. She was twenty-seven.

Eight and a half years of marriage and two children and she was looking like a tired old hag. At thirty-four, Joe was getting a bald spot on top of his head, but otherwise his body seemed little worse for wear, despite the endless late nights and his excessive drinking. On the other hand, let her have a single restless night or a crying spell, and this was the inevitable result.

All this time she'd been blaming Leona, but Leona was vulnerable and alone in this world . . . It was too easy to blame her and her too-short skirts, but it wasn't her fault men were attracted to her, and certainly it was to her great misfortune that men like Joe existed. Bet she didn't count on someone like him. Rebecca had begun to convince herself that in the bigger picture, Leona was a victim as well—made to believe she must dress a certain way to get herself a man. And rather than brainstorming solutions as Rebecca did, she was terrified to go it alone.

Poor, poor girl must feel so desperate to catch herself a man.

Smoothing a finger over the lines forming on her brow, Rebecca considered the two of them together . . . Leona and Joe. It was easy to see how this could happen. As much as Rebecca disliked Joe—now—she too had been blinded by his charming smile. He had a way about him . . . even now. On Rebecca's worst days, all it ever took for him to soothe her raging belly fires was to offer up a smile. Sighing, she remembered the way he'd wooed her, pouring on the charm.

Joe Frazer was not the sort of person people disliked at first glance. Rather, he was the sort of man it took years to despise. Leona never had a chance.

She thought about Mary Claire. Was Mary Claire one of those rare individuals who could see behind Joe's facade? Or rather, had he earned her enmity after all? Trying hard to remember how it was when those two first met, she didn't believe there was any rancor between them way back then. No, Mary Claire hadn't always been a bitter hag—not to Joe, and certainly not to Rebecca. A mental image flashed before her eyes—Mary Claire blushing prettily as Joe complimented her dress.

But no, it couldn't be . . .

Disgusted with herself—with the sudden turn of her thoughts—Rebecca flipped off the bathroom light, returning to the living room to pace. Whatever was wrong with their marriage, it was most assuredly a casualty of all their own dealings. She couldn't go about blaming everything on everybody else. Rebecca was sick and tired—so tired of putting on airs, tired of acting like nothing was wrong while everything was falling apart. For heaven's sake, even after all he'd done, she hadn't been a hundred percent certain she would march those boys off to the bus stop . . . until she'd opened her eyes this morning and found herself alone in their bed, not for the first time.

No doubt, he was with her—and everyone must know. Quashing the urge to pick up the phone, she nevertheless eyed it with rancor.

No wonder Sheriff Taylor had been looking at her so strangely. Joe was making her old before her time—and then, after he was gone, nobody would want her. She'd be left with two rambunctious boys, a ranch that had seen better days, and a tired, used-up old body that no man would look at twice.

What in God's name was she thinking when she married that man?

Then again, nineteen-year-olds weren't famous for having more than half a brain.

Except . . . how old was Leona Fox? *Not very young.* She had a little girl back in Maine, some folks said. How old was the child? As old as Joe? As old as Jeff? Younger still? It must be unconscionable to leave a child of any age, but to leave a baby? Rebecca shook her head.

Right was right, wrong was wrong. Only, as so many things went, it was easier to make the distinction when you were talking about somebody else.

Bastard.

Liar.

Cheater.

Even beyond the gut-wrenching resentment over his leaving —not for a younger woman, but a woman as old as, or perhaps older than Rebecca—this was the thing she worried most about: the ranch. Now and again, she thought about the couple her father had bought the ranch from. *Did they ever settle into so fine a house? Did they earn back the money they'd lost?*

Motivated by self-preservation, those poor, harried folks had been in such a rush to go, they'd been willing to sacrifice their dreams. Her father justified the purchase because, essentially, they too had lost everything they'd owned back in Farwell.

"One man's misfortune is another man's fortune," her father had said. "Ain't nobody ever gonna buy that house we left. This is God's way of making it up to us."

And he must have been right.

Noble Ranch had been a blessing throughout the years—right up until the day her parents died, leaving Rebecca to share a homestead with a no-good grifter.

Unfortunately, her papa never drew up a will. That morning, her parents had left the house after breakfast to run some errands. Both were gone by noon. He'd lost control of the car, they'd said, hit a tree—the only roadside tree around for miles.

What were the odds of that?

"It's the damnedest thing," said Clarence Taylor Sr., scratching his head. "It's like he drove right into it." Father, like son, had been drawn to that badge.

Anything could happen, that's what it taught her. *Anything.* So, now . . . what would happen to the house if Rebecca died first? Would it go to her sons? Would it fall into disrepair? And even if Joe should die before her, was the house hers free and clear? What about divorce? Would the law see fit to award Joe the ranch, considering it signed sealed and delivered on the day she'd said "I do"?

These were all questions for a lawyer, but Rebecca didn't know any lawyers. Clarence, for all that he was on Joe's case right now, was the same as Joe. And that, too, got her back up—that he would sit himself at her table, eat her cookies, and all the while he was sending Billy and Joe out to harass hard-working folks.

That was wrong.

As far as the mill went, Rebecca felt no ambivalence there. While times were good, most folks she'd grown up with were perfectly content to let colored folks come in and do the dirty work they didn't want to do. But the mill was in trouble. A handful of colored men had been given jobs, and those men had settled with their families in a small block of the old Cotton Mill neighborhood.

"Where twenty Negroes are gathered," Pastor Davies had said one Sunday, "That's where you'll find trouble."

Rebecca didn't walk out that morning. She wasn't brave

enough to do any such thing, but that was the last day she'd attended church because, while she'd feared there might be truth in Pastor Davies's prediction, she'd also known instinctively that the trouble he was speaking of wouldn't come at the hands of any black men.

Truth to tell, the only Negro Rebecca ever knew was Silas. That sweet old man gave everything he had to Noble Ranch, including the chance to have himself a family. He'd died during the tornado of '48, where forty-three others were injured, and three more died. But those other folks—all white—got mentions in the paper, two men and one woman. However, more was said about Mr. McKay's amputated finger than was ever said about Silas Wright.

Knowing Silas hadn't provided for himself or for his eternal rest, her father buried him out by the pecan tree. Not once, ever, did anyone ask after a tired old black man. But then, come '54, the Supreme Court delivered its verdict ruling racial segregation in public schools violated the Fourteenth Amendment, and suddenly there was all this talk of desegregation. Her papa removed the headstone marking Silas's grave. He'd done so, he'd said, because he'd feared people would desecrate his grave. But Rebecca knew better. Really, he did it because he'd felt compelled to separate them—all their family—from any insinuation that they might be sympathizers. And Rebecca knew this not because her papa had said so, but because, despite the affection she'd felt for Silas, neither she nor anyone else under the Noble roof ever mentioned Silas again.

It made her ashamed to think she could love someone like that and not speak up on their behalf or walk out of church in their defense. But if Joe was out there stirring up trouble, for no good reason except because someone told him to, that was the final straw. If she wasn't going to speak up for herself or her boys, she must stand up for Silas.

Working herself up, she continued to pace the living room

until, by the time she heard the car pull up outside, she was right-eously livid—and even more so when she heard the clear ring of female laughter—unabashed to be showing up at a married man's house.

The car door slammed shut, and there was a tumbling sound, right onto the porch.

"No, no, let me," she heard a woman say, followed by a girlish peal of laughter and a choking sound. "Blast these crickets. I got one in my mouth."

"Close your mouth, sugar, she's gonna hear you."

In a sexy tone, the woman said, "I'm trying, honey . . . c'mere."

"Stop it," Joe said. "Leona!" But there was nothing in his tone that indicated he was the least bit displeased with her. "Mmmm," he said. "Leona, baby, you got to stop this."

"Why?" she asked with a giggle. "Don't you like it? Tell me you don't like it and I'll stop."

"Mmmm," he said again.

"See, you can't do it," she said, laughing.

Rebecca was too horrified to peer out the window, or even to advance toward the door.

"I like it fine, princess, but you know we got to wait . . . mmm," he said. And then again, "Mmmm."

Rebecca was so glad she'd sent the boys off to Farwell. And just when she thought that, the telephone screamed, silencing the pair on the porch.

Realizing it must be news of her boys, Rebecca ran quick to pick up the phone even despite her distress over the atrocity going on outside. "Hello," she said, her voice trembling.

The sound of a woman's reprimand was the first thing she heard in the receiver. "No, no, don't—don't." It was Lucinda. "Boys, you got to keep your hands to yourself," she was saying. "Rebecca?"

"Yes, it's me."

"They're here!" her cousin said cheerily. "A little antsy after spending so much time on their heinies, but I thought you should know they arrived. We're off to get milk and cookies, and then to bed for the night."

"Good, good," Rebecca said, distracted, hearing the whispers from the front porch coming closer. "Thank you for calling to let me know."

"Well, of course! Don't you worry about a thing—"

The front door swung opened, slamming against the wall. Joe stood in the doorway, fly open, his expression dour. "What the hell are you doing awake?"

"I, uh, have got to go, sweetie," Rebecca said. "Kiss, kiss."

Clearly forgetting that he had brought another woman into their home—never mind that Leona was still out on the porch—Joe lunged forward to grab the phone out of Rebecca's hands. "Who the hell is that?"

Evidently, Lucinda didn't know what to say. She hung up.

Joe glared at her. "Who was that? Clarence?" Furiously, he swung the phone, smacking Rebecca against the forehead. Stunned, she reeled backward, seeing stars.

Drunk and angry, he advanced on her yet again and, for just one instant, Rebecca forgot everything she'd meant to say. She cowered before him, raising a hand to her face. "No, please, Joe! It wasn't Clarence! It was Lucinda! I would never do such a thing to you!"

"Goddamned liar!"

"What on earth is going on here," asked a female voice from just outside the door.

Leona Fox poked her head inside, her eyes hooded, lipstick all a mess. In high heels and a skirt that was entirely too revealing, she stumbled in through the front door, entering the premise without permission. "Honey, what's going on here?"

"This whore is fucking Clarence!"

Rebecca shook her head, momentarily unable to speak, shock setting in. She blinked at the woman who came forward, smiling drunkenly, as though nothing at all could be the matter. She shook her head. "Tsk, tsk," Leona said.

Rebecca's head hurt. A trickle of warm blood trailed down her forehead and she reached up to inspect a brand-new wound, this one just a bit above the old one. She didn't have the wherewithal to ask Leona to leave.

Leona came up to stand behind Joe, placing a manicured hand on his shoulder. Her long nails were painted fire-house red. "Leave her alone, baby. Let's go get your stuff and go away, like we said, okay?"

Joe turned on her. "What? You crazy? She's screwing Clarence. What if she tells him?"

Leona turned her face up to Joe with heavy lidded eyes. "Tell him what?" She turned her palm up. "What could she possibly know?"

Blinking back in confusion, Rebecca stepped back, away from the pair, straightening her spine. It galled her that they thought her so gullible and stupid. "Once and for all, I am not screwing Clarence!" It was embarrassing to even say the word. Everything was wrong. This was not the way it was meant to go.

Joe put his hands on his hips. "Yeah, sure you're not—kiss, kiss," he said with mock affection. "Kiss, kiss." He turned to Leona and said contemptuously, "Kiss, kiss."

Leona had the audacity to giggle—a shrill sound that cut through Rebecca's skull. Nevertheless, she must keep things under control.

"Joe, please, listen . . . it was my cousin, Lucinda. I sent the boys off to Farwell this morning." She shot a glance toward Leona, forgetting her resolve. "Not that you seem to care whether they're home or not—how dare you bring this slut into my home!"

"Your home?" Joe dropped one hand to his side. He turned to look at Leona, incredulously. "You hear this shit?"

Leona's head swiveled, her gaze sharpened. All pretense of

drunkenness slipped from her demeanor. "I miss nothing," she said. And to Rebecca, "Honey, who you callin' a slut?"

Her eyes were cool and hard, and it was Leona, rather than Joe, who advanced on Rebecca now. She shrugged her purse down her shoulder, slid it all the way down her arm, catching it with ease. And then she stuck her hand inside her purse, removing a gun—a dark metal handgun with an ornate wooden handle. The long barrel shimmered by the light of the moon. Rebecca inhaled sharply.

"Put that away," Joe said uneasily, but her husband's voice was gentle and coaxing, not hard.

"No sirree. Your wife's got an ugly mouth." She trained the barrel on Rebecca, right at her face, squinting to look in the sites.

Joe sounded nervous now. "Damn it, Leona. You're going to ruin everything. Put the gun away," he begged her.

Leona exhaled melodramatically. "Alright," she said, lowered the gun and aiming it at the floor. "Just for you, honey. Kiss, kiss," she said, and laughed again, her temper immediately improved. "Kiss, kiss," she said, casting a hateful glance toward Rebecca.

Well and truly in shock, Rebecca watched the pair a moment, noticing the way Joe cowed to her. No, he wasn't so much a teddy bear, but he wasn't his normal self. There was something soft in his eyes—a look of admiration.

"Go on now, sugar," Leona said. "Get your things." And then as Joe turned to face Rebecca again, his gaze hardened, sharp as blades. He glared at her, full of disgust. "You're bleeding all over yourself," he said, as though he hadn't had a thing to do with it.

Instinctively, Rebecca lifted a hand to touch her wound, revealing a smear of blood on her fingers. "You're leaving?" she asked, but it wasn't so much a question. It was all she could do not to rejoice over the thought, although it stuck in her craw that he had never appreciated the home she'd provided, and here he was being a pussycat for a whore.

"Yeah," he said. "I'm leaving. You can take the house and shove it up your big fat ass."

"What about the boys?"

"Them too," he said.

Rebecca shook her head. "It must be true then?"

Joe screwed up his face. "What are you talking about?"

"Billy Shepherd," she said, lifting her chin.

Joe and Leona peered at one another in surprise, possibly alarm. Blinking in unison, both their heads swiveled toward Rebecca, their faces mirror images, and Rebecca realized in that instant that everything Mary Claire said must have been true.

Joe cocked his head. "Clarence tell you something?"

"Yes," she said, even realizing her answer might incriminate her, but Clarence's position must account for something. At this point, if he believed she was having an affair with the sheriff, maybe he would leave her alone.

He took another menacing step toward her. "Today?"

Leona lifted her gun again, narrowing those lovely cat-like green eyes. "You'd better tell us everything you know, honey . . . or I'll plant a bullet right inside your skull."

Uncertain what to do—having never faced the business end of a gun—Rebecca lifted her hands the way she saw it done in movies. "Please," she said to Joe. "I saw him today—at the bus stop. He was looking for you."

He looked skeptical. "Why?"

Rebecca shrugged. She put the pieces together from the bits she'd overheard. "Because you and Billy were out harassing colored folk. Something must have gone wrong."

Once again, he turned to look at Leona.

"No need to deny it," Rebecca said a little more certainly. "I know everything, and I'm not the only one."

He twisted his features grotesquely. "Where you hear this crap? Not Clarence?"

"No." Rebecca lifted her chin. "I was talking to Mary Claire."

"Mary Claire? You hate that two-faced cunt!"

Rebecca straightened her spine, alarmed by Joe's language as much as his vitriolic tone. "Well, I picked up the phone while she was talking to Julia."

"Women! You were eavesdropping, weren't you? Ain't you got nothing better to do?"

Yes, it was true. Despite her fear, Rebecca was mortified to confess it, but Joe didn't linger on the subject. "What else did the old biddy say?"

"She said . . . well, she said Billy was dead." And before she offered the suggestion, she knew it must be true, "You killed him, right?"

Once again, Leona and Joe looked at one another, only this time whatever smugness Rebecca had detected in Leona's expression was gone. There was a look of genuine concern now.

Encouraged, thinking she must have some new leverage now, Rebecca said, "Listen, Joe. Clarence put you on them, right? I'll testify in your defense," she said. "I'll tell them everything. No one will blame you. I'd say you were defending those people and Billy got in the way. Isn't that what happened?" Even now, she wanted to think better of the man she'd married.

"You listening to this bullshit?" he asked Leona.

Rebecca lifted a shoulder, a little more uncertain now.

Dismissing her already, he turned to address Leona. "If all that's true, maybe we don't have to leave? Maybe we could stay here."

Leona screwed her face. "Here?"

"Yes, right here. My name's on the deed."

She waved the gun at Rebecca. "What about her?"

"What about her?"

"You know . . ." She widened her eyes, giving Joe a chicken neck. "What if she knows?"

But of course she knew everything. Hadn't she just said so? Rebecca frowned. What more could there be to know? Apparently they'd murdered a man. What in heaven's name could be worse than that? Suddenly, she was no longer following their discourse.

Leona shook her head. "No, baby, I don't trust her. For all we know, she's twisting up your head."

Rebecca said, "I don't understand."

"Shut the fuck up," Joe demanded, then returned his attention to Leona. He walked over to the telephone, picked up the receiver, ripped the cord out of the base, then tore the curly wire out of the receiver end. He walked over and handed the cord to Leona. "Keep her tight, okay?"

Leona furrowed her brow. "Where you going, honey?"

"Up to the Roadhouse."

Leona frowned. "Joe . . . I don't think it's such a good idea."

"Don't worry, baby. I know what I'm doing."

"In the meantime, what am I supposed to do?"

"Just wait."

"Wait?" Leona screwed up her face. "Wait for what? One way or another, we got to kill her. Shouldn't I just do it?"

"No, not yet," he said.

Frowning, Leona turned to Rebecca now and it was clear in that instant . . . it wasn't Joe in charge. Leona smiled thinly, her smudged lipstick making her look unhinged. "Alrighty," she said. "Alrighty, but hurry on back now." Without looking at Joe, she added, "I'll finish the BJ when you get back and we'll show this bitch how it's done, then we'll get rid of her once and for all."

16

PENTIMENTI

Gillian awoke with Bleu lying on her chest, purring loudly. She opened one eye and the cat reached out to paw her bottom lip, flexing his pickers. "Easy boy," she said, removing his paws from her mouth.

Scarcely awake, she was thinking about her grandmother's magazines again—how hard Gigi had tried to live up to the expectations of others, all those self-recriminating notes in the margins. Having dragged the box into her room, she fell asleep perusing them.

"You can do better," one note said. "Try harder." "Not for Joe." She tried to put herself in her grandfather's shoes; it must have been difficult to be the recipient of so much cloying effort. What she wondered now was whether that disingenuousness was what drove him away.

Simply as an exercise, she'd gone through the issues in the box, one by one tossing them onto the floor until they carpeted the area around her bed. There were none past the year 1960, as though Gigi had simply stopped trying. So then, had she stopped trying because her husband left her? Or had she stopped trying, and then her husband left her?

In so many ways, she supposed she was as guilty as Geeg of trying to stuff her foot into a slipper that didn't belong to her— and how difficult it must have been for Kelly to be the recipient of Gillian's resentment, never truly understanding why.

Reaching up to brush a hand over the top of Bleu's head, flattening his ears, she whispered, "Good morning, old man."

He gave her a slow blink, eliciting a smile, and Gillian scratched him around the collar. Over the course of the past few weeks, he'd become more and more a part of her routine, and now as he lay atop her, all moony-eyed, she wondered why it had taken her so long to open her home to him.

Presumably, the same reason she couldn't move forward with Kelly. She was nearly as paralyzed by indecision as she was afraid of commitment. Was she so terrified she might make the wrong choice? *Of course.* You didn't commit to an animal, then decide he was too much trouble.

And yet . . . Gillian was the one who'd walked away, not Kelly. She was the one who'd thrown in the towel—or rather, she'd never picked it up to begin with.

That was the truth of the matter.

Kelly was right. She'd married him, but kept him at arm's length, and all the while she'd poisoned their relationship with resentment—and never mind what she'd done to herself, she'd fostered resentment in him as surely as she had in herself. But still he'd tried. *"Just admit you don't love me,"* he'd said the morning she'd walked out.

Gillian had brushed his hand off her shoulder and rolled out of bed. *"Here we go again."*

"Gillian," he'd pleaded, but she was still angry because, once again, he'd dared to question her integrity and her commitment. But looking back on it, he was right to question her. And still, even angry, she hadn't been able to say she didn't love him; because it wasn't true.

The truth was she loved him more than she knew—far more

than her actions ever conveyed. Only why couldn't she say those words out loud? *I'm sorry. I was wrong. I don't know what's wrong with me. I don't know why I feel like a wild, desperate animal locked in a cage. I don't know why I need to push you away. I don't know, Kelly! I don't know!*

Was it too late to say those things now?

"What would you do, Bleu?"

The cat blinked again, and Gillian couldn't quite tell whether it was an expression of boredom or affection. She thought maybe affection, based on the volume on his purr box, but he turned away. "I hear you," she said. There's nothing worse than relationship troubles. "I mean, it's all about me, and I'm boring myself." Probably because nothing ever changed. It was the same thing, day after day, with no conscious change for the better. In a sense, Gillian was living the definition of crazy, expecting something different—as though magically, one day she was going to wake up and Kelly would be Kelly again, and she was sixteen, flirting with the idea of love.

All those years ago, she'd wanted so desperately to be in love —and she had been in love—but the instant it got real, complete with day-to-day problems, Gillian retreated like a coward.

Because, well . . . *Admit it. You are a coward.* She was a dreamer afraid to dream, and ultimately because of this, she remained unfulfilled. She had ignored her own needs and desires, settling into a role Kelly had dictated instead of choosing for herself— exactly like Gigi, she'd lied to herself on a daily basis, more and more altering herself to fit into a stranger's slipper.

It was that truth that made her feel like ducking her head beneath the pillow . . . or anesthetizing herself. *Looking for myself, sober*—Pink knew how she felt.

But Gillian didn't need a drink. She simply didn't know how to find herself without a glass of wine, or tequila, or champagne . . . or whatever.

And if she wasn't drinking, no amount of aspirin was going to deaden the pain she felt being alone. Nor was it any kind of proof against fear. What was it they said? Heroes weren't born fearless; they were created by the impetus to do what should be done, despite fear.

And you're a chicken shit, Gillian.

Face it.

"I know what you're thinking," she said to Bleu, wading through the chaos of her thoughts. "You're thinking . . . addiction is addiction, no matter what kind it is, and the first step to changing it is to fess up."

You are an addict, Gillian. Through and through. You're addicted to your fear and your pain. If you weren't, you wouldn't live this way. You're addicted to aspirin, and yes, even despite the fact that you haven't had a drink in weeks, you're addicted to alcohol as well. You can't deal with life sober. You can't face facts—kisses aren't contracts, and people disappoint. People leave. People die.

"People die," she told Bleu, opening herself up to the emotion. "People die." She said the word "die" as though it were an outrage, and her eyes began to sting. Only this time, despite the proximity of her cat, she couldn't and wouldn't blame it on allergies. But if the revelation had any impact on the cat at all, no one could have guessed. He was a cat, after all.

Fat tears welled in Gillian's eyes as she wondered if Bleu missed his dead owner. His blissful expression said no.

But wasn't that her true fear? That she wasn't good enough to hold onto a good man.

For Christ's sake, she wasn't important enough to hold onto parents; how could she hold onto Kelly? You put all your love into one man, and eventually he moved on—out of sight, out of mind. It wasn't possible to deny it any longer.

Gigi's husband left; it stood to reason Gillian's would as well. Her grandfather took up with some bimbo the instant he could. But Kelly hadn't, she reminded herself. He'd stayed faithful for three long years, even after their divorce . . . waiting and waiting and waiting.

Now he was through waiting, and thinking of him with someone else made Gillian heartsick in a way that even Gigi's illness didn't trigger—mostly because, at eighty-four, Gigi's health was bound to fail and Gillian had been bracing herself for that inevitability for a long, long time. The simple fact that Gigi had insisted on remaining active, up until the end, shoveling horse shit out of Baby's stall, had only managed to give her a false sense of security.

But it shouldn't have.

People die.

Tears slipped past her lashes, rolled down her cheeks, and into her hairline. But there was hope here; she could take a page out of Bleu's book and enjoy the moment while she could . . . or she could worry about the inevitable outcome . . . and sleep alone.

Bleu's ears shot up suddenly and he leapt away, digging sharp claws into the tender flesh of Gillian's breast. Her tears dried up at once. "Damn," she said. "What's wrong with you, dude?"

That was exactly the sort of thing she was trying to avoid, and even so she wouldn't have traded those moments of bliss for anything in the world. Clearly not as moved as Gillian was by their time together, the cat raced away, unfazed. Groaning, she lifted her pajama shirt to inspect the scratch he'd left on her breast—about an inch long.

It was just like a man—wait for you to relax, then bound away, ripping your heart from your breast. *Such melodrama, Gillian. Get over it.*

Groaning, she rolled out of bed, sliding her foot onto the slippery cover of a *Life* magazine—1958 issue, with Jaqueline, Caroline, and Jack Kennedy on the cover. She nearly lost her footing and frowned at the poignant reminder that life could end so swiftly. Five more years and Jackie would be clamoring over the trunk of a car right here in Dallas, Texas, searching for pieces of her husband's skull.

She bent to pick up the magazines and put them safely back into the box. Meanwhile, she heard Bleu bound up the stairs.

By now, she'd come to recognize his bathroom routine, and for some reason, he was unnerved by his need to defecate, bouncing off walls like a crazy, deflated balloon. She heard him run around upstairs and then suddenly stop, and she assumed he was in his box. Maybe one of these days he would relax and realize Gillian wasn't going to track him by his poop and murder him. Only for the time being, it was a good thing she'd left the box upstairs—which reminded her, it was time to change the litter. Thinking idly about yesterday's conversation with Eli, scratching the left cheek of her rear, she emerged from the bedroom and sleepily made her way up the stairs, meanwhile rubbing at the fresh wound beneath her breast. And then she froze with the realization that she wasn't alone. Standing in the doorway of her childhood bedroom, Eli Fox stood staring into the room. He turned to look at Gillian, giving her a half smile.

"What are you doing here?" All this time, she'd been lying in bed thinking she was alone.

He shrugged. "Last I knew, I still worked for you." Stunned, Gillian didn't know what to say. Her silence prompted his question. "Don't I?"

"No, I mean, what are you doing here—here!" She pointed at the floor, incensed. "In my house?"

His smile faded. "Would you rather I pissed in Baby's stall?"

As far as Gillian was concerned, he was purposely being obtuse. "Upstairs," she said, clarifying. "What are you doing in my house . . . wandering around upstairs?"

His green eyes glinted.

Gillian placed a hand on her hip, demanding answers. "There's a full bathroom downstairs. You've used it before, remember?"

Never mind that she hadn't even expected him after yesterday's conversation. Never mind, too, that it would have been unnerving enough if he were to be wandering around downstairs while she was dead asleep, or bearing her soul to her cat. But she didn't appreciate the fact that he seemed to feel so justified in wandering around a single woman's home. And to be sure, that wasn't the only reason she was annoyed. After all, she wasn't entirely certain he didn't lock Bleu down in the basement.

As he stood there looking at her unapologetically, she realized something wasn't right about Eli Fox. Unfazed by her irate tone, he flicked a bored glance through the bedroom door, studying the room a long moment before returning his gaze to Gillian, purposely avoiding her question. "You have a strange cat," he said and Gillian's jaw dropped.

She meant to tell him to get out, but he went on to say, "You know, wolves do this sort of thing in the wild to mask their scent . . . mostly so they can stalk prey. But I have never, ever seen a cat do it." He scratched his head. "It's a new one on me."

Gillian stared at the man, aghast. Despite her outrage, and driven by her curiosity, she ascended the remainder of the stairs and walked over to peer into the room to see what he was on about—nothing, really. Bleu was preoccupied with the stupid stain on the floor. With his butt in the air, he rubbed his face over the floor, then flopped onto his back, rubbing himself over the spot, flipping back and forth, from side to side. "So?" she said. "He's an animal. He's doing what animals do."

"Exactly."

Gillian tossed a hand into the air, palm side up. "What do I care? Seriously, Eli, this is out of line. How dare you come into my house first thing in the morning, without even bothering to tell me you're inside, and then wander all over like you own the place?"

His jaw went taut. "Gillian," he said, ignoring her. "Have you ever actually looked at that stain?"

Gillian peered into the room—the room she'd lived in for most of her childhood—at the wood floor, where a mess of splotches, all in clusters, all amassed together in the middle of the room. It was no wonder her grandmother had covered it. It was an eyesore. The wood was cracked. Clearly the wood had been eaten away by something corrosive—probably bleach.

"Look hard," he demanded, and drew a phantom figure in the air. "Arms, legs . . . head. If you look close, you can make out the vague outline of a man . . .

A man?

"Or woman," he said.

Woman?

Gillian screwed her face. *Did he mean his grandmother?* "What are you saying, Eli?"

"Exactly what you're thinking."

Gillian said, "It's a goddamned stain! You know what, Eli, I think it's past time for you to go." He said nothing, allowing her to speak. "I'll finish whatever needs finishing on my own. Send me a bill and I'll send you a check."

"Is that right?" he asked, but he still didn't budge. In fact, he leaned back into the door, regarding Gillian with narrowed eyes.

"Yeah," she said, feeling sick. "I think you need to leave. Now!"

He straightened finally, shaking his head. "Keep your panties on. I'm leaving." And then he shrugged past her, heading downstairs. On the way out, he shouted, "If I were you, I'd get a blue light on that floor. You might be surprised at what you find."

Blue light?

Gillian followed Eli down, intending to see him out.

And then it occurred to her why he was here. He wasn't here to help. He was never here to help out. He was here searching.

For what?

She didn't know, but she felt the truth of it down in her gut. Eli Fox knew something about the disappearance of his grandmother, and whatever it was, he wasn't in the mood to share.

Only, by the same token, whatever he thought or didn't think—whatever his problem was, it wasn't hers.

Unless of course he'd had something to do with Gigi's event, in which case—Gillian glared at his back—he'd have to answer for it. Only the instant the thought came into her head, she knew he had been there that day. The coffee cup was his. Lunging forward, Gillian grabbed him by the back of the shirt, yanking him back as he rounded the corner into the kitchen, unable to keep herself from it, she asked, "You were here, weren't you?"

He turned to face her, tugging his shirt out of her grasp.

Half expecting him to deny it or play stupid, he did neither of those things. His eyes were angry slits as he looked straight into hers. "You want to know something?" He asked. "Go ask your grandmother." And with that, he spun about and made for the back door, leaving Gillian to watch him go. Nothing he could have said could have been more insensitive.

Ask your grandmother, he'd said.

As though she could.

17

LEATHER & LACE

Gillian stood in her kitchen, stunned. Blinking away angry tears, her gaze was drawn to the small stain of blood on the kitchen floor, near the kitchen sink. *Her blood.*

There was nothing mysterious about this stain, except that Bleu had taken an interest in it yesterday afternoon, wallowing over it the same way he had the stain upstairs.

But here was the thing: Gillian had lived in that room most of her life. She had never had any reason to suspect what might lie beneath that carpet. She'd never even thought about the spot. For most of her life, it had remained covered by Gigi's rag of a carpet. The vacuum had passed over it a trillion times, and Gigi was generally forthcoming about it. *She'd used the wrong cleaner on the floor, it ruined the wood. End of story.* It was no great stretch to imagine that scenario. Her grandmother literally ruined everything with bleach—jeans, shirts, shorts, tablecloths. You name it. If you could put bleach on it, she found a way to ruin it. She'd used bleach on every type of surface imaginable—including feed bowls Gillian was compelled to caution her over. "Gigi, I don't think that's safe for cleaning things you eat out of," she'd cautioned.

"Get out of here. I don't know what you're talking about."
She'd waved Gillian away. "They use it to sanitize fruits and
vegetables all the time, it's fine."

It was true. Her grandmother was right. Gillian had Googled
it and found federal regulations specifying the proper use of
hypochlorite solutions to sanitize foods.

So, yes, the hardwood floor. No great stretch to imagine Gigi
cleaning it with bleach. Although, as much of a clean freak as her
grandmother was . . . why would she live with a dirty old carpet,
content only to vacuum it now and again. That's the part that
didn't make sense.

Out front, she heard Eli's truck start and then she heard him
take off, spinning out dust. He was angry, no doubt, but he was
wrong to take a morning stroll through her house.

How could she have been so wrong? He was so polite—
opening doors for her, chauffeuring her around. There had been
nothing about him that ever led her to believe he was anything
but a nice guy, although whatever it was that had attracted him to
Gillian, it wasn't noble.

Rather, it was the Noble house.

Jesus. Gillian had begun to consider him a friend, but his
silence had been a lie.

Frowning, she moved over to the sink to pick up a sponge,
and then, not caring all that much that she was wiping up floor
grime with a clean sponge, she passed the sponge over the
bloodstain, rubbing harder when it didn't immediately
come up.

Blood was viscous.

The floor up there was solid, nailed-down planking, but not
tongue and groove. On purpose, the boards were not evenly cut
or spaced. The seams were not entirely perfect and there were
spaces in between, where spillage might have happened.

Comparing that floor upstairs to the one in the dining and
living rooms, it was clear they were the same original flooring,

only the downstairs floors had been subjected to normal wear and tear—a few scratches here and there, but otherwise fine.

What had Gigi spilled upstairs that would prompt her to clean it up with bleach?

In a bit of a mind funk, she walked back up the stairs, ignoring Bleu as he darted again between her feet on the way down. She climbed the steps, going slowly, stopping now and again to put one thought together with the next before she put one foot in front of the other.

Get a blue light on it.

Clearly, Eli was implying something—but what? Did he believe someone had died up there? And if so, who? If it was Gillian's grandfather, Gillian should have known, because even if Gigi didn't want to tell her, her father would have spilled the beans. He wasn't a keeper of secrets; he couldn't even keep his own. He'd stolen a case of beer off a warehouse platform once and bragged about it for months. It was a miracle he didn't get arrested.

Upstairs, standing in the hall, Gillian peered at the discoloration on the bedroom floor, tilting her head one way and then the other, trying to imagine what Eli saw.

She tried to look at it as a pentimento—past the bristly scrubbing in circular patterns, mostly concentrated in one spot—past the long swishes that stretched the natural length of an arm . . .

The stain itself was as at least six feet long . . . massive in terms of spillage. No wonder Gigi had covered it with the rug. To fix it, she would have had to strip the floor and re-stain it, but then . . . it wouldn't have matched the rest of the house. And anyway, from what Gillian knew about her grandmother's circumstances, she hadn't had any money to spare. But more importantly, if she'd repaired the floor, it would have necessitated hiring help . . . she couldn't do it alone.

With a few more turns of her head, a heavy, sick feeling began to settle in Gillian's gut. Her salivary glands began to work overtime, filling her mouth with tinny saliva. She started to feel like throwing up as she walked into the room and dragged the litter box out of her way.

Fighting nausea, she stood in the middle of her old bedroom . . . and then she could see it . . . the vague shape of a human body, not entirely clear. The left side was less defined, as though it might be where Gigi had concentrated the bleach. But if she really used her imagination and thought about Gigi kneeling . . . here . . .

Gillian sank to her knees, swishing her hand over the area, mimicking what her grandmother might have done.

And then, gagging over the suspicions coercing their way into her head, she inspected the wood closer, taking her nail to the grime between the seams.

It was packed tight with years of dirt—like paste or tar. Digging her nail deep into the crack, she scooped a bit of dark paste with her thumbnail and lifted the chunk to her nose.

She dry-heaved over the sight of it, but there was nothing immediately distinguishable about the odor, except that it smelled like old carpet and mildew.

Disgusted, Gillian flicked the bit of crud from beneath her fingernail, back onto the floor, and then stood again, staring at the stain . . . circling to assess it.

The right side of the discoloration was more distinct. She could make out what appeared to be a long limb—perhaps an arm? And if she allowed herself the imagination, she could make out a head as well—but really, how many times had she glimpsed shapes of rabbits and elephants in clouds? What about the old man in the moon? It's not as though there was really a man up there. What about the ink blotches psychiatrists used—the Rorschach test? People saw any number of things in those blots. Any given answer was subjective. This was merely a spot on a ruined floor, and if you looked hard enough, you could make out any shape at all.

Eli was putting ideas into her head.

Gillian walked out of the room, shaking her head. But then she turned back around—staring at the stain. Okay, so they both had missing grandparents—maybe those horny, cheating bastards had skipped out together.

The one thing Gillian knew for sure was that Gigi was not a liar. Her grandmother was painfully honest, as Gillian was. She'd taught Gillian to be an upstanding adult.

Don't lie. Don't cheat. Don't be greedy. Don't put on airs. Be yourself. Never depend on a man. Go to school. Make good grades. Learn how to fend for yourself.

On the other hand, Joe Frazer Sr. was a lying, greedy bastard. The apple—her father—hadn't fallen far from the proverbial tree. He'd abandoned Gigi. *He. Left. Her.*

That's what Gigi said. He went away . . . but at exactly the same time Eli's grandmother disappeared—which only served to illustrate what a dirty, rotten asshole he was. He took up with a bimbo who'd abandoned her child—isn't that what Eli said? His grandmother was selfish. She'd left a baby girl in Maine to be raised by her parents, and she never came around while that child was in the hospital. And what about the house on Anthony Street? Clearly, it wasn't in his grandmother's name. It belonged to Eli's grandfather. He'd sat on it all this time. *Because why?* On the off-chance his no-good daughter would return to the house?

It seemed like a proper load of bullshit.

She realized grief made people do strange things, but it made more sense that he would hold on to an investment, or maybe if he had enough money—and clearly he did, based on her conversations with Eli—he'd simply overlooked the house all these years. After all this time, Eli was fixing it up to sell. So yes, it made sense to Gillian that if he was shut up in that house, poking around his grandmother's belongings, eventually he would begin to cook up conspiracies in his head. So then, what was he searching for here, in Gillian's house?

The gun.

He was looking for his grandmother's gun.

The instant the thought occurred to her, Gillian knew it must be true. However, what was a missing gun supposed to prove? And why would he believe it could be here, in her house?

Gillian's cell phone was in the bedroom. She turned again, walked back down the stairs, and for the first time in weeks considered calling her father. However, instead of making her way into the bedroom, she was drawn to the basement door.

"No, no, sweetie, it's not safe down there." She heard her grandmother's voice say in her head—a distant, fading memory. It was Gillian's first day in the house. "My house is your house, Gilly Pie. Only stay out of the basement, okay?"

Gillian had nodded, far too diffident to ask why. It had never been in her nature to question any edict, neither from her father nor her mother. Why should her grandmother be different? Only later—much later—she'd come to understand why: Generally, there were no basements around Dallas. These were floodplains. Much of the land was redbed clay. When the earth got wet, it swelled and when it dried in summer, it shrank. Basements weren't wise. It was for Gillian's own protection that Gigi had kept her out of that room.

Or was it?

For a moment, Gillian stood in front of the basement door. She swallowed as she opened it, turning the knob and tugging, popping the latch. A thick wave of musk smacked her right in the face, but the rising air was cool.

Eli went down there, she realized.

That's how her cat ended up behind the door. He'd been in such a hurry to get back outside before Gillian could catch him sneaking around that he hadn't even thought to be sure the cat was out of the basement—or maybe he'd never realized Bleu followed him down.

A little trepidatiously, she flipped on the light switch. A weak, flickering glow appeared in the bowels of the house. Shadows trembled at her glance.

The bulb gave off maybe forty watts. Gillian had meant to replace it with something brighter, but once the movers left, she'd forgotten. Built more than a hundred years ago, the stairs were dangerously steep and hardly constructed to code. Worse yet, there were no rails or walls to hold on to. Taking the steps slowly, she made her way down.

Once she reached the bottom, there was a clear path to the light bulb in the center of the room. A small stool lived nearby. The walls were riddled with cracks, some half an inch wide in places where the earth had shifted, cracking plaster and resettling the house.

Bleu yowled at the top of the stairs, but Gillian was too curious now to turn back . . .

Weak yellow light tinted the interior of the room—old furniture, boxes, suitcases, lamps. Like a tiny flickering neon sign, the bulb illuminated a strange little universe. The ground floor was dusty concrete, also riddled with cracks, but even in the dim light it was apparent that the floor closer to the stairs was older and the concrete poured over the rest of the room was newer.

Considering how little time Gillian had ever spent down in the basement, it was difficult to say whether anything was out of place. There was a pile of items closer to the door she could lay claim to, and it was by far the least organized portion of the room.

She recognized another pile, though she hadn't seen it in years—a stack of cardboard boxes filled with toys—Gillian's toys. No doubt Gigi had brought them down here after Gillian outgrew them. Leaning against the bottom box was Gillian's chalkboard, the surface bearing witness to some of Gillian's old artwork, anywhere the eraser no longer could erase. Another pentimento, she realized, only this one was far less sinister.

As Gillian's eyes scanned the dimly lit room, she spotted another place in the back corner that seemed messier than the rest of the basement, only she wouldn't have put any of her own belongings back there because she'd fully intended to go through everything—eventually—and she'd wanted to be able to partition the room according to what belonged to whom. Everything in the back corner . . . those were Gigi's possessions.

Gillian picked her way over boxes and furniture to reach the location in question. Once there, she could see the mess was just an old green suitcase lying askew atop a few others—as though it were singled out and dragged out from between the rest. But it was just a grungy green suitcase that appeared to be more than fifty years old. A scrap of lace appeared to be caught in the copper closure. Out of curiosity, Gillian tried to free it, but the lace was brittle and crumbled in her grasp. The lock, however, wouldn't budge. After all this time with the deteriorating lace between its teeth, it appeared to be jammed—except Gillian had the feeling the lace was only recently caught.

Someone had been tampering with the lock.

Only recently, someone had attempted to pick it with something sharp—a pocket knife? There were thin, shiny scratches over the otherwise solid patina, all near the keyhole.

With a furrow of her brow, Gillian hoisted up the suitcase. Something heavy clanked as she dragged it down to carry it upstairs.

"YOUR GOAL: TO BE SURE YOUR HOME IS A PLACE OF PEACE, ORDER, AND TRANQUILITY WHERE YOUR HUSBAND CAN RENEW HIMSELF IN BODY AND SPIRIT."
—*THE GOOD WIFE'S GUIDE, HOUSEKEEPING MONTHLY*

3:00 A.M., Saturday, July 16, 1960

. . .

"IT'S CUTE. Where'd you get it?"

"Woolworths," Rebecca answered.

Leona Fox sat at the opposite end of the kitchen table. Having worked out her frustrations on Rebecca's face after Joe's departure, her voice was more pleasant now. Her gun lay on the table as she fiddled with the camera Rebecca had purchased. There was something quite surreal about watching the woman who'd whacked her multiple times with the butt end of a gun sit down at her table as though they were neighbors chatting over coffee.

Rebecca's face hurt. Her left eye was swelling more and more by the minute—the same eye she'd injured when Joe slung her across the kitchen. Only this time, it wasn't a bruise or a scratch. She could taste blood on the tip of her tongue as she fiddled with the split in her lip.

While Leona tugged and pulled at her camera, pressing buttons, Rebecca sat, hands tied behind her back with the telephone cord. It was taut, cutting into her wrists, but Leona hadn't pulled it tight enough to restrict all the give in the cord. It was as though she'd believed her gun was incentive enough to keep Rebecca from attempting to free herself.

Well, she wasn't going to sit idly by—in the same place where her sons took milk and cookies—and allow that woman to fire a bullet through her head.

No. She wasn't going to die this way. And make no mistake, she believed Leona Fox was fully capable of everything she said.

"It's so . . . tiny."

Rebecca watched as Leona fiddled some more, pressing another button. The flash went off and she looked surprised, chortling like a dumbstruck child. "So bright! Don't you think?"

When Rebecca didn't respond, Leona peered up, frowning, and Rebecca nodded. "Yes," she said. "It's bright."

"Hey," Leona said in a conversational tone. "Did you get to

that Fourth of July picnic last year?" She furrowed her brow as though trying to remember, and then waved a hand, flashing an enormous diamond. *Did Joe give her that?* "You must have, but I can't remember. Did you know that's where I met Joe?"

Rebecca shook her head.

"Yep," she said, staring, but not really seeing Rebecca. "I wondered if you knew. Joe said you were pretty but stupid. Anyway," she said, recovering herself and offering a mischievous smile with heavy-lidded eyes. "You're not so pretty anymore, are you?" She laughed impishly. "Truth to tell, you look like something the cat dragged in.

"Hey, you know I had a cat once . . . Lucy. Named the bitch after that black-haired girl in Charlie Brown—you know the one. She's like a counselor or something. Bossy little bitch. Anyway, I didn't like her very much. Didn't like the cat either, so I won't tell you what I did, but when my daddy found her, he sent me to girl's school." She shook her head. "Self-righteous bastard.

"But whatever, that was fine. And you know that's where I got pregnant, 'cause I figured out that to get what you want, you just gotta spread your legs a little . . ." She swiveled toward Rebecca and spread her legs, sliding a hand beneath the table and giving Rebecca a naughty grin. "Like this . . .

"You know how he likes it, right?" She squirmed in her chair, fondling herself beneath the table, and she moaned.

Horrified, Rebecca's gaze flitted to the gun. Leona caught the direction of her gaze and she stopped her rude display.

"Sexual repression is for the birds. But you don't know how to please a man, so how can you please yourself. You don't know anything, do you? How the hell do you think Marilyn gets what she wants? You don't think that skirt flew up by accident, do you? That girl knows how to work it."

Bored with the one-sided conversation, Leona went back to the camera, studying it. She fiddled with the metal cone that held the flash bulb, and finally yanked the Hawkeye flash out of the port holes. "You have to get these developed, right?"

Without waiting for Rebecca's answer, she put the flash unit back. The sound of it clicking wasn't all that unlike the sound of a gun trigger depressing.

"Yes," Rebecca said.

"Yeah, I thought so." She turned the camera toward Rebecca and posed herself like a photographer, tried to snap a photo, and frowned when she pushed the button and nothing happened.

"You have to wind it," Rebecca said as Leona fiddled with all the protrusions, not quite figuring it out. "If you untie me, I'll show you."

Leona's brows shot up. Her head slid back and she laughed. "That's cute. You think I'm stupid, right? No, thank you!" Finally, she found the lever to wind the film, and ratcheted it down. Rebecca heard the tiny click once it was in place, and Leona turned the camera on Rebecca and pushed the button.

"Keepsake," she explained, putting a finger to her lips, sucking at the tip. "You know, it's gonna be better this way . . . at first, I thought we could stay in my house, but Billy got scared. He was going to snitch—but that woulda been fine, you know, 'cause Clarence already knows. Whatever, I hate my house and I'm sick and tired of answering to my father."

Rebecca said nothing.

"I got a little girl, you know. Her name is Cat, short for Caterina. I just call her Cat." She snorted inelegantly. "I'd rather have a cat. I feel sorry for you, saddled with those boys." She shook her head. "Ain't no way to live, and no one will ever want you anyway, so it's all for the best."

Rebecca didn't understand anything the woman was saying, but she was too angry to ask for clarification. Any minute, Joe would come walking through the door, and Leona had already told her what they planned to do. One way or the other, they would kill her, and then what would happen to her boys?

Once again, Leona wound the film. She snapped another photo. "God, you're boring," she complained. "No wonder Joe doesn't like you. You know, I don't know what he's thinking about this house. I wouldn't live here if you paid me. We can go anywhere we want."

"If you leave now, I won't tell anybody."

Leona sneered. "Yeah, whatever. I've heard that before. Don't worry, we aren't staying, lady. I got my suitcase out in the car, everything I need. We got money coming out of our ears now, and I don't need anything from my dad—selfish goddamn bastard."

"Leona, Joe has nothing—no money," Rebecca told her. "If that's what he told you, he's lying. The house belongs to me."

Leona laughed. "Really, you are stupid, aren't you?" She gave Rebecca a snide look out of the corner of her eyes as she continued to fiddle with the camera. "You know that heist over in Euless?" she asked, pointing to herself with a sharply manicured, red-painted finger. "That was us."

Startled by the confession, Rebecca's jaw went slack.

"Yeah, that's right," she said, as she reached over to pat her gun. "Thanks to dear old Pop, we got a nice little nest egg, and we won't have to share with Billy."

Rebecca tried not to look as horrified as she felt. She had already suspected they were responsible for Billy's death, but this was not the scenario she'd envisioned.

Leona's hand slid off her gun, back to the camera. "Ever notice how easy it is to get men to do whatever you say if you only give 'em proper motivation? Well, I'm sure Billy never would have done me. He was too tripped out about getting his share of the money to his old lady. But all I needed to do was make Joe believe he wanted to." She shrugged. "As for Clarence, well . . . you know he wants me too—and not just the money."

Clarence. He'd been coming around a lot, but never once had he implied that he'd suspected Joe of robbing any bank. There was nothing in the paper about a suspect. Was Clarence Taylor in on it as well? Or had he figured it out and decided he wanted a share?

There were so many questions rifling through Rebecca's head, but she was too upset to ask even one—never mind being afraid. Right now, as she sat staring at the massive ring on Leona's finger, she was downright furious.

Little by little she worked the cord behind her back, pulling it like an accordion. It still wasn't loose enough to slide her hand through, but even once she reached her goal, she realized she would need to do it at just the right moment.

At the other end of the table, Leona played with her new toy —winding, pointing, and clicking; winding, pointing, and clicking; winding, pointing, and clicking—each time taking photos of Rebecca while she was tied up in her chair. Judging by the expression on her face, it seemed to give her a perverse pleasure, and Rebecca wondered what she intended to do with all those photos.

If she didn't get out of this mess, someday, someone would find that camera and they would develop the film, and what might they see? A tired, beat-up old hag, who was too dumb to recognize a grifter when she spied him.

What a mess she'd made of her life. What a mess she'd made of her parents' life—of their home. And now she wondered if Joe had had anything to do with her parents' death. No, he wasn't with them on the day they'd crashed into the tree, but she remembered now that he'd offered to change the brake pads. If he'd damaged those breaks, Rebecca was as much responsible for their deaths as he was. And the longer she sat mulling over the possibilities, the angrier she became.

Leona took a few more photos, frowning now because she couldn't get the flash to go off. "Rats," she said. "How do you make this work?"

"You have to change the flash."

Frustrated, she tossed the camera onto the table. "Stupid

thing. Who cares, anyway? What's taking him so long?" She turned her palm up, curled her fingers to check her nails. "You made me chip my polish," she said, and Rebecca watched as she sank into the chair, getting comfortable.

Any second Joe would come home, and any opportunity Rebecca might have would be lost. If she didn't do something now, right now—whatever the consequences—it would be too late.

They would kill her and bury her in the basement—or some-place else—and then what would happen to her boys? To hell with the ranch. Right now, it wasn't the property she cared about. It was Jeff and Joe.

Clarence was a dirty, good old boy cop. She'd always known that. Only the memory of him seated across her table, eating jumbles, made her blood boil hotter than Texas tea.

Leona sighed, clearly bored. She toyed with the gun, but instead of picking it up, she shoved it away—not far, but a little further out of her reach—and then she sank deeper into her chair, until she was slumped so far that her face was at the level of the table. *Such an unladylike posture.*

In the meantime, Rebecca continued to pull at the telephone cord, slowly, surely loosening its grip. At long last, she set her hands free, but in the process, the cord fell to the floor, dropping with a clatter. Leona's gaze snapped to, locking with Rebecca's across the table.

It was now or never.

Before Leona could sit up, Rebecca thrust her arms up, shoving the dinette table right into Leona's jaw. The gun slid across the pearlescent surface, clanking onto the floor. The camera flew out of Leona's hands, landing with a crash.

Before Leona could recover herself, Rebecca bounded up from the chair. She sprinted for the dining room. The El Dorado was gone, and the Studebaker keys were upstairs on the sleeping porch.

"Bitch!" Leona shouted as she scurried to retrieve her gun. Somehow, despite wearing those heels, she was up fast and lunged after Rebecca, chasing her through the dining room.

Realizing she would remain in Leona's sites if she ran straight to the front door, she made a sharp left into the hall and lunged for the first door she could reach. The basement door.

The lights were off. The bulb was loose. The room was dark. Only Rebecca knew her way down, after squirreling so many of her belongings downstairs.

Taking the steps as quickly as she dared, she reached the ground level and hurried to the back of the room, hiding behind a dresser. Feeling at her back, she found one of her father's canes and lifted it into her hands—the hammer cane. Bracing herself to act, she waited in darkness for Leona to descend.

At the top of the stairs, the light switch clicked, but no light emerged. Leona cursed roundly, using words Rebecca had never heard. Cursing even more, she began to click-clack her way down the stairs, the metal in her heels sounding like little taps against the wood.

Her heart beat faster.

Her lungs ached.

Her thoughts rattled about in her brain.

God. Oh, God. She should have picked up the gun. It had been too close to Leona and she'd only wanted to get away. In the musky darkness, Rebecca's breath came in soft puffs.

She was so glad the boys were gone, but if they'd stayed, maybe none of this would ever have happened. She'd ramped herself up, looking for a fight—a fight was what she got.

Any, any moment, Joe was due to return home.

Where to go?

What to do?

The stairs creaked as Leona descended. "I know he said to wait, but you're too much trouble. When I find you, I'm gonna—"

Suddenly, Leona squealed. Rebecca heard her tumble down

the stairs. She landed with a thump. Then silence. A thick, muddy silence reached her ears.

Rebecca waited the length of two heartbeats, then emerged from her hiding place, clutching the cane, ready to smack Leona. By now, her eyes were adjusting to the darkness, and she spied the outline of a body, twisted awkwardly on the concrete bib around the stairs.

She didn't see the shining black puddle slowly emerging from beneath Leona's head, and she stepped into the oily slick and slipped, tumbling down over Leona's prostate body.

For a terrible moment, Rebecca lay in horror, sensing Leona's warmth but no heartbeat. There were no moans of distress, no sign at all that she was alive.

She's dead.

The gun was inches from Rebecca's hand. She tossed the cane and reached for the gun, getting up and hurrying toward the stairs, hurrying. Emerging into the hall, she once again bolted up the stairs toward the sleeping porch to grab the Studebaker keys.

She was halfway up when she heard the car pull in out front, and nearly fell to her knees and wept. But thinking about the boys, she kept going, all the way to the porch.

Frightened out of her mind, she opened a dresser drawer, grabbed a set of keys, and then froze in the hall as she heard Joe enter the house and call out to Leona.

Of course, Leona didn't answer.

Now what? Did she tell him she was upstairs? Did she wait to see if he found the basement door ajar and then go down, try to sneak out the door? Did she appeal to his sense of mercy?

He was the father of her children. Not once had he actually said he would kill her—that was Leona. Still, he hadn't disagreed . . .

Rebecca stood so long she didn't exactly know how much time passed.

"Leona!" Joe shouted. "Where are you?" Having assessed the

damage in the kitchen, he must have come back around to the hall, nearly silently, maybe stopping to stare at the basement door. For the longest time, there was silence—a terrible silence that hurt Rebecca's brain.

He must have realized what the silence meant—or maybe he heard Rebecca's heavy breathing—but he suddenly called her name. "You there?" he asked. When she didn't respond, he prompted again, "Rebecca?"

Rebecca's hand was trembling now. She held the gun in front of her, retreating slowly into the boys' bedroom. And then suddenly Joe seemed to realize where she was. She heard the first tap of his shoe against the hardwood stairs. Lapping at her dry, cracked, and bloodied lip, Rebecca retreated into the room and waited with Leona's gun.

"Rebecca," he said again, crossly. "If you hurt her, I'm gonna twist your neck with my bare hands."

A sob escaped Rebecca's throat and she sniffled, giving herself away. One by one, his footsteps came slapping up the stairs, every step an exclamation by itself.

I'm going to kill you, it said.

Again. And again. And again.

There was no turning back. Whatever those two had begun, it was irreversible. They'd killed a man. And now that Rebecca knew it, he couldn't afford to let her live. They'd robbed a bank too. Clarence either suspected or knew. There was nowhere to turn. Rebecca had no choice. One way or another, her babies were going to live without either a father or a mother. Or both.

If Rebecca had any hope Joe would soften—that she could talk him out of his murderous rage or convince him to turn himself in—it was lost the instant she saw his face. It was twisted with rage, his lips curled backward like a rabid dog, and she heard him growl before he spoke.

"Where is she?"

Rebecca shook her head, not wanting to tell him, not able to speak.

He took another step toward her, and she instinctively retreated, inching backward until her spine was against the wall. It occurred to her that she didn't even have a clue if the gun was loaded. *Oh, God, she didn't know.* And then everything happened in a blur. He lunged at Rebecca. She pulled the trigger. A single shot rang out, finding purchase in Joe's throat, and then once again, she put another hole through his shoulder at close range. Blood sprayed everywhere—all over her face and blouse—and then, for a terrible, uncertain moment, Joe teetered, his face contorting as though he couldn't quite believe she had done it. After a painfully long moment, he crumpled to the floor. Rebecca stared at his body, blinking.

Now she had not one but two bodies in her house. She had a dead woman in her basement and a dead husband in her boys' room. There was a gun in her hand, covered with her finger-prints, and . . . Clarence . . . was . . . dirty. What would happen to Jeff and Joe if she were arrested and sent to prison? What would happen to the ranch? What would happen to her? What about all the stolen money? What if they believed she was an accomplice? One dead body might appear to be self-defense, but two . . . what about two? Oh, God, and if you added Billy Shepherd into the mix, what about three? Long before she might be lucky enough to be tried and pronounced innocent, they would believe her guilty. And in the meantime, what about her boys?

She'd shot Joe twice already. Both bullets entered his body while he was attacking her. Surely, they would know this? But when he left the house, where did he go?

To see Clarence?

To make a deal?

Rebecca stared at her husband's still but twisted form, watching as a large slick of dark blood pooled out from beneath his body. His head was turned, and even in repose his face was horrific. His eyes were raging pools of fury. Even now, his lips curled back into a threatening scowl.

And he was breathing.

Unlike Leona, Rebecca could see his back rise and fall. She glared down at him, thinking of her parents, thinking of all the times through the past years that Joe had smacked her around. She licked her busted lip, thinking about all the ugly words he'd ever said to her.

He'd spent her money, beat her so many times, never gave a damn about their boys, and all the while he was putting his—man thing—into that whore downstairs.

She winced, as though in pain, remembering the atrocities he and Leona were committing on the front porch—her front porch. He'd brought Leona into their home, where her children might have witnessed everything—oh, God, what if they had been home? Would these two ne'er-do-wells have harmed them?

If only Leona hadn't been wearing those damnable heels . . . if blind luck hadn't been on Becky's side. . . . Immense rage overwhelmed her, and here and now she decided she was never going to be a victim again. Leaning into her husband's body, she aimed the barrel at the back of his head and, one last time, pulled the trigger.

The blast sounded like thunder, probably heard for miles. But then, she didn't have any neighbors on Old Mill Road. Not for *miles and miles and miles.* They'd buried Silas by the old pecan tree and no one ever knew.

Joe's lungs emptied one last time. She heard a gurgle come from deep in his throat, and then he pissed on her floor. Grimacing over the sharp smell, Rebecca swiped the back of her hand across her brow, coming away with blood.

Well, now . . . there wasn't any way they could mistake that for self-defense—not with one bullet to the back of his head and two more in front.

Exhaling a long breath, expelling her fear, Rebecca took the gun with her on the way to the laundry room to get the bleach.

PRESENT DAY

WITHOUT KNOWING WHY, Gillian hauled the green suitcase up to the sleeping porch, as though by rote, only belatedly recalling the key she'd found in her grandmother's drawer. Outside the sleeping porch, she turned the knob and pushed open the door, then dragged the suitcase inside and hoisted it atop a dresser. The contents shifted as she swung it through the air, and settled again as she put it down.

She'd stowed the mystery key in the vintage tin and left it on the dresser; she tilted it now, spotting the two keys inside and reaching in to pluck one out. It was exactly the sort of key that would belong to a suitcase—old-school, brass, with a notch on one side, yet another at the tip, much like a tine—she slid it into the lock and the latch popped. Cautiously lifting the lid, she peered inside.

There was nothing about the contents that seemed the least bit suspicious.

It was a jumble of women's clothing, some lace, and a pair of red leather vintage pumps. For a moment, Gillian thought the shoes must have made the *thunk* sound she'd heard, but then after rummaging through the contents, she felt something hard. Pulling an old blouse out of the way, she spotted a camera—a Kodak Brownie Starmatic.

Broken.

Why would Gigi keep a broken camera?

Even more curious now, because none of the clothes were reminiscent of anything Gigi would wear, she set the camera aside and continued rifling through the suitcase, halting when she spotted a plain white envelope.

On one side, in what appeared to be Gigi's handwriting, the envelope was marked "evidence." It was sealed, but whatever it contained was confined to one side of the envelope. An area outlining the contents revealed a squared object—or, maybe objects—about an inch and a half, by an inch and a half. Feeling around, making sure there was nothing she could tear, Gillian ripped the envelope on one side and poured the contents into the suitcase, revealing a stack of squared color photographs—a match to the two she'd found in the tin.

With a sense of horror, she lifted up the photos and flipped through them one by one—seven in total. The face depicted was barely recognizable but nevertheless unmistakable. She knew those blue eyes too well. They were the eyes of the woman who'd raised her—Rebecca Lee Frazer.

Gigi's face was beaten and bloodied. The extent of her injury made Gillian's gag reflex rear. The left eye was swollen shut, the lip split on one side. Blood spilled from one brow.

All but one of the photos was of Gigi, seated before a kitchen table—the same table Gillian kept downstairs. *Who could have done such a thing?*

Joe?

Only one of the photos revealed a different face. This one was blurry . . . and yet, the features—the ones Gillian could make out —were not masculine, but feminine. The lashes were long, thick, and black. The one eye shown was . . . green? It was difficult to say, as it was such an extreme close-up and way out of focus. It only showed the upper half of someone's face . . . as though the photograph had been an accident.

Gillian put the photos down, back inside the suitcase, atop the envelope and the clothing, and looked around the room . . . shaken by the thoughts that were vying for space inside her brain.

Eli had been searching for something—maybe proof that his grandmother's final moments had been spent in this house? Was that possible? What about her grandfather? Where was Joe Sr. during this ordeal? Had he beat Gigi? Clearly, someone had.

Evidence.

Of what? The envelope was clearly marked, though the seal had remained unbroken until Gillian tore it. Searching the suitcase for a name—any indication that it belonged to someone else, she found nothing . . .

A little more determined now, she grabbed the photos—all of them—and set them aside on the dresser, then she turned the suitcase upside down. The pair of red shoes tumbled to the floor, followed by a pile of old clothing—skirts, blouses, a cone-shaped bra, and underwear.

No gun.

She looked over the interior of the case, finding nothing. She set it down again, feeling about for slits in the interior cloth, but there was nothing.

Of course not, but why would someone leave something so incriminating, and marked so plainly, only to conceal something else. There were no hidden compartments in the lining. The satiny material was old and brittle, but remained intact.

Trying to remember everything Gigi ever told her about her husband, she set the suitcase on the floor and got down onto her knees to look through the clothing.

What had Geeg said about Joe Sr.? Word for word . . . *He was a no-good, cheating bum.* Of course, Gilly never really cared enough to delve deeper. She knew enough about cheaters and no-good bums. Her grandfather had left, because wasn't that what cheaters did? All this time she had never suspected anything more than what Gigi told her. Why? Because she was projecting? Because she found it easy to believe she and her grandmother had suffered the same fate?

Abandoning everything on the floor, she got up and walked

into the hall, only to turn in a nervous circle. She put a thumbnail into her mouth and peered into her old bedroom. And then, taking a deep breath, she stared again at the discoloration with more discerning eyes.

Eli was right. It did look like a human shape—grotesquely distorted, but human nonetheless. As she studied it, Bleu brushed past, swishing her ankles with his tail, but Gillian was too engrossed in the moment to pay him any mind.

As though by habit, she moved through the room, toward the closet, only to look inside. She used to keep crayons there, but the closet was empty now. Gigi rarely threw anything away. She would have kept everything, and stored it where?

Down in the basement.

Remembering the chalkboard, Gillian ran out the room and down the steps, then down again into the basement. The light was still on, and she immediately began rifling through old toy boxes, pulling them down one by one, pouring the contents onto the floor, searching for chalk. She wasn't even sure why, exactly, except that she was driven to find some.

Gigi probably would have melted crayons for wax—or any number of projects. And crayons wouldn't have fared too well in this heat—but chalk. Finally, she found the box of chalk, half empty, but it didn't matter. She only needed one. She flipped the lid, pulled one out and ran back up, taking the stairs in her bare feet two at a time, ignoring the pain that flared in the arch of her left foot.

Once back in her room, Gillian traced the outline on the floor with a stick of orange chalk, outlining the circumference, sticking as close to the inner border as she could—where the damage was worst. Once she was finished, she stepped back to study the drawing, and now it was clearer . . . the head, the legs, the arm— one arm. It was impossible to make out the features on the left side of the blob. Swallowing, Gillian looked over at Bleu, scratching around in his box. Frowning, she went in search of her cell phone and found it in the bedroom. For the first time in ages, she dialed her father's number, and then she sat down at the kitchen table—the same side of the table Gigi had occupied in the photos.

The phone rang, and rang. "Answer," she said, anxious for more information. She hung up and dialed the number again. This time, her father answered on the second ring.

"What do you want?"

Gillian exhaled sharply. "Daddy?"

"What do you want, Gillian?"

She might as well not hedge. She was a poor actor. There was no way she was going to manage any level of duplicity, not today. "I was wondering about something." She picked at the kitchen table with a thumbnail.

"That ain't never good," he said, irascibly.

Bound and determined not to argue, Gillian asked, "Do you remember anything at all about July 1960?"

"July?" he asked, sounding annoyed. "What'r you smokin', woman? You sound more 'n more like your crazy mama—she went batshit on me, you know. Dumb bitch. I tried to help, but, no, she wouldn't listen."

"This is a serious question, Pop." He stopped talking and Gillian pressed on. "I just need to know what you remember about July 1960."

"Not a goddamned thing. What was I, nine?"

"Eight," Gillian provided.

"Whatever."

"Dad . . . this is important." Gillian closed her eyes. "Do you remember . . ." She didn't want to ask straight out about anything she'd discovered. "What you did that summer?"

She remembered the photograph of him and Jeff, the one with the bus driver. The back of that photo was dated July 15, 1960.

He exhaled a breath. "What you ought to be doing is talking

about how much you gonna sell the house for," he said. "Mama ain't never coming home."

"I realize, Pop," Gillian said. "But Gigi didn't want to sell the ranch. She wanted me to have it."

"I'm her son," he argued. "It should be mine. Tell me what you got to say about that?"

In fact, he was one of two sons, both of which Gigi had left out of her will. "I'm not selling the house," she said again, more firmly.

He let loose a barrage of curses, all words Gillian had heard aplenty from his mouth. He warned her about the lawyer he'd hired, complained about how much it cost. He told her about the lawsuit he was planning, and then sat quietly waiting for Gillian to respond.

"Two things," Gillian said. "I have a copy of the will. She didn't die intestate. And two, I know where she hid her valuables, and . . . I'll make you a deal. You answer just a few questions—just a few, Daddy—and you and Jeff can have everything except the house."

"Why do I give a damn about a bunch of junk? That's all she ever kept, except the house."

"That's not true. She told me a long time ago she put away about twenty-thousand dollars she was saving for you and Jeff. She just never gave it to you because she said—well, never mind what she said. I know it's there."

"'Cause you seen it?"

"No."

"Well," he said, as though he thought her obtuse. "If you ain't seen it, how do you know it's there?"

"Because I just do," she said.

Her father was silent a long moment, as though thinking it over. And then he asked, "Why should I trust you?"

Gillian sighed. "Because Gigi wouldn't lie." And nevertheless, even as she said it, Gillian understood that wasn't true. If the facts emerging were real . . . not only had Gigi lied, but she was possibly an accessory to murder. Joe met her declaration with stubborn silence. "Dad?"

"What?"

"All I'm asking is for you to answer a few simple questions, and for the answers, you can have everything Gigi left, except the house."

"What questions?"

"What did you do summer of 1960?"

"Damn it. What the hell do I know!? I can't remember one summer from the next. Why the hell should I remember that one?"

"Because . . . it's the summer your father left."

Silence. And then he said, "No-good cheating bum."

Gillian waited on the edge of her seat, once again picking at the tabletop with a fingernail, her heart racing and her skin prickling.

He huffed out a breath. "We went to Farwell, me and Jeff."

Gillian swallowed. "Gigi took you?"

"No, we went by bus. Alone," he said, enunciating the word "alone" as though he'd yet to get over it. "Jeff wet his goddamned pants, I had to set next to him, and then when I tried to move to another seat, the driver made me sit back down, telling me to leave the chair for someone else. But that goddamned bus was empty the whole way, 'cept for some old hag and some nitwit who kept flicking his Zippo over and over and over, until I wished he'd set the bus on fire."

"So Gigi stayed home?"

"Yeah, Mama stayed home. She said she had to talk to my dad, and I'm pretty sure she meant to send him packing."

"How long were you gone?"

"I don't know—what does it matter, Gillian?"

"You think it was July?" she asked.

"Yeah, maybe. When do I get the money?"

Gillian inhaled a breath. "Next week."

"Why so long?"

"Because . . . I have to find it, Pop; it's not in the house."

"What you mean you got to find it?" he asked. "I knew it was bullshit. Is that all you need 'cause I got shit to do here."

"Yeah, Dad, that's all."

Without bothering to say goodbye, her father hung up the phone. Gillian sat only a moment longer, listening to the dial tone, before going in search of a hammer. She found one out by the barn, on a folded tarp. She bent to pick it up and marched it back into the house, then marched upstairs. Back in her room, she got down on her knees, set the phone down on the floor, and wedged the forked end of the hammer into the space between floor planks, then she leaned all her weight into the handle until she heard wood crack.

18

THE GOOD WIFE

"A GOOD WIFE ALWAYS KNOWS HER PLACE."
—*THE GOOD WIFE'S GUIDE, HOUSEKEEPING MONTHLY*

2 *:00 p.m., Saturday, July 23, 1960*

"YOU'RE A GOOD WOMAN, BECKY."

"Thank you, Clarence."

Sheriff Taylor sat across the kitchen table, in the same chair Leona Fox had occupied only moments before her death. With his hat in his hand, he offered another apology for her troubles. But as he sat mulling over her story, he had a tough time making eye contact.

"You know . . . I always had good respect for you, Becky. I always imagined—before Bertie." He shook his head, maybe thinking better of what he was going to say. "Well, anyhow, you don't deserve a guy like that."

"No," Rebecca said, leaning forward in her chair, purposely averting her gaze to the table. "I'm sorry," she said, looking distressed. "I have no cookies today, Clarence." She lifted a hand to her mouth, gingerly touching the cracks on her lips. It seemed to her that some men wanted a harlot. Others wanted a virgin. Maybe depending on the mood, the same man could want both.

"Don't fret none 'bout that. You've had a helluva time," he said, his face turning pink. "But I hope you don't mind . . . I need to ask a few more questions."

"Of course," Rebecca said, sliding a hand to her nape. She held his gaze, paying attention to every detail . . . the way he surveyed the kitchen floor . . .

Despite this being where the biggest struggle had occurred, she didn't believe there was any blood to be found. But just in case, she'd mopped the floor and picked up the pieces of her camera. She'd cleaned up the bloody footprints all the way to the stairs. Clarence looked up at the ceiling . . . Becky didn't. *No reason to believe there was anything there.* The chair legs . . . *None were broken.* The way he glanced about the table . . . *Nothing beneath it —not anymore.*

At long last, he met her gaze, wincing over the sight of her face. Six days later, it was impossible not to acknowledge the evidence of abuse. Rebecca hadn't bothered with a stitch of makeup, nor had she smeared lipstick over her bruised and battered lips. Instead of hiding her bruises, she wore them like badges. *Ain't no devil ever been near you,* he'd said.

Clearly, he was wrong.

The sheriff inhaled, filling his robust chest. "What'd you tell the boys?"

"Only that their father left is all—didn't say a thing about Leona. It didn't seem right."

"No," he agreed. "I don't expect it would be." He turned away. "I been suspecting he was like this for a while now, Becky. I'm sorry I never asked."

"It's okay, Sheriff. It ain't easy to talk about . . . even now." She gave a nod to the ceiling, reminding him about the boys playing upstairs. You could hear their voices arguing over something or another. But there was nothing unusual about the banter.

"I reckon not," he said, pursing his lips.

Rebecca had only recounted part of the story—lying by omission—about the way Joe and Leona came traipsing up the porch, groping each another, never caring that the boys might hear.

"That's mine!" Joe screamed.

"I'm telling Mom!" Jeff cried.

But neither of them came down the stairs and Rebecca shook her head. "Thank God, they weren't home," she said after a moment. "Only Joe didn't know it. He was gone before I could tell him." The tears that came after that disclosure were real.

"He didn't know you sent the boys to Farwell?"

Rebecca shook her head. "No," she said, wiping away tears. "I was going to . . . well . . . I was going to ask for a divorce. That's why I sent the boys to my cousin."

"I see."

Upstairs, the boys were arguing again, their words and voices clear, so the sheriff spoke lower. "And it was commonplace for him to yell and scream?" He pointed at her face. "Do that sort of thing around the boys?"

Rebecca looked straight into his eyes. There was nothing feigned about the sadness he must have spied there. "Sometimes, but never this bad. Mostly after the boys went to bed."

Clarence Taylor exhaled, shaking his head. "Atrocious," he allowed. "If I had done any sort of thing to my Bertie, she'd have me drawn and quartered. Like I said, Becky, you're a good woman."

Because she didn't report her husband for domestic abuse? Rebecca frowned, averting her gaze, lapping at her lips, and once again she began to sob, catching herself quickly and shaking it off.

None of her tears were fake. The ordeal she'd survived was imprinted in her head and in her heart. No matter what happened now, nobody could ease her pain—nothing could erase the horror.

Somehow, she'd dragged both bodies out the back door in the wee hours of the morning. She'd hauled them out to the burial place with a wagon, only it was a good eight hours longer before she could get them into the ground. She walked back in the door around two p.m. and went straight to cleaning up the godawful mess. Only by the time she'd returned, the blood upstairs had seeped into the grooves of the floorboards, and she'd had to use a whole bottle of bleach and a knife to scrape it all up. One week later her arms were still sore from the effort and her fingertips were raw.

Subconsciously, she crossed her arms, kneading the backs of them. The mess downstairs had been easier to clean; she'd scrubbed the basement, then went all through the house, top to bottom. It was a travesty—all of it—and nevertheless, given the same situation, would she have done anything any differently?

No.

The answer was no.

Clarence placed his hat on the table. "I don't suppose they told you anything about Billy . . . or"—he looked at her—"the robbery?"

Rebecca said, "No. But now I understand why they abandoned the car."

The sheriff squinted his eyes. "Yeah, and why is that?"

Rebecca blinked innocently. "Well, because . . . I'm guessing he was afraid you might know how to find him if he took it?" She gave the sheriff a sheepish look, as though to say, *you know best, what do I know? I'm just a dumb old housewife.*

"Yeah, yeah . . . I see what you mean," he said.

"I'm sure he was thinking you'd be smart enough to know what to look for." And then a thought occurred to her. "Will you be taking the car?" She hadn't asked with any real concern. *Easy come, easy go.* If he thought he needed to have it, she wouldn't stand in his way.

The sheriff shook his head, as though the suggestion surprised him. "Well, no, ma'am. We cain't exactly do that. We cain't prove Joe did anything wrong—not with the measly evidence we got. Right now, we only got witnesses for Billy, and Billy's dead."

Rebecca nodded, and the sheriff averted his gaze, glancing at the telephone cord. "So . . . you didn't happen to look out . . . see what kind of car they took off in?" He glanced back at her, narrowing his gaze. "Seems maybe you woulda glanced out the window?"

"No, sir," she said, wiping tears from her face. "I couldn't stand it. I was . . . well, I was devastated. As you might well imagine. I was thinking what in God's name I was I gonna tell my boys."

"I see. So, you drove on to Farwell to get your boys?"

"Yes, sir."

"When?"

Rebecca opted not to lie. "The next day." She covered her traitorous lips with a hand to hide the trembling, remembering the look of pity in her cousin's eyes, her insistence that Becky not return home. It was only through sheer force of will that she'd piled the boys back in the car, and there was no way she could have reassured Lucinda it would never happen again. Because she couldn't reveal the truth: that it couldn't—because Joe was already dead.

"And you drove the El Dorado?"

Rebecca's hands slid away from her face, thinking how heavy Leona's body had been . . . how her pretty head had smacked the basement stairs, time and again, as she'd dragged the body up, and up, and up . . .

At first, she hadn't wanted to get too close to so much blood, only she was forced to drop Leona and take hold of her beneath her arms, her head cradled between Rebecca's breasts . . .

"Becky?"

"Yes," she said, lifting her gaze.

For a moment, as she looked at the sheriff, tears slipping past her lashes, she was uncertain what to say. Yes, yes, she had driven the El Dorado, but it wasn't until later that day, and right this moment she couldn't be sure Sheriff Taylor hadn't come by whilst she was out digging the graves. She'd been out half the day—battling swarms of crickets. Even now she could hear them pouncing on her wagon, and later, they'd beat the screen in droves . . . like a plague . . .

"I can see this is taking a toll on you, maybe I'd best be going." He hitched his chin toward the ceiling. "The boys upstairs playing?"

Rebecca nodded, tears pricking at her eyes. Once again, she wiped them away.

"Now, now, don't go doing that. I'm here to say that fool ain't worth your tears, Becky. He's a miserable—" He stopped himself. "Well, he ain't no good. He and Leona been carrying on a long time, and I wanted to tell you that day I came by—remember? I ate too many cookies, but it was because I was trying to find a way to tell you." He gave her a sober glance. "And then you told me where to go find him and, you know . . . some people get through this sort of thing. Some people find a way to make it work, even when there's . . . well, you know what I mean."

Fresh tears flowed from Rebecca's eyes—maybe it was the tone of Clarence's voice, the illusion that someone cared—or maybe it was his reassurance that she must persevere. Or maybe it was simply relief that he seemed to be buying her tale.

"Come on, now, don't cry; you and the boys will be alright."

Rebecca nodded, wiping her face with her hands. She inhaled a trembling breath and looked Clarence straight in the face. "Sheriff? Are you positive about the bank robbery?" she asked.

And then in a whisper, "I can't believe the father of my children would do a thing like that."

"I expect not," he said, and seemed to consider what more to say. He settled for this, "Like I said, we cain't prove a thing. And to be fair, I didn't 'spect about the robbery 'til Wednesday past, and then I needed to be sure."

Rebecca lifted her head, meeting Clarence's gaze, blinking. She furrowed her brow. "But you came by . . . before then?"

The sheriff looked confused. "Before when?"

"A few nights after the robbery. Friday. The Eighth. I remember because, well, that was the first time—" She lifted a hand to her brow. "Well, not the first time."

Sheriff Taylor lifted his brows, realizing what he'd revealed. He sat back, scratching at his chin, his demeanor changing. "Yeah . . . well." He scratched a little harder. "No, that was about something else. I came by because I heard those boys were making trouble down in the old neighborhood."

He was lying. "Oh," Rebecca said.

The timeline was wrong. The robbery happened on the fourth, because it was in the paper on the fifth. The sheriff visited on the eighth. She'd heard about Billy's death on Friday, the fifteenth, and going by what she'd learned from Mary Claire, Billy had been dead for going on nine days, which meant he and Joe could not have been down in the old neighborhood making trouble. But even if he hadn't known about Billy's death until later, if he'd waited until Wednesday the twentieth to report his suspicions, it meant he'd gone at least seven days without telling anyone what he knew. And now, as she sat watching him fidget in her kitchen chair, she knew beyond a shadow of doubt . . . everything Leona said was true.

He looked nervous now—as though he were the one on trial. "You see, at first we thought Billy musta gone and made somebody mad. Later, once we connected his car to the robbery . . .

well . . ." He looked away. "I'm guessing Joe musta believed he was a liability, or wanted to keep the money to himself."

"How much?" Rebecca asked, because the paper never said.

The sheriff shrugged. "Money? Something like twenty-four thousand."

Rebecca gasped in surprise.

"He and Joe hit the bank wearing stockings. We suspect maybe Leona drove Bill's car in the getaway. Witnesses said there were two men inside the building, but Billy didn't have no gun . . . so, I don't guess you know if Joe had one?"

Rebecca shook her head. "No, sir. Only my daddy's rifle." She made a move to rise. "I can get it if you wish."

"No, ma'am, that won't be necessary." He waved her back down. "Anyway, I'm sure they are long gone by now."

Rebecca sat again. "Yes, I'm sure."

His gaze returned to the kitchen counter where the telephone cord sat in a pile. "So, just to be clear . . . you say you was gonna call the police, and Joe ripped the cord out of the wall?"

"Yes, sir."

They sat in silence a long while, and he seemed reluctant to go on. "But . . . then," he said, scratching his chin. "After he left, why didn't you call?"

Rebecca looked down at her hands, folded neatly on the table. "It's not a crime to leave your wife, is it? After all, what were you gonna do, Sheriff? Tie him down and make him stay?" She glanced over at the cord on the counter. "Anyway, he busted the phone, remember?"

"That's right," he said, and the two of them locked gazes.

"You say he smacked you with that receiver?"

"Yes."

"How many times?"

"I don't know."

For the slightest instant, Rebecca saw past the carefully

constructed veneer—lust perhaps? Or greed. Or maybe he was living vicariously through her telling of the tale?

Upstairs, Jeff screamed again. Joe Jr. hollered back.

Whatever it was she'd spied in his eyes vanished the instant he heard the children. "Mind if I go up and say hello?"

Rebecca's heart banged against her chest. "No . . . course not . . . please do."

She got up from her chair, fluffing the back of her hair, straightening her dress. The sheriff rose as well, reaching for his hat. Together, they moved through the dining room, toward the stairs. Clarence didn't notice the dining room carpet was missing. Rebecca's gaze skimmed the floor, to be sure . . . She followed, barely listening as he talked. "Anything you need," he was saying. "Whatever it is, you know who to call."

"Yes, sir," she said, praying the boys hadn't displaced the carpet she'd moved from the dining room—but no, it was too heavy for them.

At the top of the stairs, she held her breath with every step they took closer to the room. She nearly swooned with relief at the sight of her boys sitting cross-legged in the middle of the braided rug. As soon as the boys saw them, Jeff began to whine, and Joe kept his hand firmly on his truck.

"Mama!" Jeff cried as he got up and ran to her. "He won't let me play." He rubbed his pate. "He hit me on top o' my head."

Sheriff Taylor leaned into the doorway. "Now, now, boys," he said, in a voice deeper than usual. "You know your paw ain't gonna be around awhile."

Joe Jr. looked up at the sheriff and glanced toward Rebecca. Beside her, Jeff tilted his face up in alarm, because, despite what she'd said downstairs, Rebecca hadn't said a word to either of her kids about their father. "Mama?" Jeff said.

She looked at him sadly. "It's true," she said, and she reached out to smooth the hair from his face.

"So, now," the sheriff said. "You got to be sure to mind your mama, ya hear? Do everything you're told."

"Yes, sir," said Joe Jr.

"You're the man of the house now," he continued, and Joe Jr. turned his gaze back to his truck, his face sullen and his lips forming a pout.

"Okay then." The sheriff turned to face Rebecca, returning his hat atop his head. He sighed. "I'd best be getting along. But I don't suppose I need to tell you that if you hear from him, you should call me immediately."

"You, Sheriff? Or the police station?"

"Me," he said, eyeing her with some annoyance. "You call me."

"Yes, sir," she said.

"Me and Bertie . . . we got an extra phone somewhere if you need it."

"Yes, thank you," she said.

"Alright," he said, and started back down the stairs. "Call me any time, Becky Lee, and I do mean it—day or night."

"Don't worry, Sheriff, we'll be fine." He was halfway down the stairs when Rebecca said, "Oh! Wait! I nearly forgot." For a moment, she left him standing at the foot of the stairs and darted past him, into the kitchen to grab the sheet of notebook paper she'd left on the counter, and then she returned. "With all that's been going on, I nearly forgot I wrote down that recipe for Roberta. Tell her I said don't thank me, thank Silas."

His brow furrowed. "Silas?"

Rebecca smiled, not caring much that it cracked her lip. "Silas Wright," she said, lifting her chin. "He was like an uncle to me, used to live here on the ranch."

The sheriff scratched his head.

"Brave, brave man. Died the night of the tornado in '48— remember? Anyway, he helped me out of the barn, took me down to the basement." She shook her head. "I was fifteen, smack in the middle of feeding the horses. He went out to be sure the stall doors were alright and took a two-by-four to the head."

"You mean that crusty old black man?" Sheriff Taylor asked. He glanced down at the piece of paper in Rebecca's hand, scrunching his nose.

Rebecca straightened her spine. "Yes, sir. His name was Silas," she said. "Silas Wright. He's the one who taught me how to make those jumbles—fresh with pecans from the tree out back."

He stared at her, blinking. "Yeah, okay," he said, and he took the piece of paper, albeit reluctantly. "I'll be seeing you," he said. "Take care now." And Rebecca watched him leave the porch, then walk past the El Dorado. He gave the car a single glance as he crumbled the paper in his fist, tossing the ball of paper onto his passenger seat as he got into his squad car and drove away.

Only after he was gone, Rebecca walked out onto the porch, pursing her lips as she stared at the El Dorado. Somehow throughout the ordeal, she'd kept her head. She'd had just enough foresight to come out and grab Leona's suitcase from the trunk of the car . . . but she hadn't even thought to inspect the car for anything else.

If those two were planning to leave, it meant they must have had the money on hand—either that, or it was stashed somewhere else, ready to go. But then she remembered there had been a Mexican blanket in the trunk, right beneath Leona's suitcase. On a whim, she walked out, popped the trunk, then went to the back to look inside. She opened the trunk, flung aside the blanket, and right there, in front of her eyes, sat two neat stacks of bills.

With a gasp, she spun about to be sure Clarence was gone, and then she glanced up at the window to her boys' room. Two faces peered out the window, noses pressed against the glass, and Rebecca closed the trunk again.

Twenty-four thousand dollars.

There was only one reason Clarence wouldn't feel obliged to

search the car: *He believed her.* He could see no reason to doubt Leona and Joe would leave and take the money with them. Why would they leave a penny in the car? Clearly, he thought Rebecca too chaste to put a bullet through the back of a man's skull, and he'd walked past the car with barely a backward glance—but why not?

Rebecca's life, up until this point, had been conducted with an overwhelming absence of duplicity. Only now, it was as though she'd lost her virginity and the leviathan of all deceptions had been heaved from the fabric of her womb in a birth so violent she would never be the same.

From this day on, lies—all lies, white lies, lies of omission, lies and more lies, every day, every day—were destined to gestate and proliferate like damnable crickets. But she could, and would, presume to live with that.

Tonight, after the boys were asleep, she'd come down and retrieve the money, and then she'd take out what she was owed for the price of that car—a car she'd never given Joe leave to buy —and all the rest, she'd save for the boys.

She would proceed with the plans she'd conceived, create a union of women—maybe invite Mary Claire. She would save her ranch, give the women voices, and maybe then she would begin, at long last, to make up for the egregious sins of this day. She lifted her chin at the sight of the wooden bucket on the porch— filled with pecans.

Right now, she longed to smell the sugary scent of Jumbles wafting through her house—the most delicious lie of all—and she had a bucketful today.

Sweeping up the porch, she embraced the bucket and walked in the front door, calling upstairs to the boys. "Come down, boys," she said. "We gonna bake us a mess of jumbles."

THE PHONE RANG as Gillian sat knee-deep in refuse.

The floor was ripped to splinters, and she sat staring at a huge stain along the subfloor—tar-like in some places, but more like rust over the greater circumference. Bleu sat on a random piece of wood, watching Gillian with blinking eyes.

"Hello," she said, lifting the phone, barely recalling having set it down.

"Hey, I just wanted to tell you we closed the Burke account."

Gillian stared, unblinking at the floor.

"Gillian?"

"I'm here."

"I know you've been looking in on Dana. I wanted to thank you. She did a great job, and I realize you primed her for this, so it's your win as well."

"Great," Gillian said stiffly. "Great."

Half the flooring was ripped up, not very neatly. Slivers of wood lay everywhere, with bigger, jagged bits surrounding her. One sliver pricked the bottom of her left hand.

No sane person would destroy a good hardwood floor like this . . .

"Gillian? You alright?"

Kelly knew her so well—better than anyone, including Gigi. He paid attention to her moods. "Yeah," she said. "I'm fine. I think . . ."

"No, you're not," he said. "I'll be right over."

Gillian nodded. "Okay," she said, and hung up. She set down the phone and stared at the mess she'd made, realizing what she had done—what Gigi had done.

Arteries spurt, veins ooze, she thought dimly. But this . . . this . . . this had been a steady flow. The heart pumped blood at several liters per minute. The body contained four or five. What she saw here had to be the equivalent of four or five . . .

Staring at the massive rust stain beneath the floorboard, she tried to surmise how much blood was lost. And she had no idea how long she sat, staring, but it was no surprise when she heard a car pull up outside. Kelly didn't bother knocking on the door. "Gillian?" he called out.

"Up here."

She heard him take the steps two at a time, and knew when he stopped that he was standing outside her bedroom door.

"What the fuck?"

Looking up at Kelly's familiar face, grateful for his presence, Gillian began to sob.

19

THE SAFE BOX

Gigi had had a favorite saying: "False friends are like shadows. They dance with you in sunlight, but vanish when it gets dark." Outside, the sun was setting . . . and here was Kelly.

Looking terrified for Gillian's sake, Kelly swept into the room, dragging Gillian up from the floor. He held her, rocking her in his arms. "What's wrong, Gilly? What's wrong?" The tenderness in his voice buckled her knees. He glanced over Gillian's shoulder at the destruction of the floor, then down at her feet, and asked with no small amount concern, "Is it your foot?"

Gillian shook her head, sobbing against his shoulder, clinging to him. "I've been so awful to you," she said, wiping her nose on his soft blue T-shirt.

He patted her back, drawing her close. "It's okay, baby. I'm here."

He continued to rock her and she wrapped her arms about the man who'd stuck with her through addictions and divorce, through temper tantrums and more. He kissed her on the forehead, then again, and Gillian reached up, holding her arms around his neck. Whether it was simply a moment of bittersweet familiarity, or simply need, Gillian didn't know, but she pulled herself up onto her tiptoes and pressed her lips against Kelly's mouth, begging him to kiss her. The scent of his breath, the taste of his lips, was like mana from heaven. He kissed her back, although tentatively, and Gillian's tears trickled past her lashes, then down her cheeks.

She was vaguely aware that he lifted her up out of the wreckage and set her down on her feet again, over where the floor was free of debris. After a moment, he broke the kiss, then stood with her, allowing her to find her bearings.

"Gillian," he said, sounding confused.

Only now that she had composed herself, she took him by the hand and led him downstairs to the kitchen, wiping her face with her sleeve as she told him to sit.

He sat, white-faced. "Gillian, you're scaring me."

Gillian slid into the chair beside him and seized his hand—both hands, testing the feel of them in hers—strong, familiar hands. She brought them to her lips, kissing them each in turn, unbridled by anything but raw emotion. "Kelly . . . I think someone died . . ." She lifted her chin. "Up there."

His face paled. "Nooo."

"Nooooo," she said, realizing he thought she meant today.

He averted his gaze and squeezed his temples as though she'd given him a headache. "Okay, start again . . . at the beginning."

Calmer now, Gillian pushed her chair back and got up. "Stay here. Don't leave."

"I'm staying."

Leaving him seated in the kitchen, she hurried upstairs to retrieve the photographs, and then returned to lay them all face up on the table in front of Kelly, like playing cards. "That's my grandmother," she said.

He looked at Gillian with an expression of horror. "Are you sure?"

"Very."

Gillian pointed at one of the photos. "Except that one. I don't know who that is." She tapped on the close-up of a woman. "But . . . I think it was taken the same day. I found them all in an envelope. On the back, Gigi wrote 'evidence.'"

Kelly furrowed his brow, still confused. However, to his credit —or maybe to hers—he still hadn't asked if she'd been drinking. "Evidence?"

Gillian sat again, looking him straight in the eyes, realizing she'd given him only snippets of information. So she told him about Eli and their odd conversation. She told him about the house up on Anthony Street that had sat empty for sixty years. She told him about the missing cat, locked in her basement. She told him about discovering Eli wandering around her house this morning—uninvited—as though searching for something. And then she told him about Eli's grandmother and her gun going missing. She explained about the suitcase she had discovered in the basement. And finally, she told him about the discoloration upstairs, scrubbed clean, maybe with bleach, and the rusty looking stain she'd discovered along the subfloor.

"It could be rust, Gillian."

"That much? Under a wood floor?"

"Well, yeah, they're probably nailed down, right?" *The boards.* "Regardless, it'd be easy enough to get one of those CSI types out to test for blood."

Gillian nodded "That's true."

"I'm no expert, but I'm pretty sure they have ways of finding things out."

Gillian fidgeted in her chair, thinking it over. And then she looked into Kelly's warm brown eyes, daring to say what was on her mind. "What if Gigi killed them?"

He contorted his face. "Gigi?"

Gillian nodded, feeling unhinged—only what else could she feel at the thought of her grandmother killing her grandfather— and possibly some woman. "What if she did it by accident?"

Kelly put his elbows on the table, leaning into his hands, staring at the deck of photos. "How the hell do you kill two people by accident?" he said after a long moment of reflection.

"I don't know, but what if she did? Look at those pictures," she demanded, and he did so, again.

One by one, he lifted each to reexamine it, wincing as he studied the bruised and bloodied face. "She took one helluva beating."

"Yeah, so what if she did it in self-defense?"

"Hold on, now. She said your grandfather left, right?"

Gillian tilted her head, her tone rife with doubt. "Yeah, that's what she said, but what are the odds those two disappeared forever?"

Again Kelly screwed up his face. "Who?"

"Are you listening to me, Ruby?" He caught her pet name and peered up at her, lifting his brows and offering a smile, but Gillian wasn't in the mood to be derailed. "Eli's grandmother, my grandfather."

"I don't know . . . better odds than being murdered by your grandma, that's for sure."

"Yeah, well, I searched newspaper archives online and looked for mentions of them in the paper—there was nothing. Not one word."

"Yeah, but wouldn't that make sense? I mean, who puts something like that in the paper? 'My husband left me for another woman?'" He tilted Gillian a curious look, then turned up his palm, rethinking it perhaps. "On the other hand, if two prominent people from the same town turned up missing, that should be in the paper, right?"

Gillian's nod was slightly frenetic. "That's what I'm saying, Kelly. It's suspicious—not one word."

Kelly shook his head, disbelieving the possibility. "We're talking about Geeg—ain't no way I can believe she killed two people, then covered it up."

"Maybe. Maybe you're right. But maybe I know how to find out."

"How?"

"Come with me," she demanded, reaching for Kelly's hand.

Half an hour later, they stood beneath the pecan tree—Gillian with her grandmother's old metal detector in hand—a gadget Gigi had kept handy to locate her safe, because she was wholly terrified that someday she would get Alzheimer's and forget where she'd buried her safe box.

Gillian knew where it was, because she'd accompanied Gigi now and again to place valuables in the box, only to watch her bury it again—the first time when Gillian was six.

"Someday you're going to need to know where this is," Gigi had said. "Remember, under the pecan tree, six paces west. You know which way's west?"

Gillian had shaken her head as she'd dropped a cricket in her jar and then covered the jar with a lid.

"The sun gets born in the east, dies in the west. You'll only ever come looking once I'm gone, so that'll help you remember. You're six now, right?"

"Yes, ma'am," Gillian had said. But the possibility of death was suddenly a matter of grave consequence. Gillian had sat there in the prickly grass, terrified by the prospect.

Never mind the sun or the fallout of its disappearance, for Gillian, it was the first time she'd considered the tragic reality of death, and its potential fallout for her. Seated in the lowering twilight, with crickets jumping into her lap, she'd mentally prepared herself for the probability of her grandmother's demise. Realizing she was destined to be alone, she began to memorize the sunrise and sunset.

"Six paces west," her grandmother said again. Then she'd added without segue, "Never trust banks. My pa said during the depression there were ten thousand failed banks across the country. You know how much money was lost?"

Gillian was still worrying over the looming specter of death. With a sting in her eyes, she'd stared at the cricket in her jar, then turned it over the grass, setting the insect free.

"He buried his stash out in the backyard, like this. If you ask me, that's what soured him on Farwell—the notion of his valuables getting buried too deep to find."

Gillian had been going to name that cricket Charlie, but she didn't know why. Now she brushed him away, urging him to go.

"You know, we had a tractor in back those days. In no time at all, it was buried to the stacks. You don't get that kind of dirt out of an engine. Ruins everything."

That long-ago evening had been much like this one, except that instead of the cool blue tones of a clear spring sky, tonight, there was a burning sunset and a deep purple twilight.

Casting one last glance at Kelly for support, Gillian turned on her grandmother's metal detector. A cheaper model Bounty Hunter, it was sensitive to metals, but only picked up small objects, buried five inches deep. The larger the object, the deeper it could be. The safe was a simple locking cash box, plenty big enough to trigger the detector a little deeper.

"This is crazy," said Kelly, as she measured six paces from the tree. In exactly the spot she recalled, the beep went off, a single high-pitched tone.

It must be directly below, or the sensor wouldn't pick it up. "Right here," she said, and Kelly moved in with his shovel, rearing back and pushing the spade into the ground.

"Gigi said once that all her skeletons were buried under this tree. I thought she'd meant documents—or a diary. Now I'm wondering if she was being literal."

Kelly reared back again, thrusting the narrow shovel head into the thick red clay. He kept on going, and knowing the safe wasn't buried very deep, Gillian stayed out of his way. It was only another few moments before he smacked the box and the clang of metal made him stop.

Driven by a fever of suspicion, Gillian rushed forward to pull it out. It wouldn't budge, so she dug around the plastic-covered box with a small spade. Finally, with a lot of tugging and a little more digging, she freed the dented-up box and dragged it out of the ground. She tore it out of its protective bag and set it down to reach into her pocket for the key. All the while, Kelly looked on. "One thing's for sure, Gilly. Life with you is never boring."

Gillian peered up at him. "But you're still here?"

"Yeah," he said, and smiled. "I'm still here."

Standing over her with the shovel in his hand and a lopsided grin on his face, Gillian realized she never wanted him to leave. Whatever it was she was about to discover, he was the only person in the world she could imagine sharing it with.

She didn't want to sleep with Eli Fox, and couldn't imagine being with anyone besides Kelly Ruby. *He was the one.* Her one and only. She simply didn't wish to own a business with him. She hated her job—loathed not having anything new to talk about because they shared every experience on any given day. But she loved that man.

Flicking a thumbnail across the back ridge of the key, the words were out of her mouth before she could stop them. "You gonna stick around?"

Silence.

For a long, long moment, there was only the emerging sound of crickets chirping, but then Kelly asked, "You want me to?"

Tears filled Gillian's eyes as she peered up and said, "I do," and this time, those two little words were far more meaningful than they had been the first time she'd said them standing in front of a priest. There was nothing Gillian could do to change the past, but time alone to reflect had given her a clearer picture of life in general. It struck her then, as she hovered over the safe box, that she and her grandmother had both made fatal mistakes in their marriages. Both of them had worked so hard to please the men in their lives, without ever considering their own needs.

For Gigi, judging by the endless articles and the notes in her magazines, she had tried so hard to be someone she wasn't, working her fingers to the bone to serve a man who had no appreciation for her.

And Gillian . . . she'd worked tirelessly at a job she loathed, only to please Kelly. She'd been so full of resentment, and in so many ways, she was still that hurt, little frightened child, afraid to love, afraid to keep her crickets, afraid to open doors.

In the end, both hers and Gigi's decisions had killed their marriages—only Gigi's perhaps literally. Kelly averted his gaze, swallowing. "You sure have a helluva way of showing it."

Tears welled in Gillian's eyes. "I know." On any other given day, she might have shot back that all he ever cared about was the business. Pride was the damnedest thing.

Clearly filled with pent up anger, Kelly lifted his shovel up, then stabbed the ground with it. "You couldn't have tried any harder to push me away," he said. "And then you went and hired that pretty-boy shyster."

Gillian blinked. *He was jealous of Eli.* "Is that what this has been about?"

"What specifically, Gillian? Eli had nothing to do with the end of our marriage."

"Your absence—you're jealous of a guy I hired to fix the barn?"

"Yeah, okay, so what? Only after I told you I would do it for you. What am I supposed to make of that?"

Silence.

Try harder, a little voice urged. "Kelly," she said. "You always think you need to fix things. But I don't want you coming around because you think you need to fix me."

He stabbed the ground again, holding Gillian's gaze, his eyes glistening in the twilight. "It's not my job anymore. You've made that perfectly clear."

"I needed to fix myself."

Silence again . . . except for the rising cacophony of crickets. The future of their marriage depended on what he said next.

"Well, so have you?"

Gillian inhaled a shaky breath, the safe box forgotten. "If you're asking me if I'm still drinking, the answer is no. I haven't had anything since you left with my bottle."

"Really?" He eyed her dubiously, though maybe with a gleam of hope. "So . . . nothing—in what, three weeks?"

"Nothing. Not one drop. I haven't even been out of the house, except to go to the grocery store or PetSafe."

"Ah, yes, the cat," he said, with a note of wonder.

Gillian sighed. She palmed the key, closing her fist around it. "You aren't going to make this easy for me, are you?"

"Why should I?" And yet his voice was gentler now. "You're feeling good? No more partying, you're a homebody and now you've adopted an elderly cat?"

"Don't forget the horse."

"What's up with that?"

Gillian smiled. "I figured it was time."

"Gilly," he said, looking as tortured as a man could possibly look. "What the fuck do you want from me?" His voice was hoarse —the way it used to sound in the mornings after making love. But then it hardened again. "I've gotten accustomed to getting by without you. Let's be honest here, you had one foot out the door the day you said, 'I do.'"

Gillian squeezed the key in her hand, pressing it into her flesh, but she didn't interrupt.

Encouraged by her silence, Kelly went on. "Everything was better before we got married, only then it's like you were afraid I meant to trap you, and the more space I gave, the more you took."

In retrospect, Gillian realized he'd given her too much space. "You haven't been by," she said.

"I know."

"But you said you would."

Again, a note of bitterness. "You had it all covered, Gillian, and you could have called."

"I did."

"When?"

"It doesn't matter now—I have something to ask." Gillian braced herself for the question. She opened and closed her hand around the small key. "Are you seeing someone?"

"Gillian . . ."

"Just answer me. Please."

His eyes were sad. "You must have known I would . . . eventually?"

"So, you are?"

"Yes."

The admission brought a terrible pang to Gillian's heart, gripping with a ferocity she didn't expect. "Okay, so . . ." Tears began to flow, unchecked. "Is it serious?"

"Serious? As in, am I screwing her? Or, am I walking her down the aisle?"

She felt small now, like a child peeking behind a scary door. "Either . . . both."

Kelly raked a hand across his jaw. "I'm sure you know I was with her the night of your accident, nothing happened."

The confession raised Gillian's hopes. "Why?"

He screwed up his face. "Why do you think, Gillian?"

"Who is it?" she persisted.

"Does it matter?"

"I don't know . . . does it?"

"What are you asking?"

Gillian swallowed her fear. "Is it Dana?"

"No!" He sounded horrified over the prospect.

Relief washed through Gilly as forcefully as a riptide. She hadn't realized how much fear she'd held in that regard. "Good," she wanted to say. But instead, she sat in the prickly grass and wept. One by one, her tears slid past her lips, leaving a trail of salt. "I miss you," she said, her voice sounding small as more tears slid past her lashes and down her cheeks.

This time, he didn't bend to touch her, or drag her up to kiss and hold her. "I wish I could believe you," he said.

And once again, Gillian was grieving, only this time it was over the carcass of her marriage that she had exhumed. Once brought into the light, it was equally as devastating to see what she'd done to it. She wiped her tears away. "Have I . . . have I ever . . . lied to you?"

He knew the answer to that question. She was far more inclined to say what she felt, no matter whether it hurt someone's feelings. And too often, she had hurt his. "No."

"Is it too late?"

She squeezed her eyes shut, gripping the key as she prayed.

"Too late?"

"For us."

The safe was completely forgotten as Gillian met Kelly's gaze and said, "I love you, Kelly. I always have. I've been a terrible wife, but if you let me, I'll make it up to you."

He shook his head, as though denying her. And then he stood looking at her for a long, long terrible moment and Gillian feared what he might say.

But then he smiled as he put the shovel head into the dirt, and set a boot on top. "You know, I always wanted you to say that to me." He shook his head. "I just never figured we'd be standing outside at twilight, searching for corpses when you did."

Gillian gave him a watery smile, then laughed.

"Open the safe," he said, and Gillian nodded. She slid the key into the lock, turning it. The lock was gummy but the lid snapped open nonetheless.

Inside, she discovered no gun—no incriminating evidence whatsoever—just a handful of documents. Gillian moved the documents over and discovered two stacks of bills—each about an inch thick, all hundred dollar bills.

Kelly dropped the shovel. "Holy shit," he said as Gillian handed him the box. "What the hell?" He flipped a finger through the stacks. "There must be twenty thousand dollars here."

By now, it was growing dark, and the twilight made everything surreal. Gillian got up from her knees, brushed the dirt from her pants, and grabbed the metal detector, positioning it over the spot yet again. Once again, the metal detector dinged. Her head snapped up, meeting Kelly's gaze. "There's more," she said.

He set the box aside, next to the tree, and picked up his shovel. Gillian put down the metal detector and went after the spare shovel. Together, over the next few hours, the two of them shoveled dirt out of a four-by-five hole and hurled it away. Little by little, the hole grew deeper and wider. Now and again, she met Kelly's gaze, but without a word, they persevered.

Gigi used to say when someone cared, they could hear you even when you remained silent. Kelly could hear her, she realized. He knew exactly what she was thinking, even when she didn't speak out loud. Only she vowed as they worked side by side, that she would never again leave him in silence or darkness. She understood now what that felt like and it hurt.

Perhaps Gigi could no longer speak, but Gillian could hear everything in her heart as well. Every conversation they'd ever had played in her ears as she dug deeper, thrusting her shovel into the clay and pulling it back in harmony with Kelly's.

Finally, about three feet down—a total of five feet altogether, Kelly was the first to smack hard wood. The shovel passed through a half-inch of redbed clay and hit with a heart-shuddering thump. "There it is," she said, out of breath.

Only most of the box was still covered with dirt.

As a matter of fact, they had only managed to reveal a small portion of what might be a very large box. *It could be Silas.* She stared at the box for a long moment. Before losing the nerve to go on, she tossed down the shovel and sat, swinging her knees into the hole they'd created together.

Following her lead, Kelly did the same.

The two of them sat staring at one another for a long time—so long, in fact, that the last orange threads of sun vanished behind a tangle of mesquite trees to the west.

"We didn't bring a flashlight," Kelly lamented.

Gillian remained silent, eyeing the exposed wood in the hole.

"Whatever's down there has to be big enough to trigger the detector."

Usually, the items people searched for were little bigger than the size of a quarter—mostly jewelry. Gold had another sound entirely, not a beep, exactly. It was more like that sound an old computer made when it was locked and you hit a wrong key—a deep drone, twice in succession. The beep they'd heard indicated regular old metal. *Steel.*

"Could be the gun."

"Should we keep going?"

Until now, Kelly had been holding his shovel. The handle rested in his lap, though now he gently set it aside and looked straight into Gillian's eyes with that deep, familiar gaze. "It could be a belt buckle, too. Didn't you say they buried some old guy under this tree?"

Gillian nodded. "Silas."

"Maybe it's him. Maybe that's all this is, Gillian. Maybe we should stop right here."

"Shouldn't we know for sure?"

"Why?" The question was an outright challenge. "Let's say you're right and you find what you think you might find. We're talking about an old lady sitting in a nursing home, unable to communicate or defend herself. Who's she going to answer to, Gilly?"

Once again, Gillian peered into the hole. "But . . ." She furrowed her brow. "What if it's my grandfather?"

"What if it is?" Kelly asked. "Judging by the photos, I'd say he deserved it."

"What about Eli's grandmother?"

Kelly shook his head. "I don't know Eli's grandmother, I only know Gigi, and that woman doted on you, Gillian. She loved you deeply. I can't believe someone like her could do a thing like . . ." He waved a hand toward the hole. "That."

Gillian looked down at the sliver of wood they'd revealed, unsure what to do. One thing was certain, if they kept going, neither of them would retain the option of walking away. They would be honor-bound to tell someone—likely the police.

Only then, what would happen? Gigi's name would be dragged through the mud and she wasn't in any condition to defend herself. How fair was that?

Furthermore, what if it was Silas? What then? What right did they have to desecrate an old man's grave? Innocent as his death might have been, they'd have the police out again, poking through DNA, trying to turn it all into a mystery, where none was intended.

As Gillian sat, weighing the need to know against the consequences of knowing, even without even realizing it, she'd picked up a handful of dirt and crumbled it over the spot of bare wood. "The past is the past," she said, looking at Kelly.

He nodded in agreement. "The past is the past."

In some ways, the grave they were digging was symbolic of their marriage—a giant black hole filled with so much fury and fear—remnants of all the poor decisions they'd made before this moment in time and space.

Glancing up, she looked at the branches overhead, the way they stretched out over a patch of verdant green—all beneath this tree, unlike the rest of the field, which lay burnt up beneath the heat of the sun. It was so easy to imagine they'd put an old man to rest here, and why would Gigi desecrate his grave by interring two more people in the ground with him. It was far more credible that she would bury her valuables close to him. The love she'd borne for Silas was clear in her voice every time she mentioned him—every single time she baked his jumbles. "We can start over —you and me. Right now."

Kelly regarded her curiously. "You really think it's possible to put everything behind us? Just like that?"

"Why not?"

He seemed to consider the question a long moment, and then said, "You got me. I can't think of one good reason why not."

Gillian smiled at the man she'd married, then divorced—his sandy blond hair and warm caring eyes. She thought about him lying beside her in bed, and longed to see him look at her the way he used to. *Only one thing could keep her from trying again.* "Can you still love me?" she asked.

"Yes," he said. "I never stopped."

Seated at opposite sides of what could easily become a widening chasm between them, it seemed an insurmountable task to piece together a failed marriage—all the fighting, all the disappointments, all the betrayals, all the resentment, all the lies —so many lies. Not huge ones, but little ones, the kind you told every day. She glanced again into the hole they'd dug. "What about life, liberty, and the pursuit of truth," she said. "Isn't that a thing?"

His lips spread into a slow grin. "Happiness, Gilly. It's life, liberty, and the pursuit of happiness."

"Oh," she said.

His smile warmed her, even across the pit. "You want to know what I think?"

Gillian nodded.

"Seems to me . . . if you keep going . . . you're hell-bent on looking for something to cry about. You've got no proof of anything, no gun, despite what Eli said. You've got two old geezers shagging, who might or might not have taken off together back in 1960, and you've got a weird stain on your floor."

"Not anymore."

He shrugged. "Well, there you go."

"What about the envelope?"

"What about it?"

"It says evidence, must be evidence."

"Of what? That the deadbeat smacked her around? Yeah, well, no man should ever hit a woman, and if he did that, Gillian, maybe he got exactly what he deserved. Though if I were a woman and my husband left me like that, I'd keep photos, too, just in case he tried to take away my kids."

Gillian blinked. "What about the floor?"

"Easy to replace," he said, brushing it off. "We can do it together."

It would necessitate pulling out every board and starting from scratch. "You sure?"

"Very. What about the cat?"

"What about him?"

"You planning to keep him?"

Gillian grinned slowly. "You can't make commitments and walk away."

Kelly grinned, too. "Yeah?"

"Yeah."

"You gonna marry me again?"

"Depends on if you're asking."

"What if I am?"

"Well, then . . . maybe I'm saying yes."

With that, Kelly got up, offered Gillian a hand, and pulled her up. Without a word, he bent to retrieve his shovel and began to refill the hole with dirt.

Gillian followed his lead, picking up her shovel, and then, scoop by scoop, one heap at a time, side by side, together they refilled the hole.

20

BABY'S GOOD

"I'll always be here," Gillian said, patting her grandmother's hand. "Like you were for me." Gigi never blinked. Her hand rested easily over Gillian's palm, completely elastic, her ancient fingers spotted with age, and Gillian continued to talk to her as she caressed the limp hand. "Baby's good," she reassured. "So is Kelly. He wanted to come today, but he'll be here tomorrow."

The sight of her grandmother, unchanged, tugged at Gillian's heartstrings.

She'd brought cookies today—pecan jumbles—a baker's dozen. Not that her grandmother could eat them, but the smell would reach her deep, deep down. Even if she couldn't acknowledge the simple act of love, Gillian took heart that somehow she might know.

"We're getting married again," she said, rambling because she could. "This time, we're going to the JOP. Anyway, it's not like we ever really divorced," she said, picking up one of the jumbles and putting it into her mouth. The taste was exactly like she remembered. Not once had Gillian ever baked for Kelly, but she would bake for him a lot now. There was nothing like the scent of toasted butter and sugar to make a house feel like home. Besides, she wasn't working any longer so, at least until she was finished with the restoration of the upstairs rooms, she had a lot of catching up to do.

Dana had taken her place at work, and the two of them rarely talked. Gillian was living a different life now. As her grandmother had done, she'd forged ahead with plans to create a haven for rescue horses. The M-Street house she and Kelly owned had a "For Rent" sign in the yard, and she knew it would be snapped up fast. She put an ad in the paper for a permanent ranch hand and vowed to be more careful in the hiring. Hopefully she'd find someone more like Silas.

A caretaker came into the room and walked over to the bed to fluff Gigi's pillow. Gillian asked, "Has there been any change at all?"

It was the same thing she'd asked every other visit, and every time she received the same answer. But she kept on asking.

The woman, a lovely blond named Stephanie, who gave as much attention to her grandmother as she did to her pristine nails, sadly shook her head. Steph was an interesting dichotomy. With her perfectly dyed, straight blonde hair and flawless makeup, she appeared to Gillian to be the sort of person who was too into herself to pay much attention to anyone else, much less the octogenarians in her care. But it wasn't what Gillian had witnessed. What she'd witnessed was a young woman who gave tirelessly to her profession. "Thank you, Steph," Gillian said. "I appreciate everything you do for her."

Stephanie smiled. "You're welcome," she said. And then noticing the cookies, she asked, "You bake them yourself?"

"I did."

"They smell amazing."

"Go ahead and take one."

The girl's eyes lit up. "You sure."

"Very sure."

"Don't mind if I do," she said, and reached over to pluck up a cookie with her perfectly manicured fingers. When she took a bite, her eyes rolled back in her head. "Pecan sandies?" she asked.

"Something like them. But, no, they're jumbles."

"Mmm. So good," the nurse said, and then she waved as she made her way back out of the room. Once the nurse was gone, Gillian reached into her purse and pulled out a newspaper clipping, just to look at it. She stared at it a long moment.

It was a clipping she'd discovered in one of her grandmother's unsent letters.

The headline read: "Investigation Ends: Missing Persons Suspected in Euless Heist." Side by side were two three-by-five-inch photographs of a man who looked like her father. Beside him was the photo of a blonde with a familiar gleam in her eye.

Gillian's next stop today was Anthony Street, where she intended to put the clipping in Eli's mailbox. No matter what he'd done, at least he deserved to know what she knew—even if he hadn't returned the favor. Not that the clipping proved much, but it gave Gillian a pretty good notion that those two took off together rather than face a prison sentence. She didn't know whose money it was she'd found in the safe box, but that wasn't Gillian's story to tell. It was Gigi's, and Gigi would be taking her secrets to the grave.

She returned the clipping to her purse, and then rose from her seat beside the bed, lifting up the cookies she'd brought on one her grandmother's fine china plates. She moved them to the bedside table and then bent to kiss Gigi on the forehead, saying, "I love you," before following the nurse out the door.

RECIPE FOR PECAN JUMBLES

½ cup soft shortening (part butter)
½ cup sugar
1egg
1 tsp. vanilla

1 ½ cup sifted self-rising flour
2 cups chopped pecans

Mix all ingredients. Drop rounded teaspoons of dough about two inches apart on lightly greased baking sheet. Bake at 375 degrees until browned (eight to ten minutes). Remove from oven while cookies are still soft. Cool and remove from baking sheet.

ALSO BY TANYA ANNE CROSBY

The MacKinnon's Bride

Lyon's Gift

On Bended Knee

Lion Heart

Highland Song

MacKinnon's Hope

GUARDIANS OF THE STONE

Once Upon a Highland Legend

Highland Fire

Highland Steel

Highland Storm

Maiden of the Mist

THE MEDIEVALS HEROES

Once Upon a Kiss

Angel of Fire

Viking's Prize

REDEEMABLE ROGUES

Happily Ever After

Perfect In My Sight

McKenzie's Bride

Kissed by a Rogue

Thirty Ways to Leave a Duke

A Perfectly Scandalous Proposal

ANTHOLOGIES & NOVELLAS

Lady's Man

Married at Midnight

The Winter Stone

ABOUT THE AUTHOR

Tanya Anne Crosby is the New York Times and USA Today best-selling author of thirty novels. She has been featured in magazines, such as People, Romantic Times and Publisher's Weekly, and her books have been translated into eight languages. Her first novel was published in 1992 by Avon Books, where Tanya was hailed as "one of Avon's fastest rising stars." Her fourth book was chosen to launch the company's Avon Romantic Treasure imprint.

Known for stories charged with emotion and humor and filled with flawed characters Tanya is an award-winning author, journalist, and editor, and her novels have garnered reader praise and glowing critical reviews. She and her writer husband split their time between Charleston, SC, where she was raised, and northern Michigan, where the couple make their home.

For more information
Website
Email
Newsletter

Lightning Source UK Ltd.
Milton Keynes UK
UKHW012331170620
365183UK00002B/127/J

9 781648 390111